COLD IN THE LIGHT

By Charles Gramlich

The Invisible College Press, LLC
Arlington VA

Copyright ©2002 Charles Gramlich

All Rights Reserved. No part of this publication may be reproduced, stored in a retrieval system or transmitted, in any form or by any means, electronic, mechanical, photocopying, recording or otherwise, without prior written permission of the copyright holder.

Publisher's Note:
This is a work of fiction. Names, characters, places, and incidents are either the product of the author's imagination or are used fictitiously, and any resemblance to actual persons living or dead, events, species, or locales is entirely coincidental.

ISBN: 1-931486-05-2

Cover Art ©2002 Juliana Peloso
Cover Design Michael Yang
First Printing

The Invisible College Press, LLC
P.O. Box 209
Woodbridge VA 22194-0209
http://www.invispress.com

Please send question and comments to:
editor@invispress.com

Cold in the Light

PROLOGUE
(April 29-30: Night & Morning)

There were cracked places amid the ruin's stones, and the droppings of small beasts who tried to use the cracks to hide from their hunters. The hunters didn't bother with the cracks. They knew how to wait.
           --In the Memory of Ruins

--- **1** ---

Cold in the light, her thoughts shrieked. *It's so cold in the light; I don't wanna go in there.*

But they were rolling in the corridor and she knew where it ended. She knew *how* it ended. Her legs were spread, strapped down and she couldn't move them, couldn't close them. The table beneath her was wet and slick as a glacier, and pain ached in her back from the metal chill against it, and from the needles. She lifted her head, fought the drugs that chained her mouth.

Don't make me go in there. I can't live in there.

White faces hung over her in the disinfected air, crisp and shaven, and voices murmured soothing things that did not sooth. Someone put a hand on her gestation-swollen stomach, patted her chest where it rose and fell. She wanted to scream at them not to touch her.

None of us can live in there.

Doors slapped open then, at the end of the corridor. Banks of white and blue incandescents bloomed overhead. Livid faces seemed to drip and run in that fire, seemed to grow halos of rainbow spikes. She felt herself being lifted from one table to another. This one was padded and stank of old sweat. It was no less cold. The lights were worse though, feathering their touch down on her skin and crawling across it like tiny live wires.

"For your own good, Raina," she heard them say. "...sterilize your skin." She didn't think her skin would sterilize. She thought it would suppurate, begin to rot if she didn't get free of the light.

Charles Gramlich

A plastic mask was placed over her face. She heard the cool hiss of anesthetic gas, did not want to breathe but could not fight the urge. A lassitude began to coat her muscles, her lips and thoughts. Something slipped between her legs, a hand with a tool that glittered. The object slid inside of her, began to unravel and move. She tried to arch her back to push the thing out again, but no part of her body would obey her. Even her mind began to slow, despite her steady fight to stay alert.

Behind her she heard the door explode inward off its hinges. She heard a sound like a zipper being closed. *Gunfire!* She smelled the powder burning. Lights shattered, spilling multicolored glass down around her in a rain. There was still enough illumination to see.

The man who had his hand between her legs seemed suddenly to sprout wings as he was picked up and thrown by some *thing* moving incredibly fast. The oiled voices were no longer murmuring; they were loud with hoarse-throated shouts. The zippering sound was there again, and then again.

A scarecrow man came from nowhere to dance madly in a hail of bullets. In a moment he was gone and the wall where he had stood began to stitch itself with holes. Above the holes lay a filmed window that shattered outward, and behind that opening shone the sapphire tints of evening, of a jeweled dark that seemed to glow before her eyes.

The night is warm, she thought. And she wanted to be there, wanted to nestle within the forested hills that surrounded this bleak and isolated place.

A black shape came up beside her carrying a rifle, three lighter shadows hanging behind. They were all males, but it was the biggest and closest male who ripped away the straps that bound her legs to the operating table. He put his hand over her mouth and pulled off the anesthesia mask.

She saw that hand clearly before it moved around under her shoulders to lift. Its three, razor-nailed digits glistened dark with blood, and the burrowing spike growing from the right side of the hand looked curved and deadly, and used. She felt herself being raised, being wrapped in roughened cloth and tucked against a massive body that throbbed with heat. She closed her eyes and let the lassitude take her.

She was safe now.

Cold in the Light

--- 2 ---

Michael Russo woke up instantly when the chime went off in his ear. It sounded once before going dead. He rolled over and glanced at the ceiling, at the time reflected there in foot-high orange numerals from the clock on his dresser. 2:47 a.m. Good news didn't come this late.

Russo slid quickly out from the sheets and found his robe without a glance. His wife had not stirred and he moved quietly so as not to wake her, the main reason why he wore a micro-pager in his ear at night. His calls often came late.

He went out in the hallway and down it, past the rooms of his two boys and toward the door of his office. No sound came through that door into the hall, though he knew that behind the wall there would be the chattering of printers and the hum of computers. Six inches of padded and reinforced steel made for effective soundproofing.

He tapped in his access number and the lock read him and opened under his palm. Behind the door were racks of equipment and tables full of printers. A Hewlett Packard DeskJet cranked out pages of numbers; a color plotter fed and devoured paper with a faint shush-shush as it inked out charts and graphs that were the modern day-equivalent to Mayan stelai. He ignored it all, knowing that the important stuff, the stuff that could get him out of snug blankets at 2:47 in the morning, would never appear on a printout.

The focus of the office was the huge, half-moon of his work desk. Russo headed there. The rest of the room might be cluttered but his desk never was. The newest COMPAQ professional computer sat on an anti-static mat in the center of the false-wood surface. A laser printer squatted to one side. And at the far end gleamed the shiny black of a fax machine. Nothing else was allowed except a lined yellow writing pad and a dozen sharpened pencils tucked into an enameled toothbrush holder.

He wanted space around him when he worked.

Right now, though, he wanted to see what was inscribed on the Compaq's big screen. He didn't bother to go around behind the desk, just spun the monitor toward him and leaned close. The message was there all right, a single line of code, like an electronic rune sketched in the air. Long practice made the translation easy.

Charles Gramlich

FIVE GUESTS LEFT DEERHAVEN HOTEL. HARBINGER TAKEN. NORMAL PROCEDURES REVEAL NOTHING. AWAITING RESPONSE.

Russo had expected bad but not this bad. He closed his eyes and tried to swallow the bile rising in his throat. They had known this might happen, though. They had planned for it back when Leonard Suskind still directed the Harbinger Project. And he himself had kept the plan intact when he'd taken over. Now, he used the keyboard to tap out two coded words before setting the machine to transmit.

The words were: "Night Hunt."

--- 3 ---

They stood in a faint hiss of rain, restless within the lyre winds stirred up by the beating rotors of the choppers that awaited them. It was night, two hours before the dawn. The word was given; go now while the heat trail is fresh. And they wanted that heat, wanted to trample it underfoot, wanted to take it into themselves. Their voices moaned with the need as they moved and swayed together.

Petaled armor wrapped their forms, insectile, patterned in zebra stripes for the hunt. Hands moved ceaselessly on rifles, on knives and on bayonets, and on other more exotic weapons. In another moment the helicopters were loaded and headed up into the dark sky. The Institute fell behind them, a flood of whiteness amid the black of the reigning forest.

Faint lights probed the trees below, and in a few places squads of hunters stepped out of the hovering choppers and dropped the remaining thirty or forty feet to the ground. There, they spread out to search. A rough circle was drawn, centered on a little town called Deerhaven, Arkansas, and then it began to tighten like a garrote.

But the radius of the circle was many miles long and the noose was nowhere near closed by the time dawn began to awaken the sun. At the first true brightness of the morning the hunters went to ground. There would be another night. As many as it took.

Cold in the Light

--- 4 ---

Helen Russo woke up to find her husband packing his suitcase. A glance at the ceiling showed her the time, 3:41 a.m. She had started out hating the way her husband's clock reflected the hours and minutes on the ceiling. But she had gotten used to it by now. She had even grown to appreciate it after all the mornings when he'd left their bed before it grew light.

"Michael?"

Her husband looked up from the extra underwear that he was trying to mash into one corner of his grip. He had turned his bedside lamp onto the lowest setting, and in that gauzy light she could see him force the smile that curled up his lips.

"Honey. I'm sorry but I'm going to have to fly down to Arkansas this morning. I got a call. Some of the Harbinger experiments are reaching a critical stage and I really need to be there to oversee them."

"When will you be back?" Five years ago there would have been a hint of petulance in her question. Two years ago there would have been anger. Now there was nothing.

Her husband had never noticed the petulance or the anger. Things hadn't changed now. He just zipped up his bag, picked up his suitcase, and came around the bed to kiss her on the cheek. His IBM portable was already slung over a lean shoulder.

"I don't know exactly, Hon. I'll be staying at the compound so I'll call you when I get there and let you know. Give the boys a hug for me."

"All right."

He kissed her again and she watched him walk out of the room. He didn't glance back. A few minutes later she heard the garage door open and pictured Michael's gray Lexus as it backed down the driveway and onto the street. He'd be heading toward Washington National Airport and the private jet that always waited for him.

If only it was another woman, she thought. *He'd get tired of her. He'll never get tired of his work.*

Helen threw back the covers and sat up, knowing that she would sleep no more tonight. The anger that she had thought gone suddenly came back. She stood and went to the window, glancing off toward the southwest where she knew the airport lay. She'd give him a day to "oversee" his experiments. Then she'd take the boys and fly down to Arkansas to confront him.

Things were going to change!

PART ONE

THINGS BEGIN ALONE

Amid the dregs of a man's soul
one finds many things,
dust and empty tin whistles,
the wheels off a hundred matchbox cars,
a mother's face and the whisper of silk
that passed away.
It is a world of tombs, of coffins,
filled with bones and stones and sins.

And it's always quiet there,
in the memory of ruins.

CHAPTER ONE
(April 30: Afternoon/Early Evening)

----

*Going up the river the explorers saw a raft,
and on the raft a corpse's shell. It came
down with the current, from the far distant
mountains where they were headed. Its passing
left them cold with foreboding*
--In the Memory of Ruins

--- 1 ---

The two big yellow and white road signs seemed to glow with a warm welcome under the fading evening sun. That is until Kyle Dupree got close enough to read the message they carried. Then the sun seemed to die a little more swiftly and the faintly cool temperature of the evening grew chill.

**VERY CROOKED AND STEEP NEXT 17 MILES
6 PEOPLE KILLED PAST 3 YEARS. DON'T YOU BE NEXT**

It had been five years since Kyle had driven up Arkansas Highway 71, back when he was majoring in political science and running track at the University of Arkansas at Fayetteville. He had forgotten about the periodically updated signs and the curvy Ozark Mountain roads they warned about. Eighteen years as a Creole kid in below sea level New Orleans, and the last five as a cop in Bay St. John on the Mississippi Gulf Coast, had never prepared him for hills. Certainly not the kind that carried their own obituary notices.

Still, Kyle had learned to love the mountains during his few years at the U. of A. Dangerous they could occasionally be, but they also owned a startling beauty for a southern Louisiana boy. They actually showed all four seasons rather than just the summer and winter that were so common in New Orleans.

The trees were green now in the spring, but they would turn a hundred colors come the fall, dark gold and pale yellow, saffron and rust, scarlet in a dozen shades. And later in the year there would be snow, though usually not more than a few inches at a time.

In New Orleans the plants were always flowering and that made the old city lovely, but there was also a kind of glory to be found in the changing moods of an Ozark Mountain forest. It was one reason why he'd wanted to come back to Arkansas.

Kyle had thought about moving back up here a dozen times during the last five years, and with his father dead and the older Dupree's debts finally paid off, nothing remained to hold him in either Bay St. John or New Orleans. A job opening with the police department in Deerhaven, Arkansas, not twenty miles from the University at Fayetteville, had given him the excuse he needed to make a fresh start away from places strewn with bad memories. And other than the countryside and the job, there was one even more powerful incentive for Kyle to come back to the Ozarks--Cain Duplessis.

Uncle Cain--Kyle called him uncle though grand-uncle would be the actual term--had saved Kyle's life. Almost literally. There had been a period after his mother's death when an eighteen year old Kyle could easily have slipped over into the same kind of life his father was leading at the time. He could handle the drinking, and he liked the gambling and the women. He'd even started wearing a blade because the bars he went in with his father, while OK for his father, were not quite so OK for a son who carried the "taint" of colored blood.

Then Cain Duplessis had come for him and had put him into school at the U. of A. where any relative of the Art Department's most famous son automatically got a chance to earn his own measure of respect. Kyle would always owe his uncle for that chance, just as he owed him anew for the casually dropped hint that had led to an application and a job with the Deerhaven police force. It would be good to see the old man again.

But first I have to get there alive, Kyle thought, as an eighteen wheeler whipped past him going downhill in the left lane.

The '92 Chevy Blazer that Kyle drove was heavy but it still shuddered and rocked in the backwash, partly because the vehicle sat up high enough so that it practically sailed in the wind. Kyle had almost bought a car, but if he was going to be a cop in the Ozark Mountains then there would surely come a time when he'd have to be out on streets covered with ice or snow. Besides, the optional four-wheel drive and the front end winch he had installed would come in handy if his uncle decided to take him "camping" in any more of the picturesque spots they had nearly died in when Kyle was going to school up here.

A second big truck followed the first, this one going a little slower, and piled up behind it ran a long line of cars. The traffic going down the mountain seemed a bit heavy, until Kyle remembered that on Friday evenings about half the kids from the University headed south to places like Fort Smith, Paris, Charleston, and Greenwood. The traffic on his side of the road was thinner, though there were still enough big trucks to keep things moving pretty slowly.

The problem was that, even though a bypass was being constructed, Highway 71 still marked the only complete route the semis could take from southern Arkansas into Fayetteville where their supplies were wanted. The big trucks dragged down driving speeds on the hills, and those same trucks were responsible for most of the deaths recorded on the signs he had seen. The roads were just a little too curvy for the heavyweights, a little too quick to ice in the winter.

Kyle had seen half a dozen trucks wrecked during his four years up here. He'd seen them jackknifed across the road and on their sides in the ditches. He'd even seen one that had gone completely over the edge of the highway to do a headstand in the timber below.

Fortunately, the last five years had seen the construction of passing lanes on many of the upgrades, and that made getting around the big trucks a little easier than Kyle remembered. He caught two of them going up the next hill but had to slip in behind a third as the extra lane ran out on him.

They crested the rise and started over, picking up speed on the falling slope. And halfway down the long hill toward a little town called Winslow, Kyle saw a quick puff of smoke corkscrew up from beneath the rear wheels of the truck in front of him. An instant later he heard the squall of the big rig's air-brakes and stomped his own brake pedal.

The Blazer had a five-speed manual transmission and Kyle downshifted rapidly as his right foot tried to find the floor beneath his brake. His tires were squealing and he drifted to the right. He

Cold in the Light

let it go. The left lane was full of college kids going home for the weekend.

I'm gonna hold it, I'm gonna hold it, Kyle thought, and then he jerked with surprise and momentarily lost his concentration as he heard the sudden whup whup of a helicopter crossing low over the road. Interspersed with the sound of the rotors came the flat and unmistakable crunch of a high-powered rifle being cut loose.

A praying mantis shadow swept over and Kyle spared one quick glimpse upward. The helicopter was there, less than fifty feet in the air, and a man leaned out the door with a semiautomatic target rifle. Even as Kyle watched, the fellow--dressed like a soldier--fired again, at something in the woods to the right of the highway. Maybe Kyle saw something moving there. Maybe he didn't. But the thought was in his mind that the thing being shot at was the same thing that had crossed the road to trigger the accident he was in the middle of having.

Then the chopper was gone and Kyle's right front tire began crunching road shoulder gravel as he fought to slow his speed. The Blazer's rear end began to come around and Kyle steered into the skid and started tapping his brakes. The big Chevy had an anti-lock system and in another moment Kyle felt his tires catch and knew he would get stopped in time.

He also knew that the eighteen wheeler in front of him, a massive Kenworth, would not. The smoke of peeling rubber poured up from the truck's matched sets of tires, but there was nowhere for the driver to go. And he'd been just a little too close to the station wagon in front of him.

Kyle was off the road as far as he dared go now, still rolling but with a perfect seat to watch the destruction unfold ahead. He saw the Kenworth strike the rear of the station wagon and drive it spinning into the oncoming lane of traffic. A pickup missed the car, and then a little sports piece, a British Spitfire, planted its nose under the wagon's right front bumper. The heavier automobile went airborne, slicing over and through the soft middle of the sports car as if it were a boiled and peeled egg.

Behind the eviscerated Spitfire, two more cars mated in a rending of metal, and on Kyle's half of the road the Kenworth was sliding down into the ditch, smashing through a thin silver rail and plowing up dirt and small trees as it began to go over on its side.

Kyle's Blazer shuddered to a halt on the raw, red edge of the drainage ditch, and the trucker behind him got stopped as well, though his rig sat across both lanes of traffic. The station wagon had come down on the far side of the road--Kyle hadn't seen it hit-- and the Kenworth in front of him looked like a big refrigerator box that had been crumpled in on one edge.

The evening had gone quiet, fading into a silence defined by the lack of screeching tires and tearing metal. The accident was over, the aftermath about to begin. Kyle shoved open his door and jumped out onto the highway.

--- 2 ---

Running. Wanting darkness. Wanting warmth. The Lone shouldn't have felt cold in the dull evening shine, but his mind told him he was, told him that the light was a symptom of ice and snow and pain. He understood the cold pain as an ancestral memory, a genetically coded warning that had no place in the world he lived in now. But that didn't mean it was easy to ignore. Only the fact that the light was dim and that a more dangerous ache hunted him from above kept his legs moving when all his body wanted to do was lie in soft darkness and entwine with the Podcyst and the Mother.

The Mother! She had to be protected. Only an hour ago the day-hunters had come close enough to the Podcyst to nearly startle them all into flight. Someone had needed to lead those hunters away. And he was the natural choice to do so. As the smallest and weakest of the group, he was expendable, though no other in the Podcyst would ever have laid tongue to that thought. They had all been preparing to flee when he had broken first from the Dark-home and bolted into the evening light.

His act had achieved the desired effect. The day-hunters had seen him and spun their flying machine around for the chase. And, just as he'd hoped, the dregs of sunlight had still been strong enough to keep the night-hunters, the Warkind, from joining in on the trail. They would have known not to follow a Lone. As it stood, the Podcyst now had a better chance than before of surviving the coming night. That was all he had really hoped to gain.

But, even as his fears for the Mother and the Podcyst receded, the sound of the helicopter grew closer and louder above him, turning his thoughts to his own survival. He had known how thin his chances were before he ran, but that wouldn't stop him from trying to live.

Maybe crossing the highway had helped. People had seen him there, and that might make the hunters a little more cautious. Then he heard the snap of a rifle being fired at him and realized his hopes were lies. The Project's security troops couldn't afford to let anything distract them from the Podcyst's recapture or destruction. A few people seeing something odd in the mountains of Arkansas just wasn't the same as a whole world knowing.

The sound of a second shot sent the Lone to his belly where he fought his way into a huge patch of blackberry brambles that might hide him for a moment. The helicopter swirled overhead. A flurry of bullets whipped through the briars to pepper the ground around him, and he took that as a sign to double back on his trail.

He came out of the briars through the same hole where he'd gone in, and the helicopter was past him now, moving toward the far end of the berry patch where the hunters were expecting him to emerge. A trooper with a gun stood silhouetted in the chopper's door and the Lone could have taken him with a shot from the M-16 he held in his own hands.

He chose not to. It wasn't from a lack of killing instinct--for the Mother he would do whatever necessary--but because he knew that shooting a single hunter would do nothing to further his escape. Maybe this was even his chance to lose them.

He took off at a right angle to his previous path, stumbled into the ankle deep bed of a dry runoff and went flat in hopes the leaf strewn channel would camouflage him. It seemed to, at least for the moment. The chopper pilot gave up on the blackberry patch and cruised back up the hill toward the empty creek where the Lone hid. But it went past without slowing and the Lone got up on all fours an instant later and headed downstream toward the valley below.

The channel he was in soon joined another dry streambed, and he stayed with the steadily widening way until he began to come upon oily patches of stagnant water. A sharp granite cliff had risen up along one bank of the creek, and as soon as it was arched out above the stream enough to hide him the Lone stood up and began to move more swiftly in its shadow. He liked the dark of the cliff, and the dark growing in the world around him as evening fell. But the coming of the dark also scared him. He might have lost the helicopter but the Warkind would be out soon.

He had gone several hundred yards along the creek when the helicopter made an exploratory run in his direction, driving him under a stony overhang that would hide him from the infrared scopes the day-hunters were forced to use when they searched at night. He heard the chopper begin quartering back and forth in a standard pursuit pattern and squatted back on his heels to wait for them to move away. Then a pebble rattled down the cliff and fell into a green pool of water at his feet.

The Lone leaped up instantly, hands going wet on the plastic stock of his M-16. He hoped the pebble had been dislodged by one of the many squirrels he had seen foraging in the woods around him today, but there was no way to be sure that the noise didn't mark something bigger and more dangerous.

He took one step away from the back of the overhang and glanced up at the cliff face above him. Nothing moved and his heat pits picked up no more than the flow of sun warmth from the slowly cooling rock. But there was something here around him, something that stirred the faintest of winds and startled the quiet fall of leaves.

He spun around, scanning the forest for anything unnatural. Across the streambed grew a darkness filled only with trees, and up and down the channel there was a clear opening that held the last glimmer of the day. The helicopter still searched, but well up the hill behind him now.

He stepped from his concealment and darted forward along the stream, moving quickly and easily past toppled boulders and flood-tossed sticks. The puddles of water grew more frequent as he advanced, and sometimes a trickle ran from one pool to another. A glimmer from a rising moon began to paint the upper limbs of the trees.

He stopped again at a place where a big oak had fallen across the stream. Where the roots had torn away from the soil lay a shadowy hole that reminded him of Darkhome and the Podcyst. The thought left him empty and dying inside and he understood at last how it was that all Lones eventually went insane. He fell to his knees, moaning with a need that could not be met.

Mother!

Cold in the Light

A whisper of breeze lifted the downy hair beneath his rough outer mane. His eyes went wide and he twisted around on his knees, raising the rifle as he moved. At the edge of his vision he saw something release itself from the stone face above him and come down.

A yellow-dark blur filled his senses and he pulled the trigger even as the rifle got kicked from his hands. The bullet struck nothing, and a moment later his almost 200 pounds of bulk was lifted effortlessly from the ground and slammed back against the cliff. A half dozen other shapes joined the one that held him, forming a semicircle that hemmed him in on all sides.

Warkind!

Each of the beings carried an assault rifle and an automatic pistol, and each of them had slung the advanced weaponry over their shoulders in favor of spiked clubs and curve-bladed knives. Morning stars and krisses he believed they were called. The Lone didn't really care about the names for the weapons, of course. His main thought was that he was about to die.

"Mother," he whispered to himself.

The Warkind who held him reached up with a hand and stripped off the plastisteel helm that coiled around its head. The frill of red-tipped, black spines that covered the back of the creature's domed skull rose instantly to give the impression that the being was actually growing in size. As if something already seven feet tall and weighing four hundred pounds needed to appear bigger.

The rest of the Warkind's face was much like the Lone's. There were just two major differences. The hard, yellow-brown eyes were actually larger than the Lone's, but they seemed smaller because of the deeply ridged sockets and the surrounding network of barbs that protected them. The jaw was also bigger, much bigger, and underslung to accommodate a wealth of teeth that could be used for either slashing or crushing.

The Lone had always tried to avoid the Warkind before, but now that avoidance was impossible he found himself noting other characteristics that differentiated the soldiers of his species. While his own coloration looked dark gray, the dominant theme in the hide of a Warkind was yellow on black. While his hair was whip-thin and sparse, the Warkind carried a thick pelt of hair that didn't even seem like hair. Their backs and the outsides of their arms and legs were covered with flattened, blade-like quills that overlapped each other to form a dense carapace. Almost like armor.

Yet another major difference between the two "kinds" lay caressingly against the base of the Lone's throat where the Warkind leader held him. It grew over six inches long, with a convex curve as sharp as an obsidian blade along its outer edge. It bore only a distant resemblance to the stubby burrowing spikes that grew from the Lone's three fingered hands.

The Warkind leader shifted his grip and leaned forward until his mouth was only inches from the Lone's face. His breath stank with meat and his nostrils were flared as he cocked his head to the side to study his prisoner. The thick upper lip curled back over red-stained incisors and the Lone caught a glimpse of ragged shreds of flesh caught between the teeth.

A squirrel?

The Lone tried to struggle against the grip that held him but the Warkind snapped its head forward and down and butted him in the face. Sharp spines raked his skin and he was lucky not to lose an eye, but that pain was nothing compared to the explosion of light that went off in his brain when the Warkind's wedge-shaped forehead pulped his nose and split open his cheek. He moaned but did not scream. The leader's grip on his throat pressed too tight to let that much air pass.

"The Mother," hissed the being. "Where?"

"Here," the Lone choked out. "Near here. In a stream like this."

"You lie. She is not near. The Podcyst is not near. Tell us where or I will hurt you."

"Eat your entrails."

The Warkind butted him again and the blow sounded like a melon hitting cement. The Lone tried to scream but found his mouth too full of blood and broken teeth.

"We'll eat *your* entrails," the Warkind said. "Traitor to the Sept!"

The Lone tried to spit out the blood fouling his mouth but managed no more than a thin drool of redness that wriggled down across his chin to drip on his chest. Still, it cleared his throat enough to let him speak.

"Fool. Your kind are the traitors. We must survive as a people. The Mother must live. The Mother--"

Cold in the Light

The Warkind didn't let him finish. The massive creature brought up its free hand, the fighting spike catching a stray beam of moonlight and glittering with dark intent. Then the leader rammed the spike into the center of the Lone's throat and ripped it toward the side and out. A spattering of blood misted the rock face against which the Lone was pinned, and the head lolled to the side on half of a neck. The Warkind leaned into the arterial stream that burst from the torn carotid and began to drink.

The others of his kind started to sway and moan, the sound rising in pitch until it rippled across the night like a wind. The leader knew just how far he could push them before they would lose their pack loyalty and attack, and when that point was reached he turned and hurled the Lone's corpse into their midst. The body was immediately torn apart.

The leader held up his hand to the faint gleam of the moon and watched the blood drip and fall. He had never killed one of his own species before. He had never even killed anything of intelligence, only animals such as the dogs he had been trained with, and such as the prey that he had learned to hunt. Yet, his brain and body responded exactly as they were meant to.

A fierce joy swept his frame and set his muscles quivering. He lifted his arms to the sky and screamed, and the blood ran black down from his wrist to his forearm. A thousand images ripped through his mind, of mutilation and bloody gore, of wet mouths and cracked bones and white, sharp teeth. He wanted them all.

The others did too.

And he, Kargen, would give them what they wanted.

--- **3** ---

"Might as well call it a night, friend. Nothing more you can do here."

Kyle started at the voice, then looked up from where he sat on the tailgate of his Blazer. A man-sized shadow stood in front of him, an outline painted with flashing blues and reds from the lights of the emergency vehicles scattered along the darkened highway. Kyle recognized the fellow from his drawl, and from the hat of the Arkansas State Police that he wore.

"Officer Rankin. Didn't hear you come up." Kyle exhaled slowly. "But then I didn't even realize it was dark until now. Mind's gone, I guess."

"You're only tired. Best go on now. It's gettin' late and the family will be worrying theirselves."

Kyle didn't tell the man that he had no family except an uncle who wouldn't be expecting him for a while. He had told Rankin he was a cop, though, and the young trooper seemed to believe that all cops had a family. Or maybe he just thought they needed one.

"Where will they take them?" Kyle asked.

Rankin didn't have to question who "them" was. He reached up with his hand to rub his forehead, pushing the hat back from a sweat-darkened hair line. "Most of them will go into Fayetteville," he said. "But they'll take the worst cases to Fort Smith. Facilities are better."

"And the dead?"

"The coroner's office in Fayetteville. The State'll wanna know if any of them had alcohol in their systems."

"It wasn't alcohol caused this wreck," Kyle said. And he was thinking of the words one of the survivors had screamed at him while being rescued from the ruins of her automobile.

"They'll still wanna know," Rankin said, as he turned away toward his squad car and the croak of a radio calling his name. But Kyle Dupree wasn't listening--not to the radio and not to the man. He was lost in his head, remembering.

For the first moment after Kyle had jumped out of his Blazer the earth had seemed quiet in the aftermath of the wreck. Then someone had started to scream and the world's sounds had rolled back to assault his ears with a vengeance. He began to run toward the source of the screaming. And someone ran beside him--the man who had been in the truck behind him, he realized.

Something mangled and green lay on the highway, and he was already past it before he realized it was part of an automobile that had been shredded away from the rest of its body. The main portion of the car lay a dozen feet farther on. It was the British Spitfire that Kyle had seen get smacked by the station wagon.

It took him only a second to realize that the screaming did not come from the Spitfire's driver. She had nearly been jellied by the impact of the wagon going over the top of her. Kyle caught a

Cold in the Light

glimpse of black hair and of a ruptured cheek covered with light skin that had not yet had a chance to darken in the summer sun. Now it never would. But maybe someone else still had a chance to see the summer, he thought.

The station wagon lay on its roof in the ditch beyond the Spitfire, and Kyle could see movement through the upside down rear window, a white hand slapping against glass that had somehow remained intact. Beyond the hand loomed the source of the screams, of a panic driven screech that spoke more of fear than it did of hurt.

In the next instant Kyle was there at the car, looking in through the window at a girl of eight or nine who frantically beat her fists on the glass. Her mouth gaped open, filled with sound, the voice already so hoarse from the shrieking that she sounded much older than her age.

Kyle could understand why she had panicked, why she wanted so badly to get out of the car. When the wagon had flipped and landed in the ditch, a steel fence post had been driven through the front window, past the back seat, and into the cargo area at the rear where the girl was now. The tip of the post had brought her father's head along with it--not the body, just the head.

Kyle felt something warm splash his leg, realized that the trucker who had been running with him had just puked up his latest meal. That was forgotten an instant later as Kyle's mind clicked over his options. He didn't want to break the rear window; the girl would never move far enough back to be safe from shattering glass. Instead, he ran around to the side, the side away from the father's head. The car sat almost perfectly flat on its roof and both side doors were jammed into the earth. They would never open normally.

Kyle dropped to one knee and peered in through the side window. The girl's face was right in front of him, startling him for a moment. She wasn't screaming now, just opening and closing her mouth like a fish on a pond bank.

Kyle stood up and stepped away from the door. "Distract her," he yelled at the trucker, who had remained near the back of the wagon.

"Wha...?"

"Distract her. Bang on the car or something. Anything to get her away from the door here so I can kick in the window."

"Yeah. Yeah sure," the man said, after the moment's hesitation that his mind needed before it could put away shock and act.

As people will sometimes do in an emergency, the trucker had continued to carry out the everyday actions ingrained through long habit. He had taken his keys out of the ignition and still held them in his hand. He used them now to begin hammering on the rear window.

The girl started screaming again, but she did move away from the side door and back toward the rear, scrambling on all fours in the cramped space. As soon as Kyle saw the girl's hands and head appear at the back, he stepped forward and smashed a standing side kick into the door glass. He was glad he'd worn boots as the glass shattered and his foot went through all the way up to the ankle.

In a few more seconds he had kicked out most of the jagged glass and had dropped to his knees by the window. He had just enough time to get his jacket off and spread it over the window frame before the girl came barreling out of the car and threw herself into his arms. Her screams had segued into sobs, and there were cuts and blood on her that did not seem the real source of her suffering.

"I saw it; I saw it," she sobbed. "A monster! And then Dad... And Dad...tried not to hit it. And then... And then... I saw him. I saw his head. It was there. Oh, where's my mom? I want my mom!"

Kyle had his arms around the girl and squeezed her just as tight as she did him. And he was saying "shhh, shhh" into a void that was too impossibly vast to be filled by any sounds he could muster. He refused, however, to tell her that it was "all right." He knew it wasn't. If her mother had been in the passenger seat of the car then she had died too. The whole front end of the wagon had folded up like an accordion.

Kyle started to stand, but felt the girl's arms tighten harder about him and heard her sobs ratchet higher towards hysteria. He quit moving and remained squatting where he was, even after the first cramps bit into the calves of his legs. He wanted to get up, to see if there were any more people in need of help, but he didn't think he could handle hearing the little girl start screaming again. And there were others to help the injured. He was the only one who had his arms around *this* girl.

Cold in the Light

"I'll get someone," he heard the trucker yell. But he didn't answer. He didn't fully trust his voice.

It was maybe five minutes before the trucker's "someone" knelt down beside them, someone from the long line of cars that would be building up now beyond the crash site. Kyle caught a glimpse of brunette hair over the red curls of the girl in his arms, and he heard a quietly soothing voice that seemed to know something of dealing with children. He realized he was still saying "shhh," and he stopped as he felt the newcomer put her arms around the girl and tug gently. For a moment the girl's grip tightened around Kyle's neck. Then she relaxed and allowed herself to be drawn away.

Kyle stood up slowly and stretched to relieve cramp-tautened muscles. He could see across the road to where the long-haul Kenworth had embedded itself in the red clay of the ditch. The driver had climbed out through the window and was smoking a cigarette that one of the bystanders had handed him. He seemed all right except for mincing each step that he took with his right leg.

Behind Kyle, on his own side of the road, there were people with more serious injuries from where a Chevy S10 had rear ended a Toyota Corolla. One person was dead, emptied face already covered by the loan of someone's coat. The others were being taken care of and there didn't seem much Kyle could do to add to the situation.

He looked back at the upside down station wagon, and at the crushed front end where the driver and any passenger would have sat. He had to know if that passenger seat had been filled.

By lying down on his side he found that he could see through a small opening into what was left of the wagon's front seat. There was a sweep of glass-starred upholstery, a spill of wires from under the dashboard. Beyond sat a body that seemed to have grown around the steering column embedded in its chest. The body lacked a head and Kyle actually felt a sense of relief. There was only one body. The little girl still had a mother somewhere.

Kyle remembered standing back up after that. From where he sat now, on the tailgate of his Blazer in the dark, he remembered looking over the wheels of the station wagon and seeing a state police car coming along the shoulder of the road toward the wreck site. And he remembered thinking about how much work it would take to get things cleared up and start the traffic moving again. It was natural enough for him to offer his help, one police officer to another. But now the aftermath of the wreck was over and nothing remained for Kyle to do except leave.

He went around and got behind the wheel of the Blazer and started it up. He waved once at Officer Rankin as he pulled out onto Highway 71 and headed north toward Deerhaven, Arkansas. One thought kept circulating through his mind. Three people had died on the road today, and that meant they'd have to change the signs.

VERY CROOKED AND STEEP NEXT 17 MILES
9 PEOPLE KILLED PAST 3 YEARS. DON'T YOU BE NEXT

Cold in the Light

CHAPTER TWO
(April 30: Early Evening)

In the bed of a mountain stream the men found rounded headstones from a long dead city. And needle shards of clear and fine glass. A paved floor of skulls looked up from the bottom. The sockets seemed to dream of love.
--In the Memory of Ruins

--- **1** ---

Dan Case and Tip Baldridge were up on the roof of the newspaper office when they saw the light floating in the air out over the old mining roads behind Dead Man's Curve. The roof of the *Deerhaven Journal* was a favorite weekend gathering place for the local high school kids, a place for sharing some smoke and some cold malt liquor. Maybe a kiss or two if the company was right. Tonight was Thursday, though, a school night and still a little chilly, and only Dan and Tip were there. Both were seniors and not much worried about grades.

No one knew for sure who had first used the roof of the *Journal* as a place to hang out, but it had become tradition by now to attribute it to Zeb Harkin. Old Zeb had been the only known killer ever born and raised in Deerhaven. The story had it that he used to watch his future victims from this roof while they walked unaware in the streets below. Dan and Tip didn't care if Zeb had ever climbed up on the *Journal* or not, but the crenellated wall that ran around the roof certainly stood high enough to hide a killer looking out, or two teenagers who didn't want anyone looking in while they drank some beer and rolled a few joints.

The wall was also high enough to block off most of the glow from the streetlamps below. And on this moon-bright night it wouldn't have taken much excess illumination to hide the strange floating light that promised a break in the dull evening. That light was buttery yellow and dim as a smoked bulb, but it kept moving up and down and sideways like it was riding on rails of some kind.

Both boys noticed it at the same time, and they'd had just enough beer to wonder if maybe they'd had too much.

Dan Case belched. "Typical southern attitude," he said. "What's that shit?"

"U fo?" Tip ventured.

"Yeah, 'bout as likely as you gettin' into Connie Trittum's pants."

"Then what's your guess, genius?"

"I don't guess," Dan said, as he stood up and stretched. "I find out. Come on."

"What about the stuff?"

"Hell, leave the ice-chest here. Bring the MJ and a beer apiece. We'll be back in half an hour."

"Right," Tip said, tucking the baggy-wrapped joints inside his jacket pocket and reaching down into the dregs of the ice-chest to bring up a couple of Schlitz Malt Liquors. "We take your truck, though. I'm not driving the Camaro around those friggin' roads."

"Sure, we can take the toy. Gimme a beer."

He caught the can his friend tossed over, then moved quickly to the back of the building where he slid his feet over the wall and found the top rung of the rusted old fire escape with practiced ease. There were only a few steps to the alley.

Dan's Toyota sat parked in the lot of the pharmacy next door, resting in the shadows where its black paint job kept it at least partially hidden. Dan felt proud of that paint job. He'd done it himself. And while at it he had painted over the last three letters of Toyota to render it Toy. Deerhaven wasn't very big, about three thousand people, and once Dan had finished his "toy" it meant no one else could get away with the same thing unless they wanted to look like an unoriginal asshole.

The inside of the truck was also nice, with lightly tinted glass and Captain's seats in black leather. A Browning 22 rifle hung in the back window, and only the stereo system was standard issue. It was a good one.

Tip fumbled around in the tape box while Dan started the engine and turned out onto Short Street to take the back way out of town. Tru Maclang was probably the only police officer on duty tonight, and he wouldn't give them much trouble unless he found the grass. Even so, it never hurt to be careful.

Cold in the Light

Tip finally found the tape he wanted, *Peace Sells...But Who's Buying?*, by Megadeth. He punched it in and cranked it. A song came on--called "Bad Omen."

"Shit if that don't thrash," he shouted above the thump of the bass.

Dan smiled and took a sip of his malt liquor. Life was good, he figured. Iced beer. Kick ass truck. A little mystery to season the evening. He reached over and slapped Tip on the shoulder.

"Why in the hell couldn't you a been born a good looking woman?" he yelled.

"Wouldn't matter," Tip yelled back. "I wouldn't give you any of it."

Both of them laughed, but the laughter was deadened by the music and came out sounding cold.

--- **2** ---

Truman "Tru" Maclang was sitting behind Kregg's Auto-Parts store in his patrol car when Danny Case's black pickup came off a side street and turned east onto the main drag out of town. He wouldn't have thought much about it except for two things. First, the Case boy was driving slowly and he never did that unless he was either drinking or planning some trouble. Second, today had seen a hell of a lot of strangers come to Deerhaven. That made Tru uneasy. And when Tru was uneasy with something he worried at it, like he worried at the brand new holes he always found between his teeth after the dentist cleaned away the plaque.

A couple of the strangers Tru had seen were wearing shirts and ties, though most had been dressed in what looked like army drab. Supposedly, the suit people were civilian consultants for some sort of military training exercises going on in the hills around Deerhaven. They had come into town to let the local police in on the secret, and to let them know there was no need to be concerned about the activity.

"All in the spirit of cooperation," Sheriff Hendriks had said when he came to tell his deputies.

All to keep the locals from nosing around, Tru had thought to himself. And he knew the Sheriff probably thought the same, though Seth Hendriks would never push hard enough to find out the truth of what was going on. Hendriks was no fool, and was in no way lazy--though he sometimes gave the impression of being both--but he didn't much care what happened as long as it didn't happen within the city limits of Deerhaven.

Tru could sympathize with that attitude; he felt that way himself a lot. But strange things made him curious, and right now he was curious about the fact that Dan Case, and probably Tip Baldridge, were driving out of town with what looked like a purpose behind them. He started his car and set out to follow, hanging well back so he wouldn't be seen.

--- 3 ---

About 8:00 on the thirtieth, after a miserable day of travel delays, Michael Russo stepped off a Beechcraft KingAir 200 onto the Tarmac of tiny Drake Field in Fayetteville, Arkansas. Trouble with his private jet had forced the change to the twin engine plane in Memphis, and there followed a long bumpy ride over the Boston Mountains of northwest Arkansas to get here. Russo was tired and hungry and cross, and he didn't like the looks on the faces of the three men waiting to greet him.

Two of the three were military creatures, strictly guard-dog models. The third man was Lanny Burns, on-site director of Harbinger for the past few years, and one of five government sponsored scientists who knew all the inside details of the Project.

At forty-nine, Michael Russo ranked as the youngest of what he thought of as "the gang of five" who ran the Harbinger Project. But he was overall director, had been ever since the original director--Leonard Suskind--had retired five years ago. Both he and Lanny had been there in 1974 when the Project officially began, but their roles had been reversed at that time. Then, Michael had only been working on a Ph.D. in genetics; Lanny had been ten years his senior in the field.

Under the famous Dr. Suskind they had joined together during those early exciting years, when the heavens had opened up with possibilities. It was Lanny who had first forgiven him for being Suskind's fair-haired boy, Lanny who recognized Michael's very real gifts as a researcher and theoretician and who had supported the development of his influence in the group.

Cold in the Light

Ultimately, it had been Lanny who stepped aside to allow Michael to take the directorship. The two were friends but each knew that Lanny's act had not been totally unselfish. Burns was a solid researcher and conscientious site director, but he didn't have the force of personality that the civilian head of the Harbinger Project needed. He would never have been able to resist the constant pressure from the military types who wanted to take over the whole operation, and it would have given him heart trouble and ulcers to have tried.

It had been Michael who had the will to do what needed to be done, and for five years he had walked the glacier-edge between politics and the military. So far he hadn't fallen over, though the ice seemed to be getting slicker as the days went on. And on each of those days he'd wished that Leonard Suskind still sat in the director's chair, or that at least he felt more comfortable calling up his old mentor and asking what to do. Today was no exception.

"Your face is telling me something I don't want to hear," Michael said, as the old friends shook hands in the terminal and immediately started toward the exit and the car that would take them to the research compound. The guards picked up Michael's bags and fell into step a dozen feet behind.

"I wish it were lying to you," Lanny said. "Things aren't good."

The arthritic knot of worry that was already curled up in Michael's stomach grew larger, but he forced himself to wait until they were in the car with its anti-surveillance electronics before he said:

"OK, tell me."

The soldiers sat in the front seat; Lanny and Michael in the rear, sealed behind glass. The driver pulled out onto Highway 71 and headed south toward Deerhaven, Arkansas. The Harbinger compound lay just beyond the town.

Lanny still hadn't responded; his teeth scraped back and forth over his upper lip.

"Tell me," Michael said again, his voice lower.

Lanny shook his head, but spoke as if unaware of his own denial. "Well... One of the Warkind groups seems to have a problem. They...uh...caught one of the runaways. Just a couple of hours ago. But...uh. Oh, shit, Mike. They killed the poor thing!"

Russo winced. "Dammit! Shit!" He felt his stomach sicken. "Who'd they kill?"

"Darus. The dogs found the body. We haven't been able to contact the Warkind Pod that did it, though. Probably won't till daylight when they go to ground."

"Which group was it?"

"Pod 2. Kargen's band."

Michael rubbed his forehead. "Dammit," he said again. Then: "Daylight's too far away. Pod 4 has to bring Kargen's group in tonight. That's Graye's band. He's always been steady. And I know I can trust him. He owes me one. He isn't the type to forget."

"Yeah. But it's going to play hell with our search pattern. What if the Podcyst slips through?"

"We'll have to take the chance. I won't have any more killing."

Mike looked out the window, thinking, worrying, and it took a few minutes to realize how silent Lanny had become. He looked over at his friend and felt a cold scalpel of fear slip into his spinal column. Lanny's head rested in his hands and the heavy-set scientist leaned forward in a posture that telegraphed defeat.

"Lanny," Michael called, his voice softer still. "Tell me the rest of it."

Lanny Burns looked up with a face that suddenly seemed drained and old. His brown eyes shone with a copper wetness.

"I didn't...didn't dare send it to you...even in code. I don't know. Maybe I just couldn't make myself acknowledge what happened."

Mike stiffened. "What happened, Lanny? What happened?"

"The Podcyst...killed two people when they escaped. You--"

Mike jerked as if he'd been slapped and Lanny rushed on.

"We'd talked about an emergency C-section and Mother started having some really bad contractions so I told Will Haberly to go ahead. I left to call you but never made it. Haberly started the surgery. That's when the Podcyst broke into the operating room. They must have thought he was hurting her, or the baby. They mangled him pretty bad."

It was Michael's turn to rest his head in his hands. "Oh my God," he said. For years he had tried to cultivate a sense of scientific detachment about the Harbinger Project. Now he felt that detachment slipping away and didn't know how he was going to get it back.

"Who else?" he asked tiredly.

"Drake Hammond. He tried to interfere."

"The commander of our very own Special Forces," Michael said. It wasn't a question, but Lanny responded as if it were.

"Yeah. He was in the operating room. Claimed he wanted to watch. I didn't see him but one of the nurses said the Podcyst tore him up worse than Haberly. Some of his men aren't taking it too well, either. I'm not sure bringing the Podcyst back alive is primary on their minds."

"We've got to get this stopped before it goes any further," Russo said, his voice tightening as he tried to fight the sick feeling in his gut.

Lanny sighed, closed his eyes and swallowed hard. Michael felt his face flush with quick anger and forced himself to keep the emotion out of his words.

"Lanny. I know you're hurting. But we just don't have time for me to drag everything out of you. Tell me the rest of it now!"

Burns twitched in his seat, but his voice kept steady as he replied.

"Darus was seen before the Warkind killed him. He ran across the highway in front of, I don't know how many cars. There was an accident. I'm not sure, but I think Darus caused it. Unintentionally. Three people were killed, Mike."

Michael Russo leaned back in his seat and put a hand over his face. He thought he'd been prepared for more bad news, but hearing that people who knew nothing of the Project had died because of it made him feel like throwing up.

"Jesus, Lanny. This just keeps getting worse. How the hell could this have happened? How did they escape?"

"I'll take the responsibility. They're just so damn smart. And not willing to trust us enough. Too many sides pulling at them. Us. The army. Somehow they built their own M-16s. Made some parts, stole some others. They must have pieced them together over months."

"But why now?" Mike asked.

The question was rhetorical. He thought he knew the answer. But Lanny spoke the same thoughts anyway.

"Something to do with the Mother's pregnancy," he said. "And with the male band, the Podcyst, that's formed around her." Lanny shrugged. "They're going through hormone changes related to that. Hell, we can't predict what humans in like situations will do. Much less the Whoun."

"What are we doing to get them back?" Mike asked.

"We've got an army combing the hills, the Warkind hunting at night. I gave new instructions that the Podcyst is not to be harmed. I hope the hell our people listen. I'm not very good at this. And with Colonel Hammond gone--" He shrugged again.

"How much area to search?"

"Current estimates are that they're somewhere within a twelve mile radius of Deerhaven. The sheriff there has been notified that some military exercises are being carried out around the town. I think that's at least going OK."

Russo sighed, stared out of the car window at the forested hills passing by in the dark. *Twenty minutes to Deerhaven*, he thought. *Another ten to the compound. What could happen in half an hour? A lot*, he knew.

"I'm sorry, Mike," Lanny said. "I was there with them. I should have realized how bad the C-section would bother them. Their first baby and all."

"No, Lanny. The fault is mine. I approved it. I talked to them about it. I knew they were concerned but I thought they understood how dangerous it was for the Mother, for Raina, to try and have the baby naturally. And I can hardly believe that Wahrn has turned killer. He's Raina's mate for Christ's sake. Those two have always been gentle."

"I know. I have trouble with that myself. And I really don't think they set out to do it that way. Something happened. Something in their genetics. Related to reproduction."

Lanny shook his head.

"Unless we find them soon, reproduction may not be an option," Mike said. He waved a hand at the outside darkness. "If Raina goes into labor out there she may very well die from it."

Lanny didn't have anything to say to that.

Cold in the Light

--- 4 ---

No word was spoken about it but Tip reached out and turned down the music as they neared Dead Man's Curve. It just seemed the wise thing to do, and they were both glad he'd done it when they turned off the highway to take Forest Road back into the woods where they had seen the light. That road was full of jeeps and tarpaulin-covered trucks, full of people who were dressed in dark colors. Dan's headlamps flashed across a face that looked seriously pissed. Then he swerved back out onto the highway and kept going.

"Shit!" Tip said. "Did you see the fuckin' gun that guy was carrying?"

Dan was checking his rear view mirror to make sure they weren't being followed. He glanced forward again and then quickly switched his lights to dim.

"Yeah, I saw it," he said. "Looked like an M-16. My Dad's got one from Vietnam."

"Well what the shit are they doing there? It's like the damn FBI or somethin'."

"Maybe it's your UFO."

"Hell it ain't mine." Tip lifted and spread his hands, splattering lukewarm beer over the dashboard. "I don't want no part of this. Let's head it in."

"No way. Forest Road runs to the strip mines behind the lake. And that's gotta be where that light is. We'll head over to Stone Hill and cut through Old Man Fowler's pasture. It'll take us right there."

"I don't know, Dan. Maybe we oughta leave it alone."

Dan looked over at his passenger, then whipped the Toyota off the highway and brought it sliding to a stop on the shoulder gravel. He leaned over right in Tip's face, and though they were friends Tip still felt a little scared. Both of them were seventeen but Dan was bigger than Tip, six feet and two hundred pounds, all-conference linebacker and starting fullback for the Deerhaven Warcats. Tip didn't much like to see him mad.

"I'm going down there and see what the hell is going on. If you ain't got the balls for it then get your pansy ass out of my truck. You can walk back."

"No need to turn asshole on me, man. I didn't say I wouldn't come. I said I didn't think it was a good idea."

"Then fuck you, man."

"No, fuck you!"

Tip was pissed himself now, not thinking about being scared anymore. That was just what Dan wanted. He smiled a lopsided grin and punched his buddy lightly on the arm.

"That's what I like to hear, my friend. Some testicular fortitude. Now let's go find out what's going down."

"You're driving."

"Damn straight," Dan said, as his voice dropped and he looked off into the darkness toward the strip mines that had once supplied coal for most of northwest Arkansas. He wondered what was out there as he shifted the Toyota into low gear and stomped the gas. Gravels scattered as the truck wheeled back onto the highway, and he turned his lights off so that whatever was there wouldn't know they were coming.

--- 5 ---

Tru Maclang figured he had lost the Case boy and was about to pull a U-turn and head it back into town when he passed Dead Man's Curve and saw a crowd gathered along the narrow, dirt stretch that marked Forest Road. He knew right away that it had to be the military "exercises" they had been warned about, and he knew these boys wouldn't take kindly to being interrupted while they worked, but he turned off the blacktop anyway and pulled right up to a military jeep blocking access to the road beyond. This was his backyard and he'd be damned if anyone was going to tell him different.

Just before he drew to a stop, Tru hit his blue-lights once, with no siren, to let them know they were dealing with a cop. Two men came around the jeep, their faces as cold and serious as only military faces can get. They were carrying government issue M-16s, but they were wearing uniforms and insignia that Tru didn't recognize. That bothered him a bit. He was in the army reserves these days and wore a uniform himself a lot of weekends. He had thought that he knew most of the regalia.

Cold in the Light

"Some kind of Special Forces," he muttered to himself, and that didn't comfort him at all.

By the time Tru had joined the army in 1971, the U.S. was already cutting troop strength in Vietnam and didn't need to send any more eighteen-year-old recruits overseas. Instead, they were shipping their best talent only--Special Forces Units like the Green Berets and the Navy SEALS.

Tru had watched those units pass through Fort Bragg while training briefly on helicopters in North Carolina in '71 and '72. They had scared him then, and they scared him now. And he didn't think it was just their reputations. It was more the absolutely precise way in which they fitted inside their skins, as if each part had been machined with zero tolerance for error.

Tru had always prided himself on not letting his imagination ride him too hard, but seeing the special units as they swung along the trails of Fort Bragg had touched the perfume of fear to the soft places of his body. And he was honest enough with himself, especially these days, to admit that he didn't like them because he didn't like the fact that other men could make him feel afraid.

The two soldiers who were coming toward Tru were making him feel that way right now, and it looked for a second as if they were going to walk right through the door of his patrol car and take him. Then an officer moved out from the shadows of the jeep and barked a hold order. He was a lieutenant, with that Special Forces expression that could be judged as neither young nor old. Tru didn't buy the smile sitting on the man's lips as the fellow moved to lean over the car window. Nor did he like the first words that came out of the guy's mouth.

"Excuse me, Sheriff. Can I help you?"

Tru was sure the officer recognized his badge and knew he wasn't the Sheriff. These people didn't make those kind of mistakes. And it made him mad that the fellow seemed to think flattery would sooth him. It wouldn't do any good to show anger, though. If he understood the type, his emotions would just be reflected back at him, like shouting into a barrel.

"I'm looking for a couple of kids in a black pickup," he said. "You wouldn't happen to have seen them, I guess?"

The lieutenant's lips twitched as if he had suddenly recalled the taste of something bad.

"I believe we did," he said. "About five minutes ago a vehicle fitting your description tried to turn into this road."

"And?"

"They thought better of it."

"Did you see which way they went?"

The lieutenant straightened up and stepped back from the car. He looked Tru directly in the eyes and smiled.

"I believe they turned back toward the town," he said. "I'm sure you will find them there."

Tru understood that the man was lying; he was supposed to understand. It was the officer's way of letting the local know that he wasn't wanted here. But it was also meant as a way for the deputy to save face.

Tru didn't care anything about protecting his pride in front of these people. Besides, he had taken the same leadership course years ago. He was trying to figure out a polite way to call the lieutenant a liar when distant gunfire erupted off to the north, sounding like the popping of wet logs in a fire.

Tru had thought the soldiers looked intense a few minutes ago when he had first pulled up, but now he saw them with their guard down and the predators inside of them showing. Their hands were clenched on rifle stocks and their eyes were tight on the darkness to the north. As if suddenly remembering their guest, the lieutenant looked around, almost guiltily. An attempt at a smile flickered on and off his lips, but his eyes were small and cold in the reflection from Tru's headlights.

"Ughm," the officer cleared his throat. "As you can see, the exercises have started. I'm afraid you'll have to leave. I'm...sure the boys are back in town by now."

Tru said nothing. He had heard something he wasn't supposed to hear, something more than just a war game being played out against the forested board of the Ozark Mountains. And the town of Deerhaven suddenly seemed a long way off with its warm lights and predictable troubles. None of his friends knew where he was.

You could disappear here, some deep part of his brain told him, and though he tried to make himself scoff he couldn't quite succeed.

One of the soldiers looked at his commanding officer and then half turned toward the patrol car. Tru slipped the vehicle into reverse. "I'll bet you're right," he heard himself saying to the lieutenant, pleased that his voice sounded steady. "Hope your exercises go well." The car was already rolling backwards.

Tru watched them watching him as he backed out on the road and turned his headlights toward Deerhaven. Two hundred yards away he switched off those lights and pulled over to the shoulder of the highway. His legs were shaking and he didn't think it was an overreaction. There had been a moment there when the Special Forces officer had thought about having him killed.

I should call somebody, Tru thought.

Sheriff Hendriks might believe him but had left for Fort Smith earlier this evening to go to a wedding. The others on the force? Well... Tony Banning always looked too hard for trouble. Wendell Cook never looked hard enough. And he didn't think either of the two had a mouth that could be trusted.

He found himself wishing that Kyle Dupree, the new deputy they'd hired last week, would have started work already. Tru had seen in the interview that Dupree definitely could be trusted. And not just because Cain Duplessis, Kyle's uncle, was a long time friend of Tru's.

Yeah, Tru figured Kyle would be a good cop to have at his back, and he wished he had someone like that around right now. Because in just another moment he was going to turn his car around and go looking for Danny Case and his black Toyota pickup. And he had a feeling that he might not like what he found.

--- 6 ---

The moon wouldn't be up for half an hour, and as they started across Old Man Fowler's meadow Dan thought the night looked as dark as the inside of his grandfather's fifty-year-old brass spittoon. He drove without his lights on too, so they wouldn't be spotted by anyone. Dan didn't know who might be out here to spot them, but seeing the guys with the guns back up the road had made him cautious.

Besides, the dark didn't matter a whole lot. He and Tip had been through this meadow dozens of times on their way to fish the water-filled pits left over from the strip mining that had scraped the insides out of half the mountain valleys around this area. The mining had stopped thirty years ago when the good coal petered out. But the pits were still there, tanked with water that was as bitter as chemicals to the taste, and with bass and bream that cooked up to taste just fine. They were almost to those pits now, or at least to the fence that marked the border of Old Man Fowler's property. The first water stood a ten minute hike beyond.

Dan reached out and poked the eject button on the tape player. The truck fell silent as Dave Mustaine, the lead singer of Megadeth, cut out in mid-yowl.

"It was turned down; what's the matter?" Tip asked, sitting up straight in his seat.

"Nothing's the matter. We're almost to the fence and I want to be able to hear what's going on before we start into the pits."

"Yeah, right."

Dan looked at Tip to see if he could detect any sarcasm, but nothing except a worried tension creased his friend's face, a tension that seemed just on the edge of fear. It was almost enough to make Dan spill out his own uneasiness. Maybe this wasn't such a hot idea. But he had started it now and he intended to see it through.

Dan had gotten his growth spurt late, and he still remembered as a smallish kid being afraid of almost everything. He'd stuffed that fear, even before he hit thirteen and started to put on the inches and pounds that now filled his football jersey. But he knew the fear still lived, and that he didn't dare let it out again. Then the cedar infested fence row that marked the end of the meadow came into silhouette against the faintly lighter canvas of the night sky, and even Tip seemed to sense that it was too late to turn back.

Beyond the few rusted strands of barbed wire that marked the boundary of the fence there ran half a mile of scrub brush that the friends would have to cross before they reached the first and smallest of a series of strip pits. That scrub was mostly southern blackhaw and pine, with a smattering of jack oak and persimmon. The pits themselves would be surrounded by heavier and taller growth, bigger oaks, willows, hickory.

Dan turned off the engine and got out. Tip joined him a moment later, coming around the bed of the pickup in the midst of the night sounds of crickets and wind. Dan took the Browning lever action .22 off the back window rack and chambered a cartridge. He eased the hammer down on the round and then pulled his seat forward so he could get the heavy-duty Maglite that he always carried there. He also took out a wooden box filled with another .22, a Wesson Firearms revolver that his dad had given him last year for his birthday. It carried an eight inch barrel, though there were four more interchangeable barrels of various lengths nestled in the velvet lining of the box.

"Here, take this," he said, loading the pistol and handing it to Tip with the hammer over an empty chamber. "But be damn careful with it. It's double action."

"I know how to use a gun," Tip protested.

Dan stared at Tip for a moment, then shook his head. "Sorry, man. I know you do." He shrugged. "Hey, I'm an asshole sometimes. OK?"

"Sometimes," Tip said, though he smiled as the words came.

Dan shook his head again, flipped on the Maglite and started toward the fence, wishing for a moment that he'd worn a long-sleeved shirt to fend off the cool edge of the breeze.

"Come on," he said. "Let's go find your U fo."

--- 7 ---

Forcefully putting thoughts of the car wreck behind him, Kyle Dupree turned off Highway 71 onto the two lane blacktop that would wind its way for another five miles before reaching the town of Deerhaven. Just short of the city limits would be the dirt stretch that ran up the side of the Boston Mountains to reach his uncle's place. Cain would be expecting him, and Kyle found himself wondering if his uncle had put on a pot of red beans and rice this morning. His stomach certainly hoped so.

Cain Duplessis brought his art into everything he did, and that included cooking. Most of what he fixed reflected his Louisiana Creole upbringing, jambalaya, poisson rouge, crawfish cornbread, and, of course, red beans and rice.

Kyle liked to eat, and he wasn't a bad cook himself, though he couldn't touch his uncle's skill. He planned to catch up on eating while he stayed at Cain's place over the next couple of weeks, and it seemed that half the Blazer's rear space sat filled with the raw material for that eating. Two ice chests were stuffed with crabs, crawfish, shrimp, red snapper, and half a dozen brown paper bags were loaded with garlic, filé powder, artichokes, jalapenos, bell peppers and Creole tomatoes.

Some of those ingredients would spice the pot of New Orleans chili that Cain had promised to make this weekend. That chili was for a local cookoff that Cain had won for the last three years running, but there would be plenty left over to sample.

Kyle's stomach began to growl and he turned on the radio in hopes of deflecting his thoughts from food. There was nothing but a few country stations on, so he pushed in the tape that usually sat ready at the lip of his player. The chameleon notes of traditional New Orleans jazz began to fill the cab, and what Kyle liked about this album was that it was traditional and also new, by a musician he had met recently named Michael White. The title of the album read *Live at the Village Vanguard*.

He reached out to turn the music up, and instead turned it down as a faint rattle of gunshots blew in through his partially opened window. He rolled the glass all the way down but the sound was not repeated. After a moment, he shrugged.

Somebody hunting out of season, he thought.

His fingers found the volume knob on the tape player and cranked it to the right. A clarinet worked alone. But it wouldn't for long.

Cold in the Light

CHAPTER THREE
(April 30: Late Evening)

The hair stood up on their bodies when they saw the ruins. It must have been the roar of winds through the white canyons of stone, or the cold stroke of ancestral memory. Maybe it was just the dead passing by with empty eyes.
--In the Memory of Ruins

--- **1** ---

It hurts, Raina thought.

And an instant later Wahrn stood beside her, offering his shoulder as support. She lip-curled at him, thanking him for his help as she leaned for a moment against his massive side. When the pain had passed they moved on, Wahrn matching his strides to hers as they wove deftly through the thick brush that they had sought out in hopes of camouflage. Raina could tell what Wahrn was thinking as well: *Let me take some of her pain.*

Humans were always amazed at the ability of her people to know each other's thoughts. Some of them called it telepathy, but Raina knew that word was inaccurate. It was just that any Whoun was adept at reading the nuances of any other Whoun's behavior, from the lift of belly fur to the arch of a back, from the wetness of the eyes to the perfume of the pores. And the effect was enhanced when the two were emotionally as well as physically close. Raina knew what Wahrn was thinking because she could see it in him, touch it in him, smell it in him. And he knew the same about her.

Another cramp rocked her stomach then, driving a wedge that split away thoughts from the physical response of her body. Her muscles had begun to move to their own rhythm, ignoring the mind that normally pulled their strings. Raina fought to reassert control.

Not yet, she argued with herself. *It's not time for birthing yet.*

"Mother," Wahrn said, his voice laden with empathic pain. "Please, please hold till we find a place of safety."

And where will we find such a place? Raina's thoughts asked. But she only said: "I will try, Wahrn."

The big male glanced at her, eyes luminous in the scattered faint light of the stars. She knew that he could read her doubts and had chosen not to respond in hopes of providing her comfort. But she knew that he had his own doubts. And she wished she could ease them. Then a new contraction savaged her abdomen and she could think only of a pain that was far bigger than any she had felt before. Involuntarily, she cried out, her voice high and wavering, like wind through a hollow tree.

It shouldn't hurt this much, her mind screamed. Though she had never given birth before, she knew it shouldn't hurt this much. *Something's wrong.* And in that moment of knowledge Raina collapsed to the earth and would have given up.

Wahrn wouldn't allow it. Raina had lent him strength often enough, and now she needed his. He reached down and plucked her up as if she weighed no more than a fallen leaf. Then he trotted off quickly in a direction at right angles to their previous line of march. Without being told, the two males who were following them faded back into the brush to watch for danger.

Raina's cry hadn't been very loud. But it didn't have to be for a Warkind to hear it--and follow.

--- 2 ---

By the time Dan and Tip fought their way through thickening brush to reach the first of the strip pits, the moon was starting to peek over the bulk of the Boston Mountains. It was a pumpkin moon, more suited to fall than spring, but its light spattering off the water in the pit brightened the dark night. Dan turned off the flashlight.

"What did you do that for?" Tip asked.

"Hell, we don't need it," Dan explained. "The moon's bright enough to see by. 'Sides. When you make your own light you only look where the light is pointing."

"Yeah, well maybe that's good. Maybe we shouldn't be looking anywhere else."

Dan slapped his friend playfully on the arm. "Come on! Let's find a place to sit and watch for your flying saucers."

"I wish you'd quit saying that," Tip grumbled, but he followed the larger boy as they climbed up the shale side of the pit and found a soft place to hunker down and study the nighttime world.

South of where the pair squatted, an unbroken line of hardwoods lifted black branches into the sky. In the pit to the east lay the metallic sheen of water, and across the north spread a patchwork of heavy brush. Only in front of them to the west was there any clearing, a long finger of meadow dotted with bluecurls and lobelias. The pungent mass of a sumac bush leaned down its spear-shaped leaves to break up the boys' outlines and hide them from anything crossing the meadow. The two friends didn't have long to wait before something tried that very route.

A crab-shaped cloud had just scuttled over the rising moon when Dan saw the tall grass at the border of the meadow bend aside for the passage of a shadow. At first he thought the shadow was a deer coming out onto the meadow to browse. Then he saw that it walked upright and realized that it was one person carrying another. A moment later a sliver of the moon broke free of the cloud and cast down its ancient reflection. Dan's realization changed, and with it his world.

Dan Case had never believed for a moment that the light he and Tip had seen earlier tonight was a real UFO. He'd just been enjoying a tease at his friend's expense. But now he found himself believing. The two beings he saw in the meadow were not people, though they had hind legs on which to walk and one was holding the other in what appeared to be arms. Dan's mind tried to make sense out of sizes and shapes and skins that were all wrong. His heart just rippled in his chest and his pores burst open with the sweat of fear. He grabbed Tip's arm.

They aren't human, his thoughts shrilled. And beside him, Tip had seen too and was frozen still.

Images built from years of Friday night flicks razored through Dan's awareness: *Alien, Predator, The Thing, Invasion of the Body Snatchers*, half a hundred other celluloid marvels full of screams and gore. They had been so much fun before it suddenly became possible to believe in them for real.

But then the creature who was being carried vented a plaintive cry, and the one who was doing the carrying dropped quickly to its knees to place its burden softly in the grass. In every posture and in every movement that the second creature made, Dan could sense warmth and caring. And his fear gave way to sympathy.

He started to stand, not really thinking, merely responding mechanically to someone in need of help. But before he could reach his feet a throbbing drumbeat of sound rippled across the Arkansas night and anchored him to the shale bank of the pit.

The creatures in the meadow heard the sound too, and it was clear to Dan how much it frightened them. The bigger of the two scooped the other up in its arms and began to sprint back toward the trees it had just quit. At the edge of the meadow two other shadows stepped forward, and Dan saw that they were both alien and that one of them had a rifle. Then a scorpion-shaped mass of darkness swept out of the northern sky and machine guns opened up in a vicious symphony.

A *helicopter*, Dan thought, though he had never seen one move as quietly as this one. It had been almost on top of them before he'd heard it. But it was here now, engines throbbing low like the purr-rumble of some monstrous cat, guns spitting red tracers that sparked like railroad flares. The meadow group's one rifle chattered an answer to that attack, like a man pissing in a rainstorm and expecting it to be noticed.

Dan grabbed Tip and dragged him along as he threw himself backwards into the paper-thin screen offered by the sumac's branches. His friend was muttering a soft litany of disbelief.

"They're filming a movie. It's gotta be a fucking movie."

Dan wanted to scream at Tip to shut up. He wanted to punch his friend in the mouth and keep on punching until everything grew quiet again. But he knew that Tip was only a focus for the red nightmare of emotions that swirled inside of him. The strange creatures and the juxtaposition of sympathy with violence had torn his understanding of what the world was like into shreds.

Dan was scared. "Shitless," his father would have called it.

Dan saw one of the alien-looking beings go spinning to the ground as small caliber, fast slugs from the chopper's guns ripped into its chest and through. He saw the others at the edge of the woods, dodging toward the shadows. And he saw the first line of trees rupture and turn to shrapnel beneath the slash of semi-jacketed bullets. He doubted anything could survive that metal storm, though he found himself begging under his breath for the beings to run.

Cold in the Light

A second helicopter came over the trees then, as different from the first as a tractor trailer is from a sports car. Its heavier rotors cut waves of sound in the air and Dan recognized it as the kind that carried troops. He expected it to land to release its load, and was startled when a dozen bulky figures stepped out of the chopper's doorway and dropped twenty feet into a crouch on the earth.

The machine guns had cut off a few seconds before and that tiny slice of silence had let an animal caution sweep into Dan's mind. They had to remain still, had to stay in this place until the meadow emptied itself again. To move was to be seen, was to die--because whoever was trying to kill the aliens wouldn't hesitate to kill two country boys who'd seen them.

And yet, Dan would almost rather have run and died than to sit still and watch the troopers who had come out of the chopper stand up from their crouches. They were huge, seven, eight feet, and far more alien than the other four creatures he had seen. Their hands were full of metal blades that gleamed in silver. Rifles were slung over the massive curves of their shoulders. Their bulk seemed to fill up the meadow and draw the darkness down, but when they moved it was like a battle tank morphing into a leopard.

Tip bolted.

"Don't run," Dan screamed, and realized at the same moment that he had made a mistake. One glance at the meadow proved that. Had the soldiers been human they would have hesitated a second when they heard him yell. They would have taken a moment to complete a thought, to make a decision on how to respond to a surprise. These things just came. Suddenly, without pause or doubt, they just came.

Dan's reaction was a little slower but no less inevitable. He burst from the sumac's now useless screen and took off around the banks of the strip pit, angling away from the point where Tip had gone into the brush. Whether he wanted to lead the hunters away from his friend or hoped they would follow Tip instead of him, Dan himself couldn't have said. His only coherent thought was to run, faster and farther than he had ever run before. The whispering hiss of grass moving aside for the passage of some huge bulk closing quickly behind him was all the stimulus he needed to give his feet wings. His speed wasn't nearly enough.

Dan had covered barely forty yards, barely five seconds of time, when the blow of a strange hand slapped into his back and knocked him sprawling. The .22 rifle spun from his fist, and he just managed to get his arm up to protect his face as he struck a boulder-sized clump of shale that shattered under him and sent him sliding down the hill toward the pit. His feet slid over the edge of the bank and he grabbed at a knob of greasy rock that broke under his fingers. A second later he crashed into the water on his back and went under.

His feet struck soft muck and he automatically pushed himself off the bottom and struck out for the surface. The water of the pit tasted like burnt chemicals, but it was as clear as mirror ice and Dan could see the moon shining down through it. His head broke the surface then and his lungs grabbed for air. The monster waited for him on the bank.

Dan caught a glimpse of a blunt face whose eyes were buried behind thorn-like spikes. He saw a mouth that was underslung and open, and arms that sprouted from shoulders as thick as tree trunks. He saw a predator's hands, with scarred yellow nails and a six inch bone blade where a human's last two fingers would have been. The creature came in the water after him.

Even with the drag of wet clothes and tennis shoes, Dan was a good swimmer. And he turned now and dove deeply into the black water, trying to stay under as long as he could in hopes of losing his pursuer. Something brushed his leg and he kicked it away, unsure if it were the creature that hunted him or only a floating piece of weed. He didn't want to know which.

Inside of two minutes his lungs were barbecuing in his chest and spider-black floaters were dancing in his eyes. When the need for air finally forced him to the surface, the first thing he did was glance over his shoulder for pursuit. With a spurt of both surprise and euphoria, he saw that the creature was actually falling behind. It clearly wasn't adept at swimming. But though it moved like a bathtub through the water it just as clearly wasn't going to stop.

Dan set out to lengthen his lead.

The pit was about sixty yards long and at the other end was a gently sloping bank worn down and rutted by the hooves of cattle coming to the water to drink. Beyond that was an open meadow where Old Man Fowler kept his prize rodeo bull, a huge, brindle-colored Brahman who was known on the bull riding circuit as Hammerstomp.

Cold in the Light

Dan and Tip had hung over the fence on many a day and talked about giving Hammerstomp a try. They had never done it, and now Dan's memory of the bull's massive chest and mean looking shoulder hump gave him an idea. Hammerstomp didn't like having other living things in his meadow, and he didn't care if they were human or not.

With a slim hope perched now on his shoulders, Dan redoubled his efforts to open a gap between himself and the thing that was chasing him. That gap widened, slowly, and by the time Dan dragged himself from the water at the far end of the pit he had gained almost twenty yards on his pursuer.

Picking up that lead had cost him, though. His heart was hammering far too fast and his legs were twinging with the first sign of impending cramps. He tried to ignore the pain as he staggered to his feet and took off in a stumbling run toward the fence that marked the boundary of the rodeo bull's territory.

Hammerstomp had been known to leap a fence or two and Old Man Fowler had hung his top strand of barbed wire almost six feet off the ground. Dan could never have jumped it so he went to his belly and rolled beneath the lowest strand instead. Rusted barbs grabbed his shirt, dug furrows in his shoulder, but he twisted free and came to his feet again. The meadow in front of him was bright with new moonlight. There was no sign of the bull. Behind him came a faint plash, the sound of his hunter leaving the water. Dan began to run again, though he felt close to the end of his strength.

Only a moment later Dan caught his second wind as the dark bulk of Hammerstomp loomed before him in the night. The Brahman was standing beneath a lone oak tree in the middle of the field and Dan changed course right toward him. He glanced once over his shoulder to see where his "shadow" was, and wished that he hadn't as the creature cleared the top wire of the fence in a single, soaring bound.

Desperately, Dan began to yell as he ran, hoping to attract the bull's attention. It worked, and the boy felt a sudden exaltation sweep over him as the Brahman moved out from under the tree and the moonlight caught its wicked horns and bounced off. He could almost feel his stalker slowing up behind him.

The bull's head came up as he smelled something he didn't like-- Dan hoped it wasn't him. Then Hammerstomp snorted angrily through his .44 magnum nostrils and moved his panzer bulk farther out into the field.

Dan swerved to go past the bull but he needn't have bothered. Hammerstomp had picked up the strangeness in the alien creature's odor and was just as pissed as hell about it. The boy's over-the-shoulder glance came just in time to catch the opening round of the confrontation that followed.

Hammerstomp charged and the creature seemed almost to skip aside. But the weird being clearly hadn't had much experience with rodeo bulls. Before Hammerstomp was even past the point where the being had stood, he'd pivoted off his hind legs and lunged forward in another attack.

The bull hooked with his right horn and Dan saw the point bite. The creature was driven to the side, driven a dozen feet and smashed into the tree beneath which Hammerstomp had rested moments before. Then Dan stumbled and had to look down to keep from falling.

In the next moment the woods at the far end of Hammerstomp's meadow loomed in front of Dan. His body wanted the protection that he sensed in those woods, but his head turned almost despite himself and he took one last glance into the field behind him. What he saw there carved itself like a wound into his brain.

The moon was high now and free of clouds, its light coating the night with the whiteness of bones and ghosts. The creature was limned by that whiteness, and it was still on its feet. It was holding Hammerstomp by the horns and slowly twisting the bull's head to the side. That wasn't the worst of it, though.

In the tree just above the struggling figures, there hung a kite of shadow. Dan didn't realize what it represented at first; he didn't know that it was alive until it released itself from among the branches and came down to the ground. Then he saw the effect it produced. He saw the thing that had been hunting him lose its head--saw that head detach itself from its shoulders and leap upward into the sky, spinning as it went and spitting blood like a firecracker wheel spits sparks.

Dan looked away, his gorge rising, and as he entered the woods at a run he heard two screams erupt across the night. One was in the meadow behind him and he would never have believed a bull of Hammerstomp's bulk could have produced such a high pitched sound. The other was much farther away, but he recognized it anyway. Dan had heard Tip scream before, though never with quite so much feeling.

--- 3 ---

Human running, Kargen identified, as he squatted in the tree and let the dark, warm wind slide over and around his quills. *Easy to kill.*

But now! His gaze turned downward; his muscles tightened like small animals moving beneath his yellow-on-black skin. Below, pitting himself against some beast that he had foolishly allowed to injure him, was another Warkind. A member of Hark's band. Not yet blooded. *Weak!*

The tendon at the base of Kargen's war-spike ached. He flattened the heavy quills that armored his back and sides, and stepped out of the tree to drop quietly toward the earth. Falling, his thoughts were on the weak, and on how they must be eliminated if his people were to survive. Surely the Mother would understand that.

Thoughts of the Mother energized Kargen's attack. As the second Warkind heard movement and began to turn, Kargen's clawed feet grabbed firmly at the dirt and he swung his arm from the hip. The glittering, six inch spike on his right hand cleared the other's carapaced shoulder by a micrometer and ripped into the less well protected throat behind. The spike sheared through, separating head from neck like a scythe clipping a stalk of grain. The head spun away; the leftover body fell to one side.

Blood splattered and Kargen felt as if the death had suddenly filled him with the purest of fuels. Power stroked his limbs and the muscles surged beneath his hide, straining at the bone. His eyes were locked tight on the bull that had been held by the other Warkind.

Hammerstomp snorted in rage as the restraining arms went loose on his horns. He came, homing on a scent that he hated, and Kargen moved like a ripple of wind through the grass. The Warkind brought both arms over and down, spikes a contrast of black against bloodied red.

The bull slammed him in the stomach, knocked him against the tree. And Kargen gloried in the exquisiteness of the pain. His own strike was unblunted, the bones of twin war-spikes scissoring through nerves and sinew. The bull bellowed, high pitched like a child, and dropped dead to earth. And in a pleasing synchrony there came another scream as well, distant, and human. Another of his band had made a kill.

Kargen looked down at his own kills then, and the smell of raw meat aromaed the air that filled his widened nostrils. His penis extruded, tumesced. He knelt and ripped open the dead animal's belly, spilling a miser's hoard of intestines into the cool night air. He dipped both hands into blood and brought them up cupped to his lips. A single taste burst ripe into his mouth, and then he smeared the remainder over his face and down his chest to his groin. His ejaculation was as intense as the stroke of a nail-embedded whip.

The weak must be destroyed; the strong must survive. Surely the Mother will understand that, Kargen thought. *Surely she'll understand that. When I take her.*

--- 4 ---

Tru Maclang followed Highway 265 up past Stone Hill, driving slowly with his window down and his lights off. He'd seen no sign of the Case boy's black Toyota anywhere and was about ready to head it on home. A closed gas station at the top of the hill offered the deputy a place to turn around, and he pulled into its sparsely graveled lot and brought his cruiser to a stop. That was when his ears caught just the faint impression of a shout.

Tru turned off his engine and sat there for a moment, waiting to hear if the sound was repeated. It wasn't. But as he sat there in the quiet an impression of fear crawled up on his shoulder and began to whisper in his ear. That fear came out of many things, the metronomic ticking of his car engine cooling, the blackness of a night where the moon's light seemed swallowed, the sudden stillness of the world around, like spoiled butter melting on a plate.

There should have been a wind to stir the odors of pavement and grass, Tru thought. But the wind had died. There should have been an orchestra of crickets and frogs. But they were silent. There should have been a comfort in being cocooned inside his car with a gun strapped to his hip. But he didn't feel any comfort. He felt like something wrong was happening here. Not just bad, but wrong.

Cold in the Light

Feeling halfway foolish and halfway scared, he reached a hand for the car's ignition, and stopped as a fleeting shadow caught in the corner of one eye. It was coming his way, coming fast, coming straight toward the police cruiser from across Old Man Fowler's meadow. The hair stitched itself to Tru's scalp in a cold wave. His right hand dipped for the service revolver at his belt; his left grabbed at the door latch, snapped it open. The back of the car rocked as the shadow struck it.

Tru heard broken taillight glass tinkle on gravels, and by that time he was out of the cruiser, knees locked in a defensive crouch and pistol thrust out before him. Whatever had hit the car had been knocked down by the impact, was momentarily hidden by the bumper. Tru saw a hand come up and slap on top of the trunk. He heard a faint screech as the nails of that hand slid on the metal, but there was still enough strength in the hand to pull the body up behind it. Neither the hand nor the body were human.

For the first time in his seven year career as a deputy, Tru Maclang almost fired his revolver in the line of duty. His finger had taken up the last of the trigger's slack when his eyes saw something that froze his grip on the weapon. The same hand that had scraped paint from the rear of his car had now moved to rest on a belly that was ripe and swollen with pregnancy. The other hand would scarcely move at all. It hung from an elbow that had recently mangled under the impact of a high velocity bullet.

Tru looked up to meet the other being's gaze. He saw wetness there, a reflection of moonlight that glistened like brass tears. The being was taller than Tru, probably heavier by fifty pounds, but it was also hurt and in that moment it seemed as fragile as a bone needle. Tru's finger released the trigger; his hand lowered the gun. The creature seemed to nod at the deputy once before turning and moving off toward the trees across the road. Tru watched it go, his mind vacuumed free of thoughts.

After a moment the deputy got back into his car, twisted the key in the ignition. The familiar sound of his engine coughing to life brought the thoughts back in a flood. He'd go see his old friend Cain Duplessis first, and if a man as level-headed as Cain could believe him, then they'd start calling people and getting them out of bed. Tru had a feeling that tomorrow would not be soon enough to share what he had just seen, and only in the very back of his mind did he realize that Cain's house lay in the same direction the creature had just taken.

--- 5 ---

Mother. Mother!
Wahrn's thoughts ached to be spoken. But he didn't speak them. And she couldn't have heard them if he had. Wounded and with the Warkind coming soon, he had made her leave him. And she had gone because both knew that the hope of their race lay inside her womb. Now only his thoughts could follow her, urge her on her way, though as often as not those thoughts skittered back to the moment when the forest had bloomed with gunfire all around their small band.

Wahrn had seen the other two males of the Podcyst killed in that conflagration, had felt the razor lash of bullets against his own legs and back as he tried to stay between the gunships and the Mother.

Even wounded he had still been able to run, to run with the Mother only slightly injured beside him. Until! Until something broke liquidly in his chest and he had fallen to his knees, and from there to the ground. He couldn't run anymore and he had made the Mother leave him to save herself and the child she carried.

Behind her he would wait, try to slow the Warkind when they followed. Even now he could hear them coming, coming closer.

He wondered why they were making so much noise.

--- 6 ---

Twenty minutes after reaching the Harbinger compound and walking into the building's command center, ten minutes after giving orders that he felt confident would help locate the escaped Whoun, Michael Russo was rudely apprised of the fact that the search for the Podcyst had gotten out of hand and he was now directing a catastrophe. He was pouring over maps with Lanny when the sound monitors from one of the search parties erupted with the shock of gunfire. For an instant, everyone in the center froze. And then Russo was vaulting the narrow steel rail that separated him from the technician running the radio equipment.

Cold in the Light

"What the hell are they doing?" he yelled at the man. "Tell them to stop shooting. Tell them to stop."

But by that time the technician was shoving back in his chair, ripping off his headphones as a cat-squall of feedback tore through the electronics. Russo grabbed up the dropped earphones, punched the send button. But he could feel the dead air waiting out there beyond this room.

"It's no use, sir."

Michael looked down at the technician's hand where it had gripped his arm. He started to pull free, then abruptly sagged and slid down against the equipment.

"It's no use," the tech was saying again. And: "Sorry, sir. The transmission was cut at the source."

PART TWO

THINGS COME TOGETHER

They have a place to hide,
all the scars from all the dreams
that have been given up on.
They know how much it hurts,
to face one's sins,
to be reminded of failures.
That's why they sit and wait,
till it's time to cause pain.

And you'll never see them there,
in the memory of ruins.

Cold in the Light

CHAPTER FOUR
(April 30: Night)

Marble statues lay flat under a sky of bruise-blue, toppled by one long winter after another. Even the massive towers bent down their stones, like shoulders curved by the weight of labors. There were many places to hide.
   --In the Memory of Ruins

--- 1 ---

Behind the welder's mask, the eyes of Cain Duplessis were black, with scattered rust flecks that remarked on a varied ancestry. His skin was brown, now darkened further with sweat, and the backs of his hands wore a patina of coppery ash. The bones in front of him were a contrasting white--though in the quick dripping sparks of the acetylene torch they glistened with a sapphire watering.

Like the fluted claws of a blue-legged crab, he thought.

Cain snapped off the torch and watched the settling sparks die out on the concrete floor of his workroom at home. He was smiling when he shoved back the mask and wiped sweat-wet eyes on his sleeve.

"Leave the simile to the English Profs," he snorted at himself. "It's their province. You just make things that move."

Before him lay something that moved, a wind chime of bones mated with dark iron, a skeleton of separate dancing parts filled with a viscera of golden-wire webs and dangling, metal insects that might have lived in the times of Pangea, 300 million years ago when all the continents were one. This was only the latest of his pieces. Each one had a movement, and each movement a sound. This one made him think of an ocean shore where tides and rocks wrestled in a foam of froth. He had another that sounded like tears on a griddle, and one that made you feel a winter cold when it rang. There were many sounds to capture.

Cain took up his jeweler's file and smooth/polished the weld he'd just completed, then hooked up the block and tackle and hoisted the man-sized sculpture onto the bed of the hand truck he had built just for this purpose. The truck rolled easily once he got it started, rolled easily through the workroom toward the climate controlled garage where his pieces were stored.

He hesitated before opening the door to that garage, as he always did. He knew that he was not a great artist, but he had enough favor to capture some of the same feeling he'd experienced on first seeing a Mali headdress or a Benin Bronze. He felt it again now as he slowly pushed back the door and stared into the soft darkness with blind eyes.

Faint prickles of light starred his eyes as they began to adjust. In a moment he could make out the scalloped geometries of his pieces. There were fifty of them here, counting the one on his hand truck, fifty pieces for the biggest showing he would ever have. They were made of bones and metals, of nails and tightly curled shells, of plates of slagged glass and glittering weapons that his students had brought him over the years for his anti-crime drives.

"Swords into art form," the students called it.

On the wall to one side hung the ripped out trigger mechanism of a Remington autoloader. It made a curved penis for the sculpture it served. At the other end of the room stood a work put together out of a horse's cranium and two dozen thin knives for spinning ribs. The biggest piece had a wrecked motorcycle for a body and a dozen spiny legs that were welded from rifle barrels. It was modeled after a bizarre creature he'd seen in a book once, a creature named Hallucinogenia. He had thought the name apt.

Still in darkness, Cain pushed his newest piece over to an open space already prepared for it, then looked around for the heavy-duty block and tackle that he had installed a year ago to help maneuver the bigger pieces he worked with these days. It hung in shadows against the far wall, nestled like a spider among the web of steel bars that he had built to support it, and which allowed him to position it over just about any spot in the garage.

It had taken two weeks to put that system in. While at it, he had cut a skylight and had it filled with the stained glass abstracts that a friend at the university worked with. Now the moon shone strongly through the variegated prism of the glass, giving Cain enough light to see by and turning the storage room into a Dali-esque landscape.

Cold in the Light

Strange faces of light were painted on walls and floor, dripped down like brightly colored liquids over the curves of his sculptures. They stirred with the faint, wind-powered movements of tree limbs that overhung the house and lay between the skylight and the moon. This was Cain's ideal church, a place where technology and nature had been welded together, a place where Africa and Europe and the Americas were all part of the weave. He liked it here at night.

After a moment he sighed and took a step toward his block and tackle. He had to finish here and get back to grading the final projects his art students had turned in. He stopped again as something struck him odd about a globe of yellowed moonlight that had gathered at his feet. Centered in that globe lay a fuzzy shadow that seemed to have sprouted dozens of needle-like horns.

He looked toward the skylight, eyes searching for the arrangement of stained glass that had provoked that image. But it wasn't the glass. What he saw staring down into his pseudo-church looked very much like a real demon.

Cain Duplessis couldn't remember the last time he'd been afraid. He didn't think he would ever forget this time. His heartbeat went from slow and steady to rapid and fluttering, and his skin tightened painfully as his muscles filled with blood. His eyes seemed to melt into the gaze of the creature on his roof.

Then that connection broke as the being shifted away from the skylight. Cain heard shingles rasp as something scraped across them, then heard, or thought he heard, the thud of a heavy body dropping to the ground outside. The garage door banged, rattling sculptures against the wall. Cain almost expected to see that door lift. But it was locked, he remembered.

His front door wasn't.

Cain turned in a surge of adrenaline and raced across the garage, his hand finding and flipping on the light switch as he went through into the main part of the house. The front door stood to his right and as he turned toward it he heard the wooden frame rattle-rattle as something hit lightly against it several times. He froze, trying to think what he would do if the thing came through after him.

He needed something. A weapon! He didn't own a workable gun. But there were knives in the kitchen.

Then the doorbell rang. Cain jumped, startled by the unexpected sound. Were demons ringing at doors politely these days?

In the next instant, though, Cain's flash of puzzlement mutated into more fear. *Kyle!* His nephew was due any time. Could it be him outside now? With that thing?

Cain rushed toward the door, yelling a question, but it wasn't Kyle's voice that he heard answering him from beyond the wooden panel. He threw it open and saw Truman Maclang standing beneath the porch light, lips drawn flat instead of curved into his usual smile.

Cain's eyes flicked over the darkness beyond the spread of the light. He sensed that the dark was empty of menace, but that didn't keep him from grabbing his friend's arm and ushering him over the threshold into the house. It didn't stop him from shutting and locking the door behind them.

"You're not gonna believe what I--" Cain started to say, and stopped as he realized the deputy was echoing him word for word.

Tru Maclang realized it too, and his bark of reflexive laughter sounded almost convulsive. The deputy shook his head.

"On the other hand, maybe you will believe it," he said.

"You have my guarantee," Cain replied.

--- 2 ---

Kyle took the turnoff to his uncle's place and slowed down to an easy pace on the bumpy dirt road that met him. Cain's house sat a little over a mile off the main highway, well away from any other homes and uphill most of the way along what seemed little more than a glorified logging trail. Rocks pounded the underside of the Blazer and Kyle downshifted, slowing even further. But the 4.3-liter V6 had no problem swallowing the grade.

Popping the tape out of his player, Kyle rolled down the Blazer's window to let in the night. It was an Arkansas country night, the kind he had grown to love during his college years up here. The air blew cool back past his face, and it carried with it the rip of crickets and the throat-deep rumble of frogs. There had been many nights when Kyle had sat out on car hoods with friends from school, the bunch of them drinking beer and talking, feeling the darkness around them. He felt comfortable in the dark, never afraid.

The lights of Cain's two story house came up on Kyle's right and he turned over a culvert into the big front yard. The first thing he saw was the deputy sheriff's car, and his stomach flinched. *Something's wrong,* he thought. But when his uncle opened the door and drew him into a room that smelled of Creole cooking, Kyle felt himself relaxing.

The deputy was Truman Maclang. Kyle remembered him from the interview at the Sheriff's office, remembered that the man was a good friend of his uncle's and that he had liked the fellow whom everyone called Tru. He had thought the deputy's feelings were similar, and that thought got reinforced now by the friendly way in which the man greeted him.

Kyle decided the deputy was only visiting, and when Cain brought out mounds of red beans and rice that seemed to hide the plates they were sitting on, he forgot all about his earlier apprehension and dug in with a hunger that had been building for the last ten hours. Halfway through his plate Kyle realized his uncle had taken only a few bites and that Maclang had done no more than pile his beans into little teepees. But it wasn't because they were talking instead of eating. The bite of worry returned to Kyle's stomach, and the beans suddenly seemed a cold gruel in his mouth. He pushed the plate away.

"All right," he said. "Who's going to tell me what's going on here?"

--- **3** ---

Restless they stirred--in the absence of Kargen--in movements like yin and yang symbols flowing over and around each other. Yet constrained by the tether of some object that lay in the dirt at their center. Lips were parted, tongues tasting at the night air as they drew it in over yellow-white teeth. Corded hands clenched, spasmed, pulled at the body armor that was meant to protect them but which seemed to do no more than restrain their muscles.

One of the Warkind ripped off his acrylic helmet and hurled it into the dark. Another followed that act. And a third. In a moment they were all tearing away at the human-made bindings that kept their bodies from the air. Even rifles were dropped to the ground, and only edged weapons were retained.

Their movements became quicker, almost clonic. A huge Warkind, his head-quills tipped with the scarlet that marked dominance, leaped into the center of the circle and struck the object that lay there. Another came in, circling the object in a series of fits and starts. The bone blade of its left-hand war-spike tore holes in the air, and then it was striking, striking, striking. And leaping away.

A communal convulsion seemed to grip the band, a berserk chorea. One Warkind turned on his neighbor in a frenzy of biting and snapping. Yet another bit only at himself, tearing at his arm until blood spurted into his mouth.

The biggest of the group, he who had been first to seize the center, lashed out with a taloned foot that sent a smaller beast rolling. Then the giant roared a challenge, the quills rippling along his back and arms and flushing an even deeper crimson on his head. He bent toward the object that had focused the band's attention, his head moving down and to the right as he stripped away a tithe of flesh with his teeth.

Something struck the big Warkind from the side, beneath the shoulder. The blow lifted him bodily, flipping him over onto his back to smash hard on the earth. Instantly, the giant's limbs snapped out against the dirt, levering him upward. Clawed toes grabbed at soil and he came to his feet like a cat twisting in midair.

Kargen loomed there before him, returned now to his band, blood coating him like a slime and the massive cranium of a slaughtered Warkind in one fist. Kargen's head-quills had turned darkly red, down to the spikes that arched over his eyes.

Kargen dropped the skull and snarled an answer to the challenge that the other Warkind had issued seconds before.

"I am first here, Chane. You will remember it."

But the one called Chane was beyond words now, and beyond remembering. He attacked, hands just catching the earth as he went to all fours and lunged, speed building like a muscle car going into top gear. Kargen leaped straight up in the air to avoid Chane's rush. But even airborne he struck back, the talons of his left foot ripping furrows in the other Warkind's yellow-black hide.

Chane swapped ends in a flurry of dust, and as Kargen's feet touched earth the Pod leader found himself swarmed and going under. A blunted muzzle struck at his jugular, hot with breath and spittle. A war-spike ripped toward his eyes.

The quills at Kargen's throat saved him from Chane's teeth. And his hand caught the wrist driving the spike and turned it aside. His other hand came up from beneath, driving his own spike into the bigger Warkind's belly.

Drunk on his own adrenaline, Chane didn't even recognize the pain of his wound. He lashed out with his free hand, but Kargen twisted his head aside at the last instant and Chane's war-blade grazed harmlessly past his ear, exploding its violence against the ground instead of against Kargen's face.

Kargen's spike didn't miss. For the second time, he snapped it deep into Chane's belly, twisting it as he sought for some vital organ. This time Chane grunted, shifted his weight, and Kargen gained enough leverage to flip his attacker over his head.

Chane was ready for that and he spun in the air to come down in a defensive crouch. But Kargen surged up too, on all fours, and now he was the one attacking. Chane didn't try leaping over him; he collapsed to his knees, hammering down with both war-spikes gleaming.

Kargen wasn't there.

One fraction of a second earlier, the Warkind leader's tremendous hind limbs had uncoiled, driving him forward and up. And he was in the air, turning, turning, coming down behind the other Warkind. Chane was already moving, trying desperately to throw himself forward out of the way. But he was too late to avoid the tendon-ridged arms that whipped around his neck. He was too late for anything as Kargen arched himself backward and kicked out with both feet. Scythe-like talons hooked into the muscles at the back of Chane's upper legs and peeled them to the bone.

Chane bellowed with pain, and with a sudden fear that blossomed wetly in the deepest core of his brain. He tried to push himself back against the stricture of Kargen's arms, only to find that his hind limbs flapped uselessly instead of giving him the purchase he needed. Then Kargen took out Chane's right eye, reaching in past the cirriform arcs of the socket spikes with his war-bone and plucking it out like he was using a lobster fork on the last morsel in a crab's claw.

Chane bellowed again, a halfhearted bellow laced with a whimper of helplessness. With all the fatalism of the Warkind in defeat,

Chane's will had already started its retreat from the world. His upper body slumped in Kargen's arms and his head- quills began to fade from red toward white.

Kargen's tongue flicked from between his teeth, licking up the odors of pain and dying. Then he snapped Chane's spine and pushed the body away so he could stand. The rest of the Warkind waited, twitching and swaying in absolute silence.

Deep in his own silence, Kargen moved over to stand above the object that had so recently been the center of the band's attention. His nares widened and he broke the quiet with a low rumbling growl. The war-blade of his right hand touched lightly at his cheek, then sliced down along his jaw so that the red blood welled. He flicked the blade toward the others, anointing them with scarlet droplets. A dozen mouths opened; nostrils flared for the scent. The night seemed to fill up with the promise of more violence.

"The Mother is ours," Kargen growled. "The firstborn will be Warkind. Or it will be nothing. And nothing will stop us. Not Whoun. Not Human."

Low moans of killing hunger met his words, but Kargen's thoughts had drifted and he wasn't paying attention. He was looking down and watching the living drops of his own blood as they fell on the dead and mangled face of Tip Baldridge. The contrast was beautiful.

--- 4 ---

"Remember when we first found out about them?"

Michael Russo turned away from the doorway where he stood, the doorway into a room they had planned to use as a nursery for the Mother's first offspring. He had been thinking about the report he'd just read--direct from the field--on the near destruction of the Mother's Podcyst. Lanny had come up behind him, unheard against the white noise of Michael's thoughts. But his friend's bemused gaze suggested that there were others here tonight whose thoughts were full of disorder.

"Yeah," he answered Lanny's question. "I was thinking about it. Seeing Len Suskind with that metal box. Frost all over it. Not knowing what was inside. I remember how my spine seemed to liquefy when Leonard told us where it had been found and what it held."

"I got the hiccups," Lanny chuckled. "Some big muckety-muck had to take me out in the hall for a drink of water."

Russo smiled. "Swallowed your gum or something, I think." He shook his head. "Doesn't seem like twenty years."

"We gotta do something, Mike. The Mother's out there."

Michael rubbed his nose beneath his glasses. He sighed.

"I know. At least Teagle's out in the field with his troops. Our new commander swore he'd court-martial anyone involved in firing again at the Podcyst. Drake Hammond was a bit less reasonable, if you remember."

"I guess. I'm not sure Teagle has what it takes to ride herd on those Special Forces killers of his, though. Hammond you couldn't rattle. No way. You'd almost think the Podcyst deliberately took him out. Dammit, why couldn't I have seen this coming!"

"A misjudgment. On my part as well as yours. And ordering the hunt was another. Mine alone. I thought the best way to catch a Whoun was with another Whoun. But Teagle will do. The troopers don't worship him like they did Hammond, but they'll follow what he tells them."

"And what about the Warkind? Will *they* do what he tells them? You know we still haven't heard anything of Kargen's band. What if they..."

"What if they what?"

"What if they've...reverted or something?"

"Reverted?"

"I don't know. Turned savage or something. We don't know shit about them. We watched them grow up and we still don't know shit."

"They won't hurt the Mother."

"How do you know?"

"I know, dammit! Kargen...would never...hurt...the Mother. Or let her be hurt. I've seen the way he looks at her. He'd give his life for her. Like all of them."

Lanny's voice softened. "You just wanna believe that, Mike. You don't know. I've seen that look you're talking about. And I'm not so sure it's as protective as you think. I think Kargen has always wanted Raina for himself. Whether he knew it or not."

"That's bullshit. The Warkind aren't built that way. They protect. That's their genetic pattern."

"Mike. You're a good scientist but forgive me for saying that you don't know crap about reading emotions. The Warkind are a hell of a lot more than just bodyguards. And Kargen is something more than the rest of them. He's as smart as any of the Whoun typicals for one thing. And probably more imaginative. Did you ever watch him when he was little? I saw him play-hunting one day. He killed something in the game. A pretend something. And put it in the middle of the room. An hour later! An hour later he came back into that room, started across it, and stepped over the imaginary thing he had killed. I tell you he could still see it. It was real to him!"

"So what do you want? You want me to have him shot because he's smart, because when he was little he didn't know the difference between reality and fantasy? Hell, every four-year-old in the country would have to be executed."

"No, it wasn't like with a kid. And I didn't say I wanted him killed. I'm just saying that maybe the situation is a lot more complicated than we thought. Maybe we oughta back up a step."

Russo shook his head. "Three of them dead already. Wahrn and the Mother missing. I won't see another of them damaged."

"Mike. You can't let the Podcyst getting shot up mess with you like this. You're afraid. I know that. And it's OK. But you can't act like you're afraid if we're going to get the Mother back alive. I wish I had it in me to make the kind of decisions that may have to be made. But I don't. You do. And we need that. We need you."

Russo's face heated up in an instant, and cooled just as rapidly. Had his fear been that transparent? He didn't want to admit it but he knew that Lanny made sense. He had been shying away from decisions out of fear that he might make the wrong ones. After all, the hunt that had killed three of the beings he was supposed to protect had been his idea. He closed his eyes and swallowed the taste of bile.

"I lost them, Lanny. I can't seem to get that thought out of my head."

Lanny Burns reached out and took his friend gently by the arm. "You're right, Mike. You lost them. But I lost them too. We all lost them. And there's more out there we could lose. Maybe Wahrn. Maybe the Mother. We've gotta do what we can to keep that from happening."

Russo opened his eyes again but didn't look at his friend. He looked instead at the empty room that he had hoped by now would be housing the first Whoun born on Earth in millions of years. He started to speak, then stopped. At last he nodded, more to himself than to Lanny.

"All right. You want a decision, you've got it. I want a helicopter ready in fifteen minutes. Full medical gear and communications. We're gonna go find Kargen. You and me. And then we're going to find Wahrn and the Mother. Maybe out there I'll be able to figure where she's going."

"I'm with you," Lanny said. He started to turn away, moving swiftly now that he had a goal.

Russo stopped him with a word. "Lanny."

The older man turned back to face his friend.

"One more thing," Russo continued. "Absolutely no guns. We will not go armed."

Lanny felt his skin dampen with a sudden sweat. But all he said was: "Got you."

--- 5 ---

Tip was dead! The thought kept jackbooting its way into Dan Case's awareness no matter how hard he fought to keep it out. Along with it came the guilty knowledge that it was his fault. He had *made* Tip come out here with him even when his friend had tried to hold back.

Now his own life was in danger too, and even though Hammerstomp's meadow and the aliens he had seen there were well behind him now, Dan still ran from that danger. He moved slower than before, in a near jog, but still moved because he couldn't be sure that he wasn't being followed. And he had no doubts he would be killed if he were caught. He had to get somewhere, had to warn somebody.

For a moment, Dan's mind flashed a ridiculous image of himself as star of the original *Invasion of the Body Snatchers*. What was he going to do? Run out on the highway, try to stop the cars? Yell to everyone? "You're in danger! They're here! They're here! You're next!" Maybe he should check everyone first to see if they had little tails hanging out of the back of their necks. Or was that some other movie?

Idiot. Stupid idiot.

He had to tell someone--one person who might listen and would be able to convince others. And the only person he could think of who might meet those requirements was the deputy, Tru Maclang. Unlike some among Deerhaven's finest, Maclang actually seemed to remember a little of what being young meant.

That didn't mean he wouldn't give you hell for drinking and smoking, but he was more likely to threaten a call to your parents than to haul you to jail. Maclang might at least listen to his story before bursting out laughing. Dan emphasized "might" to himself because he was pretty sure no one would believe him until they saw what he had seen. Or until it killed them.

Something grabbed Dan's right leg, sweeping his boots from beneath him.

A reflexive yell aborted as Dan's back struck the earth with numbing force. He kicked out, aiming at a shadow, at a huge dark shape on the ground. His left foot hit softness, jarred it backwards. A hiss of pain escaped the shadow and its grip on his other leg loosened. Dan scrambled away, slammed into a tree and clawed up it to his feet. He started a movement that would have segued into a run. Then behind him came a voice that seemed full of echoes and sighs.

"Human. Sorry!"

Dan wanted only to run. He wanted to run and run and run until he was home safe beneath his blankets. But something in the voice stopped him, and not just that the words were in English. He turned, his whole body shaking in an adrenaline storm. And a solid wave of goose bumps swept over his skin as the dark shape on the ground hitched itself forward into a quilted patch of moonlight.

The shape was alien all right, but not like the one that had been chasing him. This was a smaller one, like the beings he and Tip had seen in the meadow when the helicopters had started shooting.

A moment later he saw the wetness that painted the creature's side and realized that it actually *was* one of the beings from the meadow. And it had stopped at least one bullet in the fire-fight. No wonder it had been too weak to hold on once it grabbed him.

There returned the sympathy that Dan had first felt when he saw one of these beings kneel in the meadow to help another. That emotion quickened further when the creature gagged on a cough that hacked up shining bile. Dan moved forward, his thoughts just beginning to reassert control over his muscles.

"You're hurt," he said.

"Hurt. Yes. But didn't mean to hurt you. Thought you were Warkind."

"Warkind? That's what shot at you? What's been chasing me?"

The being gasped a breath, then slowly shook its head. "Humans do shooting. The Warkind have...other weapons."

Dan squatted down, close enough so that he could reach out and touch the being beside him. His fear had gone, swallowed in the other's pain.

"What can I do?" he asked.

"Do? Nothing. Dying I think." The voice had grown weaker.

"I could stop the bleeding," Dan said. "If there's nothing hurt too bad inside then that might help.

"Bleeding won't stop. I tried. Mother tried."

"Mother?"

"Gone now. Made her leave. Thought I would slow the Warkind when they came." He coughed again, harder, like his chest was being wrenched from inside. "Fool!"

Now Dan shook *his* head. "Cussing yourself won't do any good. Did you try mud?

"Mud?"

"On the wounds. If you pack it tight it should stop the bleeding."

"There is no mud."

"I can make some, if you're not too squeamish."

"Don't understand?"

Dan stood up. "I'll pee," he said. "On the ground. That'll make mud."

The creature laid its head down on one arm. Dan thought he heard the mutter of a word. It might have been "mother" again, which probably meant that this one was a "father." He was about to ask when the being spoke aloud.

"If it works. I'll not mind."

"I gotta pee anyway," Dan said.

--- 6 ---

I am the Mother, she thought. *And Wahrn always said that the Mother has strength. She doesn't falter; she doesn't weaken. Oh Wahrn I wish I could find that strength now. But I'm also Raina, and Raina is tired. And she hurts. Wahrn, I need you. I can't be...alone. Alone.*

It was loneliness that had driven Raina to the house--when she'd seen the lights moments ago, when she'd smelled gentleness in the man who lived there. But he had feared her. And she had fled rather than be the cause of more fright.

She stumbled and fell. Her fingers dug scars in the soft loam of the forest floor; her stomach heaved in a contraction that forced her over onto her side. The back of an arm stifled a scream as she shoved it across her mouth. But in the next moment the pain had passed on. She knew it would be back. There was no use in going any farther right now.

To one side of her lay a pile of shadows that had built up behind an immense toppled oak. She crawled to them, slid into them as if she were pulling a warm cloak over her shoulders. In that darkness within a darkness she lay, waiting for the baby to come.

Cold in the Light

CHAPTER FIVE
(May 1: At Midnight)

The doors of the buildings were ribbed with bone, the windows covered with oiled skin. On a table of flesh there had spilled a cup of blood. This was their religion and their strength, to drink amid violence and not be touched.
--*In the Memory of Ruins*

--- **1** ---

Half an hour ago Kyle Dupree had been thinking about how the darkness never scared him. He knew now that he had been lying to himself. And he wondered how many other lies his mind had told him, how many other beliefs about himself would also prove to be untrue.

For a moment, thinking about what his uncle and the deputy-- Truman Maclang--had told him over cooling red beans and rice, Kyle wondered if there were things about Cain Duplessis that he didn't know either. The being that Cain and the deputy had claimed to see could not exist. But in his gut Kyle believed that it did.

Kyle's uncle made a living off his imagination, and it was too well disciplined to have fooled him into such a creation. Maclang was far more literal, but had clearly seen the same thing. Whatever that thing was, it had to be out there somewhere.

Kyle planned to go find it.

The need to find, to know, had driven Kyle out of the house to his Chevy Blazer. He stood there a minute now, just off his uncle's porch where the strangely cold glow of the yard light had mixed with blackness to form a purple-tinged umbra. The others had come out on the steps and were watching him. He knew they would go with him. It was just after twelve o'clock. The night prickled.

Kyle unlocked the door of the Blazer and reached beneath the front seat to draw out his service pistol. He actually had two of them, a Colt Trooper in .357 Magnum, and a Colt Double Eagle

Officer's .45 ACP. The .357 produced a greater amount of hydrostatic shock than the Double Eagle, which meant it would do more damage to liquid filled objects like a body, but the autoloader carried eight shells to the Magnum's six. And it was faster and easier to reload. If it came to shooting in bad light then Kyle wanted all the tries he could get. He left the revolver and took the stainless steel Eagle.

The .45 hung in a Bianchi combat holster and Kyle strapped it onto his right hip. Three extra magazines filled a leather holder at the left side of the belt. The only other thing he picked up before closing the Blazer's door was the heavy-duty flashlight that he always kept handy.

Tru Maclang was leaning across the front seat of his own vehicle when Kyle turned back toward the house. Cain stood a few feet away, near the stone-slab steps of his home. Kyle walked over to join them just as the deputy came up from prospecting for tools with one hand holding a flashlight and the other the pump shotgun that had been hooked to his dash. It was a Mossberg Model 590 12-gauge.

"I figure you know a bit about how to use this thing, Cain," the deputy said, holding the gun out toward Kyle's uncle. "Seeing as how we've hunted a few birds together."

Cain took the gun by the customized pistol grip and worked the pump action to chamber a shell.

"I know how to use it. Only problem is I don't think I've ever hit anything I've shot at."

Maclang chuckled. "Well. That piece there carries three inch shells loaded with buckshot. You don't have to be too accurate."

"Now wait a minute, Uncle Cain," Kyle protested. "Tru and I can go looking for this creature. But you don't need to be out in the woods. You've had no training for this kind of thing."

Cain shook his head. "Under normal circumstances I'd agree with you, Kyle. But none of us has had any training in facing what Tru and I saw. And if it is the same creature then it's hurt and pregnant. Like Tru said. Maybe it scared me when I saw it on the roof. Maybe it still scares me a little. But the itch is in me. I have to know what it is. If it's what I think, then it'll be something I couldn't stand to miss."

"You figure it's an alien?" Maclang asked.

"I figure it's something different from anything we've ever seen before," Cain answered. "Something none of us would have believed in yesterday. I don't know about it being an alien."

"I think you're probably wrong, Uncle," Kyle said, snapping on his flash. "When we get right up to it I think it's going to be something we understand all too well. But let's go find out, shall we?"

The others nodded. Truman Maclang fired up his own flash and held it up to push back the night shadows, but Kyle led the way as they went toward the corner of the house where Cain said the creature had jumped off the roof. Right away they found jagged scratches through the brown paint of the garage door, and footprints half an inch deep in the soil below. A few liquid spatters showed black beneath their lights, but Kyle knew how blood fell from a wound and this had the right pattern. The footprints weren't right, though. They had been made by something with claws.

Kyle looked up at his uncle, expecting to hear some version of "I told you so," but Cain stood looking at the woods instead of at the prints. And Kyle understood why when a low, treble-pitched cry drifted toward them out of the black trees. Kyle shivered in the grip of a sudden wine-chill, but he knew he was going into those trees to locate the source of that sound. There was too much pain there to be ignored.

--- 2 ---

"I haven't ridden in one of these things in ten years," Lanny Burns called out to his friend over the hollow drumbeat of the helicopter's rotors. "It's like being inside some big thing's belly. You can feel the pulse; hear the breathing. Scares me a little. You?"

Michael Russo glanced over at his stocky colleague, a little surprised at Lanny's metaphorical turn. He'd never thought of the geneticist as particularly imaginative. A solid researcher, yes. But not the type to fashion strange images from the mundane. He thought back for a moment to what Lanny had said about Kargen's vivid imagination. The older scientist seemed to think it made the big Warkind dangerous. But Russo couldn't believe that. He *wouldn't* believe that.

Mike felt he understood the Warkind, their nature, their genetic role. He had watched them since 1978, as they grew from infancy to adulthood and reached the physical maturity that would allow them to fulfill their psychological need to protect the Whoun Sept.

The others, the "Typicals" like Wahrn and Raina and the members of the Podcyst, were intelligent, cooperative, and extremely social. The Warkind were very different, not stupid, but governed more by instincts and the savage loyalty of the pack. They weren't sterile but did not mate, their sexual identity being expressed through extreme identification with their War-Pod, or war-band.

There was no democracy within a War-Pod, though; there was obedience. The strongest ruled, until he showed weakness. Kargen had grown up to be one of the strongest, and he'd *always* been smart enough not to show weakness. But Mike felt sure that Kargen, and all the Warkind, would obey their instincts when it came to defending the Mother.

Mike didn't understand why Kargen's band had killed a member of the Podcyst, but it just wasn't possible that Lanny was right and that Kargen had somehow thrown off his biological programming and wanted the Mother for himself. Lanny had allowed his intellectual revulsion at the Warkind's violent tendencies to color his thinking. They just had to get to Kargen and ease him down from his adrenaline high. Everything would be all right then, and they could renew the search for Raina without worrying about what Kargen might do.

Mike looked out at the night through the windshield of the helicopter. Even the bright, new-penny radiance of a nearly full moon didn't alter the sea-like blackness of the Ozark forest below them. Only occasionally did he catch a glimpse of a sodium-vapor light like those that seemed to stand outside most rural homes.

Meant to keep back the shadows, Mike found it more likely that such lights created shadows where none had been before. He much preferred the city, though no population center around this area could be dignified with that term. The closest town was Deerhaven, with a population of less than four thousand. It couldn't be more than five miles from their current location but the countryside seemed to have swallowed it utterly. Not even a glow could be seen.

Hidden in a valley, Russo supposed.

With a guilty start, Mike realized he had never responded to Lanny's question of a few minutes earlier. He'd been lost in his own internal argument. Half turning toward his friend, he started to say something when the helicopter's engine changed pitch and the steel frame of the machine began dropping slowly beneath them. They were starting to descend.

--- **3** ---

Melissa Bowers put on her work gloves before giving the cat its shot. She had become a veterinarian because, to her, animals were the best part of life. But that didn't mean she would trust her skin to a strange cat after putting a needle into its rear end. This one squalled a little, but she held it while she worked the vaccine into the muscle. When she let it go it raced across to the other end of the wire mesh cage, getting as far away from her as it could.

"Sorry," she told it. "Guess it wouldn't do any good to explain to you about rabies and why you need a shot to keep from getting it, huh?"

The cat hissed at her as it laid pointed ears back on its head.

"No! I didn't think so."

She looked around the small animal room and smiled. There was one other cat besides the one she had vaccinated, and four dogs. There were a couple of hamsters, a rabbit, and a turtle that had swallowed a marble. And a frog who wouldn't eat, or at least who hadn't eaten for two days while she worked at removing the superglue its young owner had squirted in its mouth.

Other than a Rottweiler with a copperhead bite, most of the animals had minor problems. Their numbers showed that she was being accepted by the town, though, which had proven to be more important to her than she would have thought. Deerhaven had been her home for her first fifteen years, but she hadn't left it on the best of terms. And she'd come back to set up her office only six months earlier, after twelve years away--just drifting at first, then in veterinary school at Louisiana State University in Baton Rouge. She had almost forgotten how warm small towns could be, though she would never forget how vicious.

Melissa shut off the light, then opened the door and went out into her office. It was a neat and tidy room, from desk, to medicine cabinets, to padded examination table. She locked the outside door, turned off the rest of the lights, and went through into the adjoining part of the house. This was her kitchen, with a workroom, den, and bedroom beyond. Her living quarters were considerably less tidy than her office, but long practice let her navigate easily through the piled books and the piled clothes that she hadn't yet had time to fold. At last she made it to the bedroom and collapsed onto her quilt.

She was trying to decide whether she really had to have a shower or not when the sound of a distant helicopter floated in through her open window. She looked at her watch. 12:07; May 1. She wondered why anyone would be flying this late but fell asleep before her mind could generate any possibilities.

--- **4** ---

Kyle stood up from where he had been squatting by the strange, clawed tracks, his hand dropping to touch the butt of his pistol while goose bumps pimpled his back and arms. The moaning sound came again, not as loud this time, but still full of recognizable pain.

"It's hurt," Tru Maclang said. "I knew it was hurt."

"Or," Cain muttered softly, and Kyle heard and wondered if his uncle was thinking about the creature being pregnant.

Something occurred to Kyle then, something a little girl had said to him earlier today when he pulled her out of the wrecked car where her father had been killed. "I saw it; I saw it. A monster." At the time he had given it little thought. Now he knew what that monster had to have been. A being like the one Cain and Tru had seen. Not the same creature. Surely the wreck site was too far away. There must be more than one of them. Where had they come from? And if there were others here, out in the forest...

"Come on," Kyle said.

And the others followed as he moved quickly toward the woods, his light sweeping over spring grass and the beginning of the trees. A plank fence separated his uncle's property from the untenanted land beyond, and Kyle slipped between the middle boards, then took a short jump-step over the drainage ditch that had been plowed once and allowed to grow up with weeds ever since. He stopped there, the other two at his heels, though they had moved a little more cautiously. Kyle wasn't sure which way to go. Sound got hard to localize at night, and there had been no further moans to guide them.

The dark lay thick away from the house, and the pale light from the flashlights seemed swallowed up in a black sheath. Overhead spilled a tremendous canopy of stars, with the milky way running through them like a backbone. Kyle flipped off his light while he waited for...something. Maclang followed suit.

The darkness seemed even deeper for a moment, but only for a moment. As their eyes adjusted the night seemed to grow a texture of low brush and individual trees. This was a hardwood forest and the taller oaks were actually pale where they stood out above their neighbors. The lower mass of trees, shagbark hickory, red cedar, yellow oak, seemed dense as a wall, and Kyle's memory supplied the rich green that his eyes couldn't detect.

The moaning sounds had stopped, but the woods weren't silent. The wild mountain orchestra racketed on stage, made up mostly of frogs this late at night, their voices as loud and insistent as tiny jackhammers. Behind the chorus of frogs wove the rustle of a cool breeze as it quested among leaves and twigs.

In nights past Kyle had heard the dark wind rushing so hard through the upper reaches of the Ozark forests that the sound ran like a waterfall. Tonight it reminded him more of a dog sniffing for a track, and when he opened his own nose to the darkness he picked up a scent that shouldn't have been there.

Kyle had always had a good sense of smell. He loved the odors in humidors and in Creole kitchens full of garlic, filé, and cayenne. Smell was one of the reasons he enjoyed cooking. Even odors that others found unpleasant, Kyle found interesting. The scent that his nostrils picked up now was not unpleasant, though it could get that way if it grew much stronger. It was wet and acrid, like sweaty fur, but underneath lay a copper and bone roux that lent it substance.

After a moment, Kyle started forward, trailing the smell, his right hand tight on the butt of his pistol, his body sweating despite the spring chill. The others followed and Maclang flipped his light back on.

Kyle turned on his own flash, though he would have preferred to leave the lights off for now to save their night vision. Things that lived in the dark always hid away from the light anyway. But, if Maclang had his flash on then it would be better to have two.

An open lane between the trees beckoned and Kyle moved along it, his boots swishing through grass wet with dew. A spiderweb curved itself suddenly around his head and he stopped to claw the sticky stuff away. He felt a hard knot move within the strands and threw it from himself quickly, knowing it for the spider and shuddering despite the fact that there weren't any poisonous varieties building webs in these trees.

Behind him, faintly, he heard his uncle curse and figured another spider had lost its home to the blundering of a giant who shouldn't be here at night. Then he heard a sound to his front, a rattling of dry tree limbs maybe.

Maclang had heard the sound too, and came up beside Kyle.

"What the hell was that?" the deputy whispered.

Kyle felt as if he could almost hear Tru's heart pounding in fear. His own heart had surged at the noise but had steadied now, though he could taste the metallic tang of adrenaline in his mouth. In his case it was more from excitement than from being afraid. But then, he hadn't seen the creature. Maclang had.

"I don't know," he said. "But you'll notice there's no frogs singing around here now."

"Maybe this isn't such a good idea," Maclang said. But Kyle could tell from the way he said it that he would carry the search through.

Cain had come up too. "It's here," he said. "I can smell it."

Kyle looked over at his uncle, seeing him as only a broad shadow within the greater shadows of the night.

"Yeah. I can too. Straight ahead, I think." He pointed with his light.

About twenty yards in front of them, right across their path, lay a fallen tree, a tremendous oak whose roots hadn't bitten deep enough into the rocky soil to hold it upright when a storm wind hit its bulk. Those same roots curved outward from the trunk like a thousand reaching fingers, each still grasping its tithe of dirt and creating a sheltered grotto that could hide almost anything from their view.

Kyle motioned the others to follow him as he started circling to the right, trying to reach a point where he could shine his flash into the black hole behind the uprooted oak. He didn't want to get any closer if he could help it.

Cold in the Light

A few more steps took him to where he wanted to be, in line with the base of the dead tree's trunk. He lifted his flashlight, and heard a moan that segued into a low growl as the cone of white light began to creep among the roots. His heart slammed into a higher gear, heating the blood that rushed toward his muscles, and then the light fell into the hole and bounced back from twin orbs that seemed to float like chips of violet ice in the middle of the air.

Eyes, Kyle thought.

And he palmed his pistol as a sudden movement uncoiled from the shadows. He heard Maclang yell out beside him, "Shit," and saw the deputy's service .38 come into his fist. Both of them cocked hammers at the same time but neither of them fired. Cain hadn't even moved.

A being stood less than a dozen feet in front of them, washed in the gleam of the two men's flashlights. The rational part of Kyle's mind had still been holding on to the thought that his uncle's "creature" would be human when he finally saw it. Strange maybe. Big, and ugly, and covered with enough dirt to hide its nature. But he had thought it would be human. It wasn't.

Kyle saw six feet of corded muscle suspended on a gray-black hide sparsely cloaked in thin hair. He saw jaws as heavy and thick as a male gorilla's, with canines that looked as if they could crack spines--and had. But on the chest below those jaws were the convex curves that marked breasts, one of which was larger than the other. And further down lay the ripe and distended abdomen of a late-term pregnancy.

One of the being's hands was up to keep the glare from the flashlights out of its eyes. The other hung down like a sleeping bat from a mangled elbow. When Kyle's light played across that elbow it played across bone and blood that glistened in yellows and reds. Kyle looked away, and when he did he found himself looking into the being's face instead. He saw intelligence there, knowledge that had mated with fear and pain.

"Don't be afraid," he said into that intelligence. He lowered his flashlight. "We only want to help."

As Tru followed Kyle's lead and pointed his flashlight at the ground, the being put down its raised hand and stood looking from one to the other of them, as if it could see through the shadows to make out their features. When it finally did speak, its words were in English and were perfectly enunciated. Kyle found that he wasn't surprised.

"My child is not for you," the being said. "It is not something to be used."

Moving slowly, Cain stepped forward past Kyle and the deputy. He laid his shotgun on the ground and stood up with his hands lifted and open near his shoulders.

"Uncle," Kyle warned, but the older man shook his head.

"It's all right, Kyle." To the being he said: "We're not the people who shot you. We don't want to harm you or the baby. We'll help if we can."

The being looked down at its mounded stomach, moving its good hand slowly to rub against the hurt there--the gesture so human that it made Kyle blink.

"I... I think I need your help," the being said. "Something's wrong. The baby won't come. But I...can't...go back to the compound. They'll take my child away and I may never see it."

"We won't let that happen," Kyle heard himself promise, though he was unsure what the "compound" was, or who "they" might be.

"The Institute!" Tru Maclang said. "Yeah." He looked over at Kyle and Cain. "They built it...oh, must be twenty years or more now. The government I mean. Supposed to have something to do with tracking weather patterns for NASA, I heard. Everybody calls it the Institute. I don't know what the real name is."

"Yes," the being said. "What you call the Institute. I can't go back there. Ever."

"You won't," Tru said. He gestured at the being's wound. "Not back to anyone who could have something to do with shooting a pregnant lady."

Kyle almost laughed at Tru's gallantry, then noticed that for some reason the being was looking directly at him. Its eyes reflected even the dimmest light. It seemed to be waiting.

"We'll do what we can," Kyle heard himself say.

"All right," the being said. And moving like an old and fragile grandmother it walked very slowly forward to join them.

Cold in the Light

--- 5 ---

As the helicopter carrying them began its slow descent, Mike Russo forgot about any apology he'd been planning to make to Lanny for ignoring him. Instead, he turned his attention below, to the geometric grid of white lights that marked the military encampment from which Major Wayne Teagle, new commander of the Harbinger Special Forces, directed the search for the Mother. Drake Hammond, the previous commander, had been difficult, a charismatic leader with a gift for strategy and tactics, but also with a touch of paranoia that made him a pain in the ass to deal with.

The situation between Harbinger's civilian directors and its military guardians had always been delicate. It had been that way on the day that Leonard Suskind dropped the recombinant DNA work predicted to win him the Nobel Prize and agreed to take over the Harbinger Project instead.

It had been that way when Michael Russo had followed in his mentor's footsteps. It hadn't changed. While he, Mike, was officially in charge, as a civilian he didn't have authority to give orders to the military. Such orders had to come from the military commander on-site. Hammond had been very aware of that fact, and had been happy to make others aware of it as well.

During his directorship, Mike had seldom experienced any open conflict with Hammond, but the colonel had never bothered to hide his opinions on having civilians in control of the Project. He hadn't liked it. And he'd tried to do whatever he could to change it.

Hammond's death at the hands of the Podcyst had allowed Major Teagle, the colonel's second-in-command, to take charge. Mike liked the change. He felt like he could deal with the major. Teagle had certainly been willing to act on every suggestion Mike had made so far.

As the helicopter touched down to be met by a dozen troopers, Mike started to plan the wording of his next suggestion to ensure that Teagle would accept *it* too. He thought about it while they were moved efficiently through the darkness toward the command tent. But once they bowed beneath the tent's flap and entered the well-lighted interior Mike forgot everything he'd been planning to say.

Wayne Teagle was there, standing beside a map table with half a dozen other officers, but so was another person who Mike had never expected to see again. Seated at the table, appearing quite comfortable in his camouflage khakis, lounged Colonel Drake Hammond.

--- 6 ---

Dan Case slipped between the middle strands of a barbed wire fence and crouched in the drainage ditch beside Highway 265. The sky overhead showed a wet black that swallowed the moonlight and the road seemed chilled and empty. Dan still felt naked to prying eyes. He'd read enough *Popular Science* to hear about the army's see-you-in-the-dark technology; he figured there were a lot more advanced things that he hadn't heard about. And Wahrn, which was the name of the being he'd decided to help, had made it clear that the military would not stop until he and all the Whoun who had escaped with him were either captured or dead.

Yet, it really did feel as if he were alone with the road and the night. Staying doubled over in the ditch, Dan scouted up and down the highway for thirty yards in either direction, and when nothing threatening appeared he slipped back through the fence and made his way to the edge of the trees where he'd left the injured Wahrn.

"Near as I can tell it's clear," he told the Whoun. "We don't have much choice anyway but to try."

"Yes. The Warkind will smell my blood soon. They'll follow. Don't know why they aren't here already."

Dan's mouth went cotton-dry at thought of the Warkind, but he said nothing. He reached down and gripped Wahrn beneath one oddly jointed shoulder, half lifting and half acting as anchor for the Whoun's own strength. Wahrn groaned slightly as he got his clawed feet under him and took a step. But he didn't complain.

"You should not help me," Wahrn said. "You can't fight them if they come. And too late then to flee."

The second step came a little easier for both of them.

"Then we better not let them catch us," Dan said. "Because I'm not leaving you."

They struggled forward--two steps and a pause, two steps and a pause. Slow progress. But Wahrn seemed to be holding his own for now.

"This woman you spoke of. Your friend. She will help us?"

Cold in the Light

"I don't know," Dan said. "Maybe. And she's not really a friend. I've met her a time or two is all."

He thought that Melissa Bowers had better help them because no one else was likely to. Though a veterinarian, her training would surely have included some experience with gunshot wounds. Hunting dogs got shot sometimes, and Dan knew of a few cows who had been mistaken for deer, both in and out of deer season.

The woman also lived on the outskirts of town, only a few minutes walk from where they were now. The Deerhaven Emergency Clinic stood five miles farther away. Doc Shelton's house was a little closer but he was supposed to be camping this week.

Besides, Rudy Shelton had never struck Dan as the type to listen much to teenagers. Or to aliens. He remembered a visit the doctor had made to school to talk about drugs. Respect for authority had been a theme. In Wahrn's case the authorities were the problem. And Dan didn't think the clinic staff would be much different. They'd probably call the military as quickly as Shelton would.

Dan had only seen Melissa Bowers a few times, had talked with her only twice, but he thought she would be the type to listen before she acted. He remembered the easy way she'd handled Jake, Dan's Blue Tic hound, when he had taken the dog in for a rabies shot. There had been kindness in her fingers.

The fence loomed suddenly in front of them, and Dan lowered Wahrn to the ground and lifted the lowest strand of the barbed wire so that the Whoun could slide beneath it. He slipped through himself, and this time found it much harder to get the injured being up. He didn't like the gasps that had begun to punctuate Wahrn's breathing either.

"Wounds...bleeding again," Wahrn said.

"I know. We'll be there in a few minutes." They moved from the ditch onto the road like two old men clutching each other in a windstorm.

"Can you make it?"

"She has... The doctor. She has seen bullet wounds like mine?"

"Name's Bowers. I'm sure she's seen a bit of everything."

Maybe more than she should have, Dan added in his thoughts. He had noted when he met her how awfully reserved she seemed for someone not yet in her thirties. And from the way folks acted there was something a little wrong about the woman.

Dan had overheard his dad saying how people should just leave her alone, that she had paid enough for the past. Most of the other folks in town didn't seem to feel the same way. That was part of the reason Dan had made a point of taking Jake to her for the rabies vaccination. She'd seemed appreciative, and he figured she'd listen now when he walked into her office with Wahrn hanging on his shoulder.

They were at the far side of the road when Wahrn stumbled and went to his knees, dragging Dan down beside him. Dan wrestled free of the big Whoun's bulk and wrapped his arms around the other's chest from behind. Wahrn pushed himself away from the ground, and Dan heaved upward with all his strength. They were half way to standing when lights struck them, blinding white against their dark-adapted eyes. Dan thought he heard the snick of rifle bolts working.

Wahrn moaned and slid back to his knees, covering his face with his strange hands.

--- 7 ---

John Cole and Sid August were spotlighting for deer out along Pine Chapel Road about 12:15 in the morning. They were south and a little east of Dead Man's Curve, on land owned by some rich city doctor named Sallis. Five years ago, after picking up the land dirt cheap at an auction, the fellow had brought in bulldozers and had the area along the road cleared of brush and yellow weeds.

Some people said he planned to start a winery, like those farther south at Altus, Arkansas, but John and Sid had never seen a grape vine planted. They had seen a few fruit trees set into the earth, and had even helped dig the foundations for what would have been two fairly large buildings. Grass had been planted to start a lawn, and a small pond had been dug. Then the work had stopped.

The land had quickly grown up with scrub oak and persimmon, and with blackberry brambles that sprouted into mazes of briars filled with rabbit warrens. Only the newly planted grass had held its own, and both the pond and the foundation had filled with stagnant water. No one ever saw the doctor again, though the bank still listed the land under his name.

Cold in the Light

The deer had soon discovered the readily available water and the sweet green grass, and a couple of years later John and Sid had discovered the deer. They hunted out of season, of course, but they had been doing it for a long time and had yet to be caught. The best time to spotlight was just after dusk, when the white-tail does and the young fawns came out to graze.

Being less wary than the more heavily hunted bucks, the does would often zombify for a moment when they were hit by the bright and savage beam of the halogen searchlight that Sid carried. John seldom needed more than those few seconds to drop one of them with his rifle.

The two men were running late tonight, though, because of a tractor pull they had gone to over in Fayetteville. They were in Sid's electric blue Chevy S10, Sid driving and handling the switch for the big light while John sat in the other seat with a Remington .30-06 sticking out the window. They had turned off Pine Chapel Road and crossed a cattle grate onto the doctor's land. Sid drove cautiously, with all his lights off, easing up onto the grass patch where the deer were most likely to be.

"It's too damn late," Sid whispered, shaking his head. "There ain't nothing but big bucks out now. You'll never get a shot."

"Maybe we'll get lucky," John replied.

"Sure. We shoulda done this last week. I can't believe you threw out all that deer meat we had in your freezer."

"It was going bad, I tell you. Besides, I need fresh venison for the chili cookoff this weekend. I'm gonna beat that damn Cain Duplessis this year. Him and his shit-ass Creole recipe."

Sid snorted and waved a hand out the window at the darkness. "Hell, he only lives a little piece over there. Why don't we just go shoot him. That'd be the easiest way for you to win."

"Just shut your damn ass and get ready with the light. We're almost there."

They eased up over a slight rise and as soon as Sid felt the front wheels bite on grass instead of dirt he flicked on his headlights and added the big halogen seated in a temporary mount on his hood. Nothing showed, so he grabbed the home-made handle of the searchlight and spun it to the right, slashing a razored line of blue-white across the darkness. The abandoned foundation of the never-built winery leaped into silhouette, and on its side in front of the old piles of dirt lay a huge white-tail buck.

It was being eaten.

"Son of a bitch!" John shouted. "What the hell is that?"

But it wasn't a question he would wait for Sid to answer. The .30-06 already stuck out the window, with the safety off. He punched it forward and fired. And missed because the thing squatting on top of the buck had thrown itself backward off the carcass. John swung the rifle to bear, and lost the creature in darkness as the searchlight suddenly spun wildly out of control.

"Keep the light on it!" John shouted at Sid.

He began to turn toward his friend, and stiffened as a warm explosion of fluid bucketed across him. Another of the strange creatures stood by the driver's-side window, one spiked hand buried to the wrist in Sid's face. Sid's head looked like a melon that someone had shoved a hand grenade into.

John's throat heaved with the sudden realization that he wore parts of his friend all over his shirt. He never got to the point of throwing up, though. The door on his side of the truck smashed back on its hinges and John Cole was effectively removed from the upcoming chili competition.

CHAPTER SIX
(May 1: Just After Midnight)

Everywhere in that ancient place, the men heard the sound of soft movements, a sound like chilled souls seeking for warmth. It was only mice, someone said. Only little things. Harmless. But they slept not.
--In the Memory of Ruins

--- 1 ---

Beneath candlelight, Kyle washed blood from his hands at the kitchen sink. Not his blood. It belonged to the being who sat behind him in a chair at the oak breakfast table in his uncle's house. Kyle turned to look, seeing the white of the bandage and splint that he had put on the creature's injured left elbow, contrasting the human quality of the cloth with the alien nature of the arm that it wrapped.

"Whoun," she had said they were called. And her own name was: "Raina."

Kyle dried his hands and walked over to the table; sat. Tru sprawled in a chair to his left and Cain stood at the stove pouring coffee from a scarred pot. Kyle sat where he could see the Whoun's face--Raina's face. She wasn't looking at him.

"I've done all I can," he told her. "We need a doctor for the baby."

"Rudy Shelton's out of town," Cain said, as he came over to the table with a tray on which balanced four ceramic cups of chicory laced coffee. "Sand bass are running. Half of Deerhaven's in fishing camp."

Raina reached out and took a cup with her right hand, sipped at it as if the fluid inside were not hot. Her mouth seemed to tighten around the chicory, like a plug to keep any words from coming out. Kyle wanted to hear her say something.

But Tru spoke next. "Well we can't take her to the Clinic," he said, grabbing a cup for himself. "The army'd swarm that place in ten minutes if they're looking as hard as she says."

"Then where?" Kyle asked to the room.

He watched Raina, saw her glance flick from Tru to Cain. Then her gaze met his and dropped. She was scared, Kyle realized. Scared for her baby and herself. Scared of the humans who were sitting here with her. She had no reason to trust them, no choice not to.

"Let me think," Tru said. "There's gotta be somewhere."

Cain sat down and Kyle watched his uncle's callused fingers move to touch Raina's hand, to slide gently over her knuckles and wrap around her broad wrist in a gesture of warmth. The Whoun seemed to relax. Her lips curled upward, and once again that movement was so human that Kyle was startled. Something about that bothered him. Raina wasn't alien enough.

Cain and Tru had accepted this being for what she seemed and what she'd said. As if such things happened every day. Kyle told himself they should be more cautious. What did they know about the Whoun, after all? She was pregnant. She seemed able to see in the dark but was incredibly sensitive to light, which explained the candles they were using. She'd been hunted and shot by soldiers from some mysterious place called "The Institute." That meant the government was involved. But were the Feds in the right or the wrong? Or were right and wrong even meaningful in such a situation?

Kyle looked at the bandage he'd put on Raina's arm. Red seeped through the linen. His teeth clenched as he thought of the being's pain, and he forced them to relax as he reached out for his own cup of coffee. The first thing was to see that Raina got to a doctor. An independent doctor. One who could answer a few questions that Kyle wanted to ask.

He took a small swallow from his cup, felt the bite of chicory swell in his mouth. He remembered being lost once, around age ten, in the country near a cousin's farm, and how he had followed the smell of chicory coffee home to find that he'd never been more than a hundred yards from the house. Raina was lost now. Kyle wondered how far she was from home.

"Mel Bowers," Tru said, snapping Kyle back to the kitchen and the now.

"Who's Mel Bowers?" he asked.

"Oh, someone new in town. But trained to handle things like this."

Cain and Tru exchanged a glance that Kyle didn't understand.

"Who is Mel Bowers?" he repeated. "I somehow doubt he's had experience with *these* kinds of things."

"I meant pregnancy," Tru said. "And Mel's not a--"

The table jarred as Raina shoved suddenly forward, hunching over as her face contorted with the pain of a massive cramp. The coffee cup lurched from her hand, spilling, spinning on the table.

Cain grabbed her good arm as she spasmed again. Kyle jumped up, pulled the table back a little to give her some room. More coffee spilled. Tru stood too, hands out but not knowing what to do with them. Raina groaned, clutched hard at her abdomen, then quieted. Sweat had started on her face. On everyone's.

"Let's get her into the living room," Kyle said. "Put her down on the couch. Tru and I'll have to go get Bowers." He turned to Cain. "You all right with her till we get back? I hate to leave you alone but two of us should probably go. We don't know what's out there."

"I'll be fine. Just get Bowers. Here, help me get her up."

With Kyle and Tru each taking some of the Whoun's weight, they got Raina to her feet and helped her into the living area where an ancient but comfortable looking sofa ruled among the lesser pieces of furniture from a more modern age. She moaned weakly as they laid her down, but seemed to recover a little strength as Cain brought her a tumbler of water and some blankets for cover. He spread the blankets over her legs and chest and then pulled up a chair and sat down beside her.

"You ready?" Kyle asked Tru.

"Yeah. Just let me get my jacket from the kitchen. It's got my car keys in it."

"Fine on the jacket. But let's take the Blazer. OK?"

"Why?"

"Hunch. It's got a blue-light if we need it. And four-wheel drive."

"Right. I'll meet you outside."

As Tru turned away, Kyle looked at his uncle. "We should be back in thirty, forty minutes. There anything I can get you before we leave?"

Cain shook his head. "Just be careful."

Kyle nodded and went out the front door to find Tru waiting for him on the porch. In the light there he checked the loads in his Colt Double Eagle, slipping the magazine free into his hand. It was an act bordering on superstition, he knew. The gun hadn't unloaded itself since the last time he'd checked. But seeing the dull gray noses of the bullets gleaming against the brighter brass of their casings gave him comfort anyway. With a soft click he shoved the magazine home again.

"You expecting trouble?" Tru asked.

"Yeah. Yeah I think maybe I am. Come on."

They got in the Blazer and Kyle backed up in the drive, then pulled out on the dirt road leading down from Cain's house to the main highway. The windows were down, letting in the cool, and the trees closed quickly in around them. Neither man broke the quiet until they turned off dirt onto Highway 265 into Deerhaven.

"Now will you tell me who Mel Bowers is?" Kyle asked.

Tru didn't answer for a moment, and when he did his voice sounded to Kyle as if it were somehow troubled.

"She a... Mel is short for Melissa, by the way. Anyway, she grew up around here. Left in '81, '82. Came back a couple months ago. She's a vet."

For a moment Kyle was confused. He flashed on an image of a hard-muscled, short-haired woman in army greens. Then realized what Tru meant.

"She's a veterinarian!" he said.

"Yeah. And I'm bettin' she's a pretty good one. I've been over to her clinic a couple times. It's an old house off Fairground Road. I'll show you."

"And you think she's strong enough to deal with what we've got coming?"

Tru looked over at Kyle, his eyes shadowed. "I figure she's strong enough to deal with pretty much anything," he said.

"Then I guess there's something about her you're not telling me."

Tru looked away, out into the night as it flashed past the windows. "Something," he agreed. "But it's nobody's business but hers. Not for me to talk about."

Kyle nodded to himself, smiled. He was really starting to like Truman Maclang. Then his smile turned to a frown as around a curve in the road ahead of them he saw lights. He took his foot off the gas, let the Blazer slow. They were doing no more than thirty when they rounded the corner.

--- 2 ---

Kargen pulled a spiked fist out of the human's chest and tossed the ruptured heart away from himself into the darkness. And the dead man's head, nearly destroyed by Kargen's other fist, fell forward to strike the steering wheel, triggering the horn into one long blaring note.

The sound startled Kargen, angered him. In a burst of adrenaline-fueled rage he grabbed the wheel with one hand and wrenched it loose from the steering column, silencing the horn and knocking the body sprawling across the seat to lodge against the inert form of the second human, the one who had fired the rifle and had died for that mistake at another Warkind's hands.

But a little taste of destruction wasn't enough to fill Kargen up. He lashed out with a foot, caving in the side wall of the pickup, then crouched and locked his grip beneath the frame of the truck. He stood up, slowly, the muscles bulging into relief maps across his back and shoulders.

The driver's side of the truck rose off the ground, six inches, a foot, two feet. A last surge of strength carried it over onto its side to smash down in a groan of metal and a shower of glass. The hood-mounted searchlight broke free of its tether and hit the ground like a soft explosion.

Kargen hooked his heel spurs over the engine mounts beneath the truck and vaulted atop the cab. Metal screeched under his claws, electric blue paint peeling back to reveal gouged silver metal. He scanned through the darkness, looking for some sign that would guide him to the Mother.

He found it.

A few miles to the east Kargen could see the aurora glow that marked the town of Deerhaven. Closer--much closer--there gleamed the purple haze of a single halogen yard lamp. He didn't know how, but he knew the Mother was there, close around that one lonely light. It was like a smell, but not quite a smell, like something that settled out of the air and slithered in through his pores. Suddenly calm, his nictitating eyelids shuttered closed and he looked out at the world through the white film of that distortion.

From behind those membranes the night seemed to thicken with phosphor shapes and the distant light started to throb like a heart. Those perceptions didn't go away when he opened his eyes fully again. On every side of him he heard the whisper of dark veils being lifted, and the world had grown depth and detail that he had never known before. It had become sacred. A holy place. A fit chapel for the sacrament of his joining with the Mother.

Kargen stepped off the truck and dropped solidly to earth. He pushed through the gathered force of his war-band and moved off toward the east. The others followed, puzzled. Their leader's spoor had changed abruptly, segueing from blood-bitter rage to quill-flat calm. But another quality had entered his scent as well, something much more disquieting and which none of them had ever smelled before--something tainted.

--- 3 ---

Dan stepped in front of Wahrn. He didn't know why. Nothing he could do would protect the Whoun from whatever was behind the sudden glare of lights that had pinned them like night moths to the road. As his eyes adjusted he saw that the lights were attached to a Jeep, and there were shadows in the seats that he took to be soldiers. Confirmation came as two men in camouflage khakis stepped from the vehicle and came forward with M-16s at the ready. A third man remained sitting in the dark bulk of their machine.

The first two soldiers were alike in size but different in mien. One moved with quick jerky steps, his head constantly turning, peering to one side or the other. The second man was...precise, with no wasted motions and no hesitation. When the two stepped forward into the frame of their own headlights Dan saw that the jumpy one had red hair. The other's hair gleamed as black as his skin or as the stock of his M-16.

"Well damn me to hell," said the red-haired one. "Everyone's looking for Whoun in the hills and here we find one on the road into town." He gestured over his shoulder at the man who still sat in the Jeep. "Lucky, Tom there broke his leg and we got tapped to haul his ass to the clinic, huh Byron?"

"Right," Byron said, his eyes never leaving Dan and Wahrn.

"Hey, fuck you guys," the one who had been called Tom yelled. "This thing hurts like a son of a bitch."

Byron's eyes still didn't move. His voice was low when it came, and Dan knew it was directed at him. Just as he knew what the man was asking.

"How bad?"

"I'm no doctor. But he'll bleed to death soon if he doesn't get one."

"Let 'im bleed," the red-haired soldier snarled. "The fucker tried to ice the colonel."

At last Byron blinked, and turned his head. "Shut up, Glen. Get the restraints out of the Jeep. Tom's leg is going to have to wait while we take these two back up the hill."

"You can't do that, man," Dan said, speaking directly to Byron. "They'll kill him. They already tried once."

"Not my concern," Byron said. "Lay down and put your hands behind your back."

"No way!"

Byron shifted the rifle in his hand until the barrel pointed directly at Dan's stomach. "Or not," he said.

--- 4 ---

Kyle was holding the Blazer at around thirty miles per hour when they came around the curve in the highway and saw a military-style Jeep in the road in front of them. Beyond it stood two men with rifles, and another man unarmed. A dark bulk huddled like a clot at the unarmed man's feet.

Kyle took his weight off the gas peddle, let the Blazer coast.

"My God, it's another Whoun!" Tru said.

"I see it. And there's a third soldier in the Jeep. The Whoun looks hurt."

"Sons of bitches probably shot it."

"Maybe."

The Blazer's speed dropped to fifteen miles per hour as Kyle pulled out in the other lane to pass and they came abreast of the Jeep. One of the soldiers--a black man Kyle saw--stepped in front of the Whoun, trying to use his body to block their view. A second soldier moved toward them, waved them through, his face showing impatience in the reflected glow of his own headlights.

If they just rolled on past right now nothing would be said, Kyle realized. After all, from the soldiers' point of view what had they really seen, an odd shape in a night made strange by car lights and shadows. The army would still have deniability.

"Shit!" Tru said.

"What?"

"Dan Case is with 'em." He nodded his chin toward the unarmed man, a teenager Kyle saw. "The boy. He's from Deerhaven. We can't let them have him."

Kyle didn't answer. He tapped the brakes, bringing the Blazer to a stop with its nose just over the center line about a car length in front of the Jeep.

"Be ready for anything," he told Tru, knowing that with those words he committed himself to a course of action that could easily lead to violence.

Kyle had seen violence as a young man, and as a police officer. He had never liked it, partly because it stripped its victims of dignity, and partly because he sensed a kind of intoxicating quality to it that made him afraid of his own capacity for evil. Right now he felt like he was choosing sides, though he didn't even know what colors the teams were wearing. He did know the taste that had filled his mouth, the copper bite of an adrenaline rush. Something was about to happen.

The nearest soldier to them, a red-head, stepped even closer to the Blazer, waving his M-16 angrily. "Get that piece a shit out a here," he shouted. "This is military business." He hadn't yet seen Tru's uniform and the deputy slid forward in his seat to let his badge show out the window.

"Afraid it's police business, too. That boy's a Deerhaven citizen."

Cold in the Light

The red-head laughed. "This ain't Deerhaven."

Tru pointed down the road behind them with his left index finger turned across his body. His right hand rested out of sight below the door.

"Yeah. It is. Back there about fifty yards is the city limits. Surely you saw the sign. It's kind of big and white. Got a few bullet holes in it."

The red-head stopped grinning. He looked over at the black guy. "Byron?"

"Signs don't matter," Byron said. "This is a military situation. And you two are obstructing it. No one will be harmed but I suggest you move on down the road."

The boy, who Tru had called Dan Case, hadn't said anything yet. Now he did.

"It's a lie, Tru. They won't let us--"

Byron rounded on the teenager, the butt of his rifle lifted as if to strike. "Shut up, boy!"

The soldier turned back toward the Blazer and Kyle could see that the muzzle of the M-16 had shifted to cover them. "I'm sure the boy will be released by morning. We'll let him call his parents later."

"And what about the Whoun?" Kyle asked. "You gonna let him call his parents, *Byron*? *Later*?"

He spoke harshly, deliberately emphasizing the soldier's name, and throwing out the fact that they already knew about the strange beings. Let Byron wonder how they knew and who they might have told.

Kyle spared a glance at the third soldier, who still sat in the Jeep. The man wasn't lazing back anymore, though. He was bolt upright and Kyle couldn't see his hands below the seats.

"When it happens," Kyle whispered to Tru, "you take the one in the vehicle."

Both Byron and the red-head had stiffened at Kyle's use of the word "Whoun." It changed what they thought they understood, and that made them nervous. Dan Case chose that moment to speak again, and even as Kyle wished the boy would shut up for his own sake, he knew the timing was perfect.

"They'll kill us, Tru," the boy shouted. "They've already killed--"

Without looking around, the soldier named Byron snapped the butt of his rifle brutally into the boy's face, dropping him to the highway like a wet bag of groceries. At the same time the red-head stepped forward and reached for the passenger door of the Blazer. Kyle stomped the gas and spun the steering wheel, stepping on his brakes hard to create a slide.

The Chevy's 195-horsepower V6 seemed to explode underneath the hood. The four-wheel drive option wasn't engaged, and with the brakes locked the front tires stood almost still while the back end smoked, then broke loose to come whipping around like a home run swing. Tortured rubber shrieked on asphalt; a corner of the bumper clipped the red-head, spinning him to the ground. As the driver's-side window came even with Byron, Kyle reached across his body to draw the Colt Double Eagle into his left hand.

The muzzle of Byron's M-16 was rising, the .223 bore looking dark and ugly. Kyle punched his fist straight out through the open window, his thumb cocking back the hammer on the Colt, his index finger tightening, tightening, pulling the trigger. The pistol bucked back hard into his palm and Byron was slapped sideways by the impact, the rifle cartwheeling from his grip into the darkness. Kyle had aimed for the right shoulder and gotten it. But Byron didn't go down.

Yelling like a berserker, the man grabbed for his own pistol, clawing with his left hand as the right one flopped uselessly. Everyone had forgotten the Whoun, but they remembered now as the being kicked out from the ground to sweep Byron's legs from beneath him. The soldier fell hard, losing his second weapon.

Kyle heard a shot from somewhere, shoved open his door and leaped out onto the blacktop. It was Tru who had fired, into the air as a warning for the man in the Jeep. That one had his hands up, and when Kyle stepped around the truck he saw the red-head lying on the ground in front of the deputy, face angry but hands very still and far away from the semiautomatic holstered at his side.

Kyle caught Tru's glance and nodded. "Nice," he said.

And when he looked back toward the man he'd shot, Kyle realized with some amazement that they'd won this short fight. Without anyone getting killed. Byron lay unmoving, but only because the Whoun leaned over him with the stubby spike on its right hand positioned about a quarter of an inch from the human's eye.

Cold in the Light

Kyle gathered the soldiers' weapons, taking the red-head's first and then walking over to Byron. The man's pistol lay about a foot from his outstretched hand. Kyle read the Sig Sauer imprint on the barrel--only a 9mm but still a good weapon--and picked it up to tuck under his belt at the left side. He nodded at the Whoun.

"It's OK," he said, figuring that if Raina spoke English then this being did too. He saw the Whoun relax, drop its hand, and shake its head as if to negate the violence.

"You fuckers'll cook for this," the red-head yelled, and in Byron's eyes Kyle saw an equivalent hatred, only colder, and itching for a target.

Kyle hadn't wanted to choose sides, but now that he had he figured he'd picked the right one. And there was no going back, even if he tried to.

--- 5 ---

Melissa Bowers woke from a nightmare so familiar it had practically become a part of her. She knew what all the dream images meant, the lake and voices, the feel of wet grass, the sound of frogs singing so loud and oblivious. But even if familiar, the images were unpleasant and she tried to push them away. Then a knock came again at her door and she realized with a start what had awakened her.

She got angry at the sudden spurt of fear that twisted her stomach, angry that somewhere inside she was still the scared teenager she'd been so many years ago. "It's over now," someone had told her once, but she had known they were lying. Nothing that happens to you in life is ever over until you're dead.

Mel pushed herself off the bed and to her feet. Exhausted from the past day's work, she'd fallen asleep on top of her covers, still wearing a pair of faded blue jeans and a red and black, checked cotton shirt so old it had worn smooth. She had kicked off her tennis shoes, though, and it took a moment to find them. The knock sounded again before she made it through the darkened house to the front door.

"Just a minute!"

She turned on the porch light and glanced through the peephole she'd drilled herself. The first thing she saw was a uniform and a badge. And she recognized the deputy wearing them--Truman Maclang. Beside him stood Dan Case, the local boy who had been among the first to bring her an animal to treat. His face was bloody and she gasped. Quickly pulling off the chain lock, she jerked back the door and stepped out onto the porch.

"What happened?"

"He got hit," Maclang said. "I thought you might take a look at it."

She spared the deputy a glance that asked why, but stepped forward and took the teenager by the left arm, started to lead him forward across the threshold into her home. Despite his injury the boy actually blushed when she touched him, and she felt unaccountably warmed by that.

"I've got someone else too," Maclang said. "In the Blazer."

Mel glanced over her shoulder, realized for the first time that Maclang was not in his patrol car and that a third man was with them. She saw him standing in the driveway in silhouette, next to a two-tone Blazer. She wondered if he was the one injured, or if it were someone else in the truck.

"Bring 'em," she said, and she turned to lead Dan into the house.

She was already in the kitchen, bathing the blood from Dan's face with a warm cloth, when she heard the door open and someone come through the house into the room behind her. Dan reached out and caught her wrist lightly.

"Don't be afraid," he said.

She turned around.

--- **6** ---

"You!"

Colonel Drake Hammond leaned forward in his chair to place his elbows on the map table in front of him. He clasped his hands and rested his chin on top. Then he smiled into the surprised faces of Michael Russo and Lanny Burns.

"Glad to see I haven't been forgotten," he said in response to Russo's startled exclamation.

Mike didn't take his eyes off Hammond as he asked Lanny the obvious. "What the hell is this, Lanny? You said he was dead."

Cold in the Light

"I... I...uh. He was dead. I mean...Jessup said he was dead. She even described the body for Christ's sake! I don't--"

"Nurse Jessup has been working with me for some time," Hammond said.

For a moment Lanny's mouth seemed to freeze around his next few words. Then his voice thawed in anger. "Shit! A damn spy. Of course. I shoulda known!"

Hammond shook his head as if he questioned their intelligence. "How long have you two been working for the government? Everyone. Spies. On. Everyone. It's the nature of the beast."

"Not in my business," Mike said, his voice low and sharp-edged.

Hammond actually chuckled, a sound that Mike Russo couldn't remember ever having heard the colonel make before.

"I somehow doubt you're naive enough to believe that, Russo," he said. "In fact, I suggest you drop the outraged facade."

Mike ignored Hammond's comment. The edge of his thumb had slipped between his teeth the way it did when he worked things out in his head. And tiny little facts began to click together, little pegs of information that fit into slots he hadn't previously considered. His thumb popped free.

"Haberly worked for you too," he said.

"Why, of course. Dr. Haberly was someone I counted heavily on. And now he is, regrettably, no longer with us. I'm afraid the Podcyst really *did* kill him. My own wounds were considerably less serious." Hammond patted his left side and smiled. "And I heal very fast." He seemed to be having a good time.

"Why try to hide the fact you were alive?" Mike asked.

Hammond's smile faded a little; he shook his head.

"I'm beginning to find your repeated attempts to cover up somewhat tiresome. There isn't anyone in this room who doesn't know the truth."

"I have no idea what truth you're talking about."

Hammond's lips thinned as if no smile had ever curved them, or ever would.

"You underestimate me badly if you think I'm stupid. But by all means let's get it out in the open. I'm talking about your transparent attempt to have the Podcyst kill me in their escape. Surely that hasn't slipped your mind."

Mike felt his mouth drop open, though he'd thought such expressions only happened in the movies. He glanced over at Lanny, who seemed equally bewildered, then back to the colonel.

"When did you get this crazy, Hammond? You can't seriously believe what you're saying. That I arranged for the Podcyst to escape? And ordered them to kill you?"

Hammond powered up from his chair, sending it toppling backward; his mouth wrenched into a snarl.

"I tell you there is no need to deny it further!" he screamed. "You had Haberly killed because you found out what he was doing to the embryo. And you've wanted me out of the way for a long time. This was your chance and you took it."

Michael Russo felt his chest contract and freeze. "What did you say about the embryo?" He took a step forward, fists clenching at his sides. "What the hell did Haberly do? You can't be sick enough to have messed around with the Whoun fetus."

"There were things that needed doing. Things you weren't up to."

"You son of a bitch!" Mike yelled.

He started forward, going after Hammond across the map table that separated them. Soldiers grabbed him from either side, locking his arms between theirs and dragging him backward. He struggled for a moment, then stilled when the struggle proved fruitless.

"You son of a bitch," he repeated.

Hammond came walking around the table to stop in front of Mike. He seemed to have regained control of himself. The tiny smile had grown back and the brown eyes were deceptively soft.

"You're a lucky fellow, Russo," he said. "Lucky my men grabbed you before you got close enough to actually take a poke at me. You wouldn't have liked the result. I assure you."

"Kiss my ass."

Hammond shook his head. Then, almost without seeming to move, he drove the stiffened fingers of his right hand into Mike's solar plexus. The scientist doubled over, gagging on bile.

"Hey!" Lanny shouted. He took a step toward Mike and stopped again as the barrel of an M-16 tapped lightly against his cheek.

Hammond never glanced up. He reached down and filled his left fist with Mike's hair, then dragged the scientist's head up to look into his face.

"I could have you shot, Russo. I might even do it myself."

"They're intelligent beings," Mike groaned. "You can't just manipulate them like they're some damn weapons system."

"No, you're right," Hammond said. "The Typicals are too intelligent to make good weapons. And the Warkind? Well, they are certainly savage enough. But they're prisoners of their genes, too locked into a need for social contact with their own kind. The new baby won't have any of those weaknesses."

"What did you do to it?" Mike demanded.

He could breathe a little easier now, though the nerves in his stomach still shrieked pain and he wasn't yet able to straighten up.

"You'll find out soon enough."

Hammond let go of Mike's hair and stepped back. He snapped his fingers as if a thought had just occurred to him. "Oh, by the way. Did you know your wife and kids are booked on an early flight out of D.C. in the morning? Coming down to see you, it looks like."

Mike did straighten up then as his pain was swallowed by fear.

"Don't worry though," Hammond continued. "I've already arranged to have them met at the airport."

--- 7 ---

Kyle watched Melissa Bowers work, her fingers deft and kind while probing in and over and around the bullet wounds stitched across the left side and abdomen of the Whoun they'd brought to her. She had washed off the mud that Dan Case had used to pack the bleeding, and now she touched lightly at the creature's back, only to bring her hand out painted with red. Kyle saw her shake her head, more in concentration than negation, and understood clearly that Tru had been right. This lady was strong enough to handle just about anything. He hoped she wouldn't have to.

The woman straightened up from the table where the unconscious Whoun lay. Her forehead braided itself with thinking, and in thinking she brushed back a strand of dark blond hair from her face, leaving a faint smear of blood across the pale of one cheek. She wasn't anything like what Kyle had imagined. Too young, for one thing. According to Tru she'd left Deerhaven in '81 or '82, and this woman couldn't have been more than fifteen or sixteen at that time. He wondered why she had left, and found himself having difficulty thinking of her as Mel.

She had blue eyes, he noted.

"Hard to believe," she said. "Five holes and blood everywhere. But it doesn't look like anything critical got hit. Skin and muscle mostly. Some cracked ribs. I'll have to immobilize those."

Kyle glanced toward the Whoun. It had turned out to be a male. "Wahrn," was what the boy called him. Neither Kyle nor Tru had mentioned Raina to the others yet. There'd been no time. After tying up the soldiers so they could eventually free themselves, Kyle had smashed the radio in the Jeep and cut the two front tires after he and Tru pushed it off the road. Then there had been the rush to get here, and Wahrn's collapse into unconsciousness just after Mel Bowers got her first look at him.

"My God," she had said, as the rag in her hand stilled against the cut she'd been cleaning on Dan Case's cheek.

"He's been shot," Kyle had told her. "They're still after him."

Mel's eyes seemed not to know where to look, though her feet took her a step toward them.

"What are you?" she'd asked. But at that moment Wahrn's legs folded and he nearly pulled Kyle down with him as he collapsed. Tru was there to catch some of the weight, and Mel arrived only a second later, though Kyle hadn't seen her move.

"Get him on the table," she yelled.

Dan cleared the way for them, grabbing up a salt shaker and pushing clothes off onto the floor. Between them, Kyle and Tru heaved Wahrn up on the butcher-block table that dominated Mel's kitchen.

"What is he?" the veterinarian asked again as she pushed between Kyle and the injured being. "He's not an animal."

"He's called a Whoun. We were going to ask for your help. But you should know. The military shot him. They'll be coming."

She had waved Kyle's explanation away as she bent to her examination. And all the men could do was wait, while minutes passed and one sector of Kyle's mind worked over the fact that his uncle and Raina were alone.

At least he hoped they were.

It was a relief now to have Mel's attention turned back to them. Kyle felt as if he could finally do something--could at least begin to plan.

"Can he travel?" he asked.

Mel frowned. "No. I said he's got cracked ribs. Blood loss like you wouldn't believe. He needs a transfusion but I don't have the equipment. Or a donor. A hospital might be able to synthesize something."

"Too big a chance," Kyle said.

"So you'd rather have him die?"

Kyle looked at Tru but found no answers in the deputy's face. *Dammit!* He had to think. He knew he had to do something. He wanted to. But to act meant opening up to consequences that he couldn't predict. And it wasn't only *his* life involved. He tried to picture the problem as a chess game but quickly gave it up. There were too many hidden pieces on this board, and pawns turning to queens at every move.

"I'm trying to keep him from getting killed *before* he has a chance to die," he said finally. "Or just maybe, to live."

"They'll murder him for sure," Dan Case blurted in support. "They may make it look like an accident but they'll get him."

Mel shook her head. "Look. We get an ambulance and take him to a big hospital. Fayetteville maybe. Once the doctors see him. And the nurses. The army won't be able to cover it up anymore. And it won't make sense to kill him then."

"No!"

They all turned at the voice, at the harsh croaking of it, and at the pain and emotion that filled it.

"No," Wahrn said again. "I would...rather...die. Hospitals. All my life. No more...now."

Kyle glanced at Mel's face, saw her expression change from startlement to wonder. He remembered that she had never heard a Whoun speak before. And once you heard one speak you could think of them in no other way than as human. Different, but human.

"I uh. You--" She stopped talking, shook her head again in what Kyle recognized as a habit. She lifted her hands. "But I can't do anything for you. I mean. I can stop the bleeding. Bind up your ribs. But there's at least two bullets I can't take out. And I can't give you blood. I don't know how you've avoided shock this long."

"If you stop...the bleeding. Give me adrenaline. In my body it will make blood."

"You're sure?"

"Yes."

"The bullets still have to come out."

"Later."

Mel shook her head, glanced at Kyle.

"Try it," he said. "And if you can, do it quick." He looked at Wahrn to gauge the being's reaction to what he was about to say. "At my uncle's place. There's another one. A female. Named Raina."

Wahrn stiffened as if he had been lashed. He tried to sit up and Kyle stepped forward, moving with Mel to push him back down.

"Wait," Mel said.

Wahrn ignored the veterinarian, grabbed Kyle's wrist until the press of his nails began to hurt. "She is all right?"

"She got shot in the arm but that'll be OK. The problem is with her baby. I don't know about it, but it doesn't seem to be coming right."

The Whoun released his grip on Kyle, let his own arm drop. "Yes. She thought...it was wrong. You must take me to her... Please! Now." He turned his head to look at Mel Bowers. "You can help her?"

Kyle watched the woman, too, saw the heart that was in her. *She shouldn't be so calm in all this*, he thought. *No one else here is calm*. And again he wondered about her past, about what she had been through to create her this way.

"I'll try," she was saying. "But first I've gotta take care of you."

"No time," Wahrn said.

"There has to be," Mel replied. "I treat you right now or I don't go anywhere."

Everyone in the room looked at her, and everyone knew she meant it.

Cold in the Light

"All right," Wahrn said, giving in to the inevitable. He lay back on the table so she could put a needle of adrenaline into his arm. Kyle saw the Whoun flinch but heard no sound of pain escape the being's lips, as if his thoughts and feelings were far away.

Kyle moved over to Tru, who was applying a butterfly bandage to the cut on the left side of Dan Case's face. The butt-plate of the M-16 had split the skin in a seam over the boy's cheekbone. There had been a lot of bleeding but the cut wasn't deep. Mel had already cleaned it before they brought in Wahrn. And the bone didn't appear to be cracked. The main problem would be bruising and soreness.

The boy hadn't said much after they picked him and Wahrn up. Kyle had figured it was from the shock of being so brutally struck. But when Tru had asked him about his friend another possibility had surfaced.

"Tip's dead," he had said. "They killed him and I heard him scream."

Kyle had not known about the second boy, didn't know who "they," the killers, might be. And Dan Case had volunteered all the information he was going to at the time. Until they arrived at Mel's place the teenager had sat quietly in the back of the Blazer, squeezing Wahrn's hand to lend the Whoun what comfort he could.

Tru finished putting on the bandage, turned Dan's head with his hand to see if the cut were properly closed.

"This looks OK, Son. Now I think you better head it on home. Your parents--"

"Uh uh. I'm coming along."

"Not likely. You already got busted in the face. You want worse? And what about your mom and dad?"

"They're fishing. All week. And Wahrn needs me. You need me. You don't know everything you're messing with."

"We saw the soldiers," Kyle said. "We know Wahrn's being hunted. And like Tru told you, we saw you get popped in the face too."

"Yeah. But I'll live through that. You may not live through what else is out there. You ain't seen what I've seen. You ain't seen the Warkind."

"War who?" Tru asked.

"Warkind. They're Whoun too. Only bigger and faster and a hell of a lot meaner than the ones like Wahrn. They're working with the soldiers. Wahrn told me about 'em. But I saw 'em too. I figure one of them killed Tip."

Kyle and Tru both glanced toward Wahrn, who nodded his support for the boy's words.

"Damn, this just keeps getting weirder," Tru muttered. He turned back toward Dan. "It still doesn't change the fact that you're going home," he told the boy.

"I like you, Mr. Maclang. And respect you. But I'm going with Wahrn. And I guess we better go fast. The Warkind can track the others somehow. If they find this Raina of yours they'll kill her as quick as look at her."

Kyle felt his stomach roil as he thought of his uncle and Raina alone.

"OK," he said. "We don't have time to argue."

He walked over to where Mel Bowers bent over Wahrn and used cotton swabs to clean around the bullet wounds.

"Ms. Bowers, I'm asking you to hurry."

"Ten minutes," she said. "Five if you know enough to gather up what I'll need to deliver a baby."

"I know enough," Kyle said.

His words were calm but his thoughts were racing. *Too long. We've been gone too long. Hang on Cain.* He shivered and wished there was a chill in the air to blame. There wasn't.

--- **8** ---

After his nephew and Tru left to fetch help, Cain checked the windows and doors to make sure they were locked. He couldn't quite put a name on his fear, but he did fear. And it wasn't because of the soldiers who he knew to be hunting Raina. There was something else, something undefinable. Already he found himself wishing for his nephew and his friend to hurry back.

A quick check on Raina showed the Whoun to be asleep and Cain found himself both pleased and disappointed. He knew she needed rest, but he had hoped so much for a chance to question her, about herself and any others like her.

Cold in the Light

He blew out two candles, dimming the light in the living room even further to protect the Whoun's eyes in case she awoke, then leaned over the couch to pull the blanket up lightly over Raina's injured arm. A bullet had torn away the meat over the left elbow to reveal the bone there. The bone itself was cracked, with white chips powdered through the gashed flesh. But Cain had been amazed to see that Raina still had limited movement of her lower arm and hand. It hurt her, but these Whoun were tough.

While he bent over Raina a distant car horn honked and held the note. He straightened, frowning off to the west, wondering why such a far sound made him so uneasy. But then everything seemed to be making him uneasy right now. He walked through into the kitchen and picked up the shotgun that Tru had loaned him earlier.

Where the hell are they? he asked himself. But when he looked at the clock on the stove he saw that less than twenty minutes had passed since they had gone. It would be at least another twenty before they could make it back. Probably longer.

He wandered over to the kitchen counter to pour himself a fresh cup of coffee, taking the shotgun with him. He didn't think he would put it down any time soon.

CHAPTER SEVEN
(May 1: The Dark of Early Morning)

In the night one of their number was taken. They found scuff marks in the dust and a single white chip from a human tooth. They found where the missing man's bladder had emptied--the urine still warm.
--In the Memory of Ruins

--- 1 ---

Kyle eased the Blazer down into the shallow creek bed, then took it up the other side at an angle, following a path beat out over years by the hooves of cattle coming to water. Trucks and tractors had been through here before as well, bringing hay or just checking the animals, and the Chevy's headlights picked up a dim trail of rutted grass as they topped the sloping bank of the stream. The right rear tire hit a clump of shale and the vehicle's stiff suspension bounced, wringing a short gasp from within the luggage area at the back of the Blazer.

"Sorry," Kyle called into the back. "Tru, this isn't much of a road."

"I believe my exact words were 'trail.' Besides, it's the only way to get from town to Cain's house without using the highway. And we all know what a good idea it would be to just waltz back up 265."

"How much farther?" Mel Bowers asked. She sat in the rear next to Wahrn, across from Dan Case. "Many more bounces like that and we'll all need a hospital."

"Not far now," Tru replied, turning a little in the passenger seat to face the veterinarian. "We've got this little meadow for a quarter mile or so. Then it's uphill for about another mile. Last part might be a bit rough. The logging companies clear-cut this area years back and it's eroded some since."

"Can you wedge him in with some of that camping gear back there?" Kyle asked.

Cold in the Light

Kyle had never had time to unload the Blazer at Cain's, and when they were ready to leave the veterinary clinic they'd found the rear area of the vehicle too filled with supplies for Wahrn to lie down. Quickly, they had stacked boxes and ice chests in Mel's house, leaving only things that Kyle thought they might possibly need, like camping gear, his tackle box where he kept some tools, blankets and canned foods, and his spotlight and lanterns. Most of that remaining material had been shoved aside or piled between the seats so Mel and Dan could find places to sit near the Whoun.

"Those canvas tent bags might absorb some shocks," Kyle continued.

"Maybe," Mel grunted. Or at least it sounded like a maybe to Kyle.

He turned his attention back to driving. Already the engine's growl had changed pitch, meaning they were headed up a grade. Abruptly, the meadow ended and a fence loomed. A cattle grate made an opening and Kyle took the Blazer through slowly to avoid jarring his passengers on the washboard surface of the grate's pipes.

Beyond the fence the land changed from short grass to bush-dotted hillside, with here and there the raw slash of eroded ground showing pale in the headlights. In the sun those slashes would be red clay and gravel. Now they looked like old scars.

Kyle stopped the Blazer. "Which way?"

Tru pointed just to the left and up, and after a moment Kyle made out a narrow finger of brush-less ground running up the side of the hill.

"That goes about fifty yards," Tru said. "Then we'll start crossing some gullies. They're shallow, though. After that is the top of the rise and another fence. Then a pond. Cain's place is just down from there."

Kyle took his foot off the brake, started the Blazer on its way. He rolled his window up against a chill that had begun to creep into the cab. What had been cool was now getting cold. "Front's moving in," he said.

"Yeah," Tru added. "Kinda out of season. Supposed to hit the low 40's before morning. Or so the radio was saying today."

"Makes me wish I had Wahrn's fur," Dan Case said from the back.

"No help now, friend," Wahrn replied, his voice so low that Kyle could scarcely hear him. "I...feel...very cold."

"That's blood loss," Mel said. "You need rest. And food."

"What kind of food?" Tru asked. "Is it something we can get?"

Mel laughed, the sound an abrupt and throaty chuckle that Kyle liked instantly.

"What's so funny?" The deputy's voice sounded hurt.

"Sorry." Mel cleared her throat. "I just had this sudden image of Wahrn chowing down on a bowl of Klingon Gakh."

"What?"

"From *Star Trek*. Look, you're thinking of Wahrn as alien. He's not. He probably eats the same stuff we do."

"Hamburger," Wahrn muttered, though no one other than Kyle seemed to be paying attention to the object of the discussion.

Tru turned almost all the way around in his seat. "What the hell you mean he's not an alien? He sure ain't a human."

"No! Of course not. I mean the Whoun evolved on Earth. And from his teeth I'd guess Wahrn has the same basic nutritional needs as one of us."

"But that don't make no sense," Dan protested. "They're not like anything we know."

"Yeah, they are," Kyle added. "They're mammals. Guess that's what's been bothering me. They just weren't different enough to be truly alien."

"So who cares if they're mammals," Dan said. "What difference does that make?"

"It makes a difference," Mel said, "because there is virtually no chance that something identifiable as a mammal could evolve on a planet with a truly alien environment. It just ain't gonna happen. In fact, I'd hazard a guess that the Whoun are distantly related to the wolverine and badger families."

Tru snorted. "You're gonna sit there and tell us the Whoun are a bunch of overgrown badgers?"

"No. No more than I'd tell you that you're an undergrown gorilla."

Kyle almost laughed but swallowed it into a cough. He liked Tru but didn't think the deputy would be any match for Mel in a verbal sparring contest. Still, he wanted to keep the peace.

"She just means their ancestors, Tru. We've got them too. Something like chimps maybe."

Tru frowned. "OK! Let Wahrn settle things for us. Just ask him where they come from."

"We don't...know," Wahrn said. "All of us. Our first memories are of the Institute. Of humans. We are all the same age. None younger or older. We were told that we are related to life on this world. But beyond that... I wish I could give the answers you seek. I wish I knew myself."

Wahrn's words seemed to echo in the tight confines of the Blazer. All of them there fell silent. And the silence lasted.

Kyle finally broke the quiet. "It's getting rougher here, Tru. Better talk me past this."

For the next few minutes there were only the sounds of automobile shocks creaking and the murmur of directions from Tru: "A little left here. Careful! To the right."

At the high point of the ridge Kyle pulled up to a barbed wire fence and stopped. Tru got out to open the gate. In the stillness of the moment Kyle noticed again the blackness of the country nights. Beyond the fence loomed a brood of trees, their tangled limbs suggestive and menacing. It was no night to be out.

Sitting quietly in the darkened Blazer, Kyle thought about what Wahrn had said. The being's words saddened him. Did anyone know the answers the Whoun needed? Then thoughts of Cain pushed all others aside and his earlier anxiety, temporarily swallowed by action, returned. His uncle's house lay just beyond these trees, and suddenly he wanted to be there, to see that Cain and Raina were safe.

Hurry up with the gate, Tru, he thought. *Dammit! Hurry up!*

--- 2 ---

Kargen felt the weight of a cool wind against his left shoulder as he wove through singing trees. He felt dead damp leaves beneath his claws, and every tiny imperfection in the soil. Worms were crawling there, and night insects with jewel-faceted eyes. Every odor bit sharp and bright, every image limned with a witch-fire aura.

Behind him he heard the whisper of his band following, smelled the sweat of their confusion. At this moment they should have been focused on the act of violence to come. But they were restless, in turmoil. His actions were the cause. They were sick with a need he had not fulfilled. He didn't care. Nothing mattered except the Mother, and she was so close. He could almost taste her wetness, the wetness of birth and arousal.

He stopped moving. He *could* taste her. There! To the left.

Kargen dropped into a crouch as he turned, his war-spikes pointed out from his body. The others turned with him, a sound like a collective sigh rolling among them.

They were in a narrow lane between shadowy walls of trees, where a giant oak had fallen and died. Its skeletal limbs were white like ribs. Kargen could smell the black paths of snails on the sloughing bark, and where the roots curved up around the hidden base of the trunk there sparked a weave of bright blue light that only he could see. He moved toward that light, circling. One of his band squatted in the way and he shoved him aside.

Then he was behind the tree, eyes focused into the hollow where roots had once sunk. The blue light had turned purple there, and instantly the scent of the Mother burst over him like an explosion of pollen, slapping into his nostrils, hooking to his skin, driving him to his knees. He reached out and scooped up handfuls of soil, brought them up from the hole to his face. He bit at the rich humus, tasting damp and death and Mother. She had lain in this place, hurting, wanting.

Kargen slipped down into that "Darkhome." He pulled dirt over his legs, dug his feet into soft ground. He saw himself alone with the Mother in this place. His penis extruded, lifted into the sharp curve and hook that would bind him to the female when he found her.

Somewhere through the electric sizzle in his ears he heard the sound of an engine. Very distant, but coming closer. His nictitating lids closed to caul the world. His mind centered. Everything was visible to him now; everything was audible. He rolled over. The other Warkind gathered like sculpted machines.

Meat, he thought.

"Beyond the trees," he growled at them. "Take the house that lies there. Kill everyone but the Mother. Kill them twice."

Cold in the Light

With a purpose at last, the Warkind band turned as one and flowed off through the shadows, like the inevitability of a stopped heart.

Kargen lay back again amid the muskiness of soil and leaves. For just another moment he would remain in this place. Only a moment. By then his war-band would have the Mother and he would go to her with an offering of himself. How surprised she would be to find out what he had brought her.

--- 3 ---

As soon as Tru pulled back the gate and returned to the Blazer, Kyle gunned the V6 through the opening and along the narrow white ruts of an old logging trail. Trees rose on either side, mostly shortleaf pine, their heavy-needled limbs reaching out to scratch against the hood of the passing vehicle.

Kyle knew he was driving too fast, but he had begun to recognize the area from having walked through it years back while he was in school up here and visiting his uncle regularly. In half a mile the woods ended and he'd be able to see Cain's house. He desperately wanted to see the house. He had to know that everything was all right.

Kyle's uncle didn't own any of the land they were on right now. It belonged to a farmer who sometimes used it to pasture cattle. Just beyond the pines lay a bluestem meadow and a small lake where Kyle used to fish for black bass with Cain.

From the lake, the meadow sloped down until it reached the rail fence that marked Cain's property line. Beyond rose the house, and beyond that stood the fifty acres of hardwood forest that Cain owned and had always refused to lease to the logging companies. Highway 265 ran down the other side of that woods.

The meadow showed up on cue, the lake sparkling faintly as wind-driven ripples caught streaks of silver from moon and stars. Water and light and clouds and space created a Bierstadt landscape, but Kyle had no eyes for beauty right now. Down the hill his gaze was drawn, to the sodium-vapor lamp in Cain's yard. Near it squatted the purple-limned shadow of the house.

Kyle hadn't expected to see a lot of lights on, because of Raina's sensitivity to them, but at the rear of the house there were a few that spilled a warm, buttery-yellow glow out the windows. The sight calmed his anxieties and he started to breathe easily again.

"Made it," Tru said.

Then the lights shut down like a master switch had been thrown.

Mel and Dan had been leaning forward from the back, looking to see their destination.

"What happened?" Mel asked.

Kyle didn't answer. "Hold on," is all he said.

He punched the gas and the V6 powered up, leaping ahead down the meadow. At his right hip he felt the small comfort of his holstered .45 Double Eagle. Behind his left kidney, stuffed through his belt, hung another weight--the Sig Sauer P228 that he'd taken from Byron the soldier. Two guns. Fully loaded if he needed them. He hoped to hell he didn't.

Just a blown fuse, he prayed.

He glanced quickly at Tru and his friend met his gaze. The deputy had already drawn his service .38, was cradling it in his hands. Apparently, he didn't believe the lights had gone out by accident either. *We'll get there*, Tru's eyes seemed to say. But Kyle's careening heart wasn't so sure. Cain was all he had. His mother had gone ten years before, his father only six months ago. Cain had always been there.

Despite his fears, Kyle downshifted as they approached the drainage ditch and the sturdy rail fence that girded Cain's house from this side. There was no gate here. And he didn't want to run the Blazer through the fence and risk injuring his passengers only to find that everything was OK. He'd have to get out, check the house on foot. Tru could stay with the others.

Kyle tried to calm himself, tried to tell himself that there were any number of innocent causes for the lights going out. It was the truth after all. He hit the button that powered down the Blazer's windows, to listen in hopes of hearing nothing more than the usual night sounds.

But even before the Blazer's windows were all the way down his eyes told him something that took away any hope of innocent causes. At the back of Cain's place reared a huge, glass-panel window opening onto an upstairs hallway that ran the length of the house. Through that glass Kyle saw two bright yellow stabs of flame, one after the other. He knew what they were--muzzle

Cold in the Light

flashes. And the faint pops that came after were the sounds of gunshots at a distance. Someone in the house was shooting.

Tru saw the flashes at the same moment, heard the pops and recognized their meaning. "Trouble!" he yelled. Everyone in the vehicle heard him, began making themselves ready for anything.

"I'm going through." Kyle shouted a warning.

He stomped the gas and slammed the Blazer into a higher gear, aiming straight for the fence with over a ton of metal under his hands.

The bank of the drainage ditch lipped slightly higher than the surrounding ground and acted like a ramp as Kyle took it at speed. The front tires of the Blazer went airborne, and came down on top of the fence to shatter rails into splinters. Oak posts exploded away as they hit and bounced, and Kyle struggled to keep control. He heard Mel shout from the back but had no time to worry about what she might have said.

He tapped the gas, pouring power to the rear axle, steering into the resulting skid. In the next moment the heavy vehicle was back under rein and he was forcing it around the corner of the house toward Cain's front yard. Through the Blazer's open windows came the rolling thunder of a volley of shots, four of them in quick succession.

"That's my Mossberg," Tru yelled.

Kyle didn't respond. He cut the wheel hard and mashed the brake as they burst through a line of recently planted rose bushes into the front yard. The rear end of the Blazer slid around and they rocked to a stop with the headlights splashing full on the porch. Shoving the gear shift into neutral, Kyle threw open his door and leaped out, the .45 coming into his right hand, his left snaking behind his back to bring out the Sig Sauer. He started toward the house on a run.

Mel's voice stopped him. "The roof," she shouted.

Kyle pulled up in mid-stride, and his gaze swept upward to draw in the sight of a shadow that had erupted through the wall of the house and was dropping down on top of the porch. His hands lifted, guns filling them, his thumbs drawing back the hammers. Something made him hold his fire.

The shadow hit the porch roof and leaped off again toward the ground. As it landed in a patch of moonlight Kyle saw it clearly enough to recognize Raina. She was carrying a limp bundle in her arms.

Cain, Kyle's mind screamed.

Again Kyle started to move, and again he stopped, as a sound like the hissing of pain-maddened cobras struck through to his awareness. Kyle's gaze found the porch, and behind it the row of shattered windows that had let darkness into his uncle's home. His thoughts went numb.

Framed in the squares of the ruined windows were...things. They were huge, with massive musculature spread across equally massive frames. Their hides were yellow on black, the color of hornets, and it seemed as if it were the brilliant slash of his headlights that had frozen them and wrung the hissing from their mouths. Their arms were up, blocking that brightness from their faces. But even as Kyle watched they overcame their temporary paralysis and surged forward onto the porch. There were five of them.

"Warkind!" Dan screamed from somewhere behind Kyle's left shoulder.

And when Kyle remembered the teenager's description of the creatures that bore that name, he didn't hesitate. If Cain were alive in Raina's arms? If any of them were to stay alive much longer? The Warkind had to be stopped on the porch.

Kyle's mind quickened into absolute clarity. Before, he had been distracted by worry, which mutated into fear for Cain when the lights in the house had gone out. Now the fear burned itself away in the bright, cold flame of an adrenaline high, leaving Kyle intense but in control. To act in an emergency was something he could do, partly out of training and partly out of what had been wired into his brain at birth. He leveled the pistols and opened fire. Right trigger, left trigger, right trigger, left--no movements wasted, no shots missed.

To Kyle's right came the bark of Tru's .38 revolver, but it was the hammering of the two semiautomatics that held the Warkind back. In the glow of the headlights, Kyle saw puffs of dust rise from where his slugs hit their targets. He saw Warkind hands slap at wounds in abdomens and chests. But only one of the five went down, taken out by solid hits from the .45 ACP cartridges.

As abruptly as a switch closing, the other four were gone, back into the house where the shadows hid them. Kyle stopped firing.

Cold in the Light

The smell of burnt powder and gun oil slapped his nostrils. His ears hummed. He took a step forward.

Raina's jump from the porch roof had landed her only half a dozen feet from Kyle. She had barely moved during the moments of gunfire, but now she rushed past him toward the Blazer. Mel ran out to grab her arm, taking charge despite the danger. And then Dan was there as well, helping Raina as he had helped Wahrn before.

Kyle saw Cain lying slack in the Whoun's gentle grasp. And blood flashed at his uncle's throat and chest. But Kyle wouldn't let the fear take him again. That wouldn't do any of them any good.

Raina called a warning to them all as Mel and Dan hustled her toward the Blazer: "There's more than five."

Kyle started backing toward the vehicle, eyes scanning. He spared a quick glance over his shoulder, saw Tru behind the Blazer, the .38 anchored across the hood for firing support.

"Keep an eye on the woods," he yelled to the deputy, and while his head turned for that second the Warkind on the porch, the one they had all hoped dead, suddenly exploded off the ground and launched itself toward them.

Kyle saw the creature coming from the corner of his eye and snapped around to face it. As part of the same movement the .45 came up and Kyle double-actioned the trigger. The bullet carried 230 grains of lead and when it hit between the Warkind's eyes at ten yards distance it knocked the being flat.

Still the thing wasn't dead. Hydrostatic shock should have jellied its brain. But it thrashed on the ground, trying to rise. Kyle pumped an ACP round into its throat, the slug ripping through the soft tissue there and carrying away the spine. Its movements ceased.

"Now you're dead, you son of a bitch," Kyle muttered.

"Cain's in," Tru yelled. And the awareness of their need for escape came rushing back to Kyle.

"Cover me," he shouted to the deputy, as he turned and leaped for the Blazer. He shoved the Sig into his belt as he jumped behind the wheel, keeping the Colt in his right hand. There were only two shots left in the .45 but the 9mm Sig just didn't have the stopping power against these things.

The Blazer's engine was still running and Kyle stepped down on the clutch and shifted into low gear.

"Get in!" he called to Tru.

Everyone else was already aboard.

Tru snapped a shot toward the house before diving into the passenger seat. "There's one on top of the porch," he said, already moving to reload his pistol.

Kyle looked but couldn't see the being. Didn't matter now. He popped the clutch and shoved down on the gas. Once they were moving these things would never catch them. The Blazer lurched toward the house, then turned under the pressure of Kyle's hands and headed back toward the driveway. Dirt and divots of grass spun from beneath the tires.

From the back Mel screamed in shocked surprise as something big and heavy smashed down on the roof of the Blazer with a loud whumpff. The front end of the vehicle bounced upward and Kyle fought the wheel for control. One of the side windows rattled and starred as the Warkind who'd leaped on them from the porch slammed its paw against the glass. But the beast could get no purchase for its weight and the window held.

"Drive," Tru yelled. "I'll take it."

The deputy grabbed for the seat adjustment lever and shoved himself backward into a reclining position. The .38 filled his hand and he fired twice through the Blazer's roof, bludgeoning their ears with noise but hammering the thing on the roof hard enough so that when Kyle swerved it lost its grip and went rolling off onto the gravels of the road.

Through his side mirror, Kyle saw the Warkind get up like it wasn't hurt at all. It didn't chase after them, as if it knew the gap between them was too big to close. Kyle kept his foot on the gas anyway. Highway 265 was ahead and he wanted to reach it before any more of the things came out of the woods.

Driving didn't stop Kyle from having his first chance in minutes to think rather than act, though. Immediately, his mind leaped back to Cain.

"How's my uncle?" he yelled into the back.

No answer.

"Cain!"

Cold in the Light

--- 4 ---

Cain was remembering--reliving it all. He was bending over the couch again, checking his pregnant guest. There had been a sound, a scratching and clicking on the oak boards of his front porch. At first he'd thought it was Kyle and Tru coming back, but their boots wouldn't have made that kind of noise. And it scared him when it seemed that Raina heard the sounds too, and her eyes snapped wide open. He straightened, lifting the shotgun whose stock had suddenly turned damp against his palms.

Raina sat up and Cain didn't caution her. His mouth was too dry, drier than his hands were wet. It was as if the vague fear that had ridden him all evening had crystallized and been projected as sound into the outside world. He took a short step toward the front door, cocking his head to listen.

The click, click, click came again. And he had no idea what it meant. He told himself that he didn't want to know. But now he heard it on the back porch too. Whatever it was, it surrounded them. An image came to mind, a noose tightening around a neck.

Raina stood and moved up beside him. Whether he wanted it to or not, her first steps identified for Cain exactly what sound he was hearing. His living room was floored with hardwood and when the claws on Raina's feet touched over the planks they tapped like fingernails on Formica.

"Your people!" he blurted. But he said it quietly because he could see the almost painful tension that thrummed the female Whoun's body.

She shook her head. "Warkind."

"That's bad?"

"They hunt with the soldiers." She leaned forward, her mouth opened slightly and her nostrils flared, reading the air as if it were engraved with smells. "And... There's something wrong in them. I don't know."

"What do you think?"

"Their smell is wrong. Like death. But not natural."

Cain's spine shivered, and the shivers spread as the knob of his front door turned and then released. The door rattled but did not open. How long would the lock keep them out? Cain didn't know what a Warkind was, but if they were anything close to the size and strength of Raina then no lock would hold them for long.

"Upstairs," he said. "Quick. First door on the left."

Raina's cramps seemed to have retreated for the moment and she moved swiftly to obey. Cain hurried after her, thinking that even if the doors held there were windows to worry about. But at the head of the stairs stood a bathroom with a window too small for anyone to enter. That would leave only one approach to guard, and the Mossberg 12-gauge he carried was perfect for that task. It held nine 3-inch magnum shells and he'd loaded it with buckshot. At close range it would stop just about anything living.

Raina had almost reached the bathroom, with Cain a few steps behind, when all the doors and windows in the bottom floor imploded at once and the Warkind burst through amid a welter of flying splinters and glass. Cain spun around on the stairs with the shotgun leveled, and his first thought was that the gun wasn't big enough, 3-inch magnums or not.

Even the smallest Warkind bulked a head taller than Raina and would have outweighed her by a hundred pounds. They all had musculature that seemed too massive for their skins, and yet their movements were as fluid as well-oiled pistons. They were like triggers with the slack taken out of them.

Cain took a step backward, then another, whispering over his shoulder at Raina to get into the bathroom. He didn't dare turn his head to see if she obeyed. His attention remained riveted on the single Warkind who had smashed through the door and stood closest to the stairs. There were two more that he could see, and from the sound at least one had come in the back way. There were probably others.

All three of the ones below were crouched in the dim candlelight, their heads turning back and forth as they scanned. They seemed coiled to move in any direction and Cain had the sudden thought that they were expecting resistance. They didn't know he and Raina were alone, and that might work to split their attack.

He backed up another step and felt the floor level out as he reached the top of the stairs. *Just a few more feet to the bathroom.* He should have known it wasn't going to be that easy. The closest Warkind's eyes scanned inevitably in their direction and saw Cain even through the shadows on the stairs. Soundless it came, on all fours, in a blur so swift it froze Cain like a deer in a spotlight.

"Shoot for the face," Raina yelled, and her hand snaked by his right shoulder to flip on the stairwell light.

Cold in the Light

Brightness erupted, jerking Cain from his half trance. It did worse to the Warkind, dredging from it a single hissing squeal and making it stop and throw up its head as if in pain. That gave Cain the opening he needed and he pulled the trigger on the 12-gauge. In the excitement of the moment he missed, blowing splinters from the oak railing that guarded the outside of the stairs.

The Warkind reared back on its hind legs. It hissed again, then shook its head wildly.

The light hurts it, Cain thought. *It can't see.*

He pumped the shotgun to chamber a shell, which proved there was nothing wrong with the creature's hearing. It homed on the sound, locked in, and in a single bound seemed to explode in Cain's face. He pulled the trigger at point blank range, and nothing unarmored could resist that lead hammer. Flesh seemed to dissolve and flow, then erupt out from the sides and back of the thing's head. He knew it was dead before it tumbled backward down the stairs.

Cain chambered another shell. He had seven left and there were at least three more of the creatures below. He cursed himself for not having stuffed his pockets with extra bullets. But at least for the moment the Warkind seemed to be hesitating. After seeing one of them charge straight into a shotgun blast he doubted the hesitation came from fear.

Cain felt Raina at his shoulder and pushed lightly against her to get her moving once again toward the bathroom. He took a step toward that sanctuary himself; and the lights went out. Cain's heart nearly seized. He'd almost forgotten that he dealt with intelligent creatures. They'd easily located the fuse box.

I can't handle this! Cain's thoughts shrieked.

For years he had explored violence through his art. Now it explored him. He knew clearly that he didn't have what it took to handle it. Maybe Kyle had it. Even Tru. He hoped so for their sakes. Because the Warkind lived as violence distilled. They were going to kill him in his own house. Then they'd kill Raina, though he'd promised to help her. Nothing could stop them.

"They're coming," Raina spoke into his ear, and though her voice cracked flat and low it seemed to go off in his awareness like dynamite. He fired into the blackness of the stairway, unable to see anything but hoping the spread of buckshot would stop whatever moved down there. The muzzle flash strobed the shadows and lit up emptiness.

They weren't on the stairs.

Then where?

Cain felt Raina move away from him, heard her claws skitter faintly on the hardwood floor. And then there came a second noise, a whisper of sound as faint as a breath. It arose from Cain's left and he spun hard in that direction, swinging the shotgun to bear. In the ambient light streaming through the skylights from outside he saw how stupid he'd been to think in only one dimension, to focus only on the steps. A huge Warkind had leaped twelve feet from below to grasp the stair-rail and vault its way over.

If it had not been for Raina, Cain would have died then. He would never have gotten the gun around in time. But the female Whoun was nearly as fast as the Warkind and her clawed foot lashed out even as the other being made its landing, knocking it against the railing. The thin strip of wood couldn't take the weight and splintered. The Warkind held its balance for a second, but by that time Cain had the shotgun leveled and he pulled the trigger hard. Buckshot slammed into the creature's chest, hammered it back into open space. It fell away.

"Into the bathroom now!" Cain yelled. "The door's the only opening and the gun'll stop 'em there."

Raina darted through into that room and Cain turned to follow. In the same instant a shadow materialized beside him, out of darkness, out of nowhere. Cain had a split second to realize his worst mistake. There were windows upstairs as well as down, and oak trees all around to make climbing easy. How could he have assumed that all the Warkind came in on the ground floor?

Cain tried to raise the shotgun but no Raina hung at his elbow to help this time. He was far too late. The Warkind loomed over him and the gun was slapped brutally aside to spin free of numbed fingers. He saw the creature's arm lift, saw a quick gleam of reflected light splash along something in its fist.

No! On its fist.

Then the fist fell with a movement too swift to follow and Cain felt a sharp tug at his neck. Warmth spilled out over the front of his shirt and his eyes widened. He grabbed his throat with both hands and felt the rich blood welling. His legs gave way and he collapsed to his knees.

With eyes so wide they could see everything, Cain watched the Warkind lean toward him, watched its nostrils flare as it drank in the pluming scent of his blood. Its hand drew back for another strike, a six inch spike of bone jutting toward his face like a spear's head. Cain tried to mouth an old childhood prayer but the words were fossilized on his tongue. Then the shotgun boomed almost in the Warkind's ear and the creature's arm-thrust lost all momentum as the brain behind it dissolved. It fell onto its side and quivered.

Cain's knees wouldn't work but Raina got him to his feet and pulled him into the bathroom. He tried to stand on his own--couldn't--and slumped sideways against the wall. He heard Raina pump the slide of the shotgun, then pump it again and again and again as four shots blasted into the sheetrock just beneath the narrow window. He didn't understand why she'd emptied the gun into the wall at first, until the chalky white dust scattered away and he saw the glimmer of moonlight through the shattered exterior boards. She was shooting her way out.

Cain felt his strength ebbing and slid down the wall to catch himself on the back of the toilet. He wondered why the Warkind weren't coming, thought maybe the gunshots were making them cautious.

But then, he wasn't sure he could see them if they did come. His vision was smearing, breaking up into strange pointillist shapes. The artery must only have been nicked or he would have bled dry by now. But it made no difference in the long run. He had both hands tight on his throat, trying to hold in his life, and still it spilled in a steady flow all down his front.

"Close your eyes," Raina said from some distant place above him.

He looked up, saw that her eyes were gleaming like those of a cat. She had tossed aside the shotgun, and now she glanced past him toward the open door to the hall.

"Close your eyes," she said again, more urgently. And Cain obeyed.

In all his life Cain had never felt older than he did at that moment, when a pregnant Whoun lifted him and turned his head into her shoulder like a baby. With his eyes squeezed shut he could hear the female's heart through the warm heat of her fur, its beat so different from a human's, more rapid, yet deeper. And rising from beyond her body, outside in the night, he heard another sound, the roar of an engine racing at high speed.

"Kyle," he whispered to Raina. He didn't open his eyes.

"Yes," she said. And: "Be ready."

Cain felt a surge of movement beneath him, knew somehow that Raina had launched herself at the half shattered wall. At the last second he sensed himself being turned as she struck hard with her other shoulder against cracked boards and weakened studs. She groaned in pain, but they burst through, shedding the house like a used skin and dropping three feet onto the gabled roof of the front porch.

From there Raina leaped downward to the earth, though Cain felt the jar of landing as only a distant thud through his bones. All around were the heated sounds of gunfire and of automobile doors shrieking open. But the blood at his throat was cold to Cain, and the movement of other hands over his body itched like the scrabble of spiders' legs on canvas.

Doors slammed again as Cain felt himself being laid down on a carpet of towels and blankets. The Blazer's engine growled, then rose in pitch to a scream as its rpm's built. Gravels scattered with a hiss as the driver popped the clutch, but Cain sensed no movement. The stillness was loving. He wanted it. But his ears were stung by two sudden explosions; his nose twitched against smoke.

The remembering stopped as Cain opened his eyes. Humans and Whoun both were bending over him, doing something to him that he couldn't feel. His nephew wasn't there but in the distance he could hear a voice calling his name. He knew that voice.

"Tell Kyle I love him," he said, with a faint smile to the crowd. His eyes didn't close and his smile didn't fade. But Cain Duplessis chose that moment to pass on.

--- 5 ---

Kargen breathed his rage out slowly, feeling the vapor coil up over his cheek-spines to faintly mist his eyes. He had come too late and the Mother was gone. He breathed again, forcing the heat of anger out through his mouth to let it dissipate in the coolness of the air. His band had failed against humans. They had not acted as one.

Cold in the Light

Kargen understood that a part of the blame was his. As Pod leader he held absolute control over his band. They moved as he moved, killed as he killed. Even the scent from his pores guided them. And he had let them go in ahead of him. Alone! He had failed them too, just as they had failed him. That didn't bank his anger.

Standing in the driveway in front of the human house, he watched the dust raised by the fleeing Blazer drift gently down. In that Blazer, the Mother moved steadily farther away from him. He would have to track her anew. And dawn rose only a few hours distant. He clenched his fists until the phalanges creaked. In his mouth slicked the bitter taste of sheared copper, from the tongue that he had bitten half through.

Behind Kargen the eight remaining members of his band gathered. Three others were dead, and several of the living carried wounds. Most of those were not serious, the bullets having been partially deflected by the thick overlapping quills that fused together over their inner and softer skins. All of the gathered were looking at him from beneath lowered heads, their postures holding the stillness of shame. Yet, in some Kargen detected the odor of rebellion. It would not take much now to turn them against him.

All around, the night breathed, threaded through with veins of sound. Tiny smoke shapes of distortion drifted in and out of the trees, hung gibbering from black limbs. Kargen could feel their mouths suckling over his skin, thorny snouts probing into every crevice. The Mother's scent was thick as mud in his nostrils and he snorted hard to clear them. He shook his head violently; a wave of shuddering swept his body.

Behind him came the murmuring of his band. They had begun to move again, in faint jerks and pulses, muscles rolling with the quiver of a growing tension. A crisp edge of fear scrawled quick runes down Kargen's back. It was a feeling that he wasn't accustomed too, and it drove the smell of the Mother out of his awareness, spilling in thoughts of survival as a replacement. He knew that he had to control the Pod's movement, had to break it to his own pattern--or be destroyed by it.

All the twisted strange shapes had gathered at the edge of the forest, like dead leaves piled against a winter fence. Arcs of fluorescence sparked among them, painting the night with streaks of purple and green and blue. Kargen snorted again, clearing himself of the last of the Mother. He closed his nictitating lids against the crowding white forms.

Not there, he thought. *Nothing is there.*

Then Kargen turned to face his restless Pod, his hand lifting with the fingers spread wide for silence. His war-spike gleamed dully. Eyes of bladed black locked on his, waited, and Kargen opened his mouth as if to speak. Instead, he stabbed himself through the cheek with his war-spike, puncturing the skin just where the hinges of the upper and lower jaws met. Blood sprayed outward from his face and when he pulled the spike out again it was clotted and no longer gleamed.

But he had their attention.

"We have all failed here," he said, his voice made raspy by the fluid that ran down his throat. "I most of all. Because I did not understand the power of the enemy and did not go among you to destroy them. I will make that mistake no more."

Kargen opened his pores to the fresh breeze, and his quiet words and quiet scent calmed the ripple of rebellion that had been building. The movements of the others grew slower, more synchronous, almost languid. He needed only one thing more.

"Tomorrow," he said. "While the band rests in Darkhome for the coming day. I will hunt the Mother alone. At dusk I will call you."

There came a collective sigh and the faintest increase in the pace of their swaying. Still, their chorea twisted in synchrony. They were shocked at his words--to hunt in the light was unknown--but his odor blanketed them with peace and their respect for him returned. They were his again, fully and complete.

From the woods the voiceless shapes called. Kargen ignored them, and even as he did so the buzzing sounds started to fade, as if they were moving farther away from him in the arms of the Mother. For a moment his mouth twitched in thought about that. Then he turned to let his eyes trace the road that the Mother had followed from this place with her human allies.

She would not be expecting him to hunt in the light; she would not warn those she ran with. He could find them and track them, and if he needed help he would call the Pod when it grew dark. This time he would lead the attack himself. And if the Mother resisted he would hurt her. Her blood would be nearly as much pleasure for him as her body. Though he would not kill her.

Cold in the Light

Kargen took a last long look back toward the woods. The spaces between the trees were black, devoid. The night was silent and without texture or shape. He remembered now that this was the way the world was supposed to be.

And yet, for a moment the Warkind felt emptier than he had ever felt before. He had begun to get used to what he now knew as hallucinations. He couldn't remember when they had started, didn't know why they'd chosen this time to leave. But their company had been...pleasant.

For a little while.

CHAPTER EIGHT
(May 1: Before The Dawn)

----

*In the days that followed they all began
to envy the dead ones. Some drank while
others prayed. A few passed their time
in sexual fantasies, in dreams of orgasm.
Only one sat down to sharpen his knives.*
--*In the Memory of Ruins*

--- 1 ---

They were sitting in the dark, in a little sphere of quiet. The tent floor felt damp beneath them, though Michael Russo knew it was only the cool of the ground bleeding up through the nylon. The rest of the tent hung close and hot, and he wished he could be outside where a young breeze had begun playing with grass and bushes.

Other than the breeze, the main sound was the steady throb of crickets and frogs. There weren't many close to the tent, though, where a single soldier stood guard. The human sounds were the fewest, the occasional scuff of a boot sole on rock, a faint cough swallowed behind a hand.

"How can he be so damned quiet?" Lanny Burns asked. "You know he's moving around out there. Gives me the creeps."

"He's a professional, Lanny. A different kind than us."

Russo's voice was hoarse. He still hurt from the blow that Drake Hammond had thrown into his abdomen. But that was the least of his pains.

Lanny shifted position, trying to find some non-existent comfort. "I don't believe this. This is the United States for Christ's sake. Hammond can't keep us here."

"Hammond's crazy. And out here he's like a god. He can do whatever he wants."

Lanny shifted position again. Even his movements were nervous. And the false bluster of his previous words had cracked away to show the fear beneath. His voice shook.

Cold in the Light

"You don't think he'll hurt us? Huh?"

"I don't know," Mike said.

He knew Lanny wanted reassurance, but he just didn't have any in him right now. His thoughts argued that if Hammond were willing to take it upon himself to change the whole purpose for the Harbinger Project and risk destroying the future of the Whoun race, then he might do anything.

Of course, as much as Mike wanted to blame Hammond for everything, he knew it was unlikely to be true. People like the colonel followed orders. They were machines. They didn't write new programming for themselves. Someone had turned him on and turned him loose, and had given him the technical support he needed. It had to be someone who knew enough about Mike Russo to keep him in the dark, who knew he would go public rather than let the Whoun embryo be used.

Mike thought of William Haberly, who had turned out to be in Drake Hammond's pocket. But that was the point. Haberly had been following the colonel's orders, not giving them to him. There had to be someone else! Someone among the other directors, maybe.

He shook his head. *No!* He was getting as paranoid as Hammond. If anyone had given the colonel his orders then it had to be somebody higher in the military. There couldn't be another like Haberly among the directors.

But the thought of betrayal from within the group wouldn't leave him. And it twisted itself up with another thought, with the sure knowledge that Hammond hadn't been lying in what he'd said about Mike's family coming down to Arkansas, or that he'd have his soldier boys meet them.

Hammond knew things he shouldn't know. "Everyone spies on everyone," the bastard had said. Mike wondered how many other spies were around besides the colonel's military watch dogs. Who could Mike trust? He looked at Lanny but couldn't bring himself to doubt the loyalty of his best friend. Besides, Lanny's concern for the Whoun loomed clear. The portly scientist would never get involved in anything that could hurt them. It had to be someone else. If there *were* anyone else?

"Shit," Mike muttered to himself.

He got to his hands and knees and crawled over to peer out through the front of the tent. The guard had tied the flaps loosely but hadn't closed the zipper. An eddy of delectably cool air slipped through to lave his face. He drew a deep breath, but quietly. He could see only the left leg of the soldier who stood watch in front of their prison.

"What's the matter?" Lanny whispered from beside him.

Mike shook his head. "We've gotta get out of here," he whispered back. "Get to the lab. Contact the other directors. Find out who's on our side."

"What do you think they did? To the embryo, I mean."

"No way of telling. Haberly was no geneticist. He understood the neuro stuff. But the DNA. I don't know what he could have done to that."

"You forget the techs. They're all military. Some of them are pretty damn good at genetics."

"Yeah. Maybe. What do you think about the other directors? Kimura. And Rackham. I know they were off work rotation when the Mother went into labor. But that doesn't mean anything."

"I can't believe Jackie Kimura would be involved. Anyway, she's a chemist. And she couldn't *stand* Haberly or Hammond. Rackham is pretty ambitious. But I don't know."

"He was friends with Haberly."

"Friendly maybe. I don't think Rackham has any real friends. For a psychologist he isn't the most sincere person you could meet." Lanny blew out a heavy breath. "It's just hard to believe."

"Would you have believed a day ago that Haberly was in something like this?"

"No. I mean, I never liked Haberly all that much. But no. I don't see why there'd have to be somebody else, though. Haberly saw the Mother every day, most times. And if the technicians were giving him... I don't know. I guess they could be using hormones to catalyze changes in the developmental sequence. Anyway, Haberly--"

"Would be in the perfect spot to give the fetus the injections."

"Yeah. I'd say so."

"And when the Podcyst figured out something was going on..."

"They took off. Haberly got what he deserved."

Mike slapped his fist against his leg. "But, dammit. Why didn't the Podcyst come to us if they thought something was wrong?"

"How could they know we weren't involved, Mike? It's going to be hell getting them to trust any of us again."

"I know." Mike sighed. "This would never have happened if Leonard had stayed on as director. He would have known what was going on. Would have known what to do about it."

"I don't think so," Lanny said. "Leonard was just as human as any of us. He made mistakes. Especially at the end when he burned out. Before he retired. This is not your fault, Mike. No one else could have done it better."

"I still wish he were here. To worry about this."

"But he's not, Mike. Len was like a father to us both. And to the Project. But it's me and you now. Jackie Kimura if we can get to her. We know Hammond is against us. And maybe we shouldn't trust Rackham just yet. We've got to get word to somebody who can pull the army off us, though."

"I know the people for that. But first we have to get out of here."

Lanny didn't say anything. Mike glanced again through the tent flap. He realized that for the last couple of minutes he'd been hearing a low throbbing sound without attaching meaning to it. Now he did. *Helicopter. Coming.*

Sheer luck brought the helicopter in to land in the one place where Mike Russo could see it. He watched a band of Warkind disembark. It was Graye's band, and strung between them were two body bags, zippered black, shapeless enough to hide whatever coiled inside of them.

Russo winced at sight of the bags, wondering who else was dead now. But seeing Graye, the best of the Warkind to Mike's way of thinking, also gave him an idea. He whispered as much to Lanny.

--- 2 ---

"Cain!" Kyle yelled. "Caiiin!"

He was almost screaming over his shoulder toward the back of the Blazer. The gas peddle was hammered to the floor, the vehicle shuddering with speed on the erosion-eaten dirt road. Cain's house and the Warkind that had invaded it were falling behind. But black trees loomed on either side and he couldn't know if there would be more things coming out of those shadows.

They were running and they had to keep running.

"Dammit," Kyle yelled again. "Somebody tell me how Cain is!"

An "S" curve forced him to slow down and he had to drop the Blazer into a lower gear. The limbs of twisted oaks leaped into the glare of the headlights and leaped away again, some of them slapping down toward the Chevy as if to grab and hold. From the luggage area Kyle heard movement, all of it full of stop, and go, and purpose. There was breathing and counting.

"One, two, three. One, two, three."

He was very afraid that he knew what all the movement and sound was for. He wanted to look, but didn't dare take his eyes off the road for that long. One quick glance he spared, to his right, to Tru Maclang's face. The deputy stared toward the back, no answer about Cain in his expression.

And Kyle had to fight the wheel when he turned again to the road and saw the boomerang smile of a dark curve slice through his headlight glare. They hung over the ditch for a moment before Kyle pulled them back.

Only half a mile now to Highway 265, and the dirt road from Cain's place began to straighten. Kyle inched his speed up again and shifted back into high gear.

"One minute to the highway," he muttered to himself.

And then what? his thoughts asked. But he pushed the question away. Cain might be dying in the back of the Blazer. Maybe he was already dead. It was more than Kyle could bear. Reality he could bear. The truth. But not the quiet.

"Somebody tell me," he said. His voice sounded flat and hard even to his own ears, like a lead slug dropped into the shallowness of a coffee tin.

The movement from the back ceased as its purpose was lost. A collective sigh rolled up and around him. Words hit him that he had known were coming but wasn't prepared to hear--would never be prepared to hear.

Mel's voice: "He's dead, Kyle." The words low. Full of compassion. Tired. "I'm sorry. He lost too much blood."

Kyle's left eyelid twitched. His mouth felt full of dead worms and he needed to spit. He pushed on the clutch and shifted into neutral, let the tires roll with their own momentum. The stop sign that marked the end of Cain's road had stepped out of the darkness and gleamed like a red coin in front of them.

"We're at the highway," he said. His words were precise and didn't quaver. He noticed that. He tried the same voice again. "I don't know this country. Somebody tell me which way to go."

There wasn't any other sound. For the first time he realized that Tru Maclang had grasped his shoulder in support. He couldn't care. He noticed that too.

--- **3** ---

Mel Bowers had blood on her hands. Not for the first time. And she feared it wouldn't be the last. Cain Duplessis lay dead in front of her on the floor of the Blazer. She hadn't known him. Not really. But he'd been loved by at least two people in this vehicle and that made her hurt.

Her gaze turned toward Kyle Dupree in the driver's seat. She'd heard his voice when he asked which way to go, and she knew what his iron control really meant. Inside, he raged, and that scared her a little. She had known someone a bit like Kyle once--someone capable of deep caring, and deep hurt. But would Kyle stand now? Would he be able to hold himself together, and the rest of them with him? Or would he run like the other had?

And? She asked herself another question. Would she have what it took to help him?

She looked down at Cain dead, at Dan Case beside her with his face pale in fear. She looked across at Wahrn and Raina, the male Whoun's head lying across the legs of the female. The two of them were so physically close--fingers intertwined, skin touching, gazes locked--that it was hard to tell where one ended and the other began. Even the air seemed to smell differently around them.

In the short time Mel had known about them, the Whoun had become important to her in a way that she couldn't put into words. Seeing them together quickened a little hope in her soul. Kyle, Tru, Dan, Cain. Herself. All of them had come together to help these beings who were not human. Mel knew somehow that she "needed" to help them; she wondered if the others felt the same. And though usually brutally honest in her thoughts, she didn't completely understand her reasons in this situation. She did understand the sacrifice she had to make.

"I know a place," she said. Her words shocked apart the stillness that had grown inside the Blazer. "The summer homes out past the lake. Most'll be empty this time of year. We should be able to find gas if we need it. Maybe some food. Shelter in the daylight."

"We need the gas," Kyle agreed, the words so stiff that they seemed to gel in the air. "But the army will be moving on the highway. Too dangerous."

"No!" Dan yelled. "It's perfect. We don't have to use the highway. We can take Cranberry Cut. The old road. I've been through there in my truck. We can make it."

"Right," Mel said. She saw Kyle look at Tru, who nodded.

"Might work," the deputy said. "The Cut starts barely a hundred yards down the road. Toward town." He turned in his seat to question Dan. "How do you get through? We had a fence put up there a couple of years ago."

"Well, I usually come in from the lake side. But all we have to do is cut the wires. There's a ditch but it won't be nothing for a 4x4."

"All right," Kyle said. "I've got pliers. Someone tell me where to turn." He pulled out onto 265.

Though Kyle's voice still sounded flat, Mel could almost sense his mind turning gratefully toward their new problem. She wondered how long he would be able to put off facing his uncle's death.

Tru started talking: "On your left here. Just a little..."

But Mel's thoughts had turned inward to face her own pain. She should be relieved that they had a course of action in mind; the summer houses were perfect for what they needed. Only, she didn't feel relieved. Already her throat had begun to tighten and her stomach felt ill. And they weren't even close to that area of the lake yet.

She hoped the frog chorus would be silent when they got there. She might be able to handle it if only the frogs would stay quiet.

Cold in the Light

--- 4 ---

Kargen savaged his own thoughts while he waited for dawn to spill into the world. In the light he would begin to hunt the Mother and her allies--her new Podcyst. Their guard would be down then, at least against the Warkind. And any defenses they had against their human stalkers would not keep him from finding them.

But while he waited he grappled with many things. Insanity was not the least of them. He understood that over the past few days he had been growing steadily less sane. Earlier on this night he had even begun to hallucinate, had drifted so far from reality that he had failed to lead the attack that could have gained him what he sought. He had been too caught up in the rapture, had been wallowing in his own imbalance.

Only the fear engendered by his war-band's near revolt had driven the oddness from his mind. His questions were many. Why had this strangeness possessed him? Why had it left again? Would it stay away?

At the center of all his questions stood the Mother. The closer he had gotten to her, the worse his symptoms had become. Worst of all had been when he'd actually touched and tasted the earth where she had been lying. The logical answer was that something in her scent, or perhaps in her pheromones, was affecting him, altering his hormonal balance. His surge of fear had swung the balance back toward normal. But that would change when he picked up the Mother's trail again. He'd have to prepare himself.

Still, he had to ask why. He was Warkind; the Mother was Typical. According to humans, the two subgroups of Whoun were not linked by sexual ties but by social ones. The Warkind were genetically endowed warriors. Their sexuality remained biologically repressed, demonstrated only in the emotional and physical bonds of the war-bands. The Typicals were the breeding females and males.

Kargen had learned to read English when quite young. He remembered the words of one of the human thinkers: "Biology is destiny." He had always believed those words were true. If they were, then the Mother's pheromones should have had no effect on him. He shouldn't even have been attracted to her. But he was. When the Mother had gone into her first estrus it had been all he could do to control his impulses. And those impulses had gotten much, much stronger after she'd gathered the Podcyst around her and become pregnant.

Then had come the Mother's escape. She and the Podcyst had run. And he was one of those sent to hunt her. It meant that he could possess her if he wanted. If he were strong enough. He quivered and felt the heat come over him. His nictitating lids shuttered. No matter what the humans said about Typicals and Warkind being different, he wanted the Mother. And he would have her. *His* biology demanded it.

But he would not be ruled by the female's scent. And he would not be ruled by human thinking. He sat very still, with his warspikes scratching, scratching at the roped muscles of his legs. His thoughts narrowed, focused inward, fought a war.

By the time gray dawn came creeping like a fog he had mastered himself. He lived in the place that all warriors sought, where death and life and sex and hunger were one. Where you created your own reality and no one else's could intrude. Where you became a god, or a demon. And you didn't care which.

--- 5 ---

Michael Russo watched Graye's war-band vanish from the narrow field of vision afforded him by the crack in the flap of his and Lanny's prison tent. He chewed on the side of his thumb, playing out in his mind the plan that had come to him.

"What is it?" Lanny Burns asked. "What are you thinking?"

His train of logic still distracting him, Mike turned to the older man. "I said I've got an idea."

"I know. I mean what idea?"

"Graye's band."

"So?" Lanny asked.

Mike's attention shifted, dipped back into the tent from some other place. "So! What do the Warkind value? Above all?"

Lanny crinkled his lips in the facial equivalent of a shrug.

"The integrity of the Pod, the war-band. But I don't-- Wait! You're thinking about last year. Tornik. You really believe that'll be enough to make Graye go against Hammond? They're used to obeying the military. They've been trained--"

"Tornik is Graye's second. And he would have died if not for me. Didn't matter that it was luck that I was there when he had his accident. You saw how seriously they took what I did. Graye especially. Thought for a while I'd have a dozen Warkind bodyguards behind me the rest of my days. If I can get to Graye, get a few moments with him..."

Lanny shook his head slightly. "Even if you're right about Graye, he's not likely to drop by here for a visit. How the hell are you gonna get a few moments with him?"

"I just need to see him. Get close enough to speak. Go along with what I say. OK?"

"OK. Sure. Your call."

Mike moved back toward the opening of the tent. "Guard! Hey!"

The soldier on watch turned and moved toward them, his boots slicking across grass with a wet snake sound. Too cautious to put his head in, he squatted and eased back the flap with his left arm. His right hand cradled the pistol grip of an M-16.

"What?" the man asked.

"I need to talk to Hammond," Mike said.

"Doesn't seem all that smart, to me."

"Look!" Mike tried to make his voice sound desperate. It didn't really take much effort. "Maybe you know my wife and kids are coming here. Hammond wants to know things that I can tell him. I will. I just wanna make sure my family is going to be all right."

The soldier glanced toward the heart of the encampment, a faint light slicing white along his profile, leaving the sockets of his eyes hidden in shadow. For a moment, the man's face didn't even seem human, and Mike shuddered inwardly. Then the fellow turned back toward them, nodded and stood up to pull away the canvas opening of the tent.

"Let's go," he said.

With the guard behind them, Mike and Lanny were ushered through the camp toward Hammond's tent. A few moments later, after a hasty conference between soldier and commander, the two scientists found themselves herded inside. Hammond still sat before his map table. The Warkind, Graye, squatted on massive legs nearby.

Hammond beamed almost fondly upon Mike. "I hoped you would be smart, Russo."

The colonel leaned back in his chair then--a regular chair instead of a camp stool--and templed his hands in front of him. It was a celebrity's gesture, as overly dramatic as the man himself. At another time. In another place. Mike would have laughed.

Hammond nodded toward Graye, who stood up to leave. As the Warkind passed, Mike spoke softly to him. "How's Tornik these days? We should chat about him sometime."

"That will be sufficient," Hammond stated. "Graye. Your band still has a job to do. Get them ready."

The Warkind looked neither at Mike nor the colonel. But he hesitated for a moment, and into the air spilled the faint scent of brass and frost. Then the being nodded his head gravelly and went out of the tent into the night.

"For your sake," Hammond said to Mike Russo, "I hope you weren't trying any sleight of mouth. The Warkind are mine."

"Is that right? You including Kargen's Pod in that?"

A crease appeared between Hammond's eyes. "What do you know about Kargen's band? You the reason they've gone rogue?"

The word "rogue" startled Mike; he cleared his throat to hide it. He'd meant to accuse Hammond of letting Kargen do his killing, but the colonel had misunderstood, had thought he spoke with sarcasm. That meant Kargen really was an outlier, a statistical anomaly among his own kind. Mike decided not to tell Hammond the truth, that he didn't know anything about Kargen's behavior. The man wouldn't have believed him anyway.

"I'll tell you what I know," Mike said. "But only if you guarantee that my wife and kids will be left alone."

"You're in no position to barter with me, Doctor. Give me what I ask for and I'll see to it that your family has nothing to worry about. Otherwise..." Hammond smiled.

Mike stared, trying to read the intent behind the colonel's words. *You've seen too many movies, Hammond,* he thought to himself. Then he thought of how he could use that fact. Hammond would be expecting him to play the game. And he'd been in bargaining situations before. Anybody who ran a multimillion dollar research facility had to learn the art of give and take. Mike's confidence began to build.

"You've got to give me something, Hammond," he said. "I need to know they'll be safe."

Cold in the Light

Hammond smiled again, as if they were sharing some mildly funny joke. Mike's confidence slipped a little, then bounced back as Hammond sighed like a bad actor trying to save a weak scene.

"Russo." Hammond sat up straight in his chair, dropping his hands to his sides. "You seem to have me confused with one of your pet Senators up in Washington." His voice hardened, took on a slight edge of cruelty. "You. Have. No power. Here. Are you stupid, or just a slow learner?"

"Look, Hammond," Mike started to say. He had to carry this through, had to keep control of the situation. "We each want something. I'll--"

At that point the colonel calmly slipped a pistol from the holster at his side and shot Lanny Burns once in the forehead.

--- 6 ---

The house was a one-story with two bedrooms, a living room, kitchen, and bath--not very big, but made of logs the way many of the summer folk liked. Maybe it let them feel like pioneers, Mel Bowers mused. And it didn't matter that logs weren't the cheapest way to build anymore in the Ozark Mountains. They were sturdy and didn't need much care in the months when their owners were off in the cities increasing their assets. Cost wasn't a problem.

This house was nearly perfect for what its current occupants needed, though after they had come out through Cranberry Cut onto Lake Road they had been forced to drive a good ways to find it. That had been dangerous, for the absolute lack of traffic on the main road meant that the army had shut down access to anyone outside of military personnel.

Still, when they'd found this place it had been just right, sitting well back from the paved road, almost halfway up the side of Rattlesnake Ridge where it could overlook the lake. Pine trees surrounded it for cover but there were possible exits on three sides--the road they had followed in from the east, north over the top of the ridge along a clearway slashed for the power lines, or west in the groove of a shallow streambed that ran down toward the lake.

Dense woods blocked any southern exit, but it would have made Mel nervous if things had been any better. It was even far enough away from the water so that her old anxieties remained dormant.

A freestanding garage on the property provided a place to hide the Blazer, and Tru siphoned enough gasoline out of a brand new garden tractor to top off their vehicle's tank. There even remained a little extra to take with them. A caretaker must have been coming by once in a while. The gas, the trimmed lawn and hedges, and a recently painted well-house indicated that someone had been around.

Inside the house, once the padlocks were broken off, they'd discovered warmer clothing and blankets--and food. They found a rollaway bed for Wahrn. Raina seemed to feel better, too. Mel thought a lot of that was just having Wahrn back, but the female Whoun hadn't experienced any more cramps. They had been getting steadily less frequent toward morning anyway, which didn't really make sense to Mel. Even Raina had thought her baby was coming. But it was the female's first time and who knew what differences in birthing patterns you'd see in a brand new species.

With the power shut off, working by candlelight, Mel began heating chili on the tiny Coleman stove she had carried in from the Blazer. Despite what they'd been through, or perhaps because of it, the meaty smell soon had her mouth watering. Dan seemed of like mind and began setting out plates and forks for the six of them.

"I'm not hungry," Kyle said, his voice loud as he stepped suddenly back into the kitchen from checking the house.

Mel and Dan both jumped but Kyle didn't acknowledge their startled glances, just went on through the room and out the rear door without another word. Under his left arm was tucked the white roll of a down comforter.

Mel looked at Dan.

"Should I go help him?" the boy asked. "Maybe?"

She shook her head. "No. Tru's there if he needs someone. Best for us to leave him alone."

"He seems awfully calm, don't you think? I wouldn't be taking it so well."

"Yes," Mel said, "he's awfully calm. But I'm not sure he's taking it well."

Dan's pupils were dilated in the dim light. They looked scared to Mel, and she wondered if her eyes looked the same. After a moment she smelled the chili scorching and turned back to stir it.

--- 7 ---

Michael Russo looked down at Lanny's body with sick eyes; his throat felt hot with acid. Hammond's gunshot had crumpled his friend where he stood, dropping him to the tent's nylon floor like a broken old watch. Lanny lay on his face. The bullet must have gone in through the skull. But it hadn't come out again. Lanny's head bulged obscenely from the shock of the lead, like a soft clay sculpture punched by a madman's fist.

Mike lost it, retching as he dropped to his knees. It had been long hours since he'd eaten and nothing filled his stomach except mucous and bile, but the taste burned through his mouth and nose, pulling water into his eyes. The heaves racked his chest and throat, stole away his air.

"Damn you, Hammond," Mike said when he could breathe again.

Hammond lowered his pistol to the desk and drew his hand back to tap against his lips, leaving the dark and ugly weapon sitting like a clot of frozen blood.

"Anger isn't very effective coming from a position on your knees, Russo. I'd expect people to stand up when they curse me."

"You are a foul piece of shit."

The colonel dropped his hand from his face, put it down next to the gun. A blatant threat.

"Yes, yes, yes. Enough cliches. I simply needed to inform you that I am serious when I ask you a question."

Mike glanced at Hammond's fingers where they played like a spider around the butt of the pistol. Then he looked away. The threat didn't scare him just now.

"What you informed me of is how vicious a bastard you are. Giving you anything would be like scratching the belly of a rabid dog. You know the bitch is gonna turn on you. One way or another."

Hammond's lips tried a smile, aborted it. His hard brown eyes had begun to move, had begun to trace a slow pattern around the tent.

"Maybe you won't feel that way when your family arrives," he said.

Mike felt his stomach flop in fear, then turned the fear around into a cold rage.

"I love my family, Hammond. You know that or you wouldn't threaten them. But think about that leverage. Think about the damage you've just done to it. How am I gonna trust you now? How am I gonna believe that you won't hurt them even if I do cooperate? How the fuck is anyone gonna trust anyone now!"

Hammond didn't answer; his eyes were moving faster, shifting constantly, reflecting slivers of light like darting minnows. He moved his hand off the desk and leaned back in his chair. For the first time he seemed to consider the possibility that he had miscalculated.

After a moment, the colonel waved his hand at the guard, who came forward and jerked Mike to his feet. Out into the dark they went, back across the camp to the tent where minutes ago he'd thought to hatch a plan with a living friend. Now he had no friend. And he had no plan left, nor any hope of developing a new one. But he had a need.

Mike closed his eyes, called up a wishful image of Drake Hammond on the ground with a brick smashing in his too pale face. The brick shone all wet on one side, and darker red in splotches. Hammond's mouth looked like raspberries crushed against concrete. His eyes had a distant stare.

--- **8** ---

Kyle savaged his own thoughts while he stood over Cain's grave and ached in the darkness. Tru had come, and gone. The hole had been emptied of dirt, then filled back with more dirt and with a good man's body. Kyle remained.

He stood rigid, all the blood driven from his fingers by the pressure of his grip on the shovel. He thought of the things he could have done, the things he should have done. He thought of the beings who had killed his uncle, and inside of him the anger grew until it seemed the wooden handle in his hands would snap in half.

Abruptly, he dropped the shovel and wheeled back toward the house. Tru and Dan were in the kitchen, eating chili with white bread; the others were in the living room. He ignored them all,

Cold in the Light

moving past them toward the hallway where there stood an oak gun cabinet.

The people who owned this house were sportsmen, he could see. Behind the wood-framed, glass panels of the cabinet were rifles, shotguns, and .22s. Boxes of ammunition sat on the top shelf. The door was locked.

Kyle stood looking for a moment, then lashed out with a hard kick that shattered the wooden frame and sprayed glass onto the hall carpet. He reached in through the broken panels and began pulling out guns to lean against the wall for loading.

A Browning High-Power rifle in .30-06 came first. It had only a four shot magazine but its bullets would punch through an engine block. And it had a scope, a Zeiss 4X. There was also a Browning Auto-5 Magnum Stalker shotgun, chambered for 3-inch shells It was a little long in the barrel but still usable for close work.

The last of the guns Kyle wanted was an Olympic Arms CAR-9, a military style, semi-automatic rifle that held thirty-four shells in its curved clip. He would have preferred a bigger caliber but having more shots was good too. And it used the same 9mm ammunition as the Sig Sauer pistol he'd taken off that soldier earlier this night.

Kyle was loading the first clip with shells when he heard the shuffle of feet on carpet and glanced up to see Melissa and Tru and Dan staring at him from the living room. They'd been drawn by the sound of shattering glass and must have watched him take the weapons out one by one.

He looked into each of their faces, saw their tension and fear. They weren't sure of him, he realized, weren't sure just how badly Cain's death had shaken him. And yet, they were waiting for him to get them out of this mess. What scared them was the thought that he might not be stable enough for the job.

His cheek twitched; the anger began to coil in his belly and creep up into his throat. He forced himself to look away and back to the task at hand.

The brass of the shells had warmed in his palm, felt smooth and slightly oily to his fingers. He pushed one down into the magazine, then another. The ritual focused his attention, eased his pulse.

"I'm all right," he said out loud, without looking up. "I just...need a few minutes."

He finished loading one magazine, began on a second. He heard the others moving away. The rage still cooked inside of him; he wanted to lash out. But he wasn't alone. The others needed him to be in control of himself. And he found that he cared what they thought, what they felt; he cared that the two Whoun were alone and scared. As Cain would have cared.

Cain...

He picked up the CAR-9, stared into the darkness of the blued steel. "Cain," he muttered to himself. And, "No more." Nobody was going to take anyone else away from him without a fight: not the soldiers who were searching for Raina and Wahrn, not the Warkind who had killed the only real family he had left.

Kyle slapped the clip home into the rifle and chambered a cartridge, the rattle of the loading mechanism sounding like knells in his ears.

--- **9** ---

Raina lay wrapped around Wahrn on the small bed, smelling him, touching him--exploring his contours as if to reassure herself that he was truly here and alive. And though he was far into a healing sleep, she could taste his pheromones changing and flowing in perfect response to her nearness. That normality comforted her.

Being alone around the humans had been such a strain, even though the one called Cain, and now the others, had tried to ease her anxieties. She knew what they had given. Were giving. Cain, his life. And the others were at risk now because of her and Wahrn and the baby she carried. They had broken the laws of their own kind. Raina appreciated that. And though her baby had to come first, if the need arose she and Wahrn would fight for the humans as those humans had fought for the Whoun.

But they were so alien, from their movements, to their expressions, to the scent that spilled from their sweat and bled from every pore in their bodies. Their fear tasted like chalk burning, their anger as bitter as exhausted soil. Worse, they were all so completely alone inside their skins. At times they went for minutes without touching each other. Raina couldn't understand it.

Always in the Institute she had been surrounded by other Whoun, her lips and tongue constantly tingling with the taste of

Cold in the Light

life. Licking. Touching. Fur moving against fur, hand against cheek. A cocoon of scents rising all around, wrapping her in odors like a warm robe. The outside world was a very cold place, especially to birth a child. And soon now the sun would rise.

In the Institute the days were never brighter than twilight. Fear of light was coded into Whoun genetics. Raina remembered Lanny Burns telling her that the Whoun were probably descended from a subterranean species who had ventured to the surface rarely, and then only at night. He didn't know what reasons there could have been for such an adaptation, had seemed puzzled himself. As if it were unlikely.

Of course, the reasons didn't matter. When the sun came up--and it was already paling outside--she and Wahrn would begin to experience fear. They would feel a blizzard cold creeping upon them, a bone cold that could only be assuaged by finding a dark place and curling up together. With Wahrn here maybe she could survive it. At least one advantage to her genetics seemed to be that her baby would not come in the light. Already her cramps had stopped, as had the lesser ones the day before. But she would almost rather have the cramps than the day.

Raina felt the heat of Wahrn's buttocks against her lower body. She nuzzled him lightly, licking the tiny oil ducts behind his ear. She wished he were well enough to mate with her. But that was a selfish wish. She wanted his comfort, wanted him so close that he fitted inside of her. That could not be yet. In another few days maybe; he healed quickly.

If they lived!

She had not told Wahrn what she had seen at the human Cain's house. She had not told him what she knew, that the Warkind band hunting them belonged to Kargen. Long had they both sensed the strangeness in Kargen. Wahrn instinctively hated him. Raina feared him. She had seen him watching her during the first days when the Podcyst formed. There was no doubt in her mind that he was dangerous, to Wahrn, to her, to the baby.

Raina lifted her head and looked toward the front window of the house, toward where gray light limned the gaunt shape of the human named Kyle. Around her the other humans slept. Kyle watched. Earlier this night she had smelled the tension stretched between Kyle and the others like the strands of a web. The others depended upon him, but seemed uncomfortable with the urge to violence that his loss had banked within him. For his part, he had made no attempt to ease their worries, seemed even to take satisfaction from being isolated.

Of all the humans, Kyle's actions seemed the easiest for Raina to understand. This wasn't because they were rational, but because he was the human equivalent of a Warkind. To her, he seemed the least alien among them. She knew, also, that against Kargen he made the best hope any of them had.

Raina closed her eyes, wished for sleep to take her so that she wouldn't see the sun burn its way into the sky. One thought comforted her a bit. The Warkind didn't like the day any more than the Typicals did. At least there would be no need to worry about Kargen until night came again.

PART THREE

THINGS FALL APART

Predation is in the bones, in the marrow.
The need is for food,
but even when fed carnivores will hunt.
They want the wet taste of life,
the sweetness of watermelon flesh.
Sex or beauty might distract them for a while.
They might gather shiny things
around them. But their need to kill isn't rational.

And they will not be denied,
in the memory of ruins.

Charles Gramlich

CHAPTER NINE
(May 1: Early Morning)

The ruin dwellers came at last, in a
dream of movement marked by the odor
of a vast arousal. The shrieking of
a blizzard wind filled their throats.
Their eyes dripped a cold anger.
   --In the Memory of Ruins

--- 1 ---

In the woods they had burrowed, down through fallen leaves and pine needles into the meat of the soft loam soil. There, they had created a Darkhome and covered it with branches against the terrible cold sun. Only Kargen had not entered that place with them. He sat above, on a lichen covered stone that poked like a war-claw from the ground.

For a while a mist had bathed him, its fingers silken on his quills, its cloak diffusing the gray pain within the dawn. But now that sheltering touch was going and beams of watery-yellow light were searching through gaps in the trees, dropping down to stab the earth all around him. He felt one of the beams touch his shoulder and slice down across his back, arcing through his muscles like an electric shock. Another beam crawled over his ankle, sent cold ants running in a wave up his leg.

Despite himself, Kargen shivered. The tendons of his feet and hands ached with the urge to hurl dirt up as a wall against the light. The most basic part of his mind screamed at him to dig, or to run. He did neither, only sat and gradually forced his quivering muscles to still. He knew the fear was foolish for himself, though it would not have been for his ancestors--no more than humankind's fear of the dark would have been foolish in the infancy of their species. All beings had their weaknesses.

When every part of him grew quiet, and his stained ivory nails were no longer buried in the pads of his hands, Kargen stood up. A few yards in front of him lay an open space where one tall tree had pulled down its shorter brothers in a fall. The dust-yellow sparkle of morning brimmed full in that clearing.

Kargen could feel the temperature difference between the clearing and the shaded place where he was. His skin did not want to go out to that opening, but his mind pushed his legs forward and he stepped solidly into the light. It felt to him as if he had entered a well of ice.

Kargen closed his eyes against a bright lance of pain, then slowly turned his face to the sky. For long minutes he endured there, letting the morning pierce through him, drawing it to himself as if he could fill all his body cavities with it and make the enemy his. When at last he looked down he knew that he could hunt in the light. It wouldn't stop him. And no one would be ready for him.

His eyes slitted open, nictitating lids down to help protect against the drying sun. He would have to be careful of his vision. It wasn't good in the day. Too much light and he would be glare-blind. But his nose worked, his ears worked. And he had another way of locating the Mother. He could use his own hormonal response as a homing sense. The closer he got to the female the more strangely his perceptions would twist. He could adjust for that, let it serve him as a guide.

He moved forward then, out of light into shadow and back through light--drifting slowly at first, but with increasing confidence. Gradually his stride lengthened, until his walk became a lope, and a run.

Mother, he thought. *Stay in your dark place and wait. I'll be there soon.*

--- 2 ---

When the first part of morning lay thin but strong over the surrounding trees, Kyle stood up from a chair by the cabin's picture window and stretched his muscles. Tendons popped, and the ache felt good. Kyle had run in the mornings almost every day of his adult life. Now it had been a couple of days and he missed the routine. He wondered how long it would be before he'd see *routine* again.

With a rifle in his hands, he moved quietly away from the front of the house, seeing the Whoun on the rollaway bed, their heads covered against the rising light, seeing Melissa Bowers in a pile of blankets on the floor, her blond hair like a spill of straw over her face. Dan slept across the room, at the foot of the narrow hallway leading to the cabin's twin bedrooms. His head was hidden by wadded sheets but Kyle could hear the faint 'snik' of the boy's breathing.

Too damn tense if I'm hearing people breathe, Kyle thought. *Bent tight as a fishing rod with a forty pound redfish on the other end.*

The vision came unbidden, the surge and pull of a bull red, the line cutting straight through muddy water, the shock in his arms as he set the hook. He pushed image and feeling away, knowing them for what they were. His mind was squirming, looking to escape the stress that ate at him. But he had to stay focused. He moved on, toward the rear of the house.

Tru had spent the night in the kitchen, where even in sleep he would have been able to hear if anyone, or anything, had tried to come in the back door. The deputy was awake now, though. Kyle could hear him moving around and smell the odor of instant coffee as it sat in cups on the counter and waited for hot water. The smell reminded him that he hadn't eaten when the others had last night.

Clearing his throat slightly to announce his coming, Kyle stepped through into the kitchen. Tru looked up at him, water heating on the Coleman stove behind him on the counter, the stock of the Browning Auto-5 within easy reach. Last night Kyle had given the shotgun to Tru. He'd kept the CAR-9 semiautomatic rifle for himself, along with two pistols--the Sig and his own .45. Dan had drawn the .30-06 and one of the .22s. Melissa Bowers hadn't said if she could use a gun or not, but if she wanted one today Kyle would give her his .357. It could eat .38 Special cartridges if she wanted the lighter loads.

"Coffee?" Tru asked.

"Yeah. I could use a cup."

Tru lifted the metal pot off the camp stove with a rag and poured streams of boiling liquid into two Stoneware cups with coffee crystals in their bottoms. A burned, sweet odor whirled up, touched faintly with a sharp and humid bite.

"Not too much," Tru said, handing Kyle the cup. "You're the only one hasn't slept."

"I'll grab an hour after everyone's up. Then we need to talk. Need to decide what the hell we're gonna do."

Tru shook his head, lifting and sipping from his cup.

"That's a problem, all right. We've been running too fast to think. But you gotta have sleep first. More than an hour."

Kyle sipped his own coffee, burned his tongue and didn't really care. "Yeah. I know."

Tru was a good man. All of them were. Good men and good women. *Good Whoun*! Kyle half grinned, until he remembered that Cain lay dead. Abruptly, he pulled a chair out from the kitchen table and sat down, laying his gun across his lap.

Tru joined him, and Kyle realized that the other man had seen a flicker of the aborted smile. And knew the reason.

"I can't feel exactly how you feel," Tru said. "But Cain was my friend for a long time. I never understood his art, but I knew the man. He'd have something to say to you now, to make things easier. Something better than I can say."

"You're doing OK."

Tru shifted in his chair, laced his fingers around the cup he held.

"Cain gave himself over to Raina. To me and you. I think he'd have felt that way for Mel, and Dan, and Wahrn. You've got his blood in you. I can feel that."

"I won't abandon them."

Tru shook his head again, harder. "I never thought you would. That's not what I meant. But I guess it is part of what I wanted to say."

The deputy took a long swallow from his cup, as if the caffeine would fill him with the words he wanted to know how to use.

"What you said a minute ago. About not abandoning them." He breathed out slowly, almost whistling through pursed lips. "I may be out of line, but I think last night. Maybe still today. You were doubting yourself. And that made you doubt us. Made you doubt our words. The way we looked at you. But you're like Cain. I know. The same blood."

"The same blood?" Kyle mused out loud. "Some of it maybe. But I'm a harder man than Cain Duplessis ever was. He made a good man. The best. And I understood his art. Black folk been living with violence and fear close to our guts for a long time. He wanted to understand why. But he couldn't. Oh, I think he got the fear part, but not the violence. I've got them both."

"What are you gonna do with them?"

Kyle looked up at Tru sharply, bitter words piling up like a dammed river in the back of his throat. He swallowed them down. No hint of insincerity showed in the other man. Tru wasn't trying to be cute. Not because he was incapable of guile. Just that he didn't care to use it. Kyle responded the same way.

"What I've always tried to do, I guess. Balance them. Like I've tried to balance being both black and white."

"Your mother was white?"

"Father. My mother was what they call in New Orleans a Creole. White folks call them black. Or worse. Black folks call them wannabe whites. Some do at least. What the Creoles are all about is balance."

"Your mother taught you that?"

"Yeah. And Cain."

"What about your father?"

"A few years ago I'd have told you he taught me to drink. But now I don't know. I think maybe he taught me something. I just don't know what it is yet."

"My father was sheriff in Deerhaven for awhile." Tru looked deep into his coffee when he spoke, though Kyle didn't understand why.

"Your mother?" he asked.

"Schoolteacher. School's close to the biggest employer in town." Tru laughed.

"I think that's a good thing," Kyle said.

He put down his cup at the whisper of feet moving over carpet. He looked toward the kitchen door in time to see Mel Bowers come through. She nodded to them, mumbled something that might have been translated as good morning, and headed straight for the coffee pot. The water was still hot, and she poured and stirred and drank in what seemed a single motion. Then she moved over to the table, sat down with them.

A minute passed in silence. Then another. Tru finished his coffee and stood up.

"I'm gonna go check to see if maybe the phones are working. The wife'll be expecting me home soon. I usually get off at eight."

Kyle started to say something, stopped as Tru held up his hand. "I won't give anything away. But I hate to worry her. I have to tell her something."

Kyle nodded, watched the deputy leave, then turned back toward Mel. She was staring at him, he saw, and she didn't look away like most people would have when they were caught at it. He liked that.

"He knows the phones aren't working," Mel said.

Kyle raised an eyebrow.

"I checked them last night. He saw me. He believes you and I need to talk. Though I know he's worried about his wife. You'd think in this day and age one of us would have a cell phone."

"I hate the damn things."

Mel nodded slightly, then followed with a sigh. "By the way, I didn't get a chance to tell you how sorry I am about your uncle."

"I know you are." Kyle sat down his cup, leaned back in his chair, flattened his hands over the stock and barrel of the rifle in his lap. "Something I have to live with, I guess."

"And of course those words are inadequate."

Kyle locked his eyes on hers, startled a bit at the blunt truth she had spoken.

"Yes. You're right," he said. "They are."

Mel looked away, out the kitchen window as if her own thoughts on "living with things" had suddenly burdened her too much to keep talking.

"I'm sorry we dragged you into this," Kyle said. He found that he didn't want her going too far away from him.

"I'm not." She smiled, quirkily, with the left side of her mouth twisted. "Well, maybe on the surface. Not inside, though. Wahrn and Raina are something else!"

"I know." And after a pause. "I appreciate you helping us."

Mel shrugged. "Wahrn's recovering fast. Apparently the adrenaline he wanted did trigger blood formation. I still think we should go public with this, though." She leaned forward over the table as if to push her words toward him. "Out in the open! A thousand people see the Whoun and they can't cover it up."

Kyle reached up to rub the bridge of his nose with a long index finger. "I'm not against that necessarily. Remember it was Wahrn who protested most about taking him to a hospital. But even if we wanted to do it I don't know how. By now the army knows other people are involved. They'll have the highways in and out of Deerhaven blocked off. They've got helicopters."

"Then forget Deerhaven. We can go cross country. Go at night. At least until we get around the roadblocks."

"At night they'll pick up our engine heat. For all we know they've got satellites locked all over this area."

"I don't think so."

Kyle frowned. "You don't think so? Now how the hell do you come up with that? The government controls the satellites you know. The same government that's hunting us. Trying to kill us."

Mel shook her head, not angrily--though Kyle had spoken more sarcastically than he had intended--but with her mind focused on something he didn't see.

"No," she said. "Not the government. One small piece of it. You heard Tru say the soldiers weren't regular army. And from what Wahrn and Raina have said we can bet the main part of the government doesn't know anything about them."

Mel looked straight at him. "If the government wanted us blanketed we'd be blanketed. I think all they've got is what they've thrown at us so far."

Kyle sat very still, running Mel's words over in his head and knowing they were right in the way that human beings know things sometimes. He had never been one to trust his intuition, had always wanted something more solid to bite into. He wanted something more solid now, but didn't think he would get it.

Unless...

Kyle looked at Mel Bowers. She was solid. She sat there in all her slimness, and she was tougher than he was. What he'd told Tru earlier, about being a harder man than Cain. It was a partial truth. He'd left out the fact that he was more brittle than his uncle too-- more brittle than the woman across from him. Kyle had always had Cain, even in the worst years with his father. He didn't think Mel Bowers had leaned on anyone in a very long time.

"I think you're right," he said, coming to a decision. "We have to talk with the others. Convince Wahrn and Raina. But I think you're right."

Mel leaned back in her chair. "We'll convince them. After you sleep."

Kyle nodded. "A few hours." He stood up and moved toward the door, stopped again when Mel called him.

"Yes?"

"I know how to use a gun," she said.

He nodded again. "By the window. Take the Colt on the sill. I'm gonna use one of the bedrooms."

"Sleep well."

"I hope so," Kyle said.

But inside he doubted it.

--- **3** ---

After Kyle had gone off to bed, Mel drank a second cup of coffee, then went back into the living room to find Tru Maclang writing a note to the owners of the house they were borrowing. He held it up.

"To make sure they know the destruction of their property was done officially," he smiled. "Told 'em to contact the Sheriff's Office for reimbursement."

"Good idea. What about your wife?"

Tru shrugged. "Phone's disconnected. I forgot you checked it last night."

She knew he was lying but didn't call him on it. He'd had his own reasons for wanting to leave her and Kyle alone. His genuine worry about his wife had given him an excuse.

"She'll be worried? Your wife?"

"Probably. Certainly when they find my car at Cain's and the house all torn up by the Warkind. Carlene's strong, though. She'll be OK."

Mel could tell by the way he said it that Tru wasn't at all sure Carlene would be OK. She put a hand on his shoulder.

"We'll get a message to her soon. I've met your wife. She *is* strong."

"Thanks."

"I talked with Kyle. About trying to go cross country to skirt the roadblocks. I was thinking Fort Smith."

"Be hard. There aren't many ways through the Ozarks when you're on wheels."

"But *you* know some."

"Maybe." He patted his paunch. "It's been a few years since I did much travelling in the mountains."

"We can't just let them have Wahrn and Raina. We know they're willing to kill. If they want to keep it quiet badly enough they may try to kill us too."

"I've thought of that. So has Kyle. The only thing is, we don't know exactly who *they* are. Who we trust. Who we don't."

"Wahrn and Raina know. We'll have to let them guide us."

"Yeah, there's that." And after a moment. "Kyle's hurting?"

"Yes," she said. "He's got something to keep him focused now, though. The worst for him will be when we're safe. Worst for all of us, maybe. The aftermath!" She added the last with a tinge of bitterness, though she hadn't meant to open herself that way.

Tru's stare crossed hers, lingered. "You were fifteen then. This isn't the same. And Kyle isn't like the other."

Mel blushed and looked away. She hated herself for that response. She had known that Deerhaven was a small town, a place where everyone knew everything that happened to one of their number. Even if what they knew was wrong.

That was one of the reasons she'd come back, to show that the knowing didn't matter, that she was who she was despite the knowing. But it got hard when the person in front of you could have paged personally through your nightmare. She didn't *know* that Tru had read the police report on her past. That there was one, she had no doubt. Though its facts would be wrong. And Tru's father had been Sheriff in Deerhaven when Mel was fifteen. Tru had surely heard the stories and could have read the clinical speculations if he'd been curious enough to check her file.

She looked back at Tru, met his gaze steadily. "You're right," she said. "Kyle isn't like the other."

"Neither are you," Tru said, his voice striving to be kind.

Mel nodded, not speaking because his kindness didn't really feel that way to her. Yet, she knew that he meant his words to be taken as kind.

Finally, Mel broke the uncomfortable pause by turning and moving across the room toward the window where Kyle had kept watch in the night. She sat in the chair he'd sat in, looked through the glass at daylight that suddenly seemed strange to her.

She knew Tru was right. And wrong. Kyle wasn't the same as the boy she'd once known. But she thought sometimes that *she* was still that same child she had been. And always would be.

Mel looked out the window, glad that it didn't face the lake barely a mile away down the hill. She closed her eyes, snapped them open again when the sound of night frogs boomed like drums in her memory, filling her ears and her whole awareness, as they had filled the world and covered even the atonal scratch of the screams she had tried to vent on that never gone day.

When she was fifteen.

She sat then, with her eyes open. And thought of salvation.

--- 4 ---

Helen Russo shivered as she stepped off the plane onto the gray-white Tarmac of Drake Field in Fayetteville, Arkansas. She felt glad she'd worn a sweater and had made the boys bring their jackets. It had been warmer in D.C. than it was here so much farther south, and she wondered if it were the elevation that caused the difference. She'd read that the highest point in Arkansas was under 3,000 feet. Surely that wasn't high enough to affect the temperature. It must just be a weather front moving through.

Joshua and Caleb came down the plane's steps behind her, the excitement of their early morning flight having worn off in the hours-long journey. It would come back soon--at the thought of seeing their father--but for now both were yawning. And as they moved out into the relatively bright eight o'clock day they both sneezed, one after the other.

Helen smiled. Her husband had told her that sneezing on exposure to sunlight was a genetic trait. Mike always did it himself.

And his boys, Joshua who was seven and Caleb who was four, were like him. In so many ways.

She took her boys' hands and began walking away from the small plane toward the nearby terminal. Behind her came the sound of luggage being unloaded. Caleb's excitement had come back at sight of the airport and he pulled against her grip, trying to go faster. Josh held back and kept looking over his shoulder at their bags--to make sure the one carrying his stuff still hung with them, Helen figured. She didn't let either of them go; she wanted them close to her right now.

The first thing Helen saw when she stepped into the terminal were uniforms, two of them, topped by scrubbed faces and the bristles of army haircuts.

"Mrs. Russo?" one of the soldiers asked.

"Yes."

"We're here to pick you up and take you to the compound. There's a car just outside."

Helen merely nodded and led her sons on through the small terminal, stopping just long enough for them all to use the bathroom. After that they went out to where a government issue Crown Victoria awaited them. One soldier had fetched their bags and he loaded them into the trunk while the other opened the back door for his passengers and then slid in behind the wheel. In a moment they were pulling out of the airport parking area and turning south onto Highway 71 out of Fayetteville.

Josh immediately pulled a Gameboy out of his travel pack and began playing. Caleb was busy trying to see out the windows, and trying to stretch at the seat belt in his usual bid to loosen it. Helen made sure it was tight, then leaned back and closed her eyes for a moment's rest. She hadn't slept well for the few hours that she had tried last night, knowing there would be a scene with Michael when they arrived. He had never wanted them around his work, had always been more than what she considered closemouthed. But she had already determined not to back down this time. If things didn't change she was going to take the boys and leave him.

"Is this the way to Daddy's work?" Josh asked, and the puzzlement in his small voice made Helen sit up and look around.

She saw that they had turned off the highway onto a dirt road that was fast becoming a one lane trail. Ahead of them loomed a thin stand of trees and beyond that she could see a meadow filled with wild flowers and hear a helicopter with its rotors already chopping at the air.

"Where are we going?" she asked the soldiers.

The one on the passenger side turned a bland face toward her. "Just where you said you wanted to go, Ma'am. You were planning on seeing your husband right away, weren't you?"

"Yes. But--"

And Helen Russo stopped talking as the soldier's words registered. She *had* been planning to see Mike right away. But these men couldn't know that. They couldn't even have known to pick her and the boys up at the airport.

She hadn't told anyone they were coming!

--- 5 ---

Exhaustion hit Kyle like a slaughterhouse mallet and as soon as he lay down his mind dropped into unconsciousness. At first his brain simply went blank. Later it dreamed, turned his sleep into terror. Because he didn't know that he dreamed.

He was running in the darkness, through an aisle among the trees. Just ahead of him stood an abandoned sawmill, though he didn't know how he knew that it was abandoned. Behind him came the pack, neither human nor animal, but something else--something all full of edges and sharp angles, like the steel frames of animated machines.

And they were gaining on him.

With only yards to go to the mill, Kyle could feel his lead peel away, to twenty feet, fifteen, to ten. The building loomed. He could see the entrance ramp and the door beyond with its weathered paint and broken panes of glass. He needed just a few more steps but didn't think he was going to get them.

Then, as his right arm swung back he let it continue behind him and fired his pistol into the pack at his heels. He didn't know how the gun had come suddenly into his hands, but the bullet hit something and punctured a scream, a near human scream.

The distraction slowed the pack for the seconds Kyle needed. He kicked in the last of his strength to vault the railing and slam through the door into the mill. Teeth and bodies grazed his legs as he crashed the heavy oaken panel shut and shoved home the rusted bolt with enough force to tear open his palm. Pain came. But no blood. His mind didn't stop to wonder why.

To his left stood the old supervisor's office, above the tool room, and Kyle took the stairs in a few running steps. He was at the top when the remaining glass in the door shattered inward. The door itself came apart next, with the rotten sound of an overripe watermelon splitting on concrete. Kyle fired into a roiling mass of shadows but heard only the whine of a ricochet. They would be coming in a second.

There was no door on the supervisor's office, nothing to build a barricade, but the heavy block and tackle that had once been used to unload timber trucks hung in front of his face, and holes in the roof let in enough moonlight to show him the narrow I-beam that ran the length of the building. He grabbed the rope from the block and tackle and swung the long way out onto the beam.

A pair of slanted eyes flared red at the railing of the office behind him, and the ivory gleam of incisors shone in the moonlight. Kyle fired twice, spacing his shots, and grunted in satisfaction as the creature was slammed backward by a lead fist. Satisfaction turned to dismay as the thing got up again and leaped from the railing toward the beam where he stood.

It was an impossible jump, but the creature made it, both its front feet catching on the narrow strut. Kyle glimpsed a massive hydrocephalic cranium wrapped around a blunt muzzle far too full of teeth. Then he fired point-blank into its face as it started to pull its way up. The shells Kyle used were plenty strong enough to take down a man, but this one bounced off. At less than ten feet it bounced off. Kyle saw it all. The bullet struck the creature between its staring eyes and the flesh just seemed to flow beneath it and shrug it away.

The slug's impact did knock the thing back, but didn't knock its paws loose from the I-beam. Even as those paws started to elongate into something that resembled hands, Kyle stepped forward and kicked it in the mouth. This blow snapped its hold, sending it spinning down into the darkness.

Kyle turned, and found himself standing now at the end of the beam where it wed itself to the southern wall of the mill. He

Cold in the Light

touched that wall, trying to understand how he had gotten so quickly to this point.

Just above him ran a solid row of mostly shattered windows that looked out over the night forest and flooded this end of the building with silver light. He was thinking of escape through one of those windows when the brutal sounds of tearing metal jerked his head around. That noise came from the opposite end of the span he stood on. Down there in the darkness, down there in the suddenly hard-edged night, something was using tools to rip the I-beam from its moorings.

An undulating wave passed through the steel, like a suspension bridge whipped by earthquake-powered winds, and Kyle felt metal turn to spaghetti under his feet. He leaped for the wall as the beam fell away, his flailing left hand catching a window frame and clutching hard.

Slivers of broken glass pierced his palm, wringing a moan from thinned lips, but he hooked the revolver in his other hand over the wooden frame and used it to pull himself up. Howls of disappointment rose from the shadows below him, and then his feet found purchase on the mill wall and a final surge carried him through the window to tumble free in the space beyond.

He dropped forever before his fall broke on a massive spill of sawdust that had built up over years outside the mill. Only, it wasn't sawdust. The pile "rattled" as he slid down it, tiny avalanches of clinking moving along with him. He picked up a length of white, a bone he saw, with fluted grooves along its sides where teeth had gnawed. He hurled it quickly away from him, wiped his fingers on his jeans.

The whole pile began to shake. Something moved beneath it. To Kyle's left drifted shadows that hunted; to his right lay the deepwell darkness of the mill's foundation. The latter looked too much like a grave to suit Kyle, but better a darkness he didn't know than one that he knew was deadly. He rolled into it and started to crawl.

Inside of a minute the seemingly open foundation had closed around him until he crawled in a narrow tunnel. And he could smell the animals that had dug it, could feel the slime of their passing on the floor beneath and the walls around. It was too late to turn back now, though, and the tunnel too narrow even if he tried. He began to panic.

Something grabbed his boot.

Kyle was thrown over onto his left side as a huge form filled the crawlspace behind him and a set of flensing-knife teeth ripped into the leather protecting his foot. He shoved the pistol toward his attacker and fired twice, bludgeoning his eardrums with noise and filling the burrow with ozone. The shape behind him vented a jackhammer shriek and turned tornado in the tunnel, twirling about itself like some hopped up kitten chasing its tail.

A crackling, tearing sound bloomed in Kyle's ringing ears, like Styrofoam crumpling in a man's hand. The thing he had shot went limp, seemed to deflate, and something small and whip-thin, a lot of somethings, flashed past him in the tunnel, sliding over his legs and under his buttocks, snaking past his face to kiss his cheek with slime. Their touch was worse than what had grabbed his leg, and he hooted in fear and tried to throw himself backward.

The tunnel ended abruptly and he sprawled out into an open space. A faint light shone there. It came from no source that he could detect. Kyle was in the engine room beneath the mill, *and* upstairs in his uncle Cain's house, *and* in Mel Bowers' office with the sounds of animals all around. Everywhere there was rust and the rococo shadows of equipment.

To one side stood a cement wall strung with old sawdust bags. Those shapes seemed to twitch and Kyle moved to where he could see them better. He wished he hadn't. One of the bags wore a watch, its second hand still moving. Another had tennis shoes dangling below it.

The bags were bodies, half a dozen of them arranged along the wall in strange geometric forms, some partially eaten and some intact. Most were dried out husks with the flesh like string jerky over their bones, but there were a few in better shape. Some had skin that looked almost alive. Kyle recognized Mel Bowers. And beside her were Tru Maclang and Dan Case.

Mel opened her eyes, though the pupils were rolled so far back in the veterinarian's head that she surely couldn't see anything. The mouth opened too, but not by Mel's will. Something pushed her lips apart from the inside. Kyle gagged as a fetus-sized mass of white, whipping tendrils spilled free and slid down the woman's chin to drop on the floor. A few more pale shapes forced their way out through her nostrils and followed their brethren into the shadows.

"Best work I've ever done," said a voice behind him. And Kyle spun around to see his Uncle Cain standing there, alive and whole, a smile cracked across his face.

"I understand the violence now," Cain continued. "You showed me, Kyle. Darkness is a lovely place."

"No!" Kyle shouted.

Cain only smiled, as he began to bleed from the eyes, as the pores all over his body opened and maggots began to spill forth.

"You showed me, Kyle. You showed me, showed me, showed me."

Kyle began to scream and flail. In the dream the old mill suddenly became a flooded place, and he was swimming up and up with hair and hands and feet clutching at his legs, with odd white shapes bumping at his lips, waiting for him to breathe so they could come inside.

And when his head broke the surface of the water his eyes opened and he came awake. Melissa Bowers stood beside his bed, looking at him, looking scared and worried at the same time. She reached a hand toward him, the back of it facing him as if she were going to test his temperature, and he caught it with his own and held it tight.

Melissa's glance moved to his hand, then back to his face. Kyle saw her thoughts shift across her blue eyes like drifts of dark birds. Self-doubt, fear, loneliness. Need. But there was strength as well, tempered by experience, and empathy without a trace of pity.

Kyle had his own need, strong now after the nightmare. But this woman was more than just a source who could prove him alive. Kyle wanted to feel alive. But he wanted the other too, wanted the promise that their past hours together had seemed to make. He tugged very lightly on her hand, putting pressure that would be easy to ignore, or break. But she let the tug draw her to him, all the way to his mouth.

He could feel her pulse through her lips. Or maybe it was his pulse. His other hand lifted, touched the soft, worn cotton of her shirt, her shoulder a rounded arch beneath. She shifted on the bed, let the weight of her body fall across his chest, her left breast flattening against him. Her mouth stayed locked to his, hungry, her hair falling over his face, flowing along the stubble-roughened skin of his cheek, catching on the whiskers and then moving on like the feel of soap-bubbles popping.

Kyle dropped his left hand to cup her legs and the wire-taut curve of her buttocks beneath the faded jeans that she wore. He lifted, pulled her up and over him. Her knees opened, shifted to either side of his waist. She was still clothed, but in another moment she pulled back from his embrace and began to unsnap her jeans and push them down. That task was awkward and he had to help her, but after a moment she kicked her legs free and lowered herself toward him. Kyle shoved away the sheets and let her fit herself to him.

His hands found the contours of her back above the hips; his upper body lifted, his mouth seeking her mouth, caressing over the open space between the swelling of her breasts. She kissed him, still tasting of her morning coffee, her skin still scented with last night's terror and worry. His own skin would hold the nightmare's sweat he knew, and the bitterness of yesterday's gunpowder and of a grave dug fresh for Cain.

But as he fell back on the bed, as he slipped inside of her and began to move, the mingled odors of unpleasantness blew away. In their place came warmth--a roux of good sweat, and of throats breathing hard, and of cinnamon skins learning each other.

Kyle slid his hands up from Melissa's hips, letting her need set the rhythm, losing himself in the immediacy of seeing and touching and feeling.

Sunlight through the window on a pale face.

Rounded convexity of Melissa's stomach.

Blond hair across cheek and shoulder.

Soft breasts, hardness of nipples.

Eyes and mouth opened.

Throat going dry.

Muscle clench.

They both cried out, not knowing or caring who was first.

And the moment took a long time to fade as Melissa leaned down over him, resting herself against his strength. Kyle held her as her breathing slowed, and thought only briefly of his dream. He let it lick his thoughts, then sent it away, praying that it wasn't a warning for the future.

--- 6 ---

Restful in the Darkhome.

Susurration of soft movement.

Net of scents tying all together--soil and gnawed roots and body oils, and a hundred other pungencies Raina could identify but not name.

Patterns of warmth moved across her body as the members of the Sleep-Pod shifted positions, now touching this patch of her skin, now that patch. Only her buttocks remained cold. In the course of the sleep cycle, through the steady churning of the Pod, she had been slowly pushed toward the outside of the group. Finally her temperature had dropped enough to awaken her.

She moved then, turning toward the center. Her back brushed the flattened quills of a Warkind, one of those in the circle that guarded the very outside of the Sleep-Pod. The Warkind moved in response to her movement, shifting the softest part of its body toward her, letting her push off from it as she began to swim her way inward.

She released, felt the others respond to that odor of need. A gradient opened, a decrease in Pod density, a thickening of warm-scent. The combination drew her along toward the Sleep-Pod center, the most pleasant of all places outside the womb. Safe, nestled in that symmetry, Raina relaxed completely, settled into the ground, fell off into deep, deep sleep. For a time.

Another scent jolted her away from sleep. A reek. Strange and sheared and violent. She opened her eyes, huffed in fear as she saw other eyes watching her, phosphor eyes, yellow as cut pyrite, floating near her in the heart of the Sleep-Pod. She tried to move away. Could not. The Pod itself had solidified, had formed an interlocking weave of chests and heads and limbs all around her.

The yellow eyes seemed to crawl toward her. She huffed louder, began to moan in her fear. A hand slipped along her belly, drifted lower. She felt a war-spike as it scraped her skin, its length hardened like scar tissue. She felt the curve of a wet penis drop across her thigh, moving on its own to seek entry into her body. For the first time she squealed, jolted as she tried and failed to thrust herself away from that touch.

A Warkind had worked his way inside the symmetry of the Sleep-Pod, where none had ever come before. And it was Kargen. She saw him clearly now, his head-quills brilliant red and glowing against his black and mottled hide.

Kargen twisted himself on top of her, bit into her cheek in a savage mimicry of love play. Raina cried out again, the sound escalating, echoing--and opened her eyes to find the dream of Darkhome gone and Wahrn beside her, trying to comfort her with his touch and scent.

It didn't work.

--- 7 ---

Kargen stopped running when he saw the deer move in the corner of one eye, and the ripeness of the world burst over him like a shower of pollen-rain. It was a doe, with last year's fawn slipping playfully along beside it. Both were soft brown, the fawn with a stippling of darker spots over its flanks. They followed a trail, the same trail he followed. But they moved in its center, he off to one side. Though coming toward him, they had neither seen nor heard him.

Kargen squatted, flared his nostrils wide in thinking and sensing. There was something wrong. All around the deer hung a halo of dust-mote sparks, and before them blew a redolent wave of odors. He tasted vihn, and cuumb, and texeral, picked out clavidifir and onadonjin. All were scents that he had named himself, smells without human words to give them reality, smells that no human had ever detected.

He lowered his head, let his quills brush against leaves and soil, let his face feel the plumes of cyr and deukalis as they poured from the earth. When he looked up again at the deer, he saw them rotted on the hoof, their hides unraveling, dripping long threads behind them to the ground. It wasn't real but it was beautiful, and he opened his mouth to suck in a huge swallow of the glittering air to fill his senses.

The deer heard his heavy breath, burst suddenly away from him up a small hill to the left of the trail. Kargen exploded from his crouch into four-legged pursuit, passing in a savage rush across the dirt nap of the trail, scattering dead leaves on the hill as bushes and limbs whipped at him. And whipped away.

The doe might have escaped him; the fawn was much too slow. Kargen ran straight up on its heels and caught it under one arm. The doe turned to attack and he slapped her down with his free hand. She tried to rise and he slapped her again, open palmed. This time the blow felled her into unconsciousness, leaving her flanks quivering.

The fawn bleated from under his arm, struggled but could not escape. Kargen felt its tiny, sharp hooves strike his leg. He ignored that, reached across with his other hand to cover its mouth and stop its bawling.

He pulled the small creature up toward his face. And it seemed as if he could see through its sloughing skin into the exquisiteness of its inner workings, where all was pulse and flow in a hundred shades of pink and gray. He lifted the body further, smeared it over his nose and mouth, gathering its essence into his throat.

Thus he held the fawn for a minute. Then, reluctantly, he put it softly down on its trembling legs. It collapsed beside its mother, falling into stillness as its biology demanded. Kargen thought of the other Mother, the Whoun Mother, and of the baby she carried. He wondered if he would be gentle with *it* when it was born. Could he scent-bond with it as the Podcyst did? Or would he feel the protective urge of the Warkind?

Would he hate it?

Kargen looked toward the sun, at the phosphor trails of white light burning hot through the trees. He understood that he was hallucinating. The deer existed, but the smells of them, and this strange light all around, did not. Even his thoughts had become suspect. He was closing on the Mother and her fetus. Her scent lived here, in the forest, twisting his senses. He knew he could block the effect with fear, but if he could identify the critical odor then he could block it more efficiently without emotion.

He sampled the air, resisted when the melee of scents would have dragged him off amid the ghost shapes of his own mind. He categorized the odors in his sample, isolated and eliminated them one by one until reality snapped in around him. The wind grew faint; the forest moved quietly but naturally. Sunlight had flattened to a dull yellow and once more felt cold to him. Order had returned to the world.

Charles Gramlich

Kargen opened his mouth in a smile. *Vihn*! He should have guessed. Vihn was a life odor, the smell of skins in sexual embrace. Cuumb and clavidifir and onadonjin were death odors, tissues in various stages of decay. And cyr was throat-blood when it first touched cold air after being spilled. All of them were pleasant to him. And their coming now was a promise of the near future. As his hallucination had been a promise. The Mother hid close.

Kargen began to run again.

Cold in the Light

CHAPTER TEN
(May 1: Late Morning, Toward Noon)

One man ran, just ran, down corridors that lengthened into the ice-blue of distance, through marbled courtyards where peacock statues fed their mouths on shadows. But he could not escape those who followed.
--In the Memory of Ruins

--- 1 ---

The sound of helicopters woke Michael Russo from a fitful, scarlet slumber, from a roil of dream images that he couldn't remember. And didn't want to.

Last night, after Lanny's death, Mike had toyed with fantasies of murdering Drake Hammond--stabbing, strangling, crushing. Not shooting. He wanted to be closer, wanted to be right on top of the other man when he killed him. Finally, he had fallen asleep, though passing out might have been a better term. His rest had not been restful.

Still tired, and stiff from a night on the ground, Mike climbed to his feet and paced the few steps allowed him by the small prison of his tent. He moved one way, then the other, his hands twisting and twining. He wanted to find a thing to tear or crush, but the tent loomed bare, empty as his soul. He wished for sleep again. Even at their worst, last night's dreams were surely better than the sick and certain knowledge that Lanny was dead, and that his own family would soon be in danger.

Mike cursed his own ignorance and conceit, the sins that had set this avalanche in motion. He had been walking the edge of a glacier and had fallen over the side, bringing the cold mountain down with him, on top of those he cared about.

He had misjudged Drake Hammond's paranoia and Lanny had died because of it. He'd been useless as director of the Harbinger Project, had been nothing more than a figurehead. *They* had been manipulating the Whoun all along.

Mike smashed his right leg with a fist, wanting to feel the pain. He didn't even know who *they* were, didn't know who gave the orders that might soon take his family from him. As his friend had been taken.

Outside, the helicopters had landed. Engines had silenced. Mike heard voices moving toward his tent and suddenly remembered Hammond's words about his wife and kids. "I've arranged to have them met at the airport."

Mike's eyes widened. He lunged toward the opening of the tent, wanting to see, wanting to know if his family were already here, in Hammond's possession. His hand was on the tent's flap when one voice clubbed him into stillness, a voice that he knew very well but would never have expected to hear in this place. Not family, but someone close as family. The voice was angry, and far colder than Mike ever remembered it. Drake Hammond was apologizing to that voice, making it clear who commanded whom.

No! Mike thought, speaking silently to any force outside of himself that might be listening and be powerful enough to change fate. *Don't let it be!*

--- 2 ---

"Shit!" Dan said, from where he stood his turn at watch near the front window. "Soldiers coming!"

Kyle came instantly to his feet, the CAR-9 socketed firmly into his hands as he moved swiftly across the room toward Dan's position. Tru rose only a second behind, but went toward the back, toward the kitchen and the other way into the house. Mel stayed where she was, close to the Whoun, getting them down on the floor beneath the heavy quilts that offered them protection against the ambient light. They wouldn't be much help in the day.

The Whoun and the humans had been working out a plan, eating to restore their strength and talking about nightfall when they would go across the mountain, down into the city of Fort Smith and expose the existence of the Whoun to the world. It was the only way they could think of to save themselves. But it didn't look like it was going to be that easy.

Kyle pushed Dan against the wall where the boy'd be hidden from the outside and peeked through dirty glass at a Humvee rolling up the drive toward them, the long vehicle seeming impossibly wide, impossibly squat. Inside were four men, four soldiers. Inside were M-16s. Tear gas, maybe. Who knew what else. But the faces Kyle could see through the windshield were smiling and he understood what that meant. This was a routine search. They didn't know their quarry was around.

"Stay covered," Kyle whispered to Dan. "The road ends around back. They should try there first. Maybe we can surprise 'em."

Dan nodded, his breath coming too fast, sweat already beading above his lips, on his forehead. The boy was scared and for a moment Kyle wished he hadn't given him a gun. No help for it now, though. They would all have to stand.

Kyle squeezed Dan's wrist. "Watch!" he said. "Shoot only if we shoot. I don't want anyone killed."

Again Dan nodded, and Kyle left him, moving in a crouch to stay below line of sight through the window. He stopped beside Mel long enough to warn her of what to expect, then slipped into the kitchen to join Tru. The deputy had shifted the huge, coffin-type freezer out from the wall and crouched behind it. Kyle went past him, slotted himself into a pantry-shielded corner where he could cover anyone stepping through the door without being immediately seen in return.

The Humvee stopped at the end of the long, curved drive, only twenty feet from the back door. Kyle heard the tight squeak of brakes just beginning to show wear. He heard the hiccup/growl of the engine turning off.

Four of them, Kyle thought. *Too many.*

Jeep doors slammed. There came the slap of boots on dirt, the rattle of equipment. Voices buzzed--low, muffled by the cabin's log walls. Kyle couldn't make out any words.

Somebody cleared their throat and spat. The rattle moved toward the house. At least some of them were coming this way. It looked like they were going to try the back door first. They probably knew by now which houses were empty for the summer.

A scenario began to play itself out in Kyle's head. When the soldiers tried the kitchen door it would be locked, as it should be. They couldn't know that there used to be a padlock on the outside as well. They'd relax then, turn to go around the front. He and Tru would step out behind them, catch them off guard. No fuss, no

169

blood. He'd almost convinced himself how it was going to be when things fell apart.

Feet clomped on the concrete stoop just outside the back door. The plastic stock of a rifle struck the metal rail that ran along the left side of the steps.

Come on, Kyle urged. *Try the knob.* Then someone shouted from farther away, the voice loud enough for everyone to hear.

"Wait! Shit! A Blazer! Could be the one!"

"Dammit," Kyle muttered. They'd checked the garage first.

Kyle glanced at Tru to see if the deputy had heard. He had; his eyes were like trapped ferrets. Kyle laid his rifle on the floor, drew his two pistols as he stood up, the .45 Colt into his right hand, the 9mm Sig into his left. He knew the pistols better than the rifle--if it came to using a gun.

Outside was confusion. Voices raised. Kyle figured they hadn't really expected to find anything. Their quarry had last been seen heading *toward* Deerhaven rather than away from it. Now, Kyle needed to go out the door before the confusion faded and they did the logical thing: call for reinforcements. Maybe his scenario would still play. In a slightly altered form.

"Take the front," Kyle mouthed to Tru, who caught a deep breath to steady himself and then nodded his understanding.

With the pistols growing warm in his palms, Kyle moved to the door. He tucked the Sig under his right arm, used his freed hand to twist off the knob-lock and jerk back the door, then moved quickly into the opening, drawing the Sig back into his left hand as he stepped onto the porch. There was no screen and he came instantly face to face with two soldiers. Both were staring toward him; both had heard the sound of the door coming open. But he had moved so quickly that their M-16s were still pointing downward. His pistols weren't.

"Hello," Kyle said. "Looking for me?"

Beyond the two men in front of him on the stoop, Kyle could see the garage and another soldier beside it. He could see the Humvee, the fourth man reaching in the driver's-side door for something. The radio? A gun?

Kyle's eyes narrowed as he identified that last man--Byron, the hardcase that he and Tru had taken Dan and Wahrn away from, the same soldier whose gun he had confiscated and now held in his left

Cold in the Light

hand. Kyle had shot Byron, in the shoulder, but the man didn't look as if he were hurting. He'd taken his right arm out of the sling that had been made for it, was using that arm to reach in the Humvee.

Byron's presence meant they probably wouldn't get out of this without shooting, but Kyle tried to hold onto that hope. He didn't want to kill anybody. But he couldn't let these men know that.

"Let's be friendly now," he said, loudly. He made his voice cold and flat, punctuated his words by cocking the hammers on the pistols. That last was for effect only; both guns could be double-actioned.

Kyle meant his words and his threat for Byron mostly. And they worked. For now. The tall, black soldier drew his hand back from inside the Humvee. A brand new pistol hung at his hip but he made no move toward that either. He didn't look happy, but it seemed he had developed a little caution after his first encounter with Kyle.

The other soldiers watched, their gazes shifting between Kyle and Byron. They were all young, still a little unsure of themselves despite the Special Forces' reputation for eating gunpowder and shitting bullets. Whoever ran the military side of this show hadn't figured on finding anything at the summer houses either, Kyle realized. He'd sent his rawest troops on this job. Except for Byron, Kyle knew. Wounded or not, that one would always look for a chance to be in at the kill.

Kyle smiled, on the outside only.

"You guys walked right into it," he said. "We're in the house, in the woods. All around. Let those guns drop and you'll walk back out again."

Byron smirked. "You got no more than two guys," he said. "One of 'em a kid."

"Better learn to count," Tru called from the front corner of the house. "Just me and this scattergun make half a dozen."

Byron's gaze flicked toward Tru's position, then came back to center on Kyle. Even over a distance of twenty feet that glance bruised, and Kyle realized they'd made a mistake. The other soldiers were willing to believe they were surrounded, targeted. Byron knew better. And now he knew where the two men were that he was most concerned about.

Kyle readied himself, let his body shift position slightly, as if the movement were totally natural. But now he had an open firing lane toward the Humvee. For a moment it had looked like they might just win without bloodshed. That wasn't going to happen.

Don't do it, Byron, Kyle muttered silently to himself. He knew he should cut the soldier down now, before the man acted. But in his mind that meant murder and he couldn't make himself pull the trigger. In another moment it was too late anyway. Byron dove sideways into the front seat of the Humvee. When he came out the other side, Kyle guessed he'd have a rifle.

Kyle immediately lashed out with his right foot, a straight kick into the groin of the soldier closest to him on the stoop. As that man doubled over, Kyle shot the second soldier through the chest with the Sig, high on the right side where he wouldn't hit anything fatal. The 9mm didn't have enough punch to knock the man down, but the shock of being hit started him on a long slide to his knees, making him drop the rifle whose muzzle had been lifting toward Kyle's stomach.

Tru's shotgun boomed, and boomed again, spraying the Humvee with a buckshot rain in an attempt to keep Byron bottled up in the cab. At the same time, Kyle stabbed his .45 toward the garage, snapped two quick shots at the soldier there. That man had just begun to react, and now that reaction turned into a bid for cover as he threw himself back into the garage's protection.

The man Kyle had kicked was rising, his mouth twisted, spit hanging from his lower lip. Kyle pistol-whipped him behind the ear, putting him down hard, putting him out of the fight. The other soldier was on his knees, his face stunned and defeated. He threw up a hand to block a blow from above, but Kyle snapped a knee up into his chin, knocking him unconscious down the steps.

The passenger side door of the Humvee shrieked open.

Byron!

Kyle stood at the top of three concrete steps. An open target. To his left ran a thin metal rail, a hand-guide welded to posts sunk along the side of the steps. Kyle threw himself over that rail just as shots from an M-16 whacked the wall behind where he'd stood. He landed hard on his side, partially hidden but not shielded by a short row of Ligustrum bushes.

Tru's shotgun boomed again, behind it the flat crack of Dan's .30-06. The rear window of the Humvee sprayed bits of safety glass. But the barrel of an M-16 still hung over the hood. Kyle rolled as Byron emptied half a clip into the Ligustrums, the slugs

Cold in the Light

cutting leaves and slashing dirt, thunking with an ugly sound into cabin logs.

One step ahead of bullets, Kyle surged to his feet and made a tremendous dive toward the cement block well-house that stood squarely about a dozen feet out from the corner of the cabin. He landed short, but made it to all fours and scrambled into the well-house's cover before his belly had time to notice that it had hit ground.

Rising to a crouch, Kyle fired three quick shots over the top of the well-house, two at the Humvee, the other toward the front of the garage. He had to let everyone know he was still in the fight. He used the .45, then popped the half emptied clip out and stuck a fresh magazine up the slot. He didn't have to chamber a shell. One lay under the hammer already.

Dropping the partially used clip into a pocket, Kyle made his way around the corner of the well-house. He wanted a better view of the Humvee, got it just as he heard Tru yell.

"Dan, no!"

A quick glance revealed a running figure off to the other side of the cabin. *Dan!* Trying to circle the Humvee for a shot at Byron, heading for a clump of oaks that stood just across the graveled drive from the house. In another moment the boy would be dead.

Kyle stepped away from the comforting shield of the well-house. He was behind the opening of the garage; the soldier there couldn't see him, hadn't seemed much interested in shooting anyway. But he'd be a clear target for Byron if the man were looking. He wasn't. Kyle couldn't see the barrel of the M-16 that had lain over the hood of the Humvee seconds before.

Kyle could almost feel Byron turning, drawing the rifle down into position, waiting for Dan to run into his line of fire. Shouting as loud as he could, Kyle opened up with the Sig. He'd only used one of the fifteen shells in that gun; he emptied the other fourteen into the ground beneath the front of the Humvee, hoping for a ricochet off the gravel in the drive. Or at least for a distraction.

Something worked. Dan made it to the protection of the trees without Byron even firing a shot. Kyle didn't wait any longer but sprinted for the back of the garage. He'd circle around behind it, flank Byron from the other side.

The soldier was no fool, though. Even as Kyle made it into the cover of the garage, he heard Dan yell, "he's running," and heard the .30-06 open up. Three shots cracked, one after the other. From the echoes they had been fired at different angles, following a moving target. There came no sound of a hit.

Kyle figured what had happened. Byron knew he was about to be flanked from two sides, knew his position was bad and getting worse. He'd bolted for the woods, though Kyle didn't think they had scared the man.

With Byron running, the only thing left was to take out the soldier in the garage and secure the Blazer before the man thought to damage it. If he hadn't already. Having scouted the place last night, Kyle knew there was a rick of logs cut for the cabin's fireplace piled beneath a long, wide window at the garage's rear. He slipped around to that pile, stepped up to take a look through the glass.

The soldier was inside, flat on his back, dead. One of the first shots Kyle had fired must have found its target, though he hadn't expected to hit. Now the shooting was over. He and the others had won again.

Kyle stared at the dead man and felt sick. They'd won, but it didn't feel like a victory. It didn't do anything against the ache in his soul for Cain. And he wondered how long it would be before the next death. He wondered if it would be Dan this time, or Tru. Maybe it would be Wahrn or Raina.

Maybe it would be Mel.

That last thought hurt worst of all and Kyle felt both guilt and amazement, that he could have learned to care for another so soon after Cain went cold. And that his caring didn't change after his bullet had taken a man's life. He understood that he would take one again to protect Mel and the others. He hadn't meant to do it, but the line had been crossed. Going back was not allowed.

Kyle stepped down from the logs. His eyes burned but that feeling would pass. The guns had to be reloaded; the wounded soldiers had to be seen to; the Humvee had to be disabled; they had to watch for Byron.

After a moment, Kyle went back around the garage to take care of what needed to be done.

--- 3 ---

Don't let it be him, Michael Russo prayed.

He hadn't prayed in a long time and he closed his eyes tight to help the words along. But his ears wouldn't close and they kept telling him a truth that he didn't want to know--that the voice giving orders to Drake Hammond outside this tent belonged to a man he respected. Even loved. A man he had always thought of like a father. A man who had betrayed the trust of many.

Mike felt sick. It was hard to get enough air, hard to swallow the saliva that coiled like ropes down the back of his throat. He felt like a child who'd been given a candy apple by an adored parent and had found a razor blade in it. And like that child, he didn't want to believe what he knew to be true. He wanted someone to explain how he was mistaken, to tell him how his ears heard falsely. He pushed back the flap of his prison tent and stepped through it, pleading inside for an explanation he could live with.

He didn't get it.

The guard outside his tent grabbed him and put him efficiently to his knees with his arms wricked up painfully behind his back. He didn't care. There had been enough time to *see*, and the physical pain in his arms became a blessing, a distraction from the sharp spike of seeing and knowing.

"Leonard," Mike whispered.

The older man standing next to Drake Hammond and half a dozen other officers outside the tent was a civilian. He looked sixty, though Mike knew he could claim nearly two decades more, and he wore a jacket and tie that had both gone out of style long ago. But he was the one in charge. Clearly. And the look that he turned on Mike showed neither relief nor guilt, only neutrality. And soberness. It was the way Leonard Suskind always looked when analyzing data, or when writing an article, or lecturing on genetics.

Leonard had always kept personal relationships separate from his work, and he'd taken that work completely seriously. Mike wondered if Leonard now looked upon *him* as "work."

Then a smile came to the older man's face as he walked over and squatted down in front of Mike. It was nearly the same smile that Mike remembered from when he'd served as a graduate student under this man at the University of Chicago, or from the first days of the Harbinger Project when Leonard had asked Mike to help study the Whoun. The only difference was that the smile seemed to have as much frustration as fondness in it.

"Let him up," Leonard ordered. And Mike found himself released, hauled to his feet. Leonard stood up with him.

"Mike," Leonard said, nodding politely as he held out a hand.

Automatically, Mike took the proffered handshake, then quickly released his grip and drew back. He wasn't going to let Leonard pull this "old friends" act. Too much had happened. *Was* happening.

"What the hell is going on here, Len? Surely you're not part of this shit?"

Leonard kept smiling. "I'm not quite clear on what you mean by 'this shit,' Mike. If you're talking about the work of our rather overzealous Colonel Hammond here, then I most certainly am not part of it."

Hammond's face flushed. He looked furious but said nothing.

"You know what I mean, Leonard. Manipulating the Whoun. *Fucking* with the embryo."

Leonard winced, but it didn't look to Mike as if he meant it. "Please, Mike. I don't believe you have the facts to make a judgement about what we've done or haven't done."

Mike felt his soul sickness grow. This wasn't the Len he had known. It couldn't be.

"Then it's true," he said. "You and your thugs have been doing something to the embryo. What bought you, Leonard? Money? Are you just one more greedy bureaucrat selling his principles for dollars?"

Hammond started forward and Leonard shoved his arm across the colonel's chest. "Let him finish," he said. The smile had disappeared now; the warm blue eyes were freezing over.

"You took the Harbinger position to *keep* the military from using the Whoun," Mike stated flatly. "That's what you said. Isn't it? This incredible find, you said. All the things we can learn, you said. Just cheap dialogue in some hack-written thriller, huh? How could you sell out?"

Mike shook his head before he continued. "Seems to agree with you, though. You *look* healthy. Money is good for everything but the soul, I guess. How do you live with yourself?"

Cold in the Light

Leonard breathed out heavily. He looked for a just few moments to be as old as his birthdays said he should be. But the pain didn't stay on his face. He breathed again, more easily, and Mike saw the strength of the man's convictions flow back like a tide. It was scary.

"In the first place," Leonard said. "America's defense is not a black and white issue. I've found that out. But that isn't why I got involved in changing the direction of the Harbinger Project. I--"

"Changing direction?" Mike blurted. "Tampering with another race's embryo! Lying to everyone who respected you! Killing Whoun! You call that changing direction?"

Leonard held up his hand, palm outward, a gesture used in the old days to silence the debates of his graduate students. Mike wanted to punch him for it now, but habit closed his mouth.

"May I remind you who released the Warkind," Leonard said. "*You* ordered the hunt for the Whoun. Everyone overreacted, but you did more than your share of panicking. The deaths among the Podcyst are on *your* head."

Mike's rage cooled, congealed. He understood that what Leonard said was partially true. He bore plenty of guilt here. But not all of it. And not the worst of it.

"And what about Lanny?" Mike asked, quietly. "Is it my fault your colonel there put a bullet between his eyes?"

For the first time, Leonard dropped his gaze from Mike's.

So he can still be hurt, Mike thought. But what good that would do he didn't know. It wouldn't raise Lanny from the dead.

"I regret that," Suskind said. "It should never have happened." His voice hardened as he looked at Drake Hammond beside him. "It *is* being dealt with," he continued. "I have removed *Colonel* Hammond from command. Major Teagle will take over for the time being."

Hammond sputtered as his face ripened to a watermelon red. Clearly, this marked the first he'd heard of being replaced. And he didn't like it.

"You can't do that, Suskind. Civilians don't give orders to the military here."

Leonard's voice grew even harder, seemed to Mike almost too powerful for a man of Leonard's age. "Your superiors granted me the authority to do just that, Hammond. You *will* stand down."

"Like hell I will."

Mike saw Leonard glance over Hammond's shoulder to the officers standing behind. There were two lieutenants, one named Calder Davidson, who looked like he'd be happy to kill for Hammond, and the other named William Morgan, who seemed more... neutral. There was also Wayne Teagle, the man who Mike had wanted in charge of the Harbinger Special Forces back when he believed Drake Hammond was dead.

"Major Teagle," Leonard said. "Place Colonel Hammond under arrest."

Teagle looked extremely unhappy. He glanced from Leonard toward the man he'd just been ordered to replace, then back to Leonard.

"But Dr. Suskind. I--"

Leonard held up his no-more-arguments hand. "I didn't ask for comments, Major. Your duty has been indicated to you."

Reluctantly, Mike thought, Teagle stepped toward Hammond, motioning the other officers to join him. "I'm sorry, sir," he said to the colonel. "You are outranked."

It appeared for a moment as if Hammond were going to resist. His body had stiffened to a knife-like rigidity; his eyes defied any approach from the men who had so recently obeyed his orders. But in the next instant he abruptly relaxed.

"Right," he said.

He drew his pistol out of its holster with a thumb and finger and handed it to one of the lieutenants. Then he executed a military turn and began walking away across the compound. Teagle and the officers followed.

Mike thought it was too easy. He looked at Leonard, who looked back and smiled as if he had just fixed everything that had gone wrong over the past few days.

"There," Leonard said. "Happy?"

--- **4** ---

Byron spat against a tree, cursed to the bushes. Dust rose over the cabin where the Whoun and their human allies had been hiding, staining the blue sky with a dry, cinnamon brown. His quarry was slipping away. And they would have made sure the engine and the radio in the Humvee were non-operational. Phones in the house too, he imagined. The fucker leading this group knew what he was doing.

Ex-soldier maybe, Byron thought. *Trained for sure.*

He spat again, started working his way through the woods toward the cabin, feeling sure the enemy were gone but being cautious out of habit. The sons of bitches had beaten him twice and he didn't like that. But after he'd seen two of his men shot down he'd had no choice but to retreat before they took him out too.

If any of the squad *were* still alive he'd send them back to base with the news. Then he'd follow the escapees on foot. He figured they were trying for the mountains and even with a vehicle they wouldn't make good time there. He might catch them if he took a more direct route.

A sound stopped Byron, a tiny click of non-random noise. He attached himself instantly to the side of a nearby oak, his grip tight on the pistol in his hand, his thumb flipping the safety off. He scanned the trees, looking for a source, then heard the sound again, a ping followed by a faint thud. A few more seconds passed before Byron realized he was hearing acorns falling.

He glanced up. But death came from a different direction.

--- 5 ---

The two soldiers heard sticks snapping in the forest and looked toward the sound. They had been tied to the wheel frames of the Humvee and they were expecting Byron to come walking out of the trees to untie them. But it wasn't Byron. Just at the shadowy edge of the woods stood a Warkind.

The sight startled them. They had never seen a Warkind in the day before. And there seemed something odd about this one. Its head-quills were a brilliant, brilliant red, bright as arterial blood against its yellow and black hide. It was alone too. The Warkind were never alone, never away from their bands.

The odd coloring and the aloneness weren't all that was strange, though. When they saw the creature move out of the trees toward them, they saw how its stride was deliberate and precise, coming straight at them instead of showing the jerky, darting, swaying chorea that the Warkind usually called walking. They saw its eyes, like gold rosary beads behind the thick grating of small horns that protected them. And as it stood over them they saw those eyes fill up with an intelligence that shocked in its intensity.

And still there remained something else, something darker. They didn't realize just how dark until the being squatted and turned one of its hands palm-up toward them. There were two sharpened sticks in its fist, and two dripping...things stuck on the sticks. The Warkind stabbed one end of each of the broken branches into the ground in front of the soldiers, then leaned forward until its breath smoked hot in their faces.

"You shouldn't...have run the Mother away," it said, the voice guttural as gravel but the words perfectly enunciated.

The two men glanced from the sticks to the Warkind's eyes, then back to the sticks. It took them a moment to realize that they were looking at Byron's testicles.

--- 6 ---

Holding the bodies by the necks, Kargen dragged the two dead soldiers into the cabin with him. He had to smash in the back door to get inside. But he enjoyed that. Though he wanted to control his anger, it was hard. His need for rage was great. The Mother had been here! Minutes ago!

These! He lifted the bodies. Shook them. Hurled them down. Their fault the Mother was gone.

Kargen threw back his head, his top-quills clicking together over his shoulders. He let his nictitating lids close, opened his mouth and nostrils. The Mother scent hid here, and the cyr of the two soldiers he had so recently killed. But that wasn't what he wanted now. He needed to know who else had joined the Mother, who was playing Podcyst for her.

Odors rolled in, piled up in the back of his mouth, trickled blood-warm down his throat. Most of them he had tasted before, at the house in the woods where his band had tried and failed to capture the Mother. But those smells had been scattered on the wind. In this small space they were concentrated, confined. He could make them his.

Cold in the Light

Besides the Mother, only one Typical had been here. Kargen knew him as Wahrn--wounded but healing. Wahrn had been, was, Raina's primary mate, and would fight to his death when Kargen came to take the Mother. But Wahrn had no Podcyst to fight with him now. And it *would be* his death. Kargen knew he could kill any Typical who tried to stop him.

Four humans had been in this house recently as well, one of them female. Kargen had smelled only one other human female before, a scientist on the Harbinger Project. This woman was very different, more like sweat than soap, more like blood than water. He would have to watch her, not turn his back on her. Humans claimed that their females were non-violent, but this one did not wear the scent of a pacifist.

The other three human odor trails in the cabin were males, one young and very scared, a second who seemed both strong and weak at the same time. Kargen gave them little reflection. They didn't matter.

But the last man! There was something...edged about him, something like a steel bolt at the point of shearing under a heavy load. The smell was almost like that of a Warkind and Kargen shivered slightly, not out of fear but out of excitement. This one would be a pleasure to kill. He would do so right in front of the Mother, to show her that nothing and no one could defend her from him.

Kargen put his foot on the chest of one soldier, hooked his claws into the skin and peeled it down past the abdomen. One talon sank deep, opened the man's stomach to reveal a pink-red glistening that fascinated. Kargen probed the wound with one long finger; then a faint flutter of noise pulled him from his dissection. His eyes searched, found a sheet of yellow legal paper that had been taped to the front window. A breeze through the torn-open kitchen door had moved it, and he walked forward to read its message.

The words made Kargen's nostrils flare and brought a thick rumble of sound spilling up out of his throat. He left the note on the window, moved back toward the center of the room. A wooden table stood in his way and he hacked it in half with the blade of one hand. Then he picked up the bed where the Mother and Wahrn had so recently slept and hurled it smashing into a row of glass bookshelves along one wall.

The remainder of the room, he systematically wrecked, caving in walls, crushing furniture, turning pillows and mystery novels and brass spittoons into just so much landfill. After that he painted, using the two dead men as brushes, using their blood for color. Finally, he plucked the note from its window home and nailed it with a knife to the top of a decapitated head. He read the words one more time.

   Dear Home Owner:

   Your house was inadvertently damaged during a recent investigation by the Deerhaven Sheriff's Department. Take this note to the Sheriff's Office and you will be reimbursed fully. Please forgive the inconvenience.

                               Truman Maclang,
                                 Deputy Sheriff
                                 Deerhaven, Arkansas

Then Kargen turned and left, shutting the front door very carefully behind him.

--- 7 ---

As they entered Drake Hammond's tent, Major Wayne Teagle, newly appointed CO of the Harbinger Project Special Forces, was paying more attention to his own considerations than to his ex-commander. This was a mistake.

Teagle was trying to figure out what to say to the colonel in private about having to place him under arrest. Even though his once healthy respect for Drake Hammond had begun to erode over the past several months of the colonel's increasingly erratic behavior, the man remained an important symbol of the life Teagle had chosen. He didn't want to see the officer brought low. This was part of the reason why he'd been willing to go along with Hammond when the colonel pretended to be dead to fool Michael Russo.

But, Russo had also never possessed any true power over the Harbinger Project military; there had been no conflict of duty. Dr.

Cold in the Light

Leonard Suskind did possess that power. Teagle had seen the orders, with the signatures of those whose authority superseded that of any local commander. He, Wayne Teagle, was now the man in charge of all local military forces. It became his duty to curb the excesses that Drake Hammond had allowed.

Teagle straightened his shoulders, looked toward his former commander. He would have to be firm.

Hammond, seated on the edge of his desk, smiled faintly.

"Wayne," Hammond said. "Looks like you've got to play a role for me again. You did it once, though. Should be second nature by now."

Teagle felt a faint chill stroke his groin. His mouth had dried suddenly enough to make his next swallow hard to choke down. He had expected anger and verbal abuse. Not camaraderie. Not this complete failure to accept the reality of their new situation.

Should have known, he told himself.

Out loud he said: "I'm sorry, Colonel. This time it's got to be for real. Dr. Suskind is a legitimate authority. I'm sure you'll be back in comman--"

"Suskind is an *ass*," Hammond said, luxuriating in the crudity. "He's not only half senile. He's obviously been corrupted by the enemy. Surely you're smart enough to see that, Wayne?"

Teagle shook his head. "No, sir. I *am* sorry. But until I receive orders from someone higher than Dr. Suskind, I cannot yield to your wishes. You have been relieved of command."

Hammond pushed up from the corner of his desk and started to walk toward Teagle. He moved slowly and Wayne took a couple of steps back to keep his distance, placing his right hand on the holstered butt of his pistol.

"Please stop, sir. I don't want to use force."

Hammond stopped. He did not seem angry, which confused Wayne. The colonel seemed more sad than anything, and Teagle felt a wash of irrational guilt flood over him.

"It's my duty, sir," he tried to explain. "You've always stressed that a soldier's duty is to follow his orders. I'm just doing what you taught me to do."

Hammond crossed his hands in front of his stomach, lowered his head to peer out from beneath thinning brows.

"Of course, Wayne. I understand. Duty makes us all do things we don't want to sometimes."

"Yes, sir. That's exactly it."

Teagle felt himself relax a little. And he felt also a sudden surge of confidence that was as irrational as his guilt of a minute ago. He had faced Drake Hammond! Had held his ground! Had won! Not another of this man's officers could say that.

Hammond smiled, and Wayne Teagle felt a caress of air move over him from behind as the flap of the tent opened. He started to turn, to tell the others to come on in. Then he felt the burst of a tremendous, exploding agony that seemed to axe his head open. He realized he'd been hit with something blunt, then realized he already lay on the floor of the tent with cool nylon beneath his cheek. His body was numb, his mind fading toward a single, dark point. But he heard a last exchange between Drake Hammond and the lieutenant named Davidson, who must have been the one to strike the blow.

"You want us to take out Suskind now, sir?"

"Later. First I deal with the traitor fouling my floor. Give me your knife and wait outside."

Wayne Teagle's mind abandoned him. Just in time.

--- **8** ---

Mike Russo felt like laughing. But more like crying. His friend Lanny was dead, murdered. His family had been threatened by a paranoid colonel. Humans had killed Whoun, and Whoun had killed humans. Mike's world had slipstreamed into hell's wake. And Leonard Suskind had just asked him if he were "happy" now that Drake Hammond had been removed from command.

Yeah right, Len, Mike thought, gazing at the man who stood in front of him. *Abso-fuckin-lutely.*

But he didn't let his mind's chatter reach his body's lips. He understood that Leonard was insane. He didn't know what had caused it, but his old teacher and mentor had crossed over into some vast Freudian landscape from which there would be no easy return.

If asked an hour ago, Mike would have said it impossible for Len Suskind to ever lose touch with reality. The man had fit too easily within his own skin and brain. But there was no other explanation that Mike could accept. Leonard was mad.

The thought suddenly hit him. *As Drake Hammond is mad?*

The flesh around Mike's eyes crinkled. It seemed an unlikely coincidence, two men associated with the Harbinger Project losing it around the same time. Or was he seeing relationships that didn't exist? Hammond had always been difficult and paranoid, with plenty of cold blood rushing in his veins. The big change was in Leonard and there could be many explanations for that. The man claimed nearly eighty years after all.

Mike's analytical brain began to click over possibilities. Over commonalties. He didn't get far before the sound of yet another helicopter thumped its way into his awareness. Mike was surprised to see that Leonard had heard the machine before he had. Age hadn't affected the man's hearing, it seemed.

"That should be your family, Michael," Leonard said, turning and moving in the direction of the landing area.

Mike ignored the guards standing behind him, forgot whatever had been coursing around in his head concerning Leonard Suskind and Drake Hammond. He started walking, toward the approaching helicopter, moving faster, and still faster, wanting to run but not willing to risk it with the soldiers there. And the rifles.

Leonard kept pace with him, the guards trailing just at their heels. "It'll be good to see Helen again," Leonard said. "And the boys. They'll have grown, I'm sure. Hope they haven't forgotten their Uncle Len."

You bastard, Mike thought.

But once again he didn't let such wordings surface. Other ideas, wild ideas, stormed through his mind--waving off the helicopter, screaming that it was a trap, making a break for the vehicle as it landed. He knew the thoughts were useless. The pilot would be a soldier. And Mike had no weapon, nor any promise of taking one away from people who could kill him with their hands.

He stopped walking. The helicopter settled to earth within a helix of dust. In a moment, two lithe forms burst out of that dust and rushed across to hurl themselves at him.

Joshua and Caleb!

Mike dropped to his knees, hugged them both hard, loving the sound of "daddy" in their mouths. He rubbed their backs beneath their T-shirts, spoke to them though he couldn't have said what words he used. When he stood up he still held them in his arms, their heads tucked into his shoulders.

Helen had stepped out of the helicopter now. Pink sweater. White woolen skirt. Black boots. The early afternoon sun hung behind her, highlighting her dark blond hair with its few interwoven strands of gray.

It seemed to Mike as if he'd forgotten how attractive his own wife was. He couldn't remember wanting so badly just to look at her. She made his mouth dry. And he suddenly found himself wanting to do more than just look. He wanted to make up for lost time, wanted to love her--easy, hard, all the ways in between. The thought of missed opportunities nearly strangled him and he looked away, hugging his sons tighter.

--- 9 ---

As she stepped out of the helicopter, Helen Russo saw her husband holding her sons. Beside them she recognized Leonard Suskind, Mike's old teacher and mentor. She knew Leonard had retired from the Harbinger Project, wondered why he was here and why he stood so close to soldiers holding guns. Somehow, his presence made her uncomfortable, though he was a family friend and practically a godfather to Josh and Caleb.

The day had been a weird one all around, though. It had shaken her badly to realize that the soldiers knew she was coming without her having told anyone. Made her feel as if her life was public access. All the way here she'd promised herself an easy explanation. Only, she hadn't come up with any.

And now to find Leonard in a place where he shouldn't have been, and to find Mike looking so odd and hugging the boys as if it were months rather than days since he'd seen them. It didn't quite feel real, but that didn't stop her from being afraid.

Helen walked up to her husband and the small group around him, forcing a smile and nod for Leonard, returning the hug he gave her, speaking the usual inanities about how long it had been. Then she looked at Mike.

She had rehearsed what to say to her husband when she saw him, had planned her words as carefully as any Nobel Prize winner would plan an acceptance speech. But steadily her resolve had eroded, worn away by strangeness and discomfort, and when she met her husband's gaze all the strength drained out of her.

She had never seen Mike cry before.

CHAPTER ELEVEN
(May 1: Midday)

----

*The city began to mutate all around him.
Halls and doors and corridors lost their
human-given shapes, turned into corner
and windows with too many sides. Colors
were violent, shot with streamers of pus.*
--In the Memory of Ruins

--- 1 ---

After tying up the two captured soldiers and disabling their Humvee, Tru and Kyle and the others loaded supplies of water and food and fled the summer house where they'd spent a night's poor rest. They took the Blazer up the road with a dark tobacco dust rising under the wheels--until that road faded to twin ribbons of dirt with grass between. Then they turned up Rattlesnake Ridge along a clearway cut for power lines. Kyle switched to four-wheel drive.

They all knew it was dangerous to run for it in daylight. But the soldier's search party would soon be missed and there was little choice. The path they followed was rough, through flatgrass thickets and pollen-pregnant weeds taller than the Blazer, over rocks that clanged the vehicle's undercarriage like living things trying to beat their way through the metal. Twice they skirted deadfalls of trees that had been cut and piled up in the carving of this faux road. But fifty yards short of the ridge's top they were brought to a cold stop.

End of the line.

Another deadfall lay across their path, all the way across. Taller than a man and massive as a whale, grown over with living brush that anchored the vertical forest to the ground, the fall stretched from the tree line on one side to a steep ravine on the other that would never be passable by vehicle. With its dense packing of fallen trunks and limbs, the pile would be virtually impossible to move without heavy equipment. There would be no clearing of the way for those in the Blazer.

Kyle got out; Tru and the others joined him.

"Well, that's it then," Tru said. "Have to try another way."

Kyle didn't answer. He walked around to the front of the Blazer, squatted. Tru frowned, moved to where he could see his friend. Kyle seemed to be studying the bumper.

"We'd better make it quick," Dan said.

Tru looked over at the boy, saw him fidgeting, bouncing from his toes to his heels and back. For a moment, Tru wished that Dan Case was anywhere but with them. Then he felt a quick flush of shame at the thought. Dan had done all right back at the cabin when the shooting had started. Maybe he'd been a little impatient, a little nervous. But he'd done all right and hadn't frozen like so many civilians did when they needed to act.

"Kyle knows," Tru said to Dan, trying hard for a kindness that he didn't particularly feel. "Take it easy."

Kyle still hadn't spoken, but he was no longer squatting. He'd walked over to the deadfall, was tugging on branches that didn't have much give. When the workers had piled up the trees they'd piled up dirt with them, enough to harden and turn the fall into a partial hill--but a hill too steep and slick to drive over.

Mel moved up beside Tru, met his gaze and shrugged with her eyebrows. He shook his head.

"If they've got helicopters up," Mel said. "And you can bet they do. They might be investigating dust sign."

"Yeah," Dan added. "Like *ours.*"

A sudden rattle from the front of the Blazer drew everyone's attention. Kyle was pulling heavy-gauge cable away from the bumper area of the vehicle.

"The winch!" Tru exclaimed, heard an almost echo that marked Mel Bowers saying the same thing.

Then Dan joined the act. "We winch it over the top! Yes!" He moved up to join the others, his face excited, his previous worries forgotten.

The resilience of youth, Tru thought. He didn't say it. "You want us to unload?" he called to Kyle.

Kyle shook his head. "Just you three. The pitch isn't that steep. I'll drive it. The weight won't be a problem."

"What about Wahrn and Raina?" Mel asked.

Kyle had already started up the side of the deadfall, the winch cable snaking along behind him as he sought footholds and balance. "Explain it to them," he called back. "And make sure they're tucked in nice and tight." Then he was gone over the top.

"We can do this?" Mel asked Tru.

Tru nodded. "Should be able to. This fall is old. Packed down. Be almost like a levee."

Mel said nothing, only turned and went toward the Blazer to see to the Whoun, who were well into their sunshine slumber. Tru moved to the deadfall, began to climb. He met Kyle coming back, at the top.

"I'll watch from here," Tru said.

He glanced toward the anchor point that Kyle had chosen for the winch cable. It was one of the steel towers that carried the power lines down the mountain.

"Good place to hook it," he told Kyle. "Out a ways from the fall. Going down'll be hardest you know."

"Yeah. Too slick for the brakes to grip." Kyle smiled, a brief one. "A controlled fall. Only ten feet, though. Stay out from in front."

It was Tru's turn to grin. "The thought had occurred to me."

Kyle went on down, took a few cranks on the winch to take up the slack in the cable, then got in the Blazer and started the engine. Tru didn't envy him the driving job. It seemed simple but wasn't. A lot of things could go wrong.

Melissa Bowers and Dan Case were standing off to one side, the dark line of the encroaching forest behind them. Dan looked as if he wanted to put his arm around Mel to comfort her, but feared having it bitten off if he tried. Mel seemed oblivious to the boy's dilemma, though Tru doubted that she really was.

One lady that don't miss much, Tru thought.

A mechanism began to whine, drawing Tru back to the deadfall and the Blazer. Kyle had started the winch and the cable snapped taut over the convexity of the woodpile, shooting up spurts of dust as metal bit like a whip into bark and soil. The whole pile seemed

Cold in the Light

to shiver and the Blazer started forward with a jerk. Kyle would have it in neutral, Tru knew, letting the winch do the work.

The front wheels hit the bottom of the pile, bounced on logs and small rocks, then started up the side. Kyle fought the steering to keep the Blazer straight.

The bottom of the vehicle started to drag; Tru winced at the grind of the steel frame on dirt and wood. But the rear wheels were moving forward, were hitting the bottom log, and rising over it. The Blazer's belly lifted. The dragging sound fell away. Kyle nodded at Tru through the driver's side window. All wheels were rolling, the winch not even straining. The top of the deadfall was coming up.

The forest to one side began to whisper.

Tru's scalp chilled and tightened. He turned suddenly, stared hard toward the shadow-border of the woods. Kyle hadn't seemed to hear anything over the sound of the engine, but Dan and Mel were looking too. The crowns of individual trees were vibrating, their leaves dancing and murmuring. Tru flashed on an absurd image--living trees shaking their limbs in anger over the desecration of their brethren in the deadfall.

Reality turned out less absurd but no less frightening. Lifting slowly over the trees came a black shape, matte black, with the right angles of rudimentary wings butting against a streamlined fuselage. Tru heard the sound of the rotors now, a drum-steady beat quieter than that of any helicopter he'd ever known. It was wind from those rotors that had set the trees to talking, as the gunship rose from their midst with its scorpion tail poised.

The helicopter menaced like some vast animal/human hybrid. Tinted, light reflecting windows sloped back over the chopper's nose with the look of hooded eyes; a radar array poking out below seemed an underslung muzzle. One long barreled machine gun hung as evil fruit beneath the belly. And from the stubby wings depended chain guns, like over-muscled arms.

Tru's fingers rested only inches from the butt of his pistol, and he very deliberately moved his hand further away from that empty threat. He didn't want the chopper's crew to mistake his intentions.

A quick glance at Mel and Dan showed that they, too, had the good sense to stand still. Mel carried no gun at all and Dan had leaned his rifle against a bush a dozen feet away. Tru was glad of that, but over his shoulder he could still hear the sound of the

Blazer and the winch moving. He started to turn, to signal Kyle. But the gunship pilot wasn't going to wait.

The sound of the rotors increased a half octave. The chopper dipped left, slipping sideways through the air with grace and power. It came in under the high voltage wires, surging toward the front face of the woodpile, its guns swinging on the Blazer. Tru turned, yelled at Kyle to halt, saw his friend's eyes go wide as the helicopter swept into view.

Kyle slapped the button that stopped the winch. The Blazer rocked at the very top of the deadfall. Machine guns tracked it with wicked barrels, with enough firepower to shred them all from their bones. Tru didn't even want to blink. No movement was good movement. He wished he didn't have to pee.

Mel shouted behind him. Tru turned his head, saw a sight that punched his fear level up another notch.

Dan was running for his rifle.

--- 2 ---

Kargen went still in mid-stride as the bass throb of a machine bled down through the trees from somewhere up ahead. He had crossed a road and an open place in the sun that had nearly destroyed him. Though humans would have called that sun warm, Kargen's Whoun muscles and Whoun brain still quivered with the ache of a glacial cold. But the Mother had gone this way and he would not stop his hunt.

Though the sun still came through and speared at him with shafts of light, the trees beyond the open had been a comfort to him when he reached them. It was shaded there, less exposed than the clearway through the forest followed by the Mother's new Podcyst in their vehicle. And he could smell the exhaust from that vehicle at a distance, could follow the concentration gradient with ease. Even among the boles he could move as fast as they could--or faster.

But this other sound? The machine-rapid, heart-throb beat of a mechanism in motion. Not the vehicle in which the Mother rode. Something immensely more powerful.

Kargen turned his head, let his stronger left ear reach out for the sound. In a moment he had it.

Helicopter! Military!

Cold in the Light

Kargen clicked his teeth together. His war-spike twitched. Harbinger Project soldiers had already intervened more than once in his affair with the Mother. They grew tiresome.

His upper body shook; the head-quills slapped across his back like whips. A cold rage bloomed. Out of that rage came purpose. Out of stillness came movement. In a rush he swept onward through the forest, carrying hell along with him.

--- **3** ---

Tru saw Dan racing for his rifle, yelled frantically at the boy to stop before he got them all slaughtered. But the crew of the chopper had already seen the movement, were reacting to it like a threat.

The snout of the gunship swung right. A quick feed of power to the engines thrust the machine toward the deadfall, brought its weapons on target.

Dan reached his rifle, jerked it up, fumbled for an instant with the safety. Tru was frozen. The door of the Blazer shoved open behind him but he could do nothing except stare at Dan. He knew the boy had no chance but could never get to him in time to stop him. Unbidden to Tru's mind came an image of soft flesh cut through by lead at a thousand rounds a minute. He had seen what chain guns could do.

Then a blur formed at the edge of Tru's visual field. And Mel came out of that blur to tackle Dan before he could fire. She hit him hard in the back, knocking him sprawling. The rifle did a flip as it spun free of the boy's hands and struck the ground a dozen feet away. Mel landed on top of Dan, partially holding the boy down, partially shielding him with her own body.

Tru jerked a glance toward the helicopter, saw the barrels of the guns still locked. But still silent. He breathed again as the pilot eased up on his rotors and the chopper drifted a foot lower and a foot closer to the fall. The shapes of two men, pilot and copilot, made smoky outlines behind the darkened glass of the helicopter's cockpit. They seemed to realize that no one here wanted to go up against machine guns.

Tru turned toward the Blazer, shrugged his relief at Kyle, who he had heard getting out of the vehicle.

Kyle wasn't there.

--- 4 ---

Kyle stepped out of the Blazer with his hand dipping for a pistol. He could just make out the nebulous shapes of the two men in the chopper. But their heads were turned toward Dan as the boy made a grab for his rifle.

Then Kyle's hand arced upward, the .45 caught in his fist. The soldiers weren't looking at him but he knew it wouldn't do any good to fire. At this distance the shock-resistant glass of the cockpit would not take a bullet through it. Still, his thumb dragged back the hammer. He had to make something happen before Dan got shot down.

Mel happened first. Out of the corner of an eye, Kyle saw her knock Dan off his feet, spilling the rifle from his hands. And in the next moment the pilot of the gunship relaxed, let up on the throttle so that the machine drifted lower, toward the deadfall--less than a dozen feet away.

Kyle acted.

The crew of the helicopter were distracted, hadn't noticed his movement for a gun. Mel was the cause of that. She'd risked her life to stop one attempt to shoot at them. Maybe it had convinced them the threat was over.

Kyle was convinced only that they were about to be captured. He didn't know if the soldiers would kill Raina and Wahrn, or those who had helped them. But he knew that if he put down his gun he probably wouldn't get a chance to take it up again. That would mean his Uncle Cain had died for nothing. It might mean they all would die for nothing.

The surface of the deadfall felt firm under Kyle's heels. He took three running steps and planted his right foot hard on a huge, barkless log, then leaped outward toward the helicopter, arms spread for balance, the Colt shoved back into its holster to free his hands.

The oddness of the helicopter helped Kyle attack it. The usual landing rails were missing, had been replaced by retractable rubber tires and stubby wings bulking fat with guns. Rockets could be slipped into bolted-on racks beneath those wings as well, though none were there now. On top of the wings were rows of beveled grooves, to channel air flow. Kyle locked his gaze on those grooves as he jumped, every muscle straining, trying not to think about missing, knowing that it was a possibility.

And he struck the left wing of the chopper with his chest, felt his upper body jar. His arms were flailing, hands clawing at the grooves, finding them. Fingers hooked, caught.

The gunship slid sideways under the unexpected weight. Kyle was nearly bucked loose as the shocked pilot suddenly glimpsed someone hanging off his aircraft and fought his stick for control. Then Kyle got a foot on the rocket-launch battery and heaved himself up onto the wing. The main body of the chopper loomed, only a few feet away.

The pilot's first instinct must have been to take the ship up. But Kyle could see the copilot through the glass canopy, yelling, gesturing. He knew the message. They were too close to the power lines. There was nowhere to go but to the side.

In that moment while the pilot hesitated, Kyle got a shoe into one of the wing grooves, shoved himself forward, elbows scraping. To his left, a row of black metal rails ran up the side of the chopper. Next to them stood the door, a sliding model. Kyle grabbed a rail, pulled himself against the bulk of the ship, swung one foot down to a lower rail. The rotor spun directly above him now, its thrum like a hell-borne voice, its wind hot, buffeting. None of the ship's guns could reach him here. The stench of fuel burned in his nostrils.

The helicopter jerked right, then swept back to the left, an elephant trying to shake a monkey off its back. Kyle held tight as he yelled at his friends on the ground to get down. He had no time to see if they'd heard him.

The pilot took the chopper to the right again, toward the trees. In another instant he'd be clear of the power lines and would turn the ship's nose to the clouds. But Kyle stood fully on the boarding rails now, was shoving back the door with his left hand. He could no longer see the pilot or copilot through the thin bulkhead that separated the cockpit area from the small cargo bay behind.

Kyle got a knee through the doorway, reached with his left hand for a hold. The helicopter went into a climb, not quite vertical.

Kyle's knee slipped. He crashed forward onto his stomach, right elbow hooked over the doorjamb on that side, left hand grabbing for anything, feet dangling off into space with the shriek of moving air all around. He slid backward, toward the sky. A hard ground waited below.

From in front of him came an aborted yell, a thudding sound. Kyle's grasping hand found a blowing strap and clutched it, the nylon biting into his palm. His eyes looked up.

The copilot had started around the bulkhead but had slipped as the machine was pushed into a panic-stricken climb; he'd fallen with one foot under him and the other out to the side. With both hands, the man hung on against the gravity that wanted to yank him downward across the cargo area.

Kyle had the nylon strap wrapped around his hand. With the strength in that one arm he pulled himself up, pulled his legs out of the sky and got his knees beneath him. His shoulder felt like it was coming apart. But he wouldn't let go.

The helicopter leveled off abruptly, pitching Kyle forward into the hold area. And the copilot had seen him, was dropping his hand to claw at the side arm holstered at his belt. The flap of that holster came loose, the man's hand diving inside for the butt of a pistol, the blued barrel flashing as the gun slid free of the leather.

Kyle had no time to draw his Colt. He threw himself toward the soldier as the man came to a kneeling position with the gun lifting in his hand. Kyle could see the fellow's pupils, huge in the white face, that face looming now.

A flash went off in Kyle's eyes; sound bludgeoned his ears. He felt the hot shriek of a bullet crease his shoulder, smelled cordite and skin crisped together.

Then he was there, almost on top of the soldier, left hand coming up, slapping the man's pistol out of line with his body. Another bullet fired, into the chopper floor. Whined off. And Kyle's right hand flashed in, fingers curved into a blow that had every bit of strength he owned on it. The man hung wide open, took Kyle's strike in the testicles. Kyle felt the give all the way up his arm.

The soldier let out an odd sound, part moan, part scream, part gurgle. He folded over. But he wasn't out of the fight. His gun hand tried to rise.

Kyle was deafened from the gunshot, could barely see for the aftereffects of the muzzle flash. But he had his knees under him now, a platform for his upper body to pivot off of. He came around with an elbow, driving it with a twist of his hips. The copilot wore a helmet but Kyle hit him just right in the face, missing the rim of the helmet, catching the cheekbone and slicing across. The lips pulped against the teeth, spraying red.

Kyle's left arm moved too, a fraction of a second after the right, driving a straight-hand thrust with the palm flat. The soldier was leaning into him, almost like a lover, and the blow seemed to erupt in his face. Cartilage snapped in the man's nose. Tissues ruptured with the sound of a tomato being hammered. The man crashed backward, hit the rear wall of the chopper, went down. Went out.

Kyle got to his feet, drawing and cocking his Colt, his other hand scooping up the copilot's fallen weapon. Another Sig Sauer 9mm. Like the one Byron had carried. Like the one Kyle had tucked into the small of his back now. He'd keep this one too. It might come in handy.

The sound of the helicopter's engines had dropped from a whine to a thrum. Kyle hadn't noticed during the fight, but when he stepped around the bulkhead into the cockpit he saw why. The pilot had set the auto-controls, was rising out of his seat, coming to investigate the results of a shooting. He met Kyle's two guns and quickly sat down again.

"Land it," Kyle ordered. "Gently." He used the Colt as a pointer, then put the Sig right over the man's shoulder blade where it nestled into his neck.

"And you might wanna know," he said. "I can learn to fly it if I have to."

--- 5 ---

Under the blankets she felt safe. With Wahrn beside her she felt safe. Outside there was light--cold light. But in the back of the Blazer, covered away from the sun, she abode in blackness and warmth. It was almost like a Darkhome.

Her mind drifted still and slow. She had scarcely registered when Mel had come and tucked them in tightly against movement. And now every one of those movements, every stop and go of the vehicle, felt distant. She didn't know how far they had come or what the strange sounds beyond their blankets meant. She didn't care. Her body waited only for night, to give birth. The time grew near.

But then something disturbed her.

Beside her, Wahrn stirred, dragging himself out of his daytime trance. She tried to focus her senses, tried to gather her wandering thoughts. She heard a click and slither that ripped her into awareness. Her eyes opened.

Wahrn was looking at her. And looking through her. He had drawn a knife from its sheath into his palm--the sound that she had heard. She watched as he shoved back the covers and exposed himself to the sun. She heard him moan in pain. Fear screamed into her face.

Something terrible was about to happen. Soon. Soon.

--- 6 ---

Mel watched the helicopter buck and heave in the air, her skin feeling as if it were shrinking, growing too small for her body. She'd knocked Dan down, the only way she could save him from getting shot. But now Kyle had put himself in danger. And there was nothing she could do.

She had seen him on the gunship's wing, seen him disappear inside. She had thought there were shots but couldn't be sure. She'd been scared before, when Dan had gone for his rifle. But she was terrified now, a combination of visceral *and* mental anguish.

Because it was Kyle who might be dying.

A few hours ago they'd made love. Then had come duties. And soldiers. There had been no time to talk. But she'd felt Kyle's eyes turn often in her direction. He was black; she was white. He had to be thinking about that--as she was--thinking about the voiceless criticisms in restaurants if they dared to take a table, the angry stares on the highways as they passed.

And! She wondered if Tru had told Kyle about twelve years ago. About the boy who had run.

Mel bit her finger to keep from screaming. The helicopter was climbing now. Thoughts raced around in her head, trying to escape. They had known when they gave in to their feelings that any moment might be their last. And they had responsibilities: for Dan and Tru, for Raina and Wahrn. Mel had seen Kyle worry, knew what he thought about. What if the demands of duty and... She would call it "love." What if those demands came into conflict?

Cold in the Light

What if he had to choose between her and the others, and he acted out of emotion rather than reason?

So now he had acted on his own, put himself into danger in hopes of avoiding a harder choice in the future. Mel understood because she felt the same way--despite the fact that many would call it a male sort of dilemma. Women were supposed to act out of love. Always! But it wasn't that simple.

The chopper leveled off, started to descend. Mel's heart thumped alone in a hollow place in her chest. What did the change mean? Was Kyle alive? Wounded? Dead!

All morning Kyle had tried to avoid taking her burdens on himself. Though clearly he had wanted to. Mel had appreciated his insight, his gesture of respect. But with the chopper just overhead--coming down to land, and not knowing if Kyle lived or died inside--she wished he had touched her just one more time.

Then the gunship settled to the earth like a resting wasp. Mel took a step toward it. The others were watching too. Dan and Tru, at least. She couldn't see the Whoun hidden beneath blankets in the rear of the Blazer.

The sound of the rotors softened toward silence; the cargo door slid open. Mel's throat seized as a soldier dipped his head and stepped out through that door. Another soldier followed. And then Mel's fear became a smile, as Kyle stepped off the helicopter behind the two men, a gun in his hand. She began to run, the smile spreading over her face.

Behind Kyle and the soldiers the tall grass swayed in a slight breeze. Mel slowed her run, her smile segueing into a frown. No wind touched the grass near her! She screamed a warning but it came too late.

Something red and yellow and black exploded off the ground, rising onto all fours. Huge. Moving too fast to see clearly.

Kyle tried to turn, was swarmed under, his pistol knocked flying, the soldiers going down with him in a pile. A second scream echoed Mel's, raw and hoarse, from a throat that sounded as if it had gargled with scalpel blades--a man's voice crying out as he died.

--- 7 ---

In a savage rush, Kargen came out of the grass and took the three men down who were standing near the army helicopter. Two of the men were military; the third was one of the Mother's new Podcyst. He killed one of the three--a soldier--his war-spike slicing in through an opening mouth and taking out the back of the throat, birthing the man's scream in blood. Shouts in the background barely registered against the glory of that dying voice.

A second soldier lay shocked and still beneath him, face in the dirt. But the third man had moved, had rolled to his knees, hand dipping behind his back, coming out again filled with the blued glitter of a pistol to replace the one he'd lost in Kargen's first charge.

Kargen's nostrils flared. He slapped the gun from the man's hand, the blow jarring, knocking the fellow sprawling. Kargen twisted his head to the side, watched the human kicking heels against the earth as he tried desperately to push himself away from death.

This one wanted a safe place. There wasn't any.

Kargen reached out to take the man's life, but the soldier beneath him chose that moment to struggle--and to scream. Distracted, the Warkind looked down. The soldier's arms were flailing; his body arched upward to buck off the weight sitting on his back. Kargen hissed, the sound like rain on a hot griddle, but the man only struggled more wildly.

Using his knees to hold the soldier down, Kargen reached out with a swift hand to cup the face. A quick flexing of muscles in his arm, drawing the head back, and he heard the human's spine snap across like wood splitting along the grain. Unable to resist the sudden impulse, knowing what effect it would have on the surviving man, Kargen dipped his head and closed his jaws around the dead body's neck. He bit through, tearing skin, crunching bone, letting the taste and odor of fresh blood spume between his teeth.

He looked up, mouth dripping fluid and flesh, wanting to see the fear in the last man's eyes. Only then did he realize his error. This was the dangerous one, the one he'd smelled in that house only an hour ago, scared now, perhaps, but not frozen in terror. In the few seconds it had taken Kargen to kill the soldier, the man had gotten his back against the chopper and had pushed to his feet. And he had found another pistol for his hand, was raising it, steadying his aim.

Kargen moved, rolling sideways into the grass with liquid speed. Lead spanged off rock behind him; more bullets followed, puffing up dust in miniature mushroom clouds. Then Kargen got the chopper between himself and the shooter and went flat to the ground. Scrub brush and weeds hid him where he lay in a slight hollow on the hill. The firing stopped. For the moment.

Kargen knew he had almost died in that lead hail. The shots were on target if he'd been a running human. But no human could move as fast as he could. And no human marksman would predict that he'd be so quick--at least the first time shooting at him.

Kargen imagined that this warrior would make the adjustment.

They'd each underestimated the other. Kargen had not expected the man to have three guns. His throat rumbled in half laughter. *He* would make *that* adjustment as well.

Voices called from beyond the chopper. Kargen's ears caught at the sound.

A woman's voice: "Kyle!"

A man's: "I'm OK. Tru, get the Blazer down the deadfall. Watch everywhere."

Kyle, Kargen thought. *Enemy! I'll remember you.*

Tru would be the other man that he had smelled in the house. He wondered what the woman would be called? Or the boy? He caught no scent of the Mother but knew she had to be here too, closed up somewhere in a place the tell-tale wind couldn't find.

He bellied forward, moving a foot and sinking down, then adding another foot. He couldn't see what was happening beyond the chopper. But he could hear. Boots were running on wood. An automobile engine started. A motor began to hum. Kargen caught a sudden whiff of the Mother, as if a door had opened and closed. She had to be in the vehicle. A whine bled up from deep in his chest, a sound he was barely aware of making.

Kyle's voice again: "Mel! Dan! Get in the truck. Keep your guns ready."

"What about you?"

Kargen was puzzled. A woman's voice but no woman's name. Who was she? Mel? Or Dan? He kicked the thought away, moved another foot, closing on the helicopter. Kyle waited on the other side.

Sweet enemy.

"I'll watch from here," Kyle shouted. "Pick me up. I was gonna use the chopper but we'd never get aboard with that thing out there."

Kargen heard the artificial tone in the man's voice and almost roared his mirth. Kyle had lied. For his benefit, Kargen knew. They figured he could understand English but wouldn't understand all the nuances, wouldn't know that they wanted the helicopter after all. Did they think he hadn't grown up among humans? That he hadn't paid attention?

Two mistakes, Kargen thought. *Enough to let me get close. The next will kill you. Kyle.*

Kargen shifted forward. His hand found a flat rock, palmed it. He hurled it toward the woods, heard it carom off a trunk and rustle bushes. Bullets smacked the trees at that point and Kargen launched himself forward under cover of the sound, moving low and on all fours. He reached the chopper in a few strides, swarmed up the side to the top--silent for all his quickness.

A shallow groove, wide as a body, ran down the center of the helicopter, deepening toward the rear where the oversized tail assembly lifted its blades. Kargen dropped into that channel, found it a good place to hide. Beneath him the humans were like an ant pile disturbed, guns bristling as they tried to watch the grass and the trees and everything around.

Kargen just waited...waited...waited, spending his moments shredding the wires that controlled the chopper's tail rotors.

--- **8** ---

Kyle's hands were filled with guns, the Sig 9mm taken from the chopper's copilot, the Colt he'd dropped in the first attack of the Warkind--and found again when it was over. A second Sig, he'd stuck in his waistband. But none of them had been reloaded. No time. And he couldn't remember how many bullets he had used, hadn't counted his shots. Years ago he'd taught himself to count as he fired. It was a cop's habit: to know the number of bullets expended, and the number left in case of need.

Cold in the Light

But against the Warkind his discipline had failed. He had been closer to death in that moment than at any time in his life. And more afraid than he could remember. He didn't want to face that fear again, didn't know how much more he could take before he would freeze. Or crack.

Gotta get out of here, he thought. *All of us.*

Tru had brought the Blazer the rest of the way down the as if coming to get him. The deputy had understood what Kyle deadfall, had unhooked the winch and was driving up toward Kyle wanted; Kyle hoped the Warkind wouldn't, until too late.

Dan and Mel were riding with Tru--Dan in the back of the Blazer with the Whoun, Mel in the passenger side seat with Kyle's blue steel .357 in her hand. She held it well.

As Tru brought the Blazer to a stop, Kyle stepped around in front of it, his eyes studying the grass, expecting the Warkind at any instant. He knew it would come fast when it came. He avoided looking down, though, at the two soldiers dead near his feet. He didn't want to know what the Warkind had done to them, what it could have done to him. He had seen enough already.

Mel and Tru got out of the Blazer. They didn't look at the soldiers either. Mel held her pistol like she knew how to use it--in her right fist, barrel down and her left hand bracing the wrist on her gun hand. Tru carried his service .38. To Kyle, the 4-inch barreled Smith looked pathetically small up against the enemy that hunted them. But Tru was game. He wouldn't go down easy.

"You got a plan?" the deputy asked.

Kyle jerked his head toward the helicopter. "Can you fly this thing?" he asked quietly.

Tru's eyes got wide. He shook his head, but his words said something different. "I don't know. Maybe."

"But you flew 'em before? In the army, right?"

Tru nodded, licking his lips as if they had suddenly gone bone dry. "Thirty years ago."

Kyle thought he saw movement out of his right eye and spun toward that side, swinging his pistols down into cover position. Tru jumped; Mel caught a harsh breath. Nothing there!

Kyle glanced at Mel. The whites of her eyes seemed filled with pupils, leaving only a narrow circle of bright blue around them.

"Sorry," he said. "Jumpy."

A nervous smile, tiny and fleeting, curled up one corner of the woman's mouth. Then she looked beyond him at the trees, and all around, not speaking, watching the world for any sign of the creature that wanted to kill them.

Where the hell is it? Kyle wondered. He took a quick scan himself, then looked back to Tru.

"Figured on making the pilot fly us," he said. "But that isn't gonna happen. If you can get it up. And down again in Fort Smith. It'll save us a lot of time."

Tru looked as if his clothes were suddenly too tight for him. He wiped his mouth and chin with one hand. Then did it again. Kyle could feel how scared the man was, like a fever coming off of him. But he could also feel when Tru put away the fear, when he locked it down tight inside where he could control it. For now.

"I can try. I've done some flying since the old days. Not military craft."

"We don't need anything fancy."

Tru nodded. "All right. I'll need a few minutes to check out the controls." "You got it. Just don't fire her up yet. When that thing figures we're leaving. That's when it'll attack."

Tru nodded again, moved toward the helicopter. Kyle watched him open the pilot's door and climb in.

"You want me to get Dan and get the Whoun ready?" Mel asked.

Kyle turned toward her. "Yeah."

He started to say something else, and the screech of metal grating on metal rippled up his spine to petrify his words. Mel twisted around like a cat in mid-air; Kyle's pistols came up. Then they both realized the source of the sound, the rear hatch of the Blazer being opened.

Dan stepped out.

Wahrn followed. He was hurting.

But it wasn't his bullet wounds that were tearing at the big male Whoun; they were on the way to healing. It was the sun. Kyle didn't understand why the Whoun reacted so strongly to bright light. That their eyes were particularly susceptible to light made sense---they were clearly a nocturnal species--but Wahrn looked as if he were standing in an electric field with the voltages coursing up and down his body. The muscles bunched and jumped along his arms and legs. He bent over like a tree grown in a place of heavy wind.

Cold in the Light

And a pulsing low sound, a kind of moan, poured from so deep in his body that it seemed to come from the ground beneath him.

Mel moved quickly to the Whoun's side, put a hand to his shoulder. "You shouldn't be out," she said.

Wahrn shook his head, though it seemed to cause him even more pain. He forced himself to stand up straighter. Gently, he took Mel's hand in his own, squeezed it, and let it go.

"It was Kargen that attacked you," he said. "He isn't gone. I smell him. He wants the Mother. Raina."

"We're ready for him now," Mel said. "You need rest. Let's get you lying down."

"No! Ready for any other Warkind maybe. But not Kargen. He's-- There's something you don't know about him. That you should know."

Mel looked around at Kyle, her expression asking him to back her up. He wasn't ready to. Mel hadn't been watching this Kargen's face as he took a chunk out of one of the soldiers and spit the gore in the dirt. They needed Wahrn. And maybe a hell of a lot more.

Kargen, Kyle thought. *So that's your name, you son of a bitch. I'll remember you.*

Keeping his eyes wide, scanning the grass and dust around, Kyle walked up to Wahrn. He held out a Sig, butt first, the barrel pointing down.

"Want a gun?" he asked.

Again Wahrn shook his head. He lifted his right hand. In it glittered a knife.

"This is better for me. Can't shoot anyway. In the brightness."

"Right," Kyle said.

He reversed the pistol, drawing the grip around into his fist, then looked at Mel. She was angry that he hadn't supported her, but he didn't try to smile or shrug to ease her mind. It wouldn't have worked anyway, and he didn't feel like playing the game. Their eyes met and held, and when they broke the gaze it was by some mutual agreement to let the issue slide.

"So what should we know about Kargen?" Kyle asked Wahrn.

"He's--"

"Tru's signaling thumbs up," Dan interjected.

Kyle turned, then bit his lip. No time now to learn more about their enemy. They had to get out of here. But he felt better with Wahrn beside him, just knowing the Whoun's size and sense of smell was on their side. His own nostrils could detect nothing but the odors of aviation fuel and sweat, and the bitter bite of spent cartridges.

"All right," Kyle said. "More on Kargen later. Wahrn. Stay close to Mel. You two get Raina into the helicopter. Dan," he raised his voice a little, drawing the boy's attention, making eye contact. "You watch their backs. I'll take the front."

Dan puffed air nervously through his teeth, but he looked in better control of himself than he had been for a while. He nodded at Kyle's words, gripped his rifle more tightly. Mel and Wahrn had already turned toward the back of the Blazer, toward the Mother.

Kyle moved to where he could cover the widest area when Kargen attacked; he didn't think there was any "if" involved. They would be most vulnerable after Mel and Wahrn took the Mother out of the Blazer, after they started walking her toward the chopper. The distance measured only a few feet, but it was like exposing your jugular to an enemy who was quick with a knife.

Kyle checked his guns and waited, surprised to find that his hands were steady.

--- 9 ---

Helen Russo plucked at her woolen skirt, watched her husband sitting across the tent from her with his chin in his hands and his gaze turned inward. His tears of earlier were branded into her memory.

She shushed Joshua and Caleb as they fidgeted. The boys were bored, and she envied them. They didn't understand what had happened, what *was* happening. They knew only that the "Uncle" Leonard who sent them presents every birthday and Christmas had told them they had to stay here--and that later they would all play. They wanted to play now.

"I'm sorry," Mike said suddenly. He didn't look up.

Helen blinked. She was too tired to sigh.

"Why, Daddy?" Caleb asked. "Did you do a naughty?"

Cold in the Light

Joshua snorted and rolled his eyes. "It's a grown up thing, dummy," he said.

"Josh!" Helen scolded. She pulled Caleb into her arms, squeezed him, let him go. He walked over to his older brother and promptly punched him in the arm. Helen pulled them apart before Josh could retaliate.

Mike hadn't moved, seemed as much statue as human. But his words hung there between them.

Helen didn't know what to say to her husband, wondered what she was supposed to say. She could hurt him badly with the wrong phrasing, and there was the temptation to do just that. Payback for all the times she had needed reassurance from him. And hadn't gotten it.

But she couldn't bring herself to destroy Mike any further. He was a good man. He cared about people. He cared about her and the boys. She knew that. Only, he had let the duties and responsibilities of the last few years deposit a layer of coldness and distance over his feelings. Now, fear had cracked his reserve and it must seem to him as if he had failed everyone and that it was too late to stave off disaster.

Well, maybe it *was* too late. But she couldn't accept that yet. She didn't understand everything that had happened here, only that Leonard Suskind was keeping them prisoner and that he showed every sign of being perfectly willing to hurt them. That meant, to her, that he'd gone crazy, and that something was very wrong with the Harbinger research project to which her husband had dedicated so much of his life.

She didn't doubt there was much more that no one had told her, and some of it was probably worse than anything she'd heard or guessed so far. But she couldn't accept *any* of it yet. She feared for her sons and her husband and herself, and this situation was unlike any she had ever dealt with. There was only one thing here that she knew. She knew Mike.

Helen leaned forward, touched her husband's knee. When he looked at her she spoke.

"I love you," is what she said.

--- 10 ---

Kyle and Dan watched the world around while Wahrn and Mel took the Mother out of the Blazer and let her walk. They had a blanket over her to keep away the sun, and they moved her swiftly across the open area to the chopper. Kyle paced them, a pistol in each hand, knowing that the Warkind--Kargen--would have to attack now. If Wahrn was right and Kargen wanted the Mother, this would be his best chance.

Nothing happened.

Tru fired up the engines as Wahrn climbed into the chopper's holding area and lifted Raina up to join him. Mel got in behind them, yelled "OK" at Kyle, who was scanning, scanning.

"Dan. Your turn," Kyle shouted. He began backing toward the open door of the chopper while Dan went past him quickly and climbed aboard.

It'll be now, Kyle thought. *He's gotta come now.*

Still nothing happened. Kyle's hands were wet on the guns. He wanted desperately to dry them on his jeans, but didn't dare take the chance. The back of his legs struck the frame of the helicopter's door.

"Cover me while I get in," he said over his shoulder. He heard the click of weapons behind him, heard Dan's voice: "Ready."

He turned, took a step and jumped up into the helicopter, landing with both feet solidly, spinning to slam the cargo door closed, yelling at Tru to lift off. His eyes were on the windows as the engine powered up with a whine and the rotors started to hum, building speed. The chopper shifted as Tru felt out the controls, then seemed almost to leap the first few feet into the air.

Kyle shoved a Sig into his belt, grabbed a handhold and braced himself while the chopper lurched. Everyone else was sitting but even they fought for balance. The machine seemed to settle, lost one of the precious few feet it had climbed. Kyle pulled himself toward the bulkhead that separated the pilot's area from the hold, turned the corner around it into the nose of the craft.

Tru looked scared. The ship yawed to one side, nearly striking the Blazer with its left wing. Kyle holstered his .45, dropped into the copilot's seat. Tru fought the controls, got the balance right for a moment and straightened the chopper. They gained a little height but were still no more than ten feet off the ground.

Cold in the Light

"Gotta get it up!" Kyle shouted over the sound of the engines.

Tru shook his head. "Something's wrong. I can't get the pitch right."

The machine tilted, the nose coming up too quickly. Tru fought it back down.

"Too much weight?" Kyle asked.

Again Tru shook his head, biting down on his bottom lip as his hands worked over the controls. "No, not too much. The load's distributed wrong. There's no balance. I don't kno--"

Then Kyle saw Tru's face turn a chalky shade of ugly white.

"Oh my God," the deputy said.

Kyle's heart jump-started into high gear. "What?" he shouted. "What is it?"

Tru turned his head toward Kyle, his pupils swollen with terror. "On the roof!" he nearly screamed. "The weight. It's on the roof."

"Land it!" Kyle yelled, as he realized what Tru was saying.

He powered up from the seat, drawing his pistols, thumbing back the hammers. Behind them in the cargo area came the crump of glass shattering, of metal twisting. Gunshots exploded. Humans and Whoun shouted in confusion. A roar sounded, savage as any jungle.

The smell of sudden blood shocked the air.

CHAPTER TWELVE
(May 1: From Afternoon Till Dusk)

On every side of him swirled colorless petals from dead flowers, their beauty leached by evil. And he raced among them unaware, as behind him they grew black limbs and began to scuttle.
--In the Memory of Ruins

--- 1 ---

Michael Russo heard his wife's words, heard her say that she loved him. And he could see in her face that it was true. For a moment he couldn't meet the honest shock of her gaze and had to look away. It didn't help him escape. Josh and Caleb had stopped their bored fussing and were staring at him too. It was as if the world were waiting to hear his response, at least all of the world imprisoned with him inside this tent.

He looked back at Helen, understanding what she had offered him. It didn't matter that he had let her down, or let down the boys, or anyone else. She loved him and always would. And he loved her, though he realized that it had been years since he'd shown it.

"I love you too," Mike said. "And the boys." A glance took in his sons, then brought his gaze back to his wife. "I think I forgot for a while. But I'm remembering now."

Helen smiled. She went down on a knee beside her husband, put her arms around him. Caleb came running, as he always did when anyone besides himself got attention. Joshua was more reluctant--being old enough to realize that his father was acting strangely--but he came anyway. They hugged as a family, something they hadn't done in a long time.

Helen, Joshua, and Caleb *were* his family, Mike thought. Not Lanny. Not the Whoun. He owed Lanny justice. He owed the Whoun whatever he could do to save them from Leonard's manipulations. But most of all he owed his family first.

Cold in the Light

Mike didn't doubt that this new kind of Leonard was capable of killing them all, though he'd probably try to make it look like an accident. He'd have to shut them up somehow, because it was clear that this whole incident would be buried. Mike couldn't let any of that happen.

"Wanna learn a new game?" he asked Josh and Caleb suddenly.

"Yeah, Daddy," Caleb said.

"What kind of game?" Josh asked, warily.

Mike roughed his oldest son's hair. "A fun one. Come on."

Mike always carried a pocket notepad and a pen with him. He pulled out the pad and tore off twelve sheets, block printing a simple word on each. He led the boys over to one corner of the tent and placed the sheets on the floor, face down.

"You guys remember how to play warmer-colder?"

They nodded.

"Well, this is about the same. Caleb, you pick a sheet and look at the word. Josh has to guess what it is and you tell him warm or cold. Like, if the word is cat and he says tree--"

"Then that's cold," Caleb interrupted.

"Right. But if he guesses animal you'd probably say he was a little warm. OK?"

Again the boys nodded.

"Then Josh picks a word, and that's how it goes. The idea is to see how long it takes the two of you to get all twelve words. How does that sound?"

"Like fun, Daddy," Caleb said.

Josh said nothing and Mike gave him a look. "Josh?"

"OK. I guess. Caleb'll probably mess it up, though."

"Won't neither," Caleb yelled.

"I know you won't," Mike said. "Because *Josh* is going to help if you get confused."

Mike looked again at Josh, who rolled his eyes but nodded.

"Good." Mike patted them both, then checked his watch. "Go," he told them, and Caleb immediately grabbed a sheet.

Mike went back to sit next to Helen on the floor of the tent. "Maybe that'll keep them playing for a while," he said. He leaned

211

forward with his elbows on his knees, began worrying at his thumbnail--thinking.

Helen studied her husband's face, trying to divine his worries from the creases she saw there.

"What is it Leonard wants, Mike?" she asked after a moment. "What's going on here?"

Mike shook his head, but tried to answer. "It'd take a year to tell it all. The long and short of it is that the Harbinger Project involves an intelligent race known as the Whoun. We've been raising them in secret for the past twenty odd years. But now there's been an escape."

Helen felt her jaws unhinge in surprise. This was a joke. It had to be. But Mike had never been a joking man.

"You're kidding," she said, knowing how predictable she probably sounded.

Mike met her gaze, his own eyes absolutely steady. "No," he said. "I definitely am not kidding."

"They're aliens?"

"Nope. Native to Earth. Though," he barked a short and humorless laugh, "we found them in a pretty weird place. We think they evolved maybe ten to twelve million years ago. Well before humans. We don't know for sure what happened to the race as a whole. The ones we found were all embryos."

"This is incredible!"

Mike smiled, genuinely smiled. "Yes. It is."

"But how could anyone have kept something like this secret? How many people know?"

"Nixon was President when it started. But he hid us better than he hid Watergate. He formed the Harbinger Commission and had the labs built. There were only four people set to work on the Project initially, though. All civilian scientists. Leonard was picked to head it. He brought me aboard a few months later. Lanny about the same time. There've only been a few changes in that basic group since."

"What about the soldiers?"

"They came later. Well, there were a few bigwigs. The Joint Chiefs. And some of Nixon's cabinet knew. But probably not more than ten people in the government were aware of us. We were just working with embryos then. In '78, when we decided to...grow them, we needed medical personnel and those came to us from the military. They were let in on the whole story. We also got assigned a Special Forces unit, most of whom know about the Whoun but don't have any idea how intelligent the creatures are. We've sort of encouraged their misperceptions."

"How bright are they? The Whoun I mean."

"The Typicals, the breeders, are as intelligent as a human, though much less mechanically inclined. They've all learned to talk and read English. There's a...soldier caste too. Called the Warkind. They're probably twenty IQ points below a Typical. On average. There's a lot of variability, though."

Helen frowned. "And now you say one of them's escaped? Is it a Warkind? Is that what's got Leonard so crazy?"

Mike shook his head. "It was the Typicals. Several of them actually. One of them's pregnant and somebody was messing with the embryo's genetics. Leonard was behind it. His retirement was a sham."

"But why fake retirement and let *you* take over?" Helen protested. "He knows you wouldn't go along with something like that."

"No, it doesn't make much sense. Unless..."

"Unless what?"

"Well... If Leonard wanted to be free for some other reason. We had over a thousand embryos. Didn't use them all. He could have taken some elsewhere. Not much I'd put past him at the moment. The *why* is what I don't understand."

For a little bit it had seemed as if Helen's anxiety and fear had been replaced by excitement over the Whoun. Now Mike saw the fear come back. He wondered if she were remembering Leonard's last words to them before they'd been sent into this tent as prisoners. Leonard had promised the boys fun games and had sent them ahead. Then he had put his arms over Helen's and Mike's shoulders and whispered a phrase in their ears.

"We mourn in black. Why mourn we not in blood?" And his smile had been beatific. And somehow dirty. Like the smile of a rotting angel.

"I wouldn't have believed any of this of Leonard," Helen said abruptly. "But now. It's like he's crazy! That smile of his. Stuffing us away in this tent."

"Something's wrong," Mike agreed. "But he's not just crazy. There's something else."

"Will he hurt us? Hurt the boys?"

Mike decided against lying to spare Helen's feelings. He didn't think he could pull it off anyway.

"The way he is now, I think he's capable of it. He's going to have to try and cover all this up."

"Meaning he'll have to silence anyone who knows the truth."

Mike nodded.

Helen looked at her sons playing their new game, oblivious to the danger they were in. She glanced back at Mike.

"We have to do something."

Mike squeezed her hand. I know," he said. But he had no idea what that "something" might be.

--- 2 ---

Leonard Suskind paced back and forth in the tent where his newly appointed Commander, Wayne Teagle, should have been-- but wasn't. The scientist felt frustrated. After Hammond had called on the 30th to report the problem with the Whoun, he, Leonard, had flown down here in a helicopter loaded with equipment for accessing military spy satellites. He knew the codes. They should have already had the equipment set up, had the Whoun female and her all important fetus located. But first there had been Michael Russo to deal with. Then Hammond himself. Now he couldn't find Teagle to get the work started.

Finally, Calder Davidson, the highest ranking of the two lieutenants in the Harbinger Special Forces group, brought him word that Teagle had left camp to inspect some scouting parties. Leonard threw up his hands in disgust.

"I am beginning to lose confidence in our Commander Teagle," he said, to no one in particular.

"Sorry, sir," Davidson responded.

Cold in the Light

Leonard's eyes found the man, locked on as if targeting him for a missile strike.

"Get Teagle back here right now," he said. "And I've got computers and equipment aboard my helicopter that need to be remote-linked to the Harbinger mainframes. Send me some fucking technicians."

"Yes, sir!" The lieutenant saluted, then quickly backed out of the tent to carry out his orders.

Leonard grunted, the knuckles cracking in his hands as he clenched his fists. "Fucking soldiers," he muttered to himself.

He did a few quick knee bends to stretch his muscles, to relieve his stress. He liked the feeling of strength that exercise gave him. All his life he had carried a strong mind in a weak body. Now, in his seventies, his body was finally catching up. It didn't matter that his mind had found the way.

Leonard moved to the center of the tent, took several deep breaths to focus his concentration. Then he flipped backwards into a handstand and held himself there.

Have to arrange an accident for Michael Russo, he thought. *Probably for Helen as well. And the kids. What were their names? Joshua and... And Caleb.*

He let his muscles flex slowly, lowering himself toward the nylon floor of the tent, holding himself with his face only an inch from the ground, tendons straining.

A shame about the Russos. Really. Especially the kids. And Helen. Leonard remembered when he used to like Mike Russo, when he used to visit the man's family at Christmas.

He shook the regrets away as he pushed himself back to a full handstand position, then did four quick repetitions. Down, touch the floor with a nose, back up. He flipped over onto his feet, sweat rolling smoothly, lungs pumping sweet oxygen.

"Things change," he muttered to himself.

Because of the insights gained from research with the Whoun, the next few years could see humanity achieve total mastery over its own genetic destiny. Before that could happen, though, certain...decisions had to be made. Some had already been made. Like those that would help prolong his life and let him do the important work that needed to be done. Michael Russo would never have been willing to make the right decisions, to do the necessary things. Fortunately, he, Leonard, was a different kind of man.

Leonard walked over and sat down behind Wayne Teagle's small camp desk. He laid a piece of paper on the false wood surface, took a pen and wrote the words: "Helicopter crash kills family." He closed his eyes to think about that idea, absentmindedly rubbing at a discolored knot between the knuckles of the outside two fingers on his right hand.

Suddenly, he winced and looked down to see a bright rune of blood scrawled across the back of his hand where his own fingernails had sliced like a knife. He raised the hand to examine the cut, frowned to see how deep it was. Then, slowly, he brought the wound to his mouth and licked at it, smearing the cracks in his lips with crimson.

--- 3 ----

Even as Kyle's senses were assaulted into stillness by the sudden smell/scream of blood, his muscles reacted, carrying him in a burst around the steel partition that separated the cockpit of the helicopter from the space where Mel and Dan and the Whoun were under attack. Behind him, Kyle heard Tru cursing the controls of the bucking chopper as he tried to land it; in front of him he found a nightmare that seemed to swallow his eyes whole.

The air of the cargo hold vibrated with leftover gunshots, had grown slick with fear sweat. All around was movement--Dan thrown backward from an awful blow, the stock of his rifle shattered and a wet red pulsing in wide fans from his stomach and chest; Mel diving across the Mother to protect her; Wahrn on his feet, bellowing, striking out with the knife a shining gleam in his hand. And beyond loomed Kargen, black and yellow and scarlet, the door of the chopper torn apart over the curve of his shoulder--a wind swirling in.

Kyle's guns tracked. But Wahrn bulked huge in the way, stabbing at Kargen's chest. The blow never landed. Kargen was too fast, too strong. And he had adjusted to the razor-edged light that teared Wahrn's eyes and tortured his body.

Kargen caught Wahrn's knife-hand, twisted it aside and down. Kyle heard the wrist bone snap as Wahrn was driven with a grunt

Cold in the Light

to his knees, and the knife gleamed suddenly in Kargen's hand, reversed, and thrown, flashing toward Kyle. Somehow, Kyle got his right hand up, deflecting the sliver of steel off the barrel of his Colt. His left hand gun jolted, but he was distracted, the chopper wild beneath his feet. The shot missed to one side.

From his knees, Wahrn tried his left hand in an attack, slicing at Kargen's groin-pouch with the stubby digging spike on his fist, that spike a bare echo of a Warkind's much more deadly battle-blade. Kargen caught the strike against his leg, and moving with immense suddenness dropped into a squat, his hands reaching, finding Wahrn's head, locking on the Typical's skull.

"No!" Kyle shouted. He couldn't shoot through Wahrn to get to Kargen, but his right hand gun bucked as he went for a shot over Kargen's head, trying to distract the Warkind from killing.

It didn't work.

In one brutal move, Kargen rotated his hands upward, jerking Wahrn's head back while Kargen's war-spikes sliced down through the ridged muscles at each side of the Typical's neck. Wahrn groaned as his head sagged forward on torn tendons, his hands coming up, hoping to break the Warkind's hold before death reached his throat.

Kyle fired again, desperately, aiming lower, trying for the one piece of Kargen's skull that he could see. The bullet took off one of the Warkind's head-quills, sent it spinning out of the chopper. But it wasn't enough.

Kargen screamed in triumph as the blades on his hands sliced down beneath Wahrn's chin, ripping through the carotids and then away in a shower of blood. And the shower became an explosion, a raw flood of scarlet gore spouting into Kargen's face. Kyle saw it happen, knew Wahrn was dead, and knew, finally, how superbly adapted the Warkind were to killing when he saw the translucent flash of nictitating lids closing over Kargen's eyes to keep out the blood.

Kyle screamed himself, a drawn out, choking scream. He took a step forward, balancing himself against the weave and roll of the descending helicopter, his pistols hammering, slamming back into his palms. It didn't matter if he hit Wahrn now, as long as something got through to Kargen.

A bullet clipped dust from the Warkind's shoulder but didn't slow him. From his crouch, Kargen heaved Wahrn's dead weight toward Kyle, slinging it like a man slinging a sack of straw.

Kyle sidestepped, got hit anyway with Wahrn's three hundred plus pounds. The blow slapped him against the wall, robbed him of most of his air. Kargen uncoiled from his crouch, hind legs powering the move, front limbs barely touching the chopper's floor, coming like a train. But not for Kyle. For Mel and the Mother.

A sound bludgeoned Kyle's ears from just behind, the thunder and crack of a heavy caliber gun being fired. Kyle recognized the wicked blast of a .357, knew it had to have been Mel that pulled the trigger.

The shock of the 150-grain lead slammed Kargen back onto his haunches, spittle leaping from his mouth in a roar of half pain and half rage. Kyle's right hand gun lifted--the .45--coming on line with the Warkind's head.

End it now, his thoughts were shrieking. *Hammer back. One shot.*

Out of the corner of the hold charged a torn scarecrow figure, mouth open and nothing coming out. Dan! Alive! Or dead on his feet. One arm clutched across his stomach and lower chest, trying to stop the flow of blood and tissue that pulsed like red lava from his wounds. His other hand held the broken stock of his .30-06, the tip cracked sharply along the grain until it had become a spear. His lower body was painted scarlet, but his legs were churning and he hit Kargen like a fullback hitting the line of scrimmage.

Kargen was off balance, the floor gyrating beneath him, and Dan's charge knocked the Warkind over backwards. The makeshift spear rose, but never fell. The helicopter struck ground in an uncontrolled landing, and that ground seemed to roll beneath it. Then the machine slid sideways and began to tilt to the left.

"She's going over!" Kyle shouted.

He turned and threw himself across Mel and Raina, dropping the guns that he had no time to holster, grabbing for handholds, shoving his feet against the wall, locking his knees to take the strain that he knew was coming. Mel braced too. Her eyes were crazy scared, her lips curled back and thinned. Raina did not move. Seemed tranked, or dead.

Cold in the Light

Dan and Kargen were sliding toward the torn open door of the chopper, picking up speed. Wahrn's body hurtled after. Through the mangled door, Kyle could see earth rushing up to greet them.

Dirt and logs. Brown grass and sun.

They had landed on the sloping side of the massive deadfall that they had so recently crossed in the Blazer. And the angle at which they had settled was too sharp to let them stay. They were rolling over.

The tips of the speeding rotors struck the ground, hacked into dirt and rock, fragmenting into shrapnel that whined off into distance like 20th century banshees. The thrust of the rotors against dirt whipped the chopper's tail into the air, throwing the whole machine forward onto its nose.

Dan and Kargen had nothing to grip onto. The open wall behind them seemed to suck them out of the helicopter; their momentum threw them down like cast off ballast.

Kyle held on, arms and legs wrapped across Raina and across a Mel who had latched as tightly onto him. His muscles took the strain as the chopper stood on its head, tilted past ninety degrees and came whomping down onto its spine. The blow jarred. Metal groaned and shrieked as the ceiling crumpled inward under the pressure. Bullet-proof glass imploded. It seemed to Kyle as if his bones and sockets were being jackhammered apart.

Abruptly they were at rest, upside down, with the old roof making a new floor for their feet. Dust spilled around them in a fine shower.

Kyle didn't dare wait for the dust to settle. He released Mel and the Mother, surged into a crouch, his eyes scanning for his pistols in the debris. He found the .45. And Mel's .357. The Sig was nowhere to be seen, but he had another one tucked into the small of his back, a metal bruise against his skin. Maybe Kargen was dead, but the guns felt good anyway.

Mel had moved, was halfway under the blankets that covered Raina, but as Kyle rose to his feet and turned toward her she lifted her head into the open. She shrugged in answer to his unspoken question.

"She's alive. But in some kind of trance. At least I think it is. Doesn't look like shock."

"We've got to get her to the Blazer," Kyle said. "Get her out of here."

"What about Tru?" She hesitated. "And Dan?"

She had seen the boy's wounds as well as he had, probably knew better than he did what they meant. But neither of them wanted to voice their thoughts quite yet.

"I'll check," Kyle said. He handed her the .357, drew the extra Sig Sauer from behind his back into his hand. "Yell if you need me."

The upcurve of her lips was a nervous habit, signaling nothing more than that she'd heard him. Kyle moved to the door of the chopper. His stomach roiled but he forced himself to step out into the shadeless sun. His eyes searched. Left and right. Straight ahead. This time--above. He could see where Kargen and Dan should have fallen free. Neither of them were there, though Wahrn's body lay at the bottom of the deadfall like a shed skin.

His heart stutter-stepped.

Where were Kargen and Dan? If he could see Wahrn, why not the others? They'd all been thrown from the helicopter at the same time. He studied the ground beyond the dead Whoun, hoping for an answer. He wasn't expecting one, not the one he wanted where Kargen was concerned. The Warkind lived. Had to.

But Dan? Kyle had seen the boy's wounds; Dan hadn't gone for a stroll.

Kyle turned back toward the helicopter, to check on Tru, but the deputy was already pushing back the cockpit door and climbing out. Blood ran down Tru's face from a torn ear. His uniform was ripped, his face gray as spoiled meat. Kyle saw the man's shoulders hanging down with the weight of boulders.

"Tru! You all right?"

Tru looked up, his eyes flicking across Kyle, a pain that wasn't physical rising to their surface.

"I'm sorry. I couldn't... I couldn't hold her."

Kyle grabbed Tru by the arm, hard enough to hurt.

"It's not your fault. Kargen must have done something to the tail rotors. Nobody could have flown that machine."

The pain didn't go away from the deputy's eyes. But his shoulders straightened--a little--as he realized the truth in Kyle's words.

Cold in the Light

"I wanted to get it down. Help you and the others." He suddenly looked around. "Where are the others? They're OK?"

Tru's voice had filled with a desperate urgency and Kyle squeezed his arm again, more softly this time. His voice was low as he said:

"Mel and Raina are. But Wahrn's dead. And I'm not...sure about Dan. He and Kargen were thrown out when we landed. I haven't seen them."

Tru blanched and frowned at the same time, the color that had been seeping back into his face quickly draining out again. He looked away, out at the world, his hand reaching for his service .38, pulling it for scant comfort.

"Right now we've got to get Mel and Raina to the Blazer," Kyle continued. "But we all go together. No separating."

Tru nodded, understanding that they had no time to bury Wahrn or haul the body along with them. But then:

"And Dan?" the deputy asked.

Kyle sighed. He'd have to say it. What he and Mel had both been thinking. And he found himself not wanting to speak the words that would somehow make Dan's fate real. Because Dan had become one of them. More even than Wahrn, whose life the boy had saved once but couldn't a second time. Yet, it was very possible that Dan had saved the rest of them by attacking Kargen when he did. None of that would change the horror that Kyle's eyes had registered.

"He's gotta be dead," Kyle told Tru. "I don't know where his body is but he's gotta be dead."

Tru's gaze sought Kyle's eyes and held them. "How do you know? You said he and Kargen were thrown free of the helicopter?"

Kyle felt sick. But the words came despite that sickness, rising from his throat like acid and rage.

"Because I saw the blood where Kargen hit him. And I saw him attack Kargen again with his stomach cut open and his guts hanging down to his knees. The boy was running through his own intestines, Tru. He was dead. Whether he knew it or not."

Without warning, Tru vomited, spilling bile onto the dirt by Kyle's feet. And Kyle watched the deputy's shoulders heave, and wished he could throw up beside the other man. But the poison and hate in his own belly were too deep to be gotten rid of that easily.

--- 4 ---

Drake Hammond laughed. He paced in the tent where he was supposed to be a prisoner. He wasn't one.

"So, the old kook actually believed Teagle was out checking on the troops," he exclaimed.

He laughed again, slapping his hand down on the shoulder of the lieutenant who had brought him the news. This was the same lieutenant who'd led the burial detail for Wayne Teagle's corpse. Calder Davidson. His *hammer*, the colonel liked to think. Davidson was a tool that would serve without question, with none of the scruples of Hammond's other lieutenant, William Morgan.

"The old man wanted some equipment unloaded from his chopper, too," Davidson said. "I don't know what kind. Said he needed some techs to link it into the computers."

"Probably satellite gear. They've got stuff now that can look up an ant's ass while he takes a crap."

"You want it hooked up?"

Hammond snorted, lifted a hand to scratch his chin. "Sure," he said, after a moment. "Or started anyway. Why not? Suskind won't be using anything we get out of it. And it will tell *us* exactly where the Podcyst is when we want to collect them. Put Lloyd and Haynes on it."

Davidson saluted. "Yes, sir." He started to turn, and stopped again as his Commander raised two fingers.

"Make sure the equipment does not go operational until I say it does," Hammond said. "That clear?"

"Crystal, sir."

Hammond slapped the other man on the shoulder again, then added: "You know. I've been thinking that maybe our Lieutenant Morgan isn't quite the kind of fellow we need in our little army. What's your opinion?"

Davidson didn't hesitate. "Well I didn't feel that he offered proper support of you when Dr. Suskind tried to remove you from command, sir. He showed a certain...indifference."

"Yes. I wondered if you'd noticed that." Hammond grinned suddenly. "But get on out of here now." He said the last affectionately and the soldier grinned back before saluting a second time and leaving the tent.

Hammond's thoughts followed Davidson. "A good man," he muttered to himself. But then, he'd taken care to surround himself with good men, men who hadn't blinked an eye when he told them to bury Wayne Teagle and get ready to bury a few more.

Teagle was--had been, he corrected himself--a fool. Like, perhaps, Lieutenant William Morgan. Certainly like Suskind and that idiot Russo. They all believed so hard in rationality and reason. As if those words were gods.

What had Anatole France said? "A rational army would run away." You didn't lead soldiers by reason. You didn't lead anyone by reason. Ever.

Hammond spread his legs, crossed his hands behind his back. In all their grasping after power his enemies had forgotten one thing. Loyalty. That was how you led men. Because then they would die for you. Or kill for you. And logic had never yet stopped a bullet.

Leonard Suskind needed to learn just how useless his science was in the face of violence. And after that there would be Michael Russo. Then he'd tuck away the Mother Whoun, and the politicians would see how this whole project should have been military all along.

He felt sure they would want him to run it for them.

--- 5 ---

Kargen squatted, his back against a rock while he watched the human boy die on the ground in front of him. The woods around were shaded and warm, and Kargen had brought the boy here to be out of the cold sun. He didn't worry that the others would be escaping with the Mother. They had no place to go that he couldn't follow.

Though the boy had helped keep the Mother out of Kargen's hands, it was not hate that made him watch the human's dying. It was only that he *knew* the boy, had even let him escape once. His death now was too intimate a moment to ignore. And it had been

Kargen's own war-spike that had opened this human to the world. In that way they were bound. In life. And after.

The boy watched him back, the eyes brittle bright, past the point where they could hold any fear--as the chalk face could hold no more pain. The body below the face looked a pretty mess, torn down the middle and spilled wide, colored in shades of rose and ash, and in the blue-black of skin starved for blood and oxygen.

Kargen leaned forward, curling himself into an arch above the boy, bringing their faces close together. His nostrils and ears opened, smelling copper and salt and fading heat, hearing the rush of air over torn membranes. Kargen's own respiration was far from smooth. He could feel the bullet in the left side of his chest, could feel it radiating pain every time he drew a breath.

But the pain didn't matter. He liked the pain. And the lead wasn't in a place where it could kill him. At least not right away. Besides, the Mother was more alone now, with two of her protectors gone. Only the woman and two more men were left to worry about. One of the men would be easy. The older one. The one who had sweated the most.

Kargen knew, too, that the Mother would only be a burden to them from now on. He had smelled her in the helicopter. She neared her time. The birth would come soon.

The human stopped breathing. Kargen heard the quiet, felt how still the air grew near the boy's lips. He turned his head, watching, watching, as the dullness and darkness started at the edge of the boy's eyes and swept inward, emptying the irises of pale blue. Death coming was like a wave of crystallization passing through a fluid. All softness became hard.

Kargen waited until the hardening was complete. Then he sliced away a tithe of flesh to carry with him and sought out the Mother's trail.

For a moment, he relaxed the olfactory block he'd used to shut down his oversensitivity to the Mother's pheromones, though he knew the insanity that would follow. The world began to change as those molecules invaded him anew, as they thrust tiny fingers into his brain. The air rippled and slid; in the trees were movements half-seen. His mind bloomed with strange thoughts that quested along twisted pathways.

He forced the thoughts aside, let his senses quiver in search. Dust motes swirled, changed to an electric rain that tingled along his skin. Between the boles of two black trees came a weave of yellow butterflies. It was the Mother's trail. Plain to see.

Kargen began to follow that trail, striding faster and still faster. Somewhere dim inside of him a voice warned. *Enough! Control!*

"In a moment," he whispered back.

He started to run, making a sound like hyenas laughing, as the false butterflies smashed against him in an hallucinatory wave and crushed themselves on his chest.

--- **6** ---

With silence brooding among them, and the Blazer feeling empty all around, Kyle and Mel and Tru and Raina headed deeper into the Ozarks. Kyle drove, with Tru in the passenger seat and Mel in the back next to a comatose Mother. They headed downhill now along the clearway they had been following, towards an old logging road that Tru swore was ahead of them on the far side of Rattlesnake Ridge. Beyond that, none of them knew.

The army helicopter had been their best hope of getting out of this thing alive. But it was wrecked behind them. And Wahrn and Dan had been wrecked along with it.

Kyle felt certain that Kargen wasn't wrecked, though. He had to have been the one to take Dan's body. "Why" was a question that Kyle didn't want answered, but he wished he did know where the Warkind was now, how close the being was to them. He had no doubt that Kargen still followed their trail.

"How's Raina?" Kyle called to Mel.

It was a moment before she answered, and then her voice waxed thin with loss and fatigue. That was why he'd asked her the question, to turn her mind away from Dan and Wahrn and toward the living. He needed her. They all needed her. All of them that were left.

"The same," she said. Then, in a little stronger voice: "She's in a deep stupor. I felt it when Kargen attacked. She shuddered. Just...turned off. Could be smell driven, I guess. Kargen's scent maybe."

"Will she come out of it?"

Kyle could picture Mel shaking her head to his question.

"I don't know," the vet said. "It's like a healing state. Like how an animal sleeps when it's hurt. But Raina's only injury is her arm. It's not bad enough to cause this. Could be something to do with the baby. I just don't know enough. I don't think I better try to wake her, though."

"What about when night comes?" Tru asked, his words cutting through their exchange, dropping like lead into the strange air of the Blazer.

The deputy looked at Kyle, turned in his seat to gather Mel beneath his gaze. "Her cramps have been coming at night," he continued. "What if she has the baby this time? And the rest of the Warkind come? We could have fifty. A hundred Kargens. What the hell do we do then?"

Kyle didn't have an answer.

--- 7 ---

Some part of her mind knew that Wahrn was dead. And that part grieved. But knowledge and grief were distant things, as was any fear that she had felt of Kargen. Far more immediate were the sensations of life curling within her stomach--heat and movement and pressure, odors that filled her pores from the inside out.

The night before, she had felt the baby moving, had thought her cramps meant that she was about to give birth. But only in her current trance did Raina understand what had been happening. The fetus had been positioning itself, preparing instinctively for its exit into the world. When night fell this time her infant would come.

Already she could feel her stomach muscles beginning to ripple.

--- 8 ---

When dusk came in the forested places, there arose movement. Out of high piled leaves and dark beds of soft loam, the Warkind bands climbed to wakefulness. The cold of the sun-filled day was behind them; the night held a warm promise of violence.

One band went off on the odor trail of its leader, to follow the only Warkind who had ever hunted in the light. Other groups took up their own search for the Mother, just as they had been ordered to by their human commanders.

Only one war-band hesitated, their movements tense as they coiled over and around each other, sparks of static electricity rising from the friction of their hides touching. They waited, for their leader who sat apart. His name was Graye, and he worked and tore at his head-quills as his eyes grew wilder and wilder, as his mind fought a battle between orders and duty. At last he screamed, a pure knife of sound ripping through the darkness, stilling the movements of his Pod.

The band watched as Graye rose and stood poised on clawed feet. And they followed him as he turned away from the trail of the Mother and moved off toward the camp of the soldiers. In that place they would find Mike Russo, and Graye would discharge a debt that was owed.

CHAPTER THIRTEEN
(May 1: Evening)

When the world around him had grown still, and the corridor ended in dead black and a hard sound of bells, he quit running. From behind him rose an icicle wind. He turned. Wished that he hadn't.
--*In the Memory of Ruins*

--- 1 ---

"Looks like Raina's labor's starting," Mel called, her voice loud in the long stillness that had fallen over the diminished group in the Blazer. "I can feel her contractions."

Kyle braked the vehicle to a stop, the headlights cutting a swath of raw yellow through the darkness ahead of them, limning the trees that shouldered close over the narrow logging road they were following. Hours had passed since the wreck of the chopper. Night lay solid all around them. But they had found a lonely road heading in the direction they wanted to go. Then:

"How far apart are the cramps?" Tru asked.

"Fifteen minutes maybe. I'm not sure what that means. It's different for different species. No telling how fast they'll quicken. But they're much more regular than they were the first night. That was some kind of false labor, maybe."

"Can you handle the delivery?" Kyle asked.

"I think so. Yes. But we'll have to stop. I'll need more light. A stable surface. Some room to work."

"There's camping gear between the seats. And a couple of Coleman lanterns. They're pretty bright."

"I could hold 'em for her," Tru said. "I don't know if stopping is a good idea. That Warkind is still out there. Maybe more than one."

Kyle looked at Tru, swiveled in his seat to glance toward Mel, seeing nothing but her silhouette, yet knowing how solid she was

Cold in the Light

even there in the dimness. He flicked on the interior lights so he could see her face.

"Your call," he told her. "Moving? Or still?"

Kyle heard the weight that filled Mel's silence before she replied. And when she spoke he heard how carefully she measured her words. She knew what she asked them all to risk.

"Moving would be dangerous. *If* Raina were perfectly healthy. If there hadn't been any stress. Then yes. But with all that's happened. With her in this trance that I don't understand... I'd be afraid of what the jolting might do to her or the fetus."

"All right," Kyle said. "We stop." His eyes found Tru. "We need a place to defend. A cabin. A cave. Something."

Tru made no argument. His eyebrows twitched in thought. He glanced out the window for a moment, to where the light from the Blazer's headlamps was swallowed in the tree-haunted dark.

"I don't--" he began. "Well..." He shook his head. "There's a... I think. A few miles up there's a sawmill. From the seventies. Abandoned now. We'll have to turn off this road, though. I haven't seen the place in ten years. If it's still standing. Used to hunt through here. It's near a wide place along Lee Creek."

Kyle straightened for a moment at Tru's mention of a mill; images from a nightmare licked his lips. Then he shook the thoughts away as foolish, glanced at Mel. She nodded.

"Ok. We'll try it," Kyle said.

He shoved the Blazer into gear, started them forward. Twenty-five minutes passed in near silence, the only sound an occasional moan from Raina and a soothing mutter from Mel. Then Tru pointed out the turnoff toward the old sawmill. Kyle took it.

The side-road was no more than a pair of worn dirt tracks with a median of grass and short brush. No one had driven over it in a long while. On left and right the forest's limbs raked the vehicle. Beneath it banged dead branches and wiry bushes.

A few hundred yards farther and the dirt ribbons of the road began to fade into yellowed grass. They rolled to a stop in a small meadow dotted with wild flowers that speckled the ground in white and purple blooms beneath the headlights. A few trees grew among the flowers, their shadows looming impossibly huge.

"Shit," Tru said.

"What?" Kyle asked. "What happened to the road?"

Tru turned toward him, his voice cracking. "Dammit! I forgot. I'm sorry. Shit!"

"Forgot what, Tru? Where...the hell...did the road go?"

Tru's eyes met Kyle's and held that gaze. "I screwed up," he said. "The sawmill is there." He jerked his chin toward the darkness ahead of them. "Maybe half a mile. But this road doesn't run to it. We'd have to go on foot from here."

Kyle's chest felt loose beneath his skin; his hands clenched around the slick leather curve of the steering wheel. He wanted to scream at Tru, but he knew part of that was because of fear. And that made him even madder. He didn't want to fear Kargen. The son of a bitch had taken his uncle and two others that had been under Kyle's protection. Kyle wanted Kargen dead. He wanted to do it himself. None of that changed the fact that his heart wasn't really pounding out of *hate* for Kargen.

Kyle forced himself into stillness, forced his fingers to lighten their death grip on the steering wheel.

"Where is the road that does run to it?" he asked, hoping his voice sounded more normal to the others than it did to his own ears.

Tru puffed a wave of air between his lips, but he still didn't look away from Kyle's eyes.

"There isn't one anymore," he said.

Kyle felt his control slip a little. He smashed his left fist against the dashboard.

"Dammit!"

Tru didn't flinch. And Kyle knew why. The man thought he deserved the anger. He didn't. Kargen deserved the anger. And whoever had ordered the hunt on the Whoun. Whoever had carried it out. Tru had done his best. It wasn't his fault that ten years had passed since he'd last come this way. Kyle had made his own mistakes in this thing.

"I'm sorry," Tru said again. And Kyle could tell that the apology was meant for all of them. He and Mel. Even Raina, who couldn't hear it. And for Tru himself.

The rage in Kyle's muscles bled away. His jaws unclenched. He forced a few slow breaths in and out, then turned off the engine and shoved open the Blazer's door. Leaving the headlamps on, he stepped out into the night.

"Let's take a look," he said, reaching beneath his seat to pull out the steel-handled flashlight that he kept there for emergencies. This certainly qualified.

"It's a cliff," Tru said, pushing open his own door, joining Kyle in front of the Blazer, in the twin streams of yellow-white pouring from the headlights.

"I can't believe I forgot." Tru shook his head. "There used to be a road off to the left. But they bulldozed it and planted trees. The road skirted along the cliff and the kids used to ride motorcycles out here. Kinda daredevil it. Till one of 'em rode off the side. That's when they closed it down. I haven't been here much since."

"Straight ahead?" Kyle asked, meaning the cliff.

Tru understood. "Yeah," he said. "Pretty much." He pointed ahead and to the left, then swept his arm toward the right along an imaginary line of about forty degrees.

"The drop-off curves away on the left. Where the road used to run. It fades out there but the trees are too thick for the Blazer. It gets higher as you go to the right. Turns into a real bluff farther down. Maybe four hundred feet sheer."

"All right," Kyle said. "You stay in the Blazer. Watch Mel and Raina. I'll check it out."

"Sure you don't want some company?"

"I want it. But Mel needs it more."

Tru swallowed hard, nodded.

Kyle turned away from the comforting glow of the Blazer's headlights, heading into the colder and lonelier blackness at the edge of the small meadow where they were parked. The light faded quickly behind him and he switched on his flash, holding it in his left hand, his .45 in the right, hammer already back. The beam of the flash seemed watery, and too weak to push aside the weight of the darkness. Kyle fought the urge to sweep the beam from side to side. If he did, his swings would get wilder and wilder, until panic choked him. He forced his breath and his steps to slow.

Toward the end of the meadow the grass grew taller, slapping against his jeans at calf level, letting a coolness and dampness of dew seep through to his skin. He kicked a small rock, heard it skitter in front of him—and then drop away to click against more stones below. He stopped, let his flash shine out ahead, seeing that shine swallowed in the layered blanket of shadows that lay just beyond the cliff that Tru had spoken of.

Kyle's eyes were already dark adapted, and that worried him. Because he couldn't see hardly anything below. The skin at the base of his neck prickled as he imagined something crawling up toward him from out of that darkness, something that was all bones and sharp angles. He shook the thought away, stepped closer to the edge.

Turning the light downward revealed that the "cliff" wasn't exactly a cliff. There was a lip of hard stone, then a drop of several feet. Beyond that he couldn't see much, except that the ground seemed to slope away rather than fall off sharply. He couldn't tell how far down it went, though. Or if trees were growing there.

Kyle moved to the right along the cliff, stopped again where the protruding lip of stone had cracked away in brick-sized blocks. The drop was only a foot or so here, and he could make out a flow of scree just below that was pimpled with larger boulders.

He stepped off the edge, put his foot down on ground mixed from eroded pebbles and thicker slabs of half buried granite. The whole mass shifted a little under his weight, letting him know that a slide would be easy to trigger. And there must have been such a slide not too long in the past, he figured. Because the ground where he stood was slightly concave, as if the material that had once filled this bowl had spilled down the side.

He needed more light.

Stepping back up onto the meadow, Kyle waved his flashlight for Tru, hoping the deputy would take his meaning. He knew Tru had understood when the Blazer's engine turned over with a growl and the vehicle started rolling slowly toward him. He let it get within a few feet of the cliff's edge before signaling a stop. Then he stepped to one side and slapped the hood.

"Hit the brights," he hollered.

An instant later, light flashed out over the threshold of the cliff; Kyle saw their way down. But something lay in their path besides rocks, something that shouldn't have been there.

From a distance of a dozen yards it was easy to put a name to the object. Dan's head. Sitting on a boulder. Waiting for them. The eyes were missing, the sockets filled with the fleshless white skulls of small beasts.

Cold in the Light

--- 2 ---

"The satellite gear is all hooked up and ready to go," Lieutenant Calder Davidson said, reporting to Drake Hammond in the Commander's tent. Hammond had, unofficially, made the man his new "second," to replace the deceased Wayne Teagle.

"Does Suskind know?"

Davidson shook his head. "He knows we're working on it. Not that it's done."

Hammond grinned and clapped the other man on the back. He was having a good time. "Well, go and *tell* him! And escort him there. Just give me five minutes first."

Davidson saluted, checked his watch, left the tent.

Hammond stretched the muscles that had grown stiff with waiting. He unholstered his pistol, slipped the magazine free from the grip. The 9mm was fully loaded, the casings gleaming oily and yellow in the lamp light. Warm colors. But the leads were gray and cold above the brass.

Almost over, he thought.

With the satellite hookup so generously provided by Leonard Suskind, they should be able to quickly locate the Mother Whoun and whatever asshole locals were helping her. He already had a pretty good idea of the group's approximate location, somewhere in the Ozark Mountains above Deerhaven Lake, where one of the search parties had failed to check in at the appointed time. Though, he didn't understand why the chopper that was supposed to cover that quarter of the search area hadn't followed up as ordered.

Mentally, he shrugged. The helicopter didn't really matter. He'd have Davidson look into it, but in two hours all his enemies would be finished anyway--Suskind, Russo. The whole bunch. Then he could bring overwhelming force to bear on the Whoun problem, could sew it up nice and tight.

Hammond slapped the magazine back into the butt of the pistol, then worked the slide to chamber a shell, holding the gun near his ear so he could hear the click of the bullet sliding home in front of the firing pin. His grin never faltered.

--- 3 ---

Leonard Suskind left his tent and followed the officer who had come to tell him that the satellite tracing system was ready to run. He moved quickly, restlessly, almost dancing across the camp toward the temporary, prefab structure that had been set up to house the computers and display screens that were needed to operate the satellite and interpret its data. He wanted this part over with, wanted to find the Mother and bring her in so he could get back to his own experiments at home in Wyoming.

Frustration crowded into his face for a moment. Even after the Mother was returned and the fetus extracted, there would be "loose ends" to deal with, damage to be controlled. He had no liking for such tasks, one reason why he'd faked his resignation in the first place and left the inanities to Mike Russo. There were more important things to spend his time on.

"Hell!" he muttered to himself. Would he ever be able to concentrate on his *own* work?

The sudden anger seemed to spike something hot in Leonard's brain. His eyes located the back of the lieutenant who guided him; he identified the spinal cord, marked it in his mind. And he thought how easy it would be to rip that spine apart and crush the vertebrae. Saliva spurted hot over his tongue and he had to spit to clear his mouth.

Now was not the time.

Now was *not*...the time.

But soon.

--- 4 ----

An enraged Kyle dug a hole deep to bury Dan's head, using the camping shovel he'd brought with him in the Blazer. He had not found the boy's eyes, but after finishing the hole he took out the skulls that Kargen had shoved into the emptied sockets. Weasel skulls, he thought, as he hurled them away into the darkness. Certainly they bore the right kind of teeth, and the pointed snouts with the sharp, sharp bones.

At first it had seemed almost a blessing to know that Dan was truly dead and that they had not left an injured friend to the loving care of the Warkind. And if Kargen meant his display to inspire fear in Kyle, it wasn't going to work. Kyle didn't like being manipulated. It pissed him off, and that made a better feeling than the terror that had been twisting his insides.

But the weasel skulls kept bothering Kyle, as he put Dan's head in the ground and covered it with soil, as he piled rocks on top to keep out the scavengers, as he trudged warily back up the hill toward the Blazer and the warmth of friends. And the longer he thought about the skulls the more his anger drained and something else began to bleed into his bones. Because it suddenly didn't seem so clear that Kargen had been using Dan's head and the weasel heads to scare them. It seemed more and more as if there had been some other reason, a reason that Kyle couldn't fathom, and which troubled him badly because of that.

Kyle halted as he topped the rise and stepped into the beams of the Blazer's headlights. Tru and Mel were waiting for him, standing nervously in that glow, their shadows thrown out over the distance like thin and tattered clouds. He forced a smile to ease their dread. All around the little meadow the wind sniffed in the trees. Across miles came the voice of a dog.

A memory hooked Kyle, something that Mel had said the night before, at a time when Cain still lived and it had seemed as if everything might be all right. "Wolverines and badgers." She'd said the Whoun were related to wolverines and badgers. And if Kyle recalled his biology both those species were members of the *weasel* family.

Kyle knew then that Kargen wasn't killing indiscriminately, and that he wasn't killing just to inspire fear in the ones he hunted. The message in the weasel skulls had never been meant just for Kyle, and Mel, and Tru; it had also been meant for Kargen himself. And perhaps, in a way, for Dan.

Or: Thoughts of his Uncle Cain suddenly filled Kyle's mind, thoughts of Cain's art and of how in that art a peaceable man had explored metaphors for violence and murder. Kyle remembered telling Tru that Cain had never really understood violence, but that he, Kyle, knew it like a friend. Well, Kargen knew it too. More like a lover than a friend. *That* was the message hidden in the skulls. And Kargen wasn't really trying to be understood, only to understand.

Like Cain?

Kyle shuddered at that question, but it spread out behind his forehead and lingered. He closed his lids, opened his mouth and nostrils. There was dust and old pollen, a slick dampness in the wind. Entwined with the other scents came a hybrid odor of sweat and aggression and blood. Kyle knew it as Kargen's smell, left just as deliberately as Dan's head had been.

Kyle opened his eyes again. For the first time, without wanting it, he felt a connection to Kargen, as if he knew the Warkind. Or something about him at least. And he didn't fear what he knew. But he would kill the being anyway. Because he had to.

--- 5 ---

It was dark beyond the tent where Michael Russo and his family were held prisoners, but light glowed inside from a Coleman lantern the guard had given them for playing their games. Earlier, there had been a second guard outside. But something was happening in the camp and the other had been called away.

Mike had heard a distant bustle, the sound of trucks and hammering. Then one of the guards had left. Mike thought about that, sitting still in the tent except for the racing of his mind. He thought about the remaining guard.

Helen soothed Josh and Caleb for the twentieth time, the boys having long since quit the game Mike had taught them. For the past hour they'd been restless as hungry mice. But the game had done its job. He and Helen had talked, more honestly than they had in years, about his work and how that work had pounded cracks into their marriage. Just talking had sealed some of those cracks, though there were many others to be mended.

The talking had also given Mike just the glimmer of an idea on how to get his family out of this tent and this mess. The glimmer had grown bright when the second guard left. The idea began to coalesce into a plan. When he had it all figured, Mike called Helen and the boys over and explained to them another kind of game. He hoped he was going to be good at it. He hoped they all were.

Cold in the Light

--- 6 ---

Mel thought she would have been through with being afraid, that she had been afraid so long all the emotion was burned out of her. But when Kyle told them what he planned to do she found herself afraid again, with the same brassy saliva in her mouth and the same ruffling of acid in her stomach.

"No," she said, her words rushing out. "We can take the road we were on. Raina'll be OK. I can deliver the baby while we're moving."

She didn't speak it but her thoughts added: *No need to risk yourself to get us down that cliff. Not when we've just seen Dan's head on a rock. Not when you just made love to me a few hours ago.*

Kyle only looked at her, and though she knew he had to be feeling the same fears she was, he wasn't willing to run. Even if she was willing to lie to get him to.

Mel tasted a sudden revulsion for herself, something she'd rarely felt before. She remembered when she'd *first* felt it, when at fifteen she ran from Deerhaven because a boy she cared for proved himself a coward. And because her family and friends had showed themselves to be the same. Now it was as if she were trying to mold Kyle into that old image, even though she knew that Raina's chances were worsened if they couldn't find a quiet and stable place for the baby to be born.

A little voice inside her head kept saying she was being too hard on herself, that she'd been too hard on herself twelve years ago. But it was the only way she knew how to be, and too late to change who she was.

And still Kyle's eyes were holding hers. She didn't look away, though she wanted to.

"You're right," she said after a moment. "Scares me is all. The sawmill's still our best hope."

She was glad then that she hadn't turned away from Kyle's gaze. She saw the thing that came into his eyes; she recognized it. Something slipped inside her chest, down between her ribs, something quick and tight. She did look away from that feeling, her eyes turning toward Tru.

Kyle glanced toward the deputy too. Tru shook his head at them, sighed, shook his head again.

"Fuck this," he said. "Let's roll."

Mel laughed as the tension of the moment collapsed in on itself. "Never heard you say *that* word before," she said.

"Seemed like the time."

"The perfect time," Kyle agreed. "But let's get to the 'roll' part." He strode past them to the Blazer, climbed in.

Mel caught his arm through the window before he could start the vehicle's engine. Her eyes found his again. They had made love once. And between then and now there had been hours of desperation and fear. There had been dirt and sweat and pain. But the memory of their loving was clean and good. It had meant something to her, and she'd just seen in his eyes what it had meant to Kyle.

But maybe there wasn't much time to let him know what she felt. So now she whispered those feelings fiercely through the window.

"When this is over we'll get to the part that came before roll," she said. It was Kyle's turn to look away, embarrassed but grinning.

Mel grinned too, stepping back from the Blazer so that Kyle could do what he needed to do. She was still scared, but fear wasn't that important anymore. The "thing" she'd seen in Kyle's eyes had been awareness, his first full awareness of how much she could come to mean to him. She already knew what he could mean to her.

And so Mel watched, as Kyle started the Blazer and turned it around near the edge of the cliff. She watched as he strapped the winch cable around a big-boled oak in the meadow in front of the vehicle. She saw him and Tru remove a comatose Raina, and she helped unload the rest of the packed supplies. Then she sat with Raina, a pistol in her hand, while Kyle put the winch into reverse and backed the Blazer over the side of the cliff.

--- 7 ---

They watched--Graye's band did--from the trees around the soldier camp. Graye had disobeyed the orders given to him by Drake Hammond. He wasn't hunting the Mother as he'd been told. But Hammond had made Michael Russo a prisoner. And less than a year ago Michael Russo had saved the life of a member of Graye's band named Tornik, who squatted now on a limb to Graye's right.

On the night before, in the camp, Russo had reminded Graye of the debt owed for Tornik's life. Though it was not something any Warkind would forget.

But debt alone would not have been enough to turn Graye against orders. Hammond was Kill Leader. So it had been taught to all Warkind for the last fifteen years in the Harbinger compound, taught in the blood of the hunt, taught always with the scent of Drake Hammond in their nostrils as they obeyed his commands.

Only. Graye had smelled Hammond again last night, and the man's odor had changed, had grown rotted with death. And it wasn't the clean death of the hunt or in defense of the Pod or of an ally. It wasn't the blood death given and taken in the surge of battle. It was killing for the sake of killing; it was driving the blade in with the enemy's back turned, and taking joy in the evil of useless slaughter.

Graye understood that Drake Hammond was going to kill Michael Russo. And he couldn't allow that to happen, not in the unclean way in which Hammond would do it.

The huge Warkind released his hold on the trunk of the tree and fell quietly to earth. His penis extruded; he urinated on the dirt, the scent rising rank and pungent on the air. He opened his pores, spilling violent signals to the wind. The rest of his Pod stepped out of their own trees, dropping lightly to the ground like savage black kites.

Graye moved and the others followed, through the thinning trees to the grass at the edge of the camp, through the guards at the perimeter of the tents. The guards were armed and the Warkind put them down dead. But it was clean killing, war killing. The kind that Graye liked.

--- **8** ---

The satellite gear that Leonard Suskind had brought with him to the military base camp had been unloaded from the helicopter and set up in a prefab, a small, ready made metal building knocked together by a squad of soldiers in a couple of hours. Drake Hammond stood behind some boxes in a corner of that building while Calder Davidson brought Suskind in and showed him that the tracking computers were already networked into the Harbinger Project mainframes. Everything was wired and ready to run.

"Just waiting for your word, sir," the lieutenant said to Suskind.

The comment made a nice touch of sarcasm on Davidson's part, Hammond thought. And he had to laugh. Out loud. Loud enough for Suskind to hear and spin on his heels to stare.

When he recognized Hammond, the scientist bent his knees into a half crouch. Hammond couldn't resist giving the man a clown's wave, keeping his hand still while his fingers crooked and wiggled.

"Toot-a-loo," he said, stepping out from his corner. He grinned widely, Davidson joining in.

Suskind exploded from his wide-legged stance, his left hand raking out, fingers clawed, tearing across Davidson's smiling face, tearing away the smile and the lips along with it, dragging a scream from the lieutenant's ravaged mouth. Suskind's right hand darted for the officer's holster, came out gripping a 9mm that he fired once into Davidson's throat.

Hammond's thoughts panicked. *Fast! Too fast!*

He grabbed for his own pistol but could already see the weapon in Suskind's hand turning toward him, the scientist's long finger tightening on the trigger. A shaft of bright pain punched Hammond in the chest, knocking him back and down, his gun spinning from a suddenly nerveless grasp.

His eyes kept working.

There were two other guards in the small building, and two technicians who were just soldiers in lab coats. Both guards had M-16s; both seemed frozen at the sight of a seventy- something-year-old man tearing off another man's face and shooting their commander. In the next few seconds one guard and one tech died as Suskind opened up on them with the pistol, placing his shots precisely into their heads and throats. Neither of them had even started to raise a weapon.

The second technician had his pistol buttoned underneath his lab coat. There was no time to reach for it. He jumped on Suskind from behind, trying to lock the older man's arms beneath his own—and failing. The smarter of the guards ran, screaming for help from outside.

Suskind dropped the emptied 9mm. His arms went over his head, clawing at the man on his back. Hammond saw those hands

Cold in the Light

catch at the tech's scalp, saw the fingers dig beneath the skin and the arms jerk forward viciously to break the younger man's hold.

The tech screamed as he was ripped free of Suskind's back and drawn over the scientist's head to be smashed on the hard floor with a tremendous "whumpf." Dust rose. The building rattled. Hammond *felt* as much as heard the sodden crack of the vertebrae as Suskind twisted the tech's head around till the man faced his own backbone.

The fleeing guard had reached the door, shrieked through it now for help, burst past it into the outside. Hammond felt a savage delight forcing its way through the pain racking his body. A whole platoon manned the camp. In moments they'd be coming. Ready for Suskind. The scientist would die in the midst of his own handiwork.

Already, Hammond could hear more shouts from outside, and the thud of running feet. But Leonard seemed to hear them too and Hammond saw the scientist's face turn toward him, saw the ghastly lips peel back over saliva-wet teeth.

Then something odd struck Hammond about the teeth, and it amazed him that he could think of it when he was shot and near to death. He'd known Suskind for years. The man had false teeth. Only, these weren't. Suskind had grown a new set, one that looked strangely white and sharp.

Then Leonard came for him, on all fours, on his hands and feet as if it were natural for him to move that way. All thoughts except terror fled Hammond's mind. He cried out. Or thought he did. His feet worked at the floor, trying to push his body away from danger, but they only slipped on the newly laid particle board.

The shouting from outside closed in on the building. Hammond's men were coming. But he knew they were too late.

Leonard reached him, leaned over him, grinning. Though there was no mirth in the grin.

Suskind raised his hand, brought it into Hammond's view. The fingers dribbled blood and seemed curled into a feral shape that no human hand should have. Hammond saw a large swelling, a black and blue knot that pulsed along the outside edge of the hand. He didn't know what it was, but in another moment it didn't matter.

Suskind punched two stiffened fingers into Drake Hammond's eyes, punched through the delicate pulp and through the shallow orbital bones directly into the brain. A brilliant flash of light bloomed instantly in Hammond's mind, then winked out like a firefly blinking off. Dimly, Hammond heard a wrecking sound as Suskind tore his way out through the back of the building.

And then there was only one thought.

Can't be!
Can't be!
Can't...
Be.
But it was.

--- 9 ---

"You bastard!" Helen said, her voice clear, and loud enough in the tent to carry easily beyond the nylon walls. "You endanger us! Endanger your children! What the hell did you think you were doing?"

"Mommy don't," Caleb said. "Don't yell at Daddy."

"Yeah, Mom," Josh added. He sounded scared.

"Helen, I--"

"Don't you dare try to explain! To feed me any more of your lies! There's no explanation. *No* excuse. You worthless piece of..."

Helen's voice rose, growing more and more shrill, a harridan's voice that Helen had never used on anyone before. But the guard couldn't know that.

"Hey, shut up in there," the soldier called.

"I'm finished with you, Michael!" Helen yelled. "Filled up with your whining *science*! And your lies! I wish you were dead!"

"Mommy!" wailed Caleb.

And from Joshua: "No, Mom, no!"

The sound of a slap followed, and the quick scream of a child being hurt.

"My god, Helen!" Mike shouted. "It's not Caleb's fault!"

By then the guard had burst through the flap of the tent, had seen little Caleb curled up on the floor with his hands over his head, Helen leaning over him, her cheeks on fire with anger, her voice furious. Mike was grabbing for Helen's arm.

"What the he--" the guard started.

But Helen had rounded on Mike, had slapped him hard across the face. Mike took a step back, tripped and went sprawling. Helen tried to kick him, her voice still shrieking. The soldier grabbed Helen's shoulder, spun her around to face him.

"Hey!" he yelled. "Quit it."

Helen tried to jerk away. "I'll kill him," she spat.

The soldier held onto the woman, trying to calm her down, trying to keep her from turning on *him*. And Mike stood up behind the man and snapped the T-shirt that he'd flooded with fuel oil from the lantern over the soldier's head, drawing it taut and snug. He kicked the soldier behind the knee to collapse the man's leg, then rode the fellow down.

"Get his gun!" he hissed at Helen.

The soldier struggled. His weapon had fallen under him and Helen yanked it away. The man tried to scream--Mike could feel it through the pressure he was putting on the t-shirt--but the fumes from the fuel had to be overwhelming, had to be clogging the fellow's mouth and nostrils, had to be pouring into his lungs.

Certainly the soldier had been trained, was more than a match for Mike Russo. But now he was in a panic, with Mike's weight holding him down. For a terrifying minute, Mike felt as if he were riding a shark. Then Helen reversed the rifle in her hands and slammed the butt of it desperately against the guy's skull. The man slumped, lay still.

Mike whipped the T-shirt off the fellow's head and jumped back, grabbing the M-16 from Helen's hands. He needn't have bothered with the gun. The soldier seemed to be out cold. Mike prodded him with the barrel of the rifle, and when he got no response dropped to his knees to check for a pulse.

"Is he?" Helen asked, her voice quick, her hands worrying her skirt.

Mike blew out a breath. Shook his head. "No. Just unconscious."

He took off the soldier's web-belt, dropping the belt items to the floor, and used it to strap the man's hands and feet together. A torn piece of cloth made an effective gag.

For a moment, Mike simply knelt there beside the soldier, breathing hard, looking at his family. Helen was hugging Caleb to her. Though she hadn't really hit him, even pretending to do so had upset her. It hadn't bothered Caleb. He grinned at the game they'd played. Josh grinned with him.

"Good job," Mike told them all. "But now." He sorted through the gear from the soldier's belt, came up with a knife and drew it from its sheath. The straight steel blade was black, serrated along its non-cutting edge.

"Now we've gotta get out of here," he continued. "We'll cut through the back. Then we'll have to--"

In the darkness beyond the tent a sudden volley of shots exploded, spattering the night with sound. Mike dropped the knife and leaped to his feet, his ears wide. Josh and Caleb had stopped grinning. Helen held both boys as if her touch would save them all.

"They're coming for us!" Josh said.

Mike shook his head, listening. "No. It's something else. Stay here."

He went to the front of the tent, peered out past the flap, then stepped through the opening with the rifle hanging damp in his palms. He carried the gun though he wasn't sure he could ever use it.

Outside, the gunfire had stopped. But there were running shadows at the far side of the camp--toward the helicopter landing sites--and there were shouts of anger and surprise. Somebody fired a flare. It burst and hung against the black sky, dimming the stars, painting reddish-pink edges on the few wispy clouds that floated overhead.

More shooting erupted, and ended as abruptly as the first burst had.

Now's our chance, Mike thought. *We'll have to hit the woods. The highway can't be far.*

He didn't know what was going on in the camp, didn't care as long as it helped him get his family to someplace safe. He started to turn, to call Helen and the boys to join him, and a dark hand came from behind and snatched the rifle from his grip.

Mike jumped, vented a short, sharp bleat of terror. He spun around to find a seven foot shadow looming over him, a shape that moved as silently as a leopard stalking.

Mike stumbled backward, bringing his hands up reflexively to ward off an attack. No attack came. Instead, a familiar voice rattled in his ears.

Cold in the Light

"Not let them kill you," the voice said.

"Graye?" Mike questioned, his chest still viced with fear. And the shadow moved toward him, transformed into a massive Warkind with light colored quills and fur.

"Yes."

"You startled me." Mike said.

"Sorry," Graye said. He stood very still now, as if he had carried out his assigned task by arriving here and was waiting for further instructions.

"Mike?" Helen called from inside the tent. "Mike!"

"It's all right, Hon. Maybe we've got a friend out here."

Mike looked at Graye, knowing the Warkind could see his face far better than any human would be able to see it in this light.

"Do I have a friend?" he asked.

"Not let them kill you," the Warkind said again.

"Then. My wife's inside. My sons. Can you get us out of here? Is your band with you?"

Graye nodded, a gesture he'd learned from humans. "They are seeing what the shooting is."

Mike smiled. "Good."

As if called, two more Warkind materialized out of the flickering grays and blacks cast by the flare drifting over the camp. Graye turned toward them. They moved slowly around him, their tongues clicking in their mouths. Mike's nose picked up a mesh of strange odors that blew quickly away.

Graye scraped the dirt with a foot. "Speak it," the Pod leader barked.

"Commander die," one of the other Warkind blurted.

Mike Russo's ears caught those words. He knew only one man who the Warkind might be referring to.

"Drake Hammond is dead?" he asked.

The three Warkind looked toward him, puzzled.

"That is what he said," Graye replied.

"Who killed him?"

Graye looked at the Warkind who had spoken before.

"Scientist," the being said.

"Scientist?" Mike asked. "What scientist?"

"White hair. Strange smell."

White hair! Mike thought. "You mean Leonard Suskind?"

The being clacked his teeth. "Yes. That one," he said. "The soldiers shoot at him. They don't hit him. He runs."

"My God," Mike muttered to himself.

An idea captured him. A bold and risky idea. Two days ago he never would have considered it. But things had changed. More than one thing. With Leonard fleeing and Hammond dead, the rest of the soldiers might listen to reason, especially if he had the Warkind at his back. There might be an easier way than he'd thought to get his family out of this mess. And maybe a way to save the Mother and anyone helping her.

"Graye," he said. "I want two of your band to stay with this tent and protect my wife and kids. Can they do that?"

Graye nodded.

"And the rest of you will back me up. I've gotta go to the soldiers. Talk to them. With Hammond dead I think they'll listen."

"We will kill them?" Graye asked.

Mike shook his head. "No. We kill only if they try to hurt us. I don't think they will."

Graye stood silent for a moment and Mike tried through the shadows to make out the Warkind's expression. He couldn't. The flare that had been bright in the sky was fading, and in another instant it sputtered out and night slapped down across the camp again.

The big Warkind moved closer, nodded his upper body in agreement with Mike's words. Mike stuck his head back in the tent, kissed Helen and the boys and explained what he was going to do, what he had to try. Then, with Graye beside him, he strode purposefully toward the far side of the camp and the site of the recent disturbance. Other members of Graye's band drifted to join them, moving together like clots of predatory darkness on the hunt.

Mike wished someone would strike another flare, if only so that human-made light might hide the raw flickering of Warkind eyes in the air all around him.

Cold in the Light

--- 10 ---

Leonard Suskind lay flat on his belly beneath the spreading lower limbs of a cedar tree. He watched the last of the flare's glow turn from pink to gray to dark, and it reminded him of how Drake Hammond's body had seemed to shrink in on itself in death. He never should have granted Hammond any part of what he had discovered. The man was not worthy.

Hadn't been worthy, he amended.

Barely five years into the Harbinger Project, Leonard had realized the kind of genetic treasure chest he sat on. Yes, the Whoun-- the Warkind at least--did have military applications, which was what the government primarily wanted. But there existed far more wealth in the species than just a few fancy warriors. It had taken another ten years before Leonard could extract the first tiny bit of riches from the chest. The pace of that extraction had grown, though. In the last year he'd really started to spend.

Leonard's clothes felt tight and he stiffened his shoulders and split his jacket down the back. He began chewing on his tie as he remembered the beauty that he'd discovered in the Whoun.

The Whoun had immune systems that could handle a viral load big enough to choke a horse. They had incredible physical power and incredible sensory capabilities. Their smell sense was a thousand-fold better than that of any human, their hearing as good as a dog's, their vision as capable of detail detection as a raptor's but with a wider range that extended from infrared to ultraviolet.

So they had a little problem with light sensitivity, brought on by centuries of evolution as a burrowing species. That had proved a plus actually. After he'd genetically enhanced that tendency in them as infants, the already nocturnal Whoun had even developed a kind of fear of the light. It was a method of controlling them, as well as helping to keep them away from the prying diurnal eyes of human beings.

Leonard spat as a bad taste suffused his mouth. He glanced down, saw that he'd gnawed the tip of his thin brown tie into threads. He put his hand to his mouth, ran a finger over the new teeth that had first begun to appear only a few weeks ago. He smiled. Just in the last twelve hours those teeth had filled in and sharpened. He owed the Whoun this one.

What was important about Whoun genes was that they spliced easily into modern mammalian chromosomes, and once in place they rapidly began to assert a dominating influence on the host's genetics. Leonard thought it happened that way because genetic commands in the Whoun were routed through their endocrine system and its potent hormones, and because Whoun hormones were earlier and simpler versions of those around today. It was as if the more recently evolved hormone systems still recognized all the old biological keys from the days of the Whoun. And the doors controlling physical structure were thrown open.

It had been easy a few years back to help Drake Hammond grow some unusual skin glands, just enough to give the colonel the right scent for the Warkind. Hammond had been in charge of evaluating the military capabilities of the Warkind since he'd taken over as head of the Special Forces in 1987. But having the "smell" had done more to bind the Whoun's soldier caste to him than any amount of training.

Leonard was glad now that he hadn't given Hammond any other enhancements, though the man's odd behaviors and constantly changing body odor suggested that the glands had begun to alter on their own somehow. It had felt good to bleed the son of a bitch; killing him had been a needed step anyway.

Under his cedar, Leonard shifted position. He hadn't gone far from the camp, less than a hundred yards. The soldiers had not come into the woods after him, though they had seen him fleeing and had tried to shoot him down. Without the Warkind they could never have hunted him successfully in the dark forest. Without Hammond they wouldn't even have the guts to try. Not after what the one guard had seen him do to the others in the prefab.

But now it was quiet among the tents. Silence had thrown a caul over the night. That made him uneasy. He wanted to know what was going on, what the bastards were planning. He shifted his body again, then pushed himself in anger out from under the cover of the cedar and moved in a crouch toward the perimeter of the trees.

Something was happening near the prefab building; he could see movement, soldiers standing guard all around the outside. They were restless, like dogs that could sense a storm coming. Leonard could smell their sweat; a chuckle escaped his lips. Did they expect him to attack them single-handedly? He wasn't that stupid. A Warkind might have tried it. But he wasn't a Warkind.

He was better. Smarter. And unafraid of the light.

But what were the bastards doing in that building where the satellite tracking computers were located? He moved closer, circling to his left, toward the hole that he'd torn in the back wall during his escape. He smiled when he saw that they hadn't yet thought to cover it. He'd certainly stirred them up.

Leonard went to his belly in the dew-damp grass at the edge of the trees. From there he inched forward, using fingers and knees and toes. The grass stood over him like a hunting blind, protecting him from the eyes of his prey, and he moved slowly to keep it from swaying. In a moment he could hear voices from inside the building. In another he could make out the words being said.

A lone sumac bush made a broader cover and he rose to a crouch behind it, glanced through it toward the building. He had already heard the voice, and now he saw Mike Russo through the hole he himself had ripped. His heart triphammered into a rage. Russo was no longer a prisoner. There were Warkind with him. And the soldiers were listening to what he said, as if the loss of Drake Hammond and the death of their friends had sucked their spines out like marrow.

"But the technicians are dead," one soldier protested, a lieutenant by his uniform.

Leonard wondered if this was the highest ranking officer left. Probably. With Hammond dead. And the lieutenant that Leonard himself had killed. He was almost certain Teagle was dead, as well, likely at Hammond's hands.

Russo shook his head. "Doesn't matter about the techs. I can access the satellite. In ten minutes we can be ninety-nine percent certain where the Mother is."

"But then to--" the lieutenant started.

Russo cut him off. "I already told you. We go get her. And whoever's with her. And we blow this project out of the water. I know one of the television station managers in Fort Smith. He'll put us on the air. We'll show the world a Whoun. There'll be no covering up after that."

The lieutenant shook his head now. "I don't know. The Commander--"

"Your commander is dead!" Russo snapped. "He died disobeying direct orders. He killed people for Christ's sake! And you saw what Suskind did to your men. Things are out of hand. It has to stop here. We can't afford secrecy anymore."

For a moment, Leonard thought the lieutenant would deny Russo's words. But there was no one there to stiffen his backbone. Soldiers stood all around, stroking their weapons, stroking their faces, their eyes darting. But their fear stank up the air. None of them seemed to have the will to act on their own.

And Russo wasn't finished.

"Drake Hammond was a paranoid psycho, Lieutenant. You saw his behavior. I can't blame you for obeying him. You couldn't know the whole story. Now you do. I am the director of this Project. You will do what I tell you or I will relieve you of your duties. Are we clear on that?"

Leonard watched as the soldier lowered his gaze, and the scientist knew that Russo had won. It wasn't to be tolerated. Russo had always been smart, but never strong. Leonard couldn't let him be strong. Though, he remembered a time when he'd liked the young Michael, when he'd hoped for great things from him. Before the discoveries of Harbinger.

Leonard shook the old thoughts away, let the new ones back in. He couldn't kill Russo now. Not with the Warkind in the building with him. But there would be a time when Mike wasn't expecting an attack, when he'd think himself safe. Leonard could wait for that moment. It wouldn't be long off.

The scientist dropped to his belly again, backed slowly toward the woods until he could rise within the safety of the shadows. He wondered how long it would be before Russo thought to release the Warkind on his trail. Leonard wasn't quite ready for that. He had something to do first.

He turned away from the main part of the camp, moved quickly toward the area where the Jeeps were parked. He needed one of them. There was a little more killing to do. For the first time in a long time Leonard noticed that he had an erection.

PART FOUR

THINGS END IN BLOOD

Walking, they make the sound of chimes,
and of watches melting.
They move like animated paintings
of ochre, mauve, and anil,
wailing like sand against stone
sculptures in the desert.
Their smell is ripe,
pregnant with hate in a silent place.

And one day they'll come out,
in the memory of ruins.

CHAPTER FOURTEEN
(May 1: Night)

The open space behind him had filled with crawling bones and flowers that sprouted legs. It smelled thick with vomit. He felt his chest tighten as ribs began to push out on his skin.
--In the Memory of Ruins

--- 1 ---

Kyle felt the jar as the back wheels of the Blazer slipped off the lip of stone that marked the top of the hill and dropped a foot onto the pebbled slope below. He had been expecting the bump, though, and held the vehicle straight, letting it keep rolling backward, letting the winch cable unwind in front of him.

The undercarriage scraped, an ugly, steel-wool sound, and the Blazer hung for a second. Kyle fed the engine a sliver of gas to bring the wheels up. The obstruction slipped past; they were moving again. The front end dropped abruptly off the rock lip, jarring Kyle hard a second time, but the winch sat high on the bumper and though the cable groaned and creaked it kept running straight and true up toward the tree around which it hooked. He was on the slope of the hill now.

To Kyle's left this "cliff" grew steep and sharp, but here it made more of a grade, at an angle of about 45 degrees, with the rock face worn down by years of crumble and slide, crumble and slide. He could never have driven down it. The scree was too slippery, and mixed with loose soil eroded down from the meadow above. The mass of the Blazer would have turned the combination to fluid. But with the winch holding the major part of the vehicle's weight, the side of the hill stayed solid beneath the wheels.

Mostly.

With his window down and the engine idling, Kyle *did* hear a trickle of pebbles and sand flowing past the Blazer. Bigger rocks, gravel-sized, hammered the undercarriage as they rolled beneath the truck.

Kyle prayed for the slope to hold together. The cable already held all the weight it could. If an avalanche dropped the ground out from under him then the added pressure would tear the winch system apart. The Blazer would flip over, and tough as the vehicle was, Kyle didn't know if it would keep him alive as it crashed to the bottom of the hill.

The nose of the Blazer rose slightly. The steepest part of the grade lay under him now. The trickle of the sand had grown louder, an awful whisper of friction that tightened his scalp like fingernails scraping over slate. Sweat ran on his face, down his back, into his eyes. He blinked to clear his vision, not daring to take a hand off the steering wheel to wipe away the wet.

Hold together, he thought. *A little longer.* Something wet slapped Kyle's cheek. He thought at first it was an insect. Then another object flew through the open window and dropped in his lap. He slammed on his brakes, punched the button that stopped the winch. The cable groaned. The Blazer slipped a little, the rear end twisting to one side, then caught itself and held in a shush-shush of sliding sand.

Kyle flipped on the interior lights. Looked down.

He had found Dan Case's missing eyes.

--- 2 ---

Mike Russo hunched forward over the computer keyboard and began punching in commands, watching the swift and steady scroll of electronic letters and numbers across the CRT screen in front of him. With the two military technicians dead, he was probably the only person in camp who could up-link to a satellite through Leonard's equipment. That would give them a trace on the Mother and on whomever was helping her.

The machine gave a beep to indicate that his commands were being accepted. A graphic popped up on the screen to show the satellite dish mounted on the prefab's roof. It was tracking, looking for an eye in the sky to lock on. Mike tapped in a few more orders, leaned back to let the hardware/software, which was remote linked to the big mainframes at the Harbinger compound, do the rest of the work.

For the first time in long days, Mike felt in control of something, in charge of one part of his life at least. Drake Hammond lay dead, and without their charismatic leader the other soldiers were listening again to what their civilian "Director" had to say. Mike had never before been so happy to claim that title, though he knew it helped his standing to have Graye's war-band backing him up.

A search had been conducted for Leonard Suskind but nothing had been found except a missing Jeep that Mike suspected Leonard of stealing. He could scarcely credence the other stories he'd heard about Leonard. The way the old man was supposed to have moved--like an animal. The way he was supposed to have killed-- coolly, viciously, joyfully.

It didn't seem possible. It *wasn't* possible if you followed the physical rules of what humans were supposed to be able to do. And yet, Mike had known that something was wrong with Leonard. The man was in his late seventies but hadn't looked it. In fact, he looked younger than when Mike had last seen him, three years earlier. And the man's hearing and eyesight had been phenomenal for his age.

There was only one possible answer that Mike could think of. Leonard had made a breakthrough. And it had to be genetic. The man was brilliant, after all. At fifty he'd been on track to win a Nobel prize, and only the secrecy surrounding the Harbinger Project had kept that accomplishment from him.

Mike didn't know the full story of what Leonard had achieved but he knew how to discover it, even if they failed to catch the man. While in Arkansas for Harbinger, the city-boy scientist had gotten a taste for woods, and hills and isolation. Since retiring, there was supposed to be land and a cabin somewhere in Wyoming that Leonard had bought and moved to.

Mike figured the retirement as an excuse for Leonard to get on with his own work, and the older man had always been a careful and meticulous researcher. Anyone finding his cabin would find his notes. And his secret. If they knew how to look.

All that could come later, though. The immediate need was to find the Mother and bring her in. Before the baby was born, Mike hoped. Soon after, if it had to be that way.

Cold in the Light

Then it would be time to take the Harbinger Project to the world. It was almost over. Hammond was dead, Leonard isolated. There was still Kargen's band to worry about but Mike felt sure they were no danger to the Mother, despite what Lanny Burns had tried to argue.

The computer bleeped, distracting Mike from a sudden sadness that thoughts of Lanny had conjured. Maps and statistical tables bloomed across the over-sized monitor, sending unnatural hues flickering over Mike's face. The up-link was made. The satellite responded, turned its machine gaze downward toward a small piece of a smallish state called Arkansas. Not hesitating, never tiring, it narrowed its search, eliminated irrelevant data, narrowed its search again.

Mike's own thoughts narrowed. Though the feds would never say so, he'd be cutting his throat as a government scientist if he went public about the Whoun. No more government jobs. Ever. No more money from National Science Foundation grants, or from any other such agency. He found that the thoughts didn't bother him much. There would be places to hire him. He could teach. He'd always been good with students. Or there were private labs that would pay enormous sums for his skills.

Maybe he'd write a book.

The computer screen went black in front of him, then filled again with a dense grid of lines over a background map of cool greens and blues. He knew enough to pick out the contours of hills, the winding of streams. Glowing like sharp jewels, dozens of orange-red dots stood out against that background, each one marking the heat of a running vehicle. Most were moving, crossing grid lines even as he watched.

Mike looked at the lieutenant next to him, who was now the highest ranking officer left in the Harbinger security forces. The man's name was William Morgan and Mike had appointed him new commander. The fellow stood ready with the duty logs for the search operation that still went on, and one by one he ticked off the Jeeps and choppers that were involved in the hunt for the Mother. In the end, only one bright dot remained unaccounted for. It was moving, down beyond a massive hill toward the line of a stream that Mike didn't know the name for.

"Got 'em," Morgan exulted.

Intellectually, Mike knew the lieutenant was right. They had them. So why, he wondered, did his thoughts keep saying:

Not yet.

--- **3** ---

Kyle felt himself go rigid as he looked down at one of Dan Case's eyeballs. The thing that had hit him on the side of the cheek must have been the other one. It had fallen below the seat. This one had landed in his lap. He could see it clearly. It seemed so inhuman an object, like a dull pearl or a partially melted marble. But he could see the wet spot that it left on his jeans, the wet spot that told him it had once been alive.

He wanted to brush the thing from his legs, hurl it away. He didn't. He reached down slowly and picked it up, held it where he could see it--though his skin recoiled. The pale blue of the iris looked painted on. Something punctured the pupil between the blue, like a nail in a balloon. It was the canine tooth of some small beast. Weasel or mink, he figured.

Holding the eye, Kyle turned his head to look out the Blazer's window, knowing what he would see. Kargen was there in the shadows, a dozen feet away, standing upright beside the round, gray bulk of a boulder. The creature's eyes shone yellow with odd swirls of white and red. Kyle stared hard at the being, knew he was being watched in turn. But he made no effort to draw his pistol. And the Warkind made no move toward him.

For seconds the tableau held. Then Kargen turned, stepped behind the boulder, disappeared. The smells of rust and acid hung behind, fading away more slowly than the being that had released them.

From the top of the hill came a hollow shout. From Tru.

"Kyle! You OK?"

Kyle didn't feel like answering. He blinked his headlights instead, saw Tru wave in acknowledgment. A punch of a button and the winch started again. Kyle released the brakes, felt the Blazer straighten out as he rode the machine all the way to the bottom of the grade. Old landslides had spread talus out from the foot of the hill, keeping down the trees and making an open space where Kyle could stop.

Cold in the Light

He killed the engine, got out, started back up the grade using the winch cable to pull himself along. Deciding not to tell Tru and Mel about seeing Kargen just yet, Kyle took a quick moment to bury Dan's eyes. The others already knew Kargen was around anyway, and Kyle wasn't really worried about the Warkind jumping them while they brought Raina to the Blazer. The being had moved downhill, into the trees. But that wasn't why Kyle felt the way he did.

No! Kyle knew Kargen. They had become intimate in a way that only enemies were intimate. It didn't mean they could read each other's minds. It was more a matter of acts and movements, and smells. Kyle felt sure that Kargen would not attack again until after Raina gave birth. And that would be the final attack. One way or another. It was what Kyle would have done if their roles had been reversed.

Twenty minutes later the small group was on its way. To drag Raina and the supplies down the hill they'd put together a makeshift travois by strapping a tarp between two stout limbs hatcheted from a tree. The winch had been rewound and Tru had located the piece of road that led toward the sawmill, the piece beyond where the bulldozers had cut in closing off the old cliff road. Kyle pushed the Blazer over that brush and dirt trail at the best speed he could manage. They didn't have much time.

"Seven minutes apart," Mel had told him when they'd put the Mother into the back of the vehicle "And speeding up quick."

They had to get Raina to the sawmill, get set up for the delivery, which meant light and fresh water. And they had to prepare a defense against Kargen. A barricade maybe. Or something that Kyle hadn't thought of yet.

Then they came out of the woods and Lee Creek loomed before them, a narrow, dark line with spatters of faint light breaking from small ripples in the water. To the right, along the curve of the bank, stood the sawmill. The moon had just begun to rise and the faded wood of the old mill gleamed pale under that orb.

Kyle gasped. And ignored the others when they looked at him with a question. He had never been to this place before. But he had seen this mill. Last night he had seen it, in a dream of terror and death, a dream of drowned places and torn bodies and hungry things.

"Darkness is a lovely place," Cain had said to him in that dream.

Kyle wondered for an instant if his uncle had meant *this* place. Then he shook his head.

Don't be stupid, he thought to himself. *It's coincidence. Dreams don't speak to you. Old sawmills all look alike.*

He kept driving, pulled up in front of a door that hung open on its rusted hinges to leave a gap like a missing tooth in a rotted mouth. Beyond the door the moonlight didn't enter. Kyle heard the slap of the nearby creek against its banks.

He shuddered.

--- **4** ---

Where trees faded into stream bank, Kargen crouched on his clawed feet, watching from a stand of cattails as the Blazer pulled up to the sawmill with the Mother inside of it.

My female, the thoughts savaged. *Mine!*

He had followed her easily from the site of the wrecked helicopter to the stone place where he'd laid the human boy's head--trailing the vehicle's scent, cutting across hills and hollows that those in the machine had to go around by road. At several times during the last few hours he could have swept into oblivion one or more of the humans that rode with the Mother. But there was a risk. One of the males with her--Kyle--was very good. Kargen had seen that at the chopper when he'd tried and failed to kill the man.

Yes, the human woman had shot him at the last when he might have had them all. He could still feel the pulse of her lead in his chest. But the man had been quick, and ready for him, and the outcome between them had been in doubt. And though he might have killed Kyle on the hill instead of offering him the boy's eyes, Kargen had chosen at that moment to let it go. To wait. Until the small band reached the sawmill. Until the Mother gave birth.

Kargen was not sure of his own motives. Perhaps they were legion. The human female seemed to be some type of doctor, and she could help the Mother now better than he could. He knew also that he was afraid, though he didn't think of fear as a factor. He'd felt it before, had liked it, the energy it gave.

No! There was something else. He remembered seeing the Mother's pheromones as butterflies. He remembered gibbering shapes in the trees and pale lights, and deer that ran rotted through

Cold in the Light

the woods. And there were the weasel skulls and eyes like soft acorns. And blood and semen, and canvases of flesh. He had thought some of it real and some of it not. But now he knew. All of it was real. Inside his skin. All of it had been leading to this moment.

Up ahead lay the sawmill, black inside, so much like the Darkhome where the first Whoun baby of this age *should* be born, where his female *would* become his. Even her Podcyst was with her. Not the one she had begun with. One to end with.

Kargen reached up and snapped off several cattail heads, then crushed the soft brown cylinders into a fluff that he smeared all down the length of his body. When the child was here, that would be his time. The Mother would be awake then, be ready for him to come to her. But so would Kyle be ready, and Kyle knew his scent.

The Warkind wanted to see Kyle again too, wanted to look into the man's eyes the way he had on the hill. There would be fear but no misunderstanding between them. One of them could die then. *Would* die. Kargen did not intend for it to be himself, did not intend to give Kyle any chance to know he was coming by smelling him.

And after, there would be the Mother.

Kargen felt his genital pouch spread, felt his testicles and penis extrude. He looked down on himself, at the madness of his flesh. The tip of his penis opened. A tiny head poked out, a snarling head of white bones the size of a pearl.

Kargen no longer thought in terms of hallucination versus reality. When the Mother's pheromones had first affected him in this way he had embraced the strange visions, had taken them in his nostrils and mouth. When he'd realized what was happening he had blocked them, forced them away. Now he did neither. They just *were*. Part of his body, part of his thoughts.

Everything that his mind could conceive could be made real. And he would own it all.

Kargen turned and slipped into the flowing water of the creek, pulling himself along the bank toward the Blazer and the mill.

--- 5 ---

Mike Russo watched the bright dot float over the computer generated landscape, knowing that it represented a vehicle of some kind, and that it probably contained those he sought. Just ahead of the dot on the screen ran a contour that marked a streambed, and along the bank the small light stopped moving.

"Yeah, we got 'em," Lieutenant Morgan repeated.

"Maybe," Mike said. "I want three helicopters ready to go in ten minutes. But no more than fifteen soldiers. That'll match with the numbers of Graye's Warkind."

He turned and stared at the lieutenant standing next to him. "You understand?" It wasn't a real question.

The man nodded quickly but Mike wasn't ready to let up just yet.

"There'll be court-martials all around the place when this thing is over," he said. "But just maybe they'll find that the guilty ones are already dead. If I get exactly what I want. *When* I want it. Now do you understand?"

The man nodded again, more carefully, his eyes looking at Mike but offering no challenge. Mike believed him this time. He turned to Graye, who bulked huge at his left side. Behind the Warkind stood Helen and Joshua and Caleb, surrounded by a dozen other massive gray forms.

"My friend," Mike said to Graye. "Can Tornik and the others take my family to the helicopters? Watch over them as they did at the tent? We'll be leaving in a few minutes. To make sure the Mother is safe. I'll want you with me."

Graye nodded, signaled to the Warkind guard that protected Helen and the boys.

"Mike?" Helen asked.

Mike moved over to his wife, took her hand in one of his, let his other hand stroke the heads of his sons.

"It's OK," he said. "I know what I'm doing. Maybe for the first time in a long while."

Helen smiled. It was a weak and watery smile. But Mike didn't care. It was still good to see. He squeezed her hand and let go. His sons hugged him and he hugged them back harder. Then he watched the three of them walk out of the building with Warkind all around them.

Gotta handle this just right, Mike thought. No matter what, the Warkind would protect his family. He knew that. But what about Raina? The Mother? Would she listen to him with Graye at his side? Could he even get close enough to make her listen? She had no reason to trust him.

And even if she believed him when he claimed ignorance of what Leonard and the others had been doing to her and the baby, would she agree with his plan to make the Whoun public?

"She's got to," he muttered under his breath. *It's the only way now. Fly into Fort Smith. Thirty-five miles maybe. The TV station a little farther. Let everyone see a Whoun. Make them so big God couldn't cover them up.*

A soldier hollered from the doorway of the prefab. "Sir, the choppers are ready."

Mike raised his hand to indicate that he'd heard. He walked swiftly back to the table where the satellite tracking computers were seated. A few keystrokes downloaded the main grid map onto a laptop that he could carry with him. The smaller machine was meant for that purpose, to serve as a portable memory of the Mother's location.

With the laptop closed and held in his hand like a suitcase, Mike stood for a moment, staring at the main computer system and at the auxiliaries that could help connect it to satellite spies all around the world. He thought of all the thousands of dollars that the equipment on this table must have cost. And he smiled.

Then he reached out and shoved the table over backward, not waiting to see the results before he turned and headed for the helicopters that would take him to the Mother.

--- 6 ---

Kargen's war-band followed swiftly along the scent trail of their leader, moving like an animated wind through the forest, flowing around tree trunks, leaping over fallen logs, rushing as quick as air through the night. They passed a ruined helicopter and the torn bodies of humans, one of them without a head. But they did not stop.

The kill-smell on each of the dead bore the mark of Kargen, and it injected enough of a stimulant to quiver their war-spikes and raise spines all across their heads. It made them run faster, and faster, down hills and up, until they crossed a road of bare ruts through the dark woods.

The band's warriors no longer cared about the strange odors underlying their leader's scent pattern. Blood and violence made too heady a perfume. It overwhelmed any reservations they might have had. Kargen killed, and because of that he led. They only wanted to join with him in hauling down the prey, in tearing it to froth. Their teeth hurt with the thought.

Then, as one, the band slowed, came to a drifting stop in a meadow where wild flowers of purple and white bloomed. A wetness flared their nostrils, the raw signature of a not too distant stream. And painted among the wet were the threaded fragrances of Kargen and the Mother and of humans. And, too, of a place.

A killing ground.

--- 7 ---

Kyle stared at the sawmill. And he didn't want to go in. It felt too much like his dream of last night. In that nightmare he'd seen this very door, askew on its rusted hinges with glass panes shattered. He'd seen these same weathered boards, beaten by wind and rain into a uniform gray. Even a ramp led up to the building. Just as in the dream.

Kyle shut off the engine and got out of the Blazer, leaving the headlights shining. With the growl of the motor gone, the night should have been alive with more natural sounds. They just weren't there. No birds. No frogs along the creek. All he heard was the occasional slap of a fish breaking the surface of the water. His hand slid down to the butt of his Colt Double Eagle, making sure the .45 still hung where he'd put it.

Tru had gotten out as well, was shining his flash around the tall grass and weeds that bellied up to the non-stream side of the building. Next, his light probed over the sawmill itself, checking for damage with a yellow finger.

"Still standing better than I figured it might," Tru said.

"Yeah," Kyle agreed.

He went around to the rear door of the Blazer, opened it to look in at Mel and Raina. Mel stared back at him, her hands resting on

Raina's stomach, moving softly over the mounded, pebbly surface as if to ease the Whoun's labor pangs.

"How far apart now?" he asked.

"Three minutes or so. I think we have less than half an hour total. Maybe twenty minutes."

"All right. But I have to check this place out first."

He jerked his chin toward a pile of blankets and other materials in one corner of the Blazer's rear area.

"Can you pass me that nylon bag? The green one."

He took it from her as she did so, unzipped it and reached inside to pull out two Coleman Dual Fuel lanterns. He lit one, leaving the other sitting for now, and closed the hatch as he turned back toward the mill. He'd brought camping gear with him to Arkansas as a defense mechanism--knowing how much his Uncle Cain liked to rough it in the woods. It had never occurred to him he'd be using the gear so soon, without Cain, and for a purpose such as the one that animated him tonight.

Tru had gone around to the front of the Blazer, waited there for him.

"Whatta you want me to do?"

"Stay in the truck with Mel and Raina," Kyle told him. "I'm gonna look around inside." He held up his palm with all fingers spread. "Five minutes! If I take longer. Or unless I yell for more time--"

He stopped talking, not knowing what advice to give. If Kargen took him out, and Tru and Mel couldn't use the sawmill, then he didn't know what the two of them would do. He didn't know what they *could* do.

Tru seemed to understand. He only nodded at Kyle's sudden silence and climbed back into the Blazer, getting behind the wheel in case they needed to make a run for it.

Now, faced with the reality of going in the building of his dream, Kyle found his fear intensifying. He tried to make the rational portion of his mind reassert itself. This was *not* going to be the same building inside. The world hadn't altered *that* much.

Had it?

Forcing aside the thoughts, Kyle strode up the access ramp and stepped through the gaping door, holding the lantern up in his left hand to throw its blue-white glare toward every corner of the place. The fuel-oil light couldn't quite handle the job, though it tried. Its gaseous glow was certainly far stronger and farther reaching than any flashlight. Kyle felt thankful for that as he moved into the mill, scarcely aware that he'd drawn his .45 into his right hand.

The inside of the building looked like a huge barn without stalls, its concrete floor littered with leaves, and twigs and pieces of broken junk. Just like in his dream, a narrow, metal I-beam ran the length of the old building, fading away into the shadows that still clustered thickly at the other end of mill.

But with the I-beam, the resemblance to his bad dream ended. He'd used a block and tackle in the dream. None hung here. And there were no stairs to the left of the door like the ones he'd seen himself climbing the night before. There wasn't even an office at this end of the building, though he caught the shine of glass at the far end that probably marked such a room. He started in that direction, feeling relieved despite himself at the differences between this mill and its nightmare brother.

There was little time for relief, though. Already the clock had ticked away one of the five minutes he'd allotted himself. It took him another thirty seconds to stride the length of the open area and reach the office he'd expected to find. It was fronted by a row of glass windows with all the panes intact.

Not many vandals here, he thought.

The office actually sat on a concrete slab several feet above the ground floor area. Four wooden steps led up to it and Kyle followed them to find the office door closed but not locked. He pushed it open, hearing only a faint squeal of rust. Compared to the outside, the inside of the old sawmill was in good shape--protected as it was from the elements.

Kyle stepped through into the rectangular room, his feet scuffing through dust. He saw light colored spots on the concrete where furniture had once sat. A desk probably. And filing cabinets. A broken chair leaned in one corner.

There were two other doors. The one on the right was of metal, padlocked and set flush against the outside wall--almost certainly a way for the boss to come in without walking through the work area. The other door was of wood and lay to the left, against an inside wall, and judging from the length and width of the building another room hid behind it.

Storage area, he figured.

He crossed to it, tried the doorknob and found it locked too, then stepped back and smashed a foot against the latch. The dry wood splintered all the way to the floor but the door didn't swing open. A second kick finished the job and Kyle pushed past the portal into a small room with shelves lining it on three sides.

It *was* a storage area. Empty now. But what interested Kyle was the trapdoor situated in the middle of the floor. A single bolt held it shut, not a very strong bolt.

A memory from Kyle's dream crawled up his spine and spat a chill onto his neck. He couldn't forget what had lain beneath the foundation of that other mill--the writhing bodies of his friends hanging like wet bags on the wall, and his uncle Cain grinning amid them, claiming their pain as his handiwork.

"Darkness is a lovely place," Cain had said. And: "You showed me, Kyle. Showed me, showed me."

Kyle wanted to clap his hands over his ears, wanted to scream to drown out the voice. He did neither. The voice wasn't real. The nightmare was gone and there would be no ravaged human shapes dangling like cocoons below this trapdoor when he opened it, no white worms to seek entrance through his mouth. But maybe there would be a place to hide--to defend Raina while she bore her child. The rest of the building was too open, the tin and plank walls not sturdy enough to resist a Warkind. Below his feet might lie just the haven they sought.

Kyle stepped forward, kicked the trapdoor bolt to loosen any accumulated rust. He dropped to his knees, setting the lantern down to worry at the bolt with his fingers. It resisted, then slid free. He grabbed the handle and pulled open the door, gave it a push to let it fall with a slap on its back on the concrete floor.

A smell of wet musk bled up from the blackness below. In that dark he thought he heard breathing. It had to be the wind coming in through some kind of ventilation ducts. He lowered the lantern through the hole in the floor, bending down to peer around the small area beneath. It was the engine room for powering the mill's equipment, complete with a generator that had aged badly.

Wooden stairs descended a dozen steps to the cement floor. Kyle didn't want to go down them but he needed too. Sweat had beaded on his forehead. Last night's dream piled an added weight on his shoulders. He recalled drowning in a place underground, a place like this. And it didn't help now to hear the water lapping against the creek banks outside.

"Dammit!" he muttered to himself. "Get a grip!"

He shoved one foot through the opening and followed it with the other. It took him only a few seconds to reach the bottom of the stairs. The flow of adrenaline made it seem longer.

The room nearly made a square in length and width, about twelve feet. It was maybe seven feet deep. The floor was cement, the walls cinder block. The generator sat in the center, an awkward iron monster that must have been obsolete by the time this mill closed. There were some battery racks with no batteries, and a few smaller pieces of equipment that Kyle didn't recognize.

The floor and bottom part of the wall on the creek side looked damp and moldy. Nothing to worry about right now, though. Given the depth of the building's foundation and the run of the stream below its banks, there shouldn't be any problem with flooding. He hoped.

Little doubt. This was the place they needed. No matter if it made him feel uneasy. Ventilation came in through a number of small apertures on the outside walls, near the ceiling. They weren't anything a Warkind could get through. And there was only one entrance, the trapdoor. He and Tru had the artillery to cover that opening. If they put Raina behind the generator then its massive iron bulk would provide even more protection.

The only real problem was that *one* entrance also meant *one* exit. Once they were down here, Kargen could try to trap them by piling something heavy over the door. That possibility didn't worry Kyle much. He didn't think Kargen had planned things to end that way. The Warkind wanted the Mother, and one way or another he was always going to come in after her.

Besides, the mortar between the cement blocks of this room was old and cracked. Kyle had a pry bar he could bring in from the Blazer and he figured half an hour of digging would take them through one of the outside walls if they needed to.

Kyle's five minutes to explore were up. Tru would be starting to chew fingernails about now. Quickly, Kyle climbed the stairs and took the open area of the mill at a trot. The others got out of the Blazer as he approached, listened and nodded while he explained his plan. Then they all set to work.

Cold in the Light

Kyle and Tru carried Raina between them on their tarpaulin travois while Mel loaded up with sleeping bags and blankets from the camping gear. After they got Raina situated in the engine room, Kyle made two more trips outside, the first to fetch the other lantern, Mel's vet bag, the pry bar, and the extra jugs of water that he always carried when traveling.

Then he went back again, this time to get the big halogen light he'd planned to use for night fishing. It still lay in its packing case. To run it, he removed the Blazer's battery and took it with him.

After a moment's hesitation, he picked up one other item--from his tackle box. It was the fillet knife he'd been using on speckled trout and redfish for years. He'd long since wrapped the handle in shagreen to keep it from slipping in his fingers, and the blade gleamed a sharp seven inches of carbon steel, honed like heaven to cut like hell.

He threaded the knife's sheath on his belt and slid the blade home, hoping he wouldn't have to use it. Because, if it came down to a knife instead of a gun... Well. That would mean only one thing. He'd be closer to Kargen than he had ever wanted to get.

--- **8** ---

Michael Russo glanced out of the cockpit window of the helicopter at the night land flowing beneath them. He was remembering. The last time he'd been in a machine like this, Lanny Burns had still been alive. And he, Mike, had still been innocent. He didn't regret the loss of innocence. But he wished Lanny were here to talk about it with.

At least there was *someone* he could talk with, when this was over. She sat right now in the cargo area of this chopper, with Mike's sons, a few soldiers, and half a dozen Warkind from Graye's band. He knew he could have been talking to her all along these past several years. He'd been a fool not to. Helen could have helped him then, as she'd helped him over the recent hours.

"Eighteen minutes ETA," the pilot said.

Mike heard the words clearly through the headphones he had donned when he'd chosen to ride in the copilot's chair instead of in the cargo area with his family. He'd wanted to make sure the pilot knew how to read the telemetric information supplied from the satellite hook-up; he'd also wanted to be first to see their destination.

Eighteen minutes to the Mother, Mike thought. *Already less in the time it took me to think those words. And these.*

He glanced out the window again, though he knew that with the speed the helicopter traveled they were far too many miles from their target to see anything. They were over a part of the Ozark Mountains now where nobody lived. The untamed woods spread like dark clots around the occasional clearing. There existed no light except the moon.

Behind this chopper were two others, flying in formation with enough firepower to set this whole mountain aflame. Mike hoped he wouldn't be called upon to use any of that weaponry. They had to go in and get Raina, but Mike thought he could convince her to trust him. As long as Graye went along.

"Message coming in, sir," the pilot said. "One of the search parties says they found something."

Mike frowned. Word had been sent to all the field forces that he was in command now and that reports were to come to him directly. But, he'd ordered all the Warkind bands to return to base, all the other search units to hold where they were.

He took the headphone set the pilot offered him and slipped them on.

"Russo, here," he said. "What the hell are you do--"

He stopped talking. He listened. And listened. He asked for a repeat, then took off the headphones and let them drop into his lap. His eyes burned.

When he'd sent word out to the field units, only Kargen's band had failed to respond. No one had known where they were, but someone just now had found their trail. It was blazed with torn bodies, some of which were missing their heads, or other parts.

With a belly deep chill, Mike realized how right Lanny Burns had been in saying that Kargen was dangerous. He wondered if his friend had been right in another way too. *Was* Kargen pursuing the Mother for his own purposes? Did he have no intention of protecting her?

He looked out the window into the night, wishing that he could see a light somewhere below in all the forested blackness. Even if that light didn't mark the location of Raina and her friends, at least it would prove that the world hadn't all gone away.

"How long now?" Mike asked the pilot.

"Sixteen minutes, seventeen seconds," the man said.

Too long, Mike thought. *Too far.*

--- 9 ---

Leonard Suskind sobbed quietly as he raced the stolen Jeep at its best speed down Highway 71 toward the town of Alma. From there it was only a short hop into Fort Smith on Interstate 40, where Mike Russo had said he would take the Mother. When he'd *rescued* her.

Leonard cursed at that thought, through a mouth fouled with salt tears and bile. He hammered his right fist on the steering wheel. Wished that he hadn't. The throbbing in that hand was immense, like the ringing of some vast underground bell. The pain made him cry.

At first, frustration had been the greater pain, having his goals thwarted by Russo and that idiot Drake Hammond. But as he'd driven, the physical agony had grown, overwhelming the mental. The hurt in his right hand increased geometrically, and now it was spreading--to his left hand, his neck, his shoulders, down his back. He understood the reason and it scared the shit out of him. The same thing had happened in some of his early experiments. But he'd solved that problem.

Dammit! He'd solved it all. Every equation. Every enzyme reaction. Every base pair bonding.

Unless?

"No!"

He shouted the word at nothing. The doses had been calculated exactly to his body weight. The gorillas he'd used had been as physically near to his phenotype as possible, same weight, nearly the same height. And he'd altered their genotype himself, to make them close in sequence to his own DNA code. They'd lived after the treatments. Thrived. No pain. Only youth and strength. And skills they'd never had before.

Unless? The thought/question struck again.

And he knew what that thought was even as he strove now to keep it from his awareness. All along he'd understood the major difference between gorilla and man. Gorillas were shy and retiring. Peaceful. Man wasn't...peaceful.

The thought broke through.

Aggression is the trigger. That's why the chimps--

A cramp straight out of hell rippled up his right arm and poured down into his chest like an invading horde. He gasped, lost his breath, doubled over. The Jeep swerved and he barely kept it on the highway. He tasted blood behind his tongue.

From the moment he'd set foot in Arkansas the process had accelerated. He'd thought at first it was just a normal effect of hitting the right dosage. But it was the aggression. From the Warkind. From Hammond and his military bravos. The very air was saturated with violence. His system had overloaded on it, like sugar. He rode the down side of a spiral and he knew where it ended. As meat.

There was only one chance--to get to the Mother and her fetus. Before, he'd hoped only to keep Michael Russo from destroying the Harbinger Project by revealing the Whoun to the world. But now Leonard had another reason to reach Fort Smith before Russo did. He needed to be there when Mike brought the Mother and her baby in.

He wanted to live.

--- **10** ---

Mel Bowers didn't like this place, this "engine room" under the old sawmill. There were driblets of mossy water seeping across the floor closest to the creek, and ventilation holes through which crawled the sound of frogs along the banks just outside. That sound made her nervous, sparking hints of old memories that she didn't want to recall. She'd been grateful when they'd first got out of the Blazer that the frogs were silent. That wasn't true any longer. Whatever had startled them to stillness had passed; their cacophony had resumed.

But at least the air here wasn't foul, if just a little damp and musky to the taste. And the two lanterns Kyle had brought lit the small room enough for her to work. She should have felt relatively

Cold in the Light

safe. She told herself that several times. There was only one door in, the trapdoor, and besides their guns Kyle and Tru had hooked up another weapon against the Warkind--a spotlight run off the battery from the Blazer.

Mel didn't know much about watts, but in a test the light had shone as bright as sin. It would have blinded Raina or Wahrn for sure, and even though the Warkind Kargen had been out in the daylight he hadn't faced anything as intense as this. From what she could figure out about Whoun eyes, the spotlight ought to slow him down.

Mel went to Raina and knelt beside her on the blankets. For the birthing bed they'd picked a location to the left of the old generator. The cement floor was dry there, and pipes curving overhead offered at least the illusion of protection. Sleeping bags and blankets made a soft pallet for the unconscious Mother.

Kyle and Tru were both in the open area at the front of the room, near the stairs leading down from the sawmill's office. Tru paced with a shotgun; Kyle sat quietly with a pistol in his lap and his free hand near the switch for the spotlight. Each of them had other guns as well. Behind them loomed the grime-encrusted generator, and behind that another open area, near the creek-side wall. The floor was wet there, and spiderwebbed with tiny cracks that left it feeling spongy.

Mel touched Raina's stomach, and smiled despite their predicament when she felt the baby move inside. It was a sensation that she loved, whether in a human or an animal. Or in a Whoun.

She checked her watch, timed Raina's contractions.

"One minute, thirty now," she called aloud. Tru looked at her. Kyle didn't. Neither of the men spoke. At this point there was nothing more to say. They all knew the baby was coming.

And after that? Kargen?

Mel rinsed her fingers for the twentieth time, using water from one of the plastic jugs Kyle had carried in. She'd already laid out the instruments that she might want from the bag she'd hauled along in the Blazer. Now she checked over her tools again--scalpel, forceps, scissors, sutures, umbilical clamps, bandages.

She didn't have what she needed to give Raina an epidural block, but that wouldn't matter if the Whoun stayed unconscious. In case of emergency--in case Raina woke up and couldn't stand the pain--

Mel had two syringes of sodium pentothal to knock her out again. She didn't want to use them if she didn't have to. It would be dangerous for the baby as long as the chord remained attached.

There was one other instrument in front of her that Mel hoped not to have to use--the Colt .357 magnum that Kyle had given her. She had shot Kargen with it but it hadn't stopped him. Now she *prayed* not to have to use it again. Then she forced herself to sit and tried to get comfortable. Raina's eyes opened, jolting Mel, bringing the veterinarian back to her knees only a moment after she'd left them.

"Raina?" she called. "Raina! Are you with us?"

The Whoun's eyes were looking beyond the woman's, beyond this room. Then her gaze focused downward and inward, coming to rest on Mel's face.

"The baby is coming wrong," Raina said.

Mel's heart thudded in her ears, covering a sudden lack of sound from outside the creek-side wall. She heard that silence but didn't register it.

For the second time. The frogs had stopped croaking.

CHAPTER FIFTEEN
(May 1: Toward Midnight)

The wide scream of his throat was crimson. His muscles seized with the triphammer avalanche of blood. Again, ribs pushed out on his skin, burst through. He sprouted wings.
--In the Memory of Ruins

--- 1 ---

Mel felt the blood rushing and buzzing in her ears, felt her heart hurt itself against her chest.

"The baby is coming wrong," Raina had said, her first words after hours in a coma. Terrifying words.

Mel had hoped that if Raina woke up before the birth there would be a minute to ask questions and think about the answers. She wasn't going to get an instant. A gush of fluid washed over her knees as Raina's water broke and spilled into the blankets. Immediately the Whoun's stomach heaved, the muscles rippling downward toward her genital opening. Raina grunted with pain.

Shit, shit, shit! Mel thought. In a human there would be time after the amniotic sac ruptured. But Raina was contracting as if she were in late second stage labor. The baby wanted to come right now.

"Kyle! Tru!" Mel shouted. She knew she sounded panicky. Couldn't help it. Her hands were busy, but doing nothing that had to be done.

Kyle was suddenly there, hollering over his shoulder at Tru to watch the door, dropping to his knees beside her.

"What can I do?" he asked.

Raina's contraction ended. Her stomach relaxed. Mel breathed, caught herself. She gestured toward the nearest lantern, not looking at Kyle.

Focus, she ordered her mind.

"Get the light," she ordered Kyle. "Something's wrong."

Without waiting for the lantern, Mel bent between Raina's legs, cursing again, thinking that she didn't have what she needed here. Then she thought of another time when she hadn't had what she needed, when she'd been in a motel room delivering a baby with nothing but her hands.

But now Kyle had the light up. She could see. She leaned closer. Raina groaned, still not completely alert to what was happening.

While the Mother had slept, Mel had already looked over the Whoun's genital area, cleaning, checking, probing, learning what she needed to know. Whoun females had a vagina much like a human's, though set further toward the back. Mel had propped Raina's buttocks on a pillow to take care of that difference. Now she realized it wasn't good enough.

"We have to roll her over," Mel told Kyle. "Get her onto her side."

"Raina," she called. "Do you understand? We need to get you over."

She had to repeat herself before the Whoun nodded. By then another series of cramps had arced through Raina's belly. These lasted longer than before, wringing a string of moans from Raina's lips, wringing sweat from Mel's forehead.

Mel shook her head in thought, then got her hands under Raina's legs and buttocks. Kyle worked at the shoulders and back, and with a smooth twist they rolled the pregnant female onto her right side. There came a groan. But no words.

Without prompting, Kyle moved around Raina to position the light better for Mel. Mel grabbed a sleeping bag that was still rolled up and slipped it beneath Raina's left leg, lifting the limb, making room for herself to see. She put on a pair of surgical gloves and quickly probed around the Whoun's vaginal opening, trying to visualize what the uterus looked like inside.

At least Raina was dilated. And wider than a woman would be at this point. Maybe fifteen centimeters.

Another contraction hit and Raina gave a short grunt that segued into a half bark/half scream at the end. But Mel used the contraction to slip her fingers inside the vaginal cavity to feel for the baby.

She hoped to touch the head--almost all mammals were born head first--but that wasn't what she found. A small hand lay in the way, with stubby fingers and sharp nails. Mel jerked back from that contact, her panic level starting to climb again, her fingers twisting around each other.

Focus! her mind shouted at itself. She forced a breath into her lungs, forced her fingers apart.

The contraction ended but Raina kept panting, keening slightly from her throat with each hollow breath.

She's awake now for sure, Mel thought. *And terrified!* The realization pushed away her own fears.

As powerful as Raina was, as instinctively knowledgeable as she was, the Whoun was still a first-time mother. She didn't really know what to expect, wasn't sure how much pain was normal and how much to fear. She needed Mel's reassurance, and that need turned on the switches that Mel had to have turned on.

"It's all right, Raina," she said, her voice dropping softly into well-worn grooves, the same grooves she always used. Only the words were different, because this patient could understand.

"It's all right. The baby's position is a little awkward but I've seen it before. It's nothing we can't handle."

Mel heard her own voice, heard how calm she sounded. And that calm soothed the troubled seas in her thoughts. These last nights of fear and encroaching memories had eroded the confidence that she'd worn like armor for years. Only, she realized now that what she'd once put on as armor had become her nature. Her *lack* of recent confidence was what was temporary.

And she *could* handle this baby. It wasn't like a breech delivery where the whole infant would be turned sideways in the birth canal. The baby just had its arm down the canal ahead of its skull. She could fix that.

It would take a few minutes, though. She'd hoped to give Raina a shot of sodium pentothal if she woke up like this, to knock her out again. But in the time it would take for *this* delivery, a dose large enough to put Raina to sleep might kill the fetus.

She pushed that thought aside for the moment, leaned forward to get her mouth near Raina's ear.

"It's all right," she said again. "The baby's just in a hurry to get here is all. His arm's in the way of his head but I can turn it. I'm gonna have to do something that'll hurt a little though. I have to widen your birth opening some. You OK with that?"

"Yes," Raina said, her voice sounding too young to come from someone so large. "It already hurts. Is it supposed to hurt this bad?"

Mel remembered. "Yes," she said. "It's supposed to hurt. But it comes in waves. Rest between cramps. Breathe easy then. Don't tense until the cramp hits. And don't push with your belly until I tell you."

Another contraction struck and Mel grabbed Raina's shoulders until it passed. By that time the Whoun was hiccuping sobs. She sounded very human.

"It hurts! I can't!"

"You can!" Mel said "I did. All by myself. With *no one* there."

Mel knew that Kyle had to be looking at her with shock. But she didn't have time to think about his reaction now. She just kept speaking to Raina.

"I've delivered hundreds of babies. Human and otherwise. I know it hurts but it *will* pass. Trust me. Hold on. Push when I tell you."

"I will try," Raina said. Her voice sounded a tiny bit stronger, still young and scared, but stronger.

"Good," Mel said.

She sat back on her heels, turned her eyes to Kyle. He was staring at her, his face strange. But he didn't look away.

"Can you find a place to put the light?" she asked him. "I'm going to need you to wipe up some blood. You OK with that?"

He nodded, and seemed relieved to break their glance as he searched the overhead pipes for a place to hang the lantern. He finally cut a long strip from a blanket with the fishing knife at his belt and tied the lantern up by its handle so it would throw light directly where the veterinarian needed it. Then his hands gathered towels as he slipped back to his knees and pushed up beside Mel.

Moving swiftly and surely now, Mel picked up a vial of procaine, a local anesthetic, and filled a syringe from it. She waited for the next contraction to pass.

"Raina. I'm going to give you something to ease the pain where the baby will come. You'll feel a sharp prick first. And a little tugging later. OK?"

"Yes," Raina gasped.

Mel injected the procaine into the perineum just behind the Whoun's vaginal area, massaging it in with her fingers. When the next contraction ended, she made a swift cut through the perineum with a scalpel.

Blood welled out and Kyle leaned down with a towel.

"Press a little," Mel told him. "Not hard."

"Why'd you do that?" he asked.

"An episiotomy. I need a wider opening."

Her hands were searching for something among her instruments. She found it. "Ahh." She squeezed a clear ointment into her palm from a small tube.

"What's that?" Kyle asked.

"To help with the bleeding. Move the towel for a moment."

Kyle did what she told him and Mel smeared the salve over the scalpel cut.

"OK, Raina," she said. "You're going to feel my hands now. I need to turn the baby's head a little. You all right?"

"Yes," Raina said. Mel heard the fear underlying the Whoun's answer, but Raina was fighting it, holding her own.

"You're doing great," Mel said. "Here we go."

She leaned forward. Some blood still ran and it was hard to see. But Mel didn't need her eyes as much as she needed her sense of touch right now. She put her hands to the Whoun's vagina, slipped her fingers inside. She felt the baby's hand again. It hadn't moved, despite Raina's contractions.

Not a good sign.

She shoved the thought away. Her fingers probed further. The uterine opening gaped larger than in a human. That *was* a good sign. Mel smiled to herself as she found the baby's head. The neck wasn't twisted much.

If I can just--

Another contraction struck. Mel's fingers lost the head. She knelt back for a second, brushed sweat off her face with the back of an arm. A second contraction came almost immediately.

Damn. Too close together.

Mel's momentary feeling of elation passed. She bent again to her work, slipped her fingers back into Raina's birth canal, probing deeper, deeper. She found the baby's head again, held on as a contraction rippled the Whoun's uterus. This time she'd gotten her fingers around a row of ridges on the skull.

Glad it's a Whoun, she thought. A human fetus would have had a smooth scalp, harder to handle.

Mel gave a tug. Once. Twice. Nothing happened. Another contraction came and passed. Raina rode the top of the waves now, learning how to take the pain. That didn't change the fact that the baby's arm was in the way, the head socketed in behind it. The obstruction lay at a point higher than Mel could reach.

Mel fumbled for her longest forceps, found it, probed once more inside the Whoun's uterus. She needed to push the shoulder up. Get it out of the way.

It wouldn't budge.

Kneeling back on her heels, Mel chewed her lips in thought. The sweat ran on her face and Kyle used a clean towel to wipe her dry around the eyes.

"Why's it taking so long?" he asked. "Can I help?"

His voice was gravelly, rougher than she'd ever heard it. She knew his tone came from fear, and from his inability to act. He wasn't used to sitting still while others took care of things.

Probably good for him, she thought perversely. She grinned at him then, realizing suddenly what she had to do. *She* had to act.

"The baby's just stubborn," she told Kyle. "Sure *you're* not his daddy?"

He looked surprised. Mel grinned again and bent back to the Mother.

"Raina. You're gonna feel some pressure. For just a moment. Then I'm gonna ask you to push. Five minutes and it'll be over. OK?"

"Yes," Raina said. "I'm ready."

"Good."

Mel slipped her fingers back into Raina's uterus, feeling for the arm this time instead of the head. She found it, locked her grip above the sharp blade of the elbow. With a deft twist she dislocated the tiny shoulder, knowing that she could put it back in place after the birth. Then her fingers moved to the left, found the skull again, gripped, tugged. The head turned, dropped into the birth canal.

Cold in the Light

A contraction arrived like a train.

"Push," Mel called to Raina. "Push and let's get this baby born."

--- 2 ---

"We've got problems," the pilot said, snapping Mike Russo's attention away from the moving darkness outside the helicopter's cockpit.

"What? Where?" Mike asked.

The man pointed to a multicolored display on his console. Mike hadn't paid much attention to it before. Now he did. Just a few minutes ago all its colors had been greens and blues. Now a wedge of yellow-red brightness raced across it.

Mike's forehead creased. "Infrared," he said. "Ground scan."

"Yeah," the pilot said.

"And those dots?"

"Bad news!"

Warkind, Mike thought. And only one band was unaccounted for. Kargen's!

"How much longer?" Mike asked, his lips constricting around the words. He cleared his throat, swallowed acid that rushed from his chest into his throat.

"Seven minutes to target," the pilot said. "We'll beat them by a fraction. Two minutes maybe."

Mike scratched his cheek hard, slipped a thumb in his mouth and bit down on the nail, pulled the thumb out again.

"OK," he said. "You're carrying spotlights. Right?"

"Yeah."

"Every chopper?"

"Yeah." The pilot glanced at him, not sure of where he was going with the questions.

"All right. We get between the Mother and the Warkind. Hit the Warkind with the spots. They won't go through the light. Graye's band and the soldiers go out the other side of the choppers. Secure the area. We get the Mother and fly the hell out."

The pilot nodded. "Might work. Have to be quick, though."

"Yeah," Mike said. "Get on the radio. Tell the other pilots. The soldiers too. Let *them* work out the details. But tell 'em I'm going in with them after the Mother. She'll listen to me."

I hope, his thoughts added.

There came no argument from the pilot. The man picked up his radio, made the call.

Mike continued to stare at the infrared display of a Warkind band moving through the night toward the Mother and her allies. He thought of how powerful the Warkind were, of how edged they were with aggression. He thought of what he'd so recently learned about Kargen and his band. That they were rogues. Outliers. Drake Hammond had called them killers.

But Mike thought, also, of what they'd been like when they were little. And he made a decision, a dangerous one maybe, but one he felt he had to make.

"Order the men no shooting except in self-defense," he told the pilot. "*Only* in self-defense."

The man nodded. And once again Mike let the night consume his attention. He wished the next few minutes would never have to happen. He prayed for time to stop.

--- 3 ---

Kargen lay in mud and water, in a small, dark place under the back of the sawmill. Once there must have been a drain from the mill into the creek. Time and water and muskrats had worn away at it, chewing the pipe to shreds and vastly enlarging the hole. Kargen had found the eroded channel, had squeezed through it till the end. He waited there. Only his eyes and nostrils were above the morass, and the ears with which he listened to everything that happened in the room overhead.

The Mother's baby was almost here!

Strained by the erosion of the ground beneath, strips and clumps of concrete had fallen away from the floor above Kargen. Faint skeins of blue-violet light filtered down through cracks that had formed, painting strange hieroglyphics on the ground. They seemed to wriggle and Kargen watched them intently as his mind played over the swift movements to come. He wondered if he would hesitate when it was time to kill the human female.

Cold in the Light

Mel. He'd learned her name finally.

She would surely try to get in the way of what he needed to do, as she'd already tried by putting a bullet in him. But he'd also overheard and understood what she'd done for the Mother and the baby in the last few minutes--saved them from a danger that could have killed them both. His war-spike swished the water in confusion.

Then the sudden smell of hot blood and tissue murdered Kargen's confusion and brought him to a poised crouch beneath the floor. He heard a sound, a new sound on the earth. A cry. And a flood of smells poured down upon him through the cracks above. He threw back his head, opening his mouth and nares, feeling drunkenness coming on.

Zinc, iron, serum, fat. Sanris and hemin. The scents filled him. Took him over. His muscles bunched and heaved. A growl built itself in his chest, rising, rising, toward the moment of explosion. Odor ghosts reared their heads all around, among them one he recognized intimately, one that screamed at him to act.

It was like himself. And not himself.

He smelled his son.

--- **4** ---

Mel felt the grin going wide on her face. Her hands were busy as the baby's head popped free of Raina's body. Another contraction brought the shoulders. And the rest.

Even human babies scarcely look human when they're born. This was worse, painted as it was with a thin film of blood and mucous, the placenta hanging around it like strips of wet confetti. It was still beautiful, from the inhumanly curved toes, to the three-fingered hands with their strange soft spikes, to the grooves that ran across its scalp and shoulders like plowed furrows--where the quills would grow.

Wrapping it in half a blanket she had cut for the purpose, Mel lifted the Whoun infant gently. It weighed about twelve pounds, she figured. Its hairless skin, less flexible than a human baby's, fitted tightly to its bones but still shone as pink with capillary flush as any newborn's. The small body radiated heat as it twisted and moved in her arms.

Raina lifted her head, trying to see, and Mel turned the baby toward her for a moment, letting the new mother look at her child. Raina smiled too, and the sharp yellow teeth that could crack bone didn't detract from the love that Mel saw in the Whoun's face.

But there was much to do. Mel swabbed the infant's nostrils clean of bloody fluid and clamped a hemostat over the umbilical cord. Leaving enough length to tie off, she scissored the cord apart, separating mother and child forever. Raina had a last contraction as the rest of the placental membrane spilled free. At that instant, Mel popped the baby's dislocated shoulder back into its socket and the infant gave its first cry, a sound as human as its shape was not.

Mel glanced up for a minute to see Kyle watching her with the tissue-slimy infant in her arms, her jeans half covered in Raina's afterbirth. His expression hovered somewhere between disgust and a smile. She laughed at him, saw his face change as the disgust faded into wonder and something that could have been love.

The floor behind him exploded upward, cement debris sleeting into the room, a massive shape hurtling through.

--- 5 ---

Kyle heard the crashing sound behind him, twisted on his knees to see its source, his hand snaking toward his belt. The back area of the small engine room lay smoked with sudden dust. Pebbles rained down. Kargen loomed like a troll in mist, eyes a blasted yellow in the light of the lantern.

Kyle had been looking at Mel, thinking how beautiful she was with the baby Whoun in her arms and the blood and mucous stains of a newborn all over her. And now his hand filled itself with something that wasn't beautiful, the cold knot of the .45 Colt, hammer drawn. He screamed at Mel to run as the gun bucked against his palm.

The slug hit Kargen above the hip, spattering mud and blood. It was like pic-ing a fighting bull with a hatpin. The Warkind roared, a wall of sound shrieking off the concrete. He came for them.

The gun barrel shifted in Kyle's hands, tracking on target as he locked his left hand around his right wrist to steady his aim. Kargen was a tank running on adrenaline. Only a perfect shot would stop him.

Cold in the Light

But there was no chance to take that shot. Raina threw herself past him from the left, a buzz saw shriek spilling from her mouth as she hit Kargen a hammer blow with her shoulder. The shock rattled, driving Kargen sideways into the rusted generator. Raina's arms and legs wrapped around the Warkind, churning like insane windmills. Her claws were digging, her teeth reaching for his throat.

Surging to his feet, Kyle cocked the .45, prayed for an opening to fire it through. There wasn't one. Tru yelled behind him, the words a dull roar that barely licked his ears. Raina and Kargen filled his senses, locked in a savage dance. Raina was rich with fury, wild with the need to protect her offspring.

She was no match for Kargen.

The giant Warkind's right arm wrapped itself around Raina's hips; his left hand grasped her shoulder with fingers that could crush a four-by-four. Kyle had visions of Dan's torn belly, of Wahrn's throat stripped into bloody flags by this same Kargen. All of it had happened while he, Kyle, stood helpless. He couldn't let it happen again. He leaped forward, clubbing his pistol at the Warkind's skull, knowing he was too close and Kargen too fast, but unable to shoot for fear of hitting the female Whoun.

Almost gently, Kargen tore Raina's grip loose from around his neck, shoved her nearly 300 pounds at Kyle rushing in--as if he had been waiting for the right moment to put them both down. He failed in that.

The hanging lantern shattered as Raina hit it. Then she hit Kyle. The impact shoved him back and sideways, but he'd read the maneuver and kept to his feet as Raina crashed past him to the floor. In the dim light of the last lantern, Kargen hurled himself forward, a killing shadow that moved like a hybrid of steel and silk.

With no time to aim, Kyle let the barrel of the Colt drop under its own weight as he pumped the trigger. His first shot missed; the second cut a bloodless channel through the armor of overlapping quills on the Warkind's back. Kargen reared onto his haunches, lashed out with the war-spike on his left hand.

There was no avoiding that blow. Kyle took it against his forearm, grunted as he felt the bone blade slice deep through the fatty underpart of the arm. A faint red mist spumed the air as the immense power behind that hit slammed Kyle against the generator, ringing bells in his head. The Colt arced free of Kyle's numbed grip, clattered away on the darkened floor.

Stunned, reacting only on instinct, Kyle threw himself to one side. Barely in time. A whisper of movement slid past his ear, scored a line of fire down his shoulder. He hit the cement floor hard, his body screaming at him to move. But his mind was fogged.

Tru saved his life.

Unable to use his guns for fear of hitting his friends, Tru found another weapon. He spun the halogen light around on its stand and punched the on switch. A lance of blue-white flame seared the world where Kargen stood.

The Warkind shrieked.

Even to Kyle, the brightness of the light felt like a solid weight in the air. He could hear what it was doing to Raina. She had coiled into a whimpering ball even though she wasn't directly in the path of the beam. Kyle could only imagine what it was doing to Kargen. But the Warkind wasn't stopping. Still shrieking, like a burning man, Kargen turned away from Kyle and charged Tru.

Kyle heard the sound of a shot, recognized the pop of Tru's .38. He rolled over, grabbing for the Sig 9mm holstered at the small of his back. He palmed it in his left hand, his injured right arm still numb.

The spotlight disintegrated as Kargen slammed into it, dropping a near darkness over the room. Tru shouted, the words lost in the delirium of crashing glass.

Kyle couldn't see to shoot. He staggered to his feet, hollering for Tru. There was no response. And in the last of the big brightness he'd seen that Mel was gone too. He knew she was running with the baby. Though where she could run *to* he had no idea.

Spots still danced in front of Kyle's eyes, aftereffects of the halogen's brilliant gaze. He blinked, trying to clear his vision. In the dim light of the one remaining lantern, all he could see were virtual ghosts that might mark the movements of either Tru or Kargen. Then the sound of splintering wood knifed his eardrums, letting him know which ghost was a Warkind.

The trapdoor, Kyle thought. Kargen was after the Whoun infant. And Mel!

Cold in the Light

Kyle threw himself toward the stairs, yelling again for Tru. This time there came a moan, a gagging sound that choked off into a cough. In one corner of the room there was movement, Tru pushing away a twisted frame of metal hung with wires and teeth of broken glass. His back was pressed to the wall, legs akimbo. His breathing was jagged; there was blood on him.

Kyle hesitated. Torn. His eyes on Tru, his thoughts on Mel.

Tru saw the war in Kyle's face, pushed a hand at him, croaked a command.

"Go. Kill the bastard."

Kyle went, hurling his body up the stairs. On the run he switched the pistol from his left hand to his right. That arm still bled from Kargen's war-spike but the numbness was going, the pain masked by adrenaline. He only wished the 9mm was the .45. But the Colt was lost, with no time to look for it.

Then he was through the broken trapdoor into the small storage area next to the sawmill's main office. He heard Mel scream.

--- 6 ---

Mel had run when Kyle told her to run, the blanket-wrapped baby Whoun in her arms. Kyle and Tru had to stop Kargen. She prayed they could, prayed that Raina would be all right. But the infant had to be protected.

Through the trapdoor she'd gone, throwing it closed again behind her, knowing it wouldn't stop Kargen for long if he got that far. Maybe nothing would stop him.

The baby kicked; Mel's blood pulsed. The door to the storage area stood open and she raced through it into the main office. There were two doors there. The outer one was locked and she went through the inner one instead, leaping over the steps to the hard floor of the main building below.

Running then.

She had to find a place to hide. Or to defend. She had no weapons. She'd left the .357 behind. There'd been no time to think of it. Maybe there was something in the Blazer. If it wasn't locked?

The end of the mill seemed far away. Her feet pounded on the cement, a hollow sound. Her breaths rasped. The baby began to cry, its voice rising.

Something made her look back. The inner wall of the office erupted in flying splinters of wood and glass. Kargen burst through, hit the floor and rolled. She saw him come to all fours and launch himself toward her.

A scream trembled on her lips, tore its way free into the air. It was as much for Kyle as for herself. Because if Kargen was here then...

Mel turned her head and ran harder, knowing she wasn't going to make it. None of them were going to make it.

--- 7 ---

Raina staggered to her feet, tissue still dripping from her womb to the inside of her thighs. Her eyes hurt; the whiteness of the spotlight had been so cold. Her chest and stomach and intestines felt...loose, as if her fight with Kargen had torn them free and left them floating. The muscles in her calves were like kinked wires that would never straighten. She forced them to carry her toward the stairs.

Where Kargen had gone.

The Warkind wanted her baby. She didn't know why that was, but she had to stop him. Mel would try. Kyle would try. Raina didn't think they had a chance; she had felt Kargen's power when she'd attacked him. Maybe she didn't have a chance either. But that made no difference.

Her hands found the stair railing that her eyes could barely see, pulled her up the steps and through the trapdoor. She stumbled at the opening from the storage area, nearly fell into the mill's office. To her right, the glass-fronted wall of the office stood ripped wide as if a shrapnel burst had centered there. Raina glimpsed Kyle just as he leaped through that opening to the floor below. He didn't see her.

She tried to follow, felt her legs go rubbery and drop her to her knees. She shook her head, pulled one foot forward and got it under her. Using her knee for a crutch, Raina heaved herself upright.

Cold in the Light

There was a rusted smell in the air all around that she couldn't recognize.

The hole in the wall was six steps away. Raina made five before her legs went out again and pitched her forward through the gap. She fell three feet to smash hard on the cement floor. It was cold. Her breath fled. She blinked as strange dark floaters serrated her retinas.

Nothing made sense. Kargen had not hurt her this badly when he'd thrown her down. He hadn't cut her. Or bit her. She shouldn't be this weak--hadn't been only a few moments ago. She pushed her elbows against the floor but couldn't lift her upper body.

Have to get up, her thoughts railed. *Go after my baby.*

She wiped her face with a hand, felt the smear of something wet over her mouth. And the smell bubbled into her nostrils. She recognized it now.

Raina rolled onto her side, looked down the length of her belly to her hips. Blood ran everywhere, pouring from her womb. There'd been too much movement. She was hemorrhaging. Her head fell back. She saw stars through holes in the roof. She heard a sound, a drumbeat coming fast.

"Helicopter," she murmured to herself.

She blinked again. And the insides of her lids were bright. Cold and bright.

--- **8** ---

Kargen had wanted the Mother. He still wanted her. But now he wanted his son too. *His* son. And the human woman had him, fled with him across the open expanse of the old mill's main work area.

Kargen dropped to all fours, followed, his muscles driving but carrying him slower than they should. It might have been the bullets in him. At least three. Or because he could barely see. The spotlight had struck like a lance into his eyes, like an iced stake through the sockets into the brain. And already those eyes had been hurt by hunting in the daylight. His vision watered and blurred.

But his near blindness made no difference. He could hear the woman's shoes on the concrete, could smell her skin. He could smell his child. The gap between them narrowed.

Questions roiled in his head. How? When? Why?

He had never mated with the Mother. That left only one answer to how, his sperm taken artificially during one of the many "procedures" that all the Whoun had undergone in the Harbinger compound.

The woman was almost to the outer door of the sawmill now. Kargen heard the changing echoes left by her steps. He sensed a faint increase in the moonlight. The power uncoiled in his legs, launching him forward.

The woman burst free of the mill into the night, her shoes thudding on the wooden ramp beyond the door. Kargen caught her there, rising onto his haunches, dragging her down so that she landed on her back with his baby protected in her arms. Then the Warkind straddled her waist, gripping her shoulders in his hands and looking into her face, expecting a scream that didn't come.

The woman stared back at him. Flat eyed. Her pupils hot. Kargen didn't look toward the child. Its breathing was fine, its odor tasted sweet on the air. His son was healthy--crying hard, but that didn't matter. Kargen looked only at the woman. And whispered to her face:

"Melll."

Her eyes widened but no fear crept in.

"Kargen," she spat back.

The Warkind laughed, the sound jarring, explosive, unhuman. Calculated. And he saw the fear then in the woman's eyes, saw her fight it and beat it down. He nodded his head. She was brave. Worthy. He could kill her.

He let go of her with his hands, lifted them both so she could see the war-spikes quivering with need. Not far away he heard helicopters racing to reach them. That would be the soldiers. And rolling on the wind from the south came the scent of Warkind heated with violence. His band. Coming quick.

Even sooner, Kyle would be here. That one wouldn't let this female be taken without a fight. But this was Kargen's time and all the others would be too late.

The nictitating lids closed over the Warkind's eyes.

In expectation of blood.

Cold in the Light

CHAPTER SIXTEEN
(May 2: Midnight And After)

The roof above him opened, let him out into a perse-blue sky with two silver suns. And a moon of acidic rose. He beat his still wet wings against air. Flew. Then fell.

--In the Memory of Ruins

--- 1 ---

"Three minutes ETA," the pilot said.

Mike Russo nodded, slipped out of his chair in the cockpit and stepped around the partition into the cargo area. Helen and the boys were sitting there, looking worried. Mike wished now that he'd left them in the army camp. But he'd not expected to meet other Warkind on this mission, not the wild ones of Kargen's band at least. He realized now that he *should* have expected it.

Graye stood near Helen, with Tornik and three other members of Graye's band hanging close. There were five human soldiers as well, seated against the chopper's inner skin as far from the Warkind as they could get. Both Warkind and men were armed with M-16s, and in the two choppers trailing behind this one were ten more Warkind and ten more troopers.

Kargen's band should have had fifteen in it, though from reports coming in it looked as if a few of the band had been killed, either by Kargen himself or by the people traveling with the Mother. Mike wished he knew more about those people. Who were they and why had they joined like a human Podcyst around Raina? Would they give him problems when he tried to take her?

Well, he'd soon find out. For now it felt good just to know that his little army outnumbered Kargen's.

Smiling reassuringly at Helen and his sons, Mike walked past them toward the soldiers. The leader of that group stood. Mike had wanted Lieutenant William Morgan where he could keep an eye on him.

"Everything ready?" Mike asked.

"Ready," Morgan replied. "When we come in the pilots'll hit the spotlights and drop the choppers to ground. We bail." He pointed a finger at Mike, then waved it around the bay at the other soldiers and the Warkind. "You go with us. Everyone else covers."

"And my wife and kids?"

"As soon as we're set the pilot'll take this one up. They'll be safe in the air. We catch another ride."

Mike considered for a second. Nodded. The basic idea had been his but the execution of the plan had to be handled by someone who knew tactics better than he did. Morgan seemed to be that man. And without Hammond around to give orders, Mike believed the lieutenant could be trusted. From what Morgan had let slip, he hadn't been a big fan of Hammond's anyway, too sturdy and conventional for the dead commander's flamboyant style maybe.

The pilot's voice came over the chopper's intercom: "One minute ETA."

"Here," Morgan said.

Mike glanced down at what the lieutenant offered him--a pistol, dark and ugly as a bruise. He shook his head.

"No. You keep it for me."

Mike went over and kissed Helen and Joshua and Caleb one more time. "Hang on," he told them. And winked. Surprising them. Surprising himself.

The helicopter swept over a line of bluffs and past the dark mass of the woods. A creek rushing with water came up on their left. Ahead lay a building of tin and wood. The moon hung frozen above it.

--- 2 ---

Kargen looked down at the woman, at Mel, through the translucent white of his nictitating lids. Her throat lay open to attack, ephemeral, pulsing with life underneath the skin. She held his son against her chest.

Kargen would kill the woman and take the infant, go into the mountains far away from the humans who had manipulated him and the Mother and the child. And where the child traveled, the Mother would follow. He would have them both.

His hands moved, dropped from the sides toward the woman's neck, pulled by gravity, war-blades pointed in.

He stopped.

The tips of the blades dimpled the flesh at either side of the woman's jugular. But they did not pierce. In the instant between the start and finish of his attack, Kargen had seen the woman's eyes shift, not to look away from death coming at her, but to look down across her chest to the infant Whoun who was Kargen's son. And her hands had tightened convulsively across the baby.

Resigned to her own death, the human female had made a move to protect the Whoun child. She feared for it, Kargen realized. Feared he would harm it! His own son!

Those thoughts were cold teeth burrowing into his chest, icicle lights daggering his pupils. They hurt so badly because he wondered if the woman was right.

Kargen shoved back from Mel and stood up. His eyes were wild. The muscles bunched and leaped across his body. Noise came from all around. And the stenches of oil and blood and hate spilled hot on the wind. There were Warkind up the hill to his left--two minutes away--and helicopters storming in over the trees from even closer.

The woman held his baby, protecting his baby from *him*!

He couldn't kill her for that.

Footsteps pounded the concrete floor behind him. There came a faint snick of sound, as of a hammer being drawn on a gun.

Kyle!

Kargen spun, knowing that his hesitation over the woman had cost him. A wordless shout shotgunned the air around him. Kargen's eyes caught the swift movement of a shadow near the doorway to the mill, saw that shadow drop to one knee. A muzzle flash speared his vision and a pain punched him in the face as he threw himself to the side, splintering the wooden railing alongside the ramp. He hit the ground and rolled, feeling where Kyle's bullet had torn into his mouth.

But the rage he would have expected didn't come.

--- 3 ---

Tru coughed and winced as he pulled himself to his knees, using one of the steps of the stairs that ran up from the engine room to the mill proper. He rested there for a moment. His throat and chest felt raw from breathing and he knew that broken ribs were the likely cause. He prayed they hadn't gone into a lung, was afraid that they had.

Kargen had hit him like a bull, smashing the spotlight and throwing both Tru and the light into the concrete wall of the small room. Tru's breath had gone, his bones had screamed with pain. Then a greater agony had lanced him as Kargen punched his warspike in through Tru's side and out again. That whole side felt...smashed.

Tru hooked a hand over the stairway railing and pulled himself to his feet. With his other hand he pushed against the damaged ribs in the right side of his chest, to keep them from moving. He was lucky. Kargen had not been aiming for his side. Only the shrieking brightness of the spotlight had spoiled the being's strike. Else, Tru would be trying to breath through a mouth and throat that were no longer there.

In the dim light of the one remaining lantern, Tru examined his side. Blood had sprayed across the front of his uniform and had run down his stomach to his hips. But it was hard to see the extent of the injury because his mangled shirt seemed half embedded in the wound. He didn't dare pull it away. At least with things as they were the bleeding was slowing.

Tru's eyes searched the floor for a weapon, found his .38 lying under a pile of debris. The shotgun had fallen nearby but with his side like it was he'd never be able to shoot that gun. The pistol hadn't done much good before against Kargen but it was his only choice. He leaned down to pick it up.

A wave of blackness and nausea swept him as he bent over. He fought it, refused to let it have him. And when it passed he started up the stairs, moving a little faster now.

The sawmill itself was painted faintly with moonlight that bled in through broken windows and holes in the roof. Tru saw a gap ripped in the office wall and stumbled his way toward it. Beyond was a three foot drop to the main floor of the mill, and just below lay a still form that wasn't human.

A shout and a shot distracted him. He glanced toward the front door of the mill. Could see nothing. Though it had sounded like Kyle's 9 mm going off. There wasn't anything he could do about that now.

Coughing, Tru eased his way over the drop-off to the floor, then moved slowly toward the body, letting himself slide down beside it. It was Raina.

"Dammit," Tru muttered. He reached for Raina's arm, hoping to find a heart pulse, wondering if he even knew where to look on a Whoun.

A rattle of gunfire interrupted him. Not from Kyle's gun. And a huge blossoming of light threw sudden shadows into the building. Over a bullhorn, Tru heard a voice spouting words that he couldn't make out.

Tru wanted to get up. His friends were out there. But his legs wouldn't obey him. He sagged, letting himself slip over to lie on the floor next to Raina. Whatever went on outside, he'd have to wait for it to come to him. There was no way he could go to it.

--- 4 ---

Kyle had heard Mel scream, had felt that scream in his bones. He'd followed, chasing the sound. But he couldn't find her. Though he was sure Kargen had.

He ran. Then he saw them both on the ramp just outside the mill's door. Mel was down, Kargen standing over her with his arms spread wide from his body. Fear locked a vise on Kyle's temples. The Warkind heard him coming, twisted to face him.

Dead! Mel's dead! The thoughts were hot in Kyle's brain, red embers that whirled, seared.

A bass-heavy shriek tore from Kyle's mouth. He dropped to a knee, punched the Sig forward, fired. Kargen threw himself to one side, through the ramp's railing, the rotten wood exploding as his body burst across it. Kyle didn't know if he'd hit the Warkind, didn't see the being strike the ground. The ramp sloped up to the door and below it the world lay hidden.

Kyle leaped to his feet, raced toward Mel. *Don't let her be dead,* his thoughts prayed. He couldn't have said who he prayed to. Then he saw blood on Mel's clothes, and the infant Whoun lying unquiet on her stomach.

"Dammit, no," he shouted. "No!"

From the corner of one eye, Kyle saw that Kargen no longer lay where he'd fallen. He didn't care. All that mattered was Mel. And in the next instant he dropped to his knees beside her, his hands grabbing her shoulders, feeling the wetness of her shirt.

"Mel!"

Her eyes were open. It took Kyle an instant to see that. It took a little longer for her gaze to focus on his. He laughed in relief, suddenly, the sound almost hysterical. The blood that coated her wasn't hers, just afterbirth from the infant Whoun.

"He didn't kill me," Mel said, her face pale as floured dough. She seemed surprised.

Kyle couldn't help grinning. "I noticed," he said.

Then his face swallowed the grin as fear returned to piss cold water down his spine. His ears had been registering sounds but only now did he have time to recognize them, helicopters coming from the front, and from the side the whispers of strange movements. Another spurt of adrenaline poured into his heart. He looked up just as three choppers swept like winged scorpions over the trees.

"Shit!" Kyle shouted.

He grabbed Mel's arm, to drag her to her feet. From the left came a roaring sound, like the pounding of a huge surf. Then Mel was up, holding Raina's baby. Her eyes were wide.

The Blazer sat only twenty feet away from them to the left. From the void beyond something huge leaped to its roof. More shapes followed, aligning themselves along the vehicle's top or gathering around the wheels. Their eyes burned in the moonlight; their thick bodies were rich with menace. Flensing-knife teeth clashed together.

Warkind! Nearly a dozen of them.

Mel had seen. Her nerves came alive under Kyle's hands. He let go of her, stepped between her and the Warkind, the 9mm in his fist. It felt like a toy.

"Gotta get to the choppers," he said, more calmly than he felt with his skin crawling. "Surrender. Our only chance."

Cold in the Light

As if his words had been registered, huge spotlights bloomed on the sides of the helicopters, annihilating the black all around. Machine guns chewed at the air, not aimed at anything Kyle could see. The Warkind shrieked like they'd been napalmed, threw themselves backward off the Blazer into the comfort of the dark.

Half blinded himself, Kyle seized the chance offered by the lights, pushing Mel ahead of him as he yelled for her to run toward the descending choppers. The soldiers might rough them up, might even do worse. But there was no *might* about what the Warkind would do.

One helicopter swept in to land. The others hovered a few feet above the earth, their bright eyes burning, burning. An amplified voice cracked the air, coming over a loudspeaker from the grounding chopper.

"Here! Get aboard! We'll help!"

It didn't sound like a soldier's voice to Kyle. It didn't look like a soldier when a man with a bullhorn leaped out of the helicopter to the ground, stumbled and nearly fell. There were soldiers beside him, with rifles ready, their stances screaming tension. But they were looking away from where Kyle and Mel were running, squinting against their own lights as they focused off toward the trees.

From that direction came roars and shrieks. The Warkind. Furious, but held back by brightness. For the moment.

"Here!" the man with the bullhorn shouted again. He was looking at them, at Kyle and Mel, waving them toward him.

They reached the chopper and the little knot of men in front of it. The soldiers ignored them; the man with the megaphone lowered it. His face looked scared. He glanced from Kyle to Mel, then saw the infant Whoun. His eyes, full of whites, flinched when one of the soldiers fired a warning shot into the night. For some reason that made Kyle feel better.

"Where's Raina?" the man shouted over the throb of the choppers. "The Mother?"

The soldiers had been hunting them, Kyle thought. Now it was as if they weren't. Things didn't add up. But Kyle also knew how easy it would have been to shoot him and Mel down a moment ago. It would be easy now for the soldiers to point their guns toward him instead of away. And the man who had asked the question about the Mother was certainly not military. Something had changed.

Kyle jerked his head toward the mill. "She's back there," he shouted in answer. "With a friend. We have to go after them."

The man nodded, turned to look up at the helicopter pilot, his hand lifting in a signal. Kyle was still urging Mel toward the chopper, wanting to get her aboard. He stopped, his blood congealing. He could see through the open doors of the chopper to the far side. Dark shapes were dropping to earth there from the other helicopters, gathering in a place away from the light.

Men.

Warkind.

And even closer, crouched in the chopper within feet of them all, more Warkind waited, their eyes blinking tigerishly with reflected light.

Kyle closed his hand hard on Mel's shoulder, brought her to stillness. He spun toward the fellow with the bullhorn, his face going cold.

"You can trust us," the man was saying, his palm still raised toward the helicopter. "Things are diff--" He bit his words off as Kyle's pistol kissed his temple. The soldiers who saw jolted in surprise.

"Move and I'll kill him," Kyle told the troopers.

The man cut his eyes toward Kyle as if he could look the Sig's barrel away. He was shaking. Then out of the night came a hail of hard objects thrown incredibly fast. One of the spotlights burst in a coruscation of firefly sparks. A swath of darkness cut a road through the light.

--- 5 ---

For many reasons, Kargen had chosen not to remain for Kyle to find him. He'd rolled away into the all-cloaking black, knowing the helicopters would be over him in an instant. And knowing, as well, that his war-band approached.

Before he could reach the Warkind of his Pod, though, Kargen had seen them gather around the humans' vehicle, had seen some of them leap upon it with scraping claws. He'd also seen them hurled back from that place as the spotlights flared from above.

At the edge of the trees he met them.

"Smash the lights," he told them. "Take the prey."

--- 6 ---

Kyle saw the gun in his own hand, the man with the bullhorn looking scared behind the barrel. He saw one of the spotlights shatter and heard the glass drip on the ground. The soldiers stared, not knowing what to do. Kyle didn't know either.

Mel stood beside Kyle with the infant Whoun in her arms. There were Warkind in the chopper next to her, and more Warkind in the woods. Some were with the soldiers, some against. But what did the soldiers want? Was it different now than what it had been? Were there friends here? Or only foes? And if so, which were which?

The man under Kyle's gun turned his head very, very slowly to stare straight at Kyle over the barrel of the pistol. He spoke as if his words added weight to Kyle's finger on the trigger.

"My wife and sons are in the helicopter," he said. "I love them. Only one Warkind band went rogue. The one in the woods. My name is Michael Russo. I'm here to help Raina." His eyes flicked toward Mel and back. "And her baby."

Still Kyle hesitated, thinking of too many lives held in balance here. It was Mel who broke through.

"Believe him, Kyle."

Kyle lowered the gun, letting the hammer click down.

"Then we go after the Mother," he said. "Now!"

More rocks flashed from the outside shadows. The last two spotlights shattered. The soldiers opened fire on the night as it came alive to take them.

--- 7 ---

With a flex of his wrist, Kargen tore off the door at the back of the sawmill and pushed his way inside. To his right lay the Darkhome beneath the mill where his son had been born. Behind him stalked three members of his band; the others would be attacking the helicopters now. Gunfire and shouts were already lifting there.

But none of that mattered when Kargen scented the Mother. Straight ahead of him she lay, beyond a ragged-edged hole in the inside office wall that he himself had torn a short time earlier. He moved in that direction, tasting the wealth of her blood on the air. A human was near her, one of her new Podcyst. Badly hurt. But it wasn't Kyle or the woman called Mel. It was the other man.

Kargen stepped through the hole, dropped the few short feet to the floor of the mill's main room. The other Warkind were just behind him, eager in their quills and sweat. Claws clicked on the cement and the human struggled to sit up, reaching for the gun at his side.

Kargen slipped into a crouch beside the man, caught the glinting weapon as it rose. He twisted it free of the human's weakened grip, tossed it away to scrape on the concrete floor in a tiny shower of sparks.

"Damn you," the man said, the voice calm and still at the edge of dying. His breathing was harsh. Kargen could hear the froth of blood-bubbles in his throat. The other three Warkind could hear it too. They began to sway, their teeth clacking, their claws skittering.

"Lung's punctured," Kargen said to the man. But he looked toward the quiet bulk of the Mother, smelled the faint flow of vapor down from her nostrils that told him she lived. Barely. His mouth felt torn with the truth that her pain was his fault. He had not wanted *this* kind of pain for her. Not for her.

The man coughed. "Tell me something I don't know."

Kargen turned back to face the human. In his chest came a twist of anger that segued into sorrow, and then into something else, something vastly more empty.

"You can live," he said. "Just get up and walk out of here."

The man shook his head, very slightly. "Can't leave the Mother."

Kargen leaned closer to the man, letting him see the teeth that wanted his throat.

"You can't help her."

The Warkind's mouth opened wider; the glands behind the cheeks spilled their odors of blood and rot. The man sat so close that even he would be able to detect the smells and know: death sat here beside him.

"No," Kargen continued. "You can't help. But Kyle might."

The Warkind stood and moved around the human to pick the Mother up gently in his arms.

"Go. Tell Kyle I'll be waiting. In the Darkhome below."

Kargen watched as the man pushed himself slowly to his feet, first hands and then shoes scraping on the concrete, red saliva dripping from the pale mouth. Kargen didn't offer to help. But he kept the other Warkind back with a snarl when all they wanted was to tear the human apart.

The man shuffled off toward where the choppers had landed outside. Kargen turned with the three from his band and leaped back up through the hole in the wall into the old mill office. He explained very slowly and clearly to the others what he wanted, then let himself down into the engine room beneath the building. The light of one lantern still burned there, and he turned it higher despite the pain it caused his eyes.

He wanted Kyle to see him when he came.

In the right-hand corner of the room, with an open lane between himself and the stairs, Kargen squatted with the Mother's body over his legs. He did what he could to stop her hemorrhaging. And he cleaned her as well as he could of blood. With his fingers. With his tongue.

--- 8 ---

As the last spotlights shattered and the soldiers opened fire at nothing in the dark, Kyle turned to Mel, picked her and the infant Whoun up, nearly threw them into the chopper. For the first time he saw the woman who was already there, with two children. All their eyes were scared. Warkind made a wall in front of them. One of those beings stepped forward, reached to help Mel and the baby with no threat in its posture.

"Wait! Kyle!" Mel shouted, ignoring the creature that grasped her shoulders and lifted her into the helicopter.

But Kyle had already turned away, was yelling at Michael Russo to send the chopper up. He couldn't listen to Mel's words. Or he might not go back in the sawmill. And Tru was there. And Raina.

Kyle knew Mel wouldn't follow him. Not while she held the baby Whoun.

Russo gestured wildly to the helicopter pilot; Kyle felt the rotors picking up speed. The craft shuddered. A rush of movement sounded in the darkness away from the chopper. Kyle smelled a stench like freshly sharpened steel. A wave of sound followed, an immense, undulating rage pouring off the night.

Kargen's war-band was here, among them.

Kyle saw the shadows leaping in. Mike Russo stood directly in their path. Kyle shoved him to the ground, punched his Sig forward and fired. The helicopter was lifting behind him.

Three soldiers were swarmed under. Kyle saw blood spray, black in the darkness, felt it slap across his face like a heated whip. One soldier fired his M-16 into the shrieking mass, his own mouth wide around a scream. A Warkind leaped past the rifle, clubbing the soldier down and dropping to tear at his face.

Kyle emptied his clip between another set of predatory eyes, the volley of lead doing what no one shot could do against these creatures. The concussion hammered the Warkind, knocked him to his knees.

Tasting someone else's blood in his mouth, the gun empty in his hand, Kyle grabbed for Mike Russo's collar, trying to drag him back, the man trying to get his feet under him. More shots sounded from the right.

The dead gray of the chopper's underbelly was even with Kyle's shoulders now. The Warkind who'd been aboard it leaped to earth, growling and shrieking like a train wreck. And as the helicopter cleared the level of Kyle's head the Warkind who'd gathered on the far side of it swept through too.

There were ten or twelve of the new Warkind, allies with the soldiers. They outnumbered those who'd attacked from the outer dark, and they threw down their rifles and charged with claws and teeth. The Warkind Kyle had wounded went down under three of the new ones, torn into meat. And beyond, where humans were dying or dead, the rogue 'kind and the soldier allies came together in a shock of blood and savagery.

Kyle jerked Mike Russo to his feet, stepped in front of the man as he thumbed the Sig's ejector, letting the emptied 9mm magazine fall free. He let go of Russo, his hand coming up from his belt with a new clip, slapping it in. He ripped the slide back, chambering a shell.

One of the rogue Warkind shook free of its attackers, skin and quills gone at the left side of its body. Kyle shot it through the throat, a liquid sound. The last living soldier from the first chopper shot it too; Kyle hadn't seen the man come up beside him but he welcomed the help. The injured rogue went down, allied Warkind mauling him to shreds.

More men arrived. From the second and third choppers. The soldier beside Kyle took charge. He looked tough and efficient. "Lieutenant Morgan," Mike Russo called him.

The tattered remnants of Kargen's band tried to flee. Only a few of them made it. Kyle looked away, looked up to see that the helicopter with Mel and the others aboard had reached a safe height. His gut twisted. He wanted Mel here; he was glad she wasn't.

Russo seemed unable to control his breathing. Even in the washed out light of the moon his face gleamed pale.

"The Mother..." Russo said, the air ragged in his throat. "The Mother... She's..." He tried to breath.

"Still in the mill, I hope," Kyle said.

Lieutenant Morgan's hard little eyes shifted to Kyle. Kyle met them with his own gaze, let the other man look.

"We go in after her *now*," Kyle added. "And another friend. A cop."

"Yes," Russo got out.

Kyle saw the man, Russo, struggling with his fears. And winning slowly. It was something to respect. The guy was no soldier. No cop. But he wasn't running. It didn't matter, though. There wasn't time for any of this.

"I don't think--" Morgan started to say.

Kyle had already turned and was moving toward the sawmill, breaking into a trot. Kargen had not attacked with his band. Kyle would have recognized him. Which meant the big Warkind was elsewhere. Maybe where Raina and Tru were. Especially since the charge by the rogues smelled clearly of a diversion.

Behind Kyle, others followed. Michael Russo was among them; Kyle recognized his scared breathing. But the man was still coming. Half a dozen soldiers were coming too. But only four of the

Warkind. The rest of the allied Warkind had gone after the rogues. Maybe the diversion had worked.

The group entered the mill, Kyle first and the others behind. Flashlights splashed on and scattered light across the empty room--to show that it wasn't quite empty. Kyle saw movement. His gun hand came up. Held. The movement came from Tru.

Kyle rushed over to his friend, the soldiers more cautious behind him, the Warkind sniffing the air like stark gray wolves. Blood speckled Tru's lips. His face was wet with pain as he hugged himself with both arms against some agony inside. Kyle caught his friend as he stumbled, saw the wince on Tru's face.

"Ribs?" he asked.

Tru nodded.

The soldiers had gathered, Russo with them. The Warkind stood apart, their nostrils flared.

"We have to get this man to a chopper," Kyle said.

"I need my men," Morgan replied.

Russo pushed through. He was breathing a little better, moving a little better all the time. "Detail two of your troopers, Morgan," he ordered. "To take this man back to a helicopter."

Morgan looked as if he were going to refuse. Didn't. He signaled two men, who stepped forward.

Kyle held up his hand to stop the soldiers. For a moment. "Where's Raina?" he asked Tru softly.

"He's got her," Tru answered. "Kargen. In the engine room. Called it a Darkhome." Tru coughed, spilling a bloody film over his lower lip to run down his chin like red wax. "Wants you to come to him." He grasped Kyle's shoulder. "There are others with him. Three that I saw."

Kyle nodded, gripped Tru's hand and held it. He looked toward the other end of the mill. Where Kargen waited.

One more time, you son of a bitch, he thought. *One last time.*

--- 9 ---

Kargen held the Mother in his arms, her blood all over him, her smell like wet mud in his nostrils. He rocked her, his hands beneath her head and legs.

Cold in the Light

Kyle was coming. He sensed it.

Everything now was empty. The Mother was dying. His fault. His son was gone from him.

Perhaps he could have fought harder for the infant, could have warred with Kyle while the helicopters swept down upon them and turned loose their ravening guns. But even if he had won the child he could not have kept it, could not have cared for it as it needed. It was not in his nature. Mel's reaction to him had proven that. And he would have had to kill her to take the child. He would have had to tear the baby out of her arms as if he were tearing it out of her womb.

He couldn't have done that; he didn't quite know why.

With his gaze, Kargen followed the contours of the Mother's body to the place where blood seeped from between her thighs. He wanted her still, wanted to possess her. And in possessing her he would have made her bleed. But not like this. Never like this. And yet, this bleeding *was* his fault. He had destroyed everything he thought to save.

And Kyle was coming nearer.

He could taste it.

The Warkind's jaw clenched and unclenched, working the mandible bone against the bullet from Kyle's gun that had lodged there. As the lead moved, the sound grated loud inside his head, like a tiny hard skull sliding back and forth in the joint.

Kargen thought of skulls then. He thought of when, as a child, humans had first taught him his ancestry--first taught all the Whoun. Though what had happened to the race remained unknown, the human scientists made it clear that the Whoun had evolved on Earth, and that their kindred still lived on the land, as minks, and ferrets, and weasels and wolverines. Just like human kindred lived on as chimpanzees and gorillas.

Kargen remembered how the Typicals had listened and marveled at the revelation of their history. And how afterward they'd gone casually back to the business of eating and sleeping and defecating. As if the questions of the past had no bearing on them.

The other Warkind had been even worse. They did not even marvel. There seemed no room in their narrow consciousness for more than thoughts of food and the play of aggression.

Only Kargen had cared.

A few nights after, Kargen had gone to his favorite place within the Harbinger compound, a small dirt cave little bigger than *he* was in those days. He'd excavated it himself in a copse of trees not far from the wall, though well away from the huge spotlights that the humans had aligned all along that brick perimeter to keep the Whoun inside.

Always among the trees there had been small animals. Birds. Squirrels. Several times he'd seen a weasel. That night he had hunted the weasel and caught it, and stripped it of its skin all the way to the bones. He'd held the small skull up to his face, looking for anything of himself within the dark and emptied sockets. Then he'd eaten it, crunching through the skeleton like it was hard candy.

In years to come he'd built a shrine of such bones, as he had grown and had gradually deepened and enlarged his Darkhome. And he'd gone there often to sit throughout the interminable nights and think.

As he was thinking now.

Sex and love and his child were denied him. Because he was Warkind instead of Typical. And the Warkind did not mate. They only killed. Kargen did not know why that should be. Or why he felt differently--had been used differently.

The Mother had been impregnated with his seed. Without his knowledge. That act had set many things in motion; biology was a harsh mistress. Yet, within the constraints of his nature, what Kargen had done he had chosen to do. *He* had killed. *He* had hunted the Mother to this point, to this place. Life had been his to lose or win.

He swung his head slowly back and forth. It no longer mattered. Death alone remained. Whether it was his death or someone else's. Whether it was one death or many.

Kyle was coming. And Kargen would wait for him here. Kyle understood. In his own way, the human was a Warkind. When Kyle had seen the head of Dan Case with weasel skulls in the sockets, and had felt the dead eyes that Kargen had thrown through the window of his vehicle, the man had understood and had not been afraid. Kyle had known that this moment would come. Where they'd each have their chance. For redemption or oblivion. Or both.

From all around him now came the smell of bones and ghosts. And the glint of white shapes moving. They gathered to watch him. To wait. To judge. He welcomed them as old friends, and as old enemies who would never let him down.

Kyle was coming. He was almost here

The Warkind stopped rocking the Mother back and forth. His jaws stilled in their movements. In the near silence he could hear no other breathing than his own.

--- 10 ---

There was no surprise when the three warriors from Kargen's war-band attacked. Kyle and the others were nearing the mill's office, Kyle watching their own Warkind, the allies of the soldiers. He saw them stiffen, muscles and nostrils quivering, and then he smelled it himself--ozone and burnt cherries.

He shouted a warning, for the human soldiers not the allied Warkind. The rogues were in the sawmill office. Then they came. Leaping. Spikes and claws skittering. Teeth wide and white under flashlights' glow.

One of the soldiers opened up with his M-16. A rogue 'kind staggered in the lead stream, but lashed out, war-spike tearing across the man's throat. The other two rogues were met by the allied Warkind. Kyle *felt* the impact of the heavy bodies coming together, saw the whirl of an engagement. A rogue picked up a smaller Warkind, threw him into the soldiers crouched behind. The burnt cherry scent turned copper red.

No one touched Kyle. And he knew why. Kargen awaited him, had identified him for the others somehow.

Kyle raced past the melee, M-16 fire blossoming all around him in the darkness. But the soldiers and their allies would have to handle the rogues. Raina might still be alive. And Kargen belonged to Kyle.

He reached the office, burst through it into the storeroom. The trapdoor to the engine room stood open like a hungry mouth-- behind it a glow from the lantern that still burned below.

For a moment in the sick light, the world warped sideways into nightmare. Kyle heard water beneath him and the eel-like splash of twisting bodies. He smelled the crawling spaces of worms.

Cain stood at his shoulder, whispering dream words in his ear: "I understand the violence now. You showed me, Kyle."

Kyle felt the rage seeping up out of fossilized places inside of him.

"Not yet," he whispered back.

He went down the stairs.

--- 11 ---

Raina felt the distant rocking cease. It had been so cold in the light. But the light was fading, going out like a candle guttering over the last of its wax. And the warmth was coming to replace the cold, coming like a smoke rolling through the trees.

Hands touched her then. Arms and legs drew her toward the warmth. Wahrn whispered her name as his bulk filled the space beside her. And there were others whom she knew, guiding her into the Darkhome, into the softly heated coils of the sleeping Pod.

Scents flowed over her--the richness of soil, the sharp bite of roots--the sweat signatures of each individual Whoun. At one with the night tangle, she let her lips curl. As the smells welcomed. As the darkness welcomed.

Welcomed her.

--- 12 ---

Darkhome, Kyle thought, as his feet touched the concrete floor of the engine room and he looked to the right in the dim lantern glow and saw Kargen sitting very quiet with Raina in his arms. Upstairs the battle still raged between Kargen's allies and Kyle's. But whatever was to happen here would be over before help could come to either of them.

Kargen lowered the Mother to the ground and stood up, his huge form filling the corner of the small room, his skin dark and mottled, and stained in many places with crimson. Kyle waited, the Sig 9mm in his right hand. In his left hand, palmed, with the seven inch blade extending up his sleeve, he held the fillet knife that he'd drawn from the sheath at his belt.

Kargen stepped out from behind Raina's still body, but not yet moving toward Kyle. The man's glance flicked toward Raina and back to Kargen. The Warkind caught the look, understood it.

Cold in the Light

"She's dead," Kargen whispered, the voice like chainsaws cutting at a distance in the trees. "I killed her."

Yellow-brown eyes filmed and brightened, the nictitating lids closing over them and flashing open again.

"I didn't mean to," Kargen said.

"You killed a lot of things," Kyle said. "What you meant doesn't matter."

Kargen's eyes seemed to shrink even further behind the thorny facial spikes that protected them. The savage mouth twisted.

"Oh, I meant to kill the others, Kyle. All the others. I enjoyed it."

"And now you want to kill me."

Kargen took a step closer and Kyle raised his pistol, aiming it at the wide chest. The Warkind halted, swaying slightly. His nictitating lids closed again, a little longer, then opened like a blind going up on a window. The Warkind swallowed and Kyle saw liquid red on the inside of the being's lips. He knew what ran down Kargen's throat. The Warkind was wounded. Badly.

Kyle knew his slugs had hit Kargen twice already, and that Mel had shot him once earlier today with a .357. It looked like there were other injuries. And the being's eyes could not seem to focus clearly.

Damaged by light, Kyle thought.

No telling how bad Kargen's physical problems were. But maybe they were enough to slow him. Kyle hoped so.

Kargen snorted a faint film of blood through his nostrils, turned his head slightly to one side as he responded to Kyle's statement of moments earlier.

"*One* of us has to die here. In this moment. In this place. There was never any other choice."

Kyle nodded. "I know. I want it this way."

"You've already marked me," Kargen said, pointing to his side where a .45 shell had ripped through, pointing to another cut on his shoulder. Then lifting his head to show the damaged jaw where Kyle had shot him with the 9mm.

"As you've marked me," Kyle replied. "Dan Case. Wahrn. Raina. My Uncle Cain."

Kargen nodded, as he very slowly sank down into a crouch. "We owe each other much."

Kargen's glance flicked toward the Mother and beyond, toward the other side of the small room, to the place where the infant Whoun had been born. The nostrils flared as if in memory. Then the gaze came back to focus on Kyle. And Kargen let his war-spikes scrape on the concrete.

"Tell me, Kyle. How many bullets in your gun?"

"Enough."

Kargen twisted his head from side to side. "You know that's not true."

Kyle braced himself, locked his knees, his hand steady on the pistol. "Then we'll both die here. Doesn't matter who goes first."

Kargen laughed. A deep and bone-grinding laugh, so empty that it wasn't even remotely human.

"No. It doesn't matter," he agreed. His nictitating lids closed. Stayed closed.

Kyle opened up instantly with the 9mm, the muzzle sleeting fire as he double-actioned the trigger. One shot. Two.

Kargen was already coming, the huge muscles in his legs uncoiling like whips, hurling the Warkind forward.

Kyle saw his first shots impact, spraying petals of blood. He threw himself to one side, bracing himself, pistol hammering against his palm as he fell. Three shots. Four. More hits. He struck hard on his back; his fifth bullet went wild.

Kargen shrieked, whirled in mid-stride, closing on Kyle's new position, reaching. Damaged eyes unfocused. At point blank range now. One more shot. Into the face. Into the mouth. The gun flying, knocked aside by Kargen's hand.

Kyle heard the 9mm carom off the concrete wall. He felt the impact of Kargen's body, like an adrenaline rush. His leg tore where a war-blade sliced--agony a caress.

Scarlet spittle hit Kyle's face. Kargen's eyes loomed, large as cups now. The Warkind's teeth were yellow and red. Half the lower lip was gone. And all the tongue. The mouth hung wide.

Kyle spun the fillet knife around in his hand. Only time for one movement. One place to hit. Kargen's head swept down, jaws carrying oblivion. Kyle slammed the knife upward, between the protective spikes and deep into the Warkind's right eye. He heard the sound it made, like punching a pool cue into a watermelon.

Cold in the Light

Absolute stillness.

For two seconds, absolute stillness.

And silence.

Then Kyle heard the snap of the Warkind's mouth closing. And he saw the nictitating lid open over Kargen's remaining eye. He saw the surprise in that eye, saw the yellow-brown iris narrow, the pupil shrink. Saw the void gathering. As Kargen's war-spike stroked feather light over his throat and fell away.

Blood began to rain down on Kyle's face.

CHAPTER SEVENTEEN
(May 2: Through Toward Morning)

The ground swirled up to meet him, all
colored for the autumn months. Blood
rust, jaundice yellow, in beauty white
as bones and ghosts. It smashed him in
the face. Broke his wings forever.
                          --In the Memory of Ruins

--- 1 ---

    Kargen saw himself squatting in his Darkhome, with the walls and floors paved with skulls, and the cracks between running wet with blood. But above him shafts of sun pierced the ceiling, bright and hot as incandescent flares, dripping pain across his body. Sharp nails of ivory light shrieked upon him, over him, with the sound of ice cracking, daggering his skull, his eyes.

    From within the last warm depths of his brain, Kargen fought the sun's shine, staggering to his feet, throwing back his head, roaring hate at the descending white void. The odors of death and glory erupted all around him, lifting him on calling winds, as the roof fell away and he passed through into the horror of the day. His war-spikes flashed, dark as a sin. But useless. And it didn't matter.

    And he hung there hurting.

    And he hung there laughing.

    And he let the cold light come and take him.

--- 2 ---

    Kyle made his way up from the depths of the mill to discover Michael Russo and Lieutenant Morgan waiting for him. From there they all found their way to a helicopter that lifted and flew south toward a television station in Fort Smith, and the end of this nightmare. Raina was dead. Kargen had killed her. Kargen was dead. Kyle had killed him. But Mel was alive, beautiful and warm in this same chopper.

Tru lived, as well. An army medic had bound the deputy's ribs, had given him something for the pain, had said that Tru would be all right. In time. But Tru wasn't here now. He had been taken into Fayetteville, to the hospital there.

It was all over but the healing.

Kyle winced as he stretched his injured leg out in front of him. The wound left by Kargen's war-spike sliced deep through the side of his left thigh. But he could move the leg and walk on it, with a limp.

The army medic had wanted to send Kyle to the hospital too. Kyle had refused. He had to see this thing through. For the same reason, he'd turned down pain killers, had allowed only a topical anesthetic to be used beneath the tight white bandages that wrapped the leg.

Mel's arms went around Kyle, a comfortable weight, and he tried to smile for her but couldn't. He felt like crying, like lying down and sleeping for a year. But they had one more thing to do: make sure the Whoun became public knowledge, make sure Mike Russo didn't lose his nerve and no one tried to stop him.

Kyle's glance found Russo's wife--Helen. She cradled the infant Whoun. Raina's child. It was an ugly little thing of greens and blacks and pebbly skin, but already wide eyed and curious, with disconcerting irises of yellow. The baby was an orphan now. It couldn't know that, of course, and it didn't cry. It did little at all, other than look, with its pupils like coal flecks and the nictitating lids opening and shutting.

A flashback hit Kyle, sudden as a punch in the stomach. The engine room beneath the mill. Kargen. Blood slicking down the handle of the knife where it stood out from the Warkind's eye like an obscene totem.

He remembered shoving the body aside. Standing. The anger pounding inside him like a contained explosion. Like shrapnel. He remembered Kargen. Emptied. Raina dead and cold with her blood pooled around her on the floor in a sticky sheet.

Then the sickness of ashes had filled his mouth as the adrenaline burn faded and his pulse slowed. And the graveyard hole opened under his ribs, the vacancy that he always felt in the aftermath of violence. He had stood there wondering why the dream ghost of his Uncle Cain didn't show. But he'd known. Looking at Kargen's husk, he'd known. He'd exorcised his demons. Some of them at least.

Mel sneezed. Kyle jumped, looked around at her, smiled with her for a moment. Until sad thoughts returned. All the dead! With no chance to mourn. Not even time to bury Raina's body, or to bring it back with them. But they could do that tomorrow, he told himself. After the secrets were revealed.

It was all over but the healing. It had to be. He couldn't stand any more.

--- **3** ---

Leonard Suskind parked his stolen jeep in an open space on the fourth floor of the attached parking garage for WLOS, the major TV news station in Fort Smith. The army drab jeep was conspicuous as hell but he didn't care. He wouldn't be coming back to it.

He got out, staggering, nearly falling. Cramps continued to rock his body. He needed to get to the Whoun fetus soon. Had to get to it. And before long Mike Russo would bring it here, to *this* TV station. To him. He was sure of that.

Ten years ago a young newsman from Fort Smith had started asking tough questions about the Harbinger Project. His name had been Robert Ward. Ward had put a lot of things together, had come up with some dangerously accurate speculations. Only a budding friendship with Mike Russo, and Leonard's promise of first access for the future, had kept Ward from going public with what he knew. The Project would have been destroyed.

Now, Ward was news director for WLOS--Channel 9. And more dangerous than ever. Because he knew and trusted Mike Russo and would leap to be here if Russo called. As Leonard was sure Mike would.

When he'd overheard Russo back at the army camp talking about a station manager in Fort Smith, Leonard had known that only one name made sense. Only Bob Ward. And if Mike succeeded in getting to the Mother, then this would be the place he'd bring her to expose the Harbinger Project. Leonard had to be waiting. Because if he failed to reach the Mother's baby soon he would die.

Cold in the Light

Leonard moved away from the jeep, trying to straighten his tattered tie, trying to look like the scientifically cultured seventy-seven year old man he was supposed to be. It was going to be hard. His coat was split down the back and torn from brambles. Dirt splotches covered his pants and the front of his shirt. He imagined there were a few dried daubs of blood on him somewhere, though they'd hardly be recognizable among the other stains.

He hoped his age would help him. It had before. At this time of the morning there would be few people around other than security anyway. At worst, maybe they'd think him an escapee from an Alzheimer's ward. They'd handle him carefully. Until he killed them.

The first door that he tried from the garage into the main building was locked. He moved on, searching for a way in. And he'd find that way, even if it meant smashing his way through somewhere.

If-- When, Leonard corrected himself. *When* Russo came with the Mother they would probably arrive by helicopter, and the landing pad was most likely on the roof. That meant they wouldn't be coming through the garage. He'd have to get close to the studios where the actual taping would be done. He'd have to wait for them there.

The throbbing in his right hand was vast now, evil, and he slammed it against the wall, trying to shut down the pain. He looked at it then, at his fist. And the blood was running down it, dripping from the fingers. Over the blue-black knot on the outside of the hand, a crack had formed. The skin was splitting, something ugly and white showing through beneath.

Leonard felt a rage crawling up from inside of him but he forced it down. He couldn't release it. The time wasn't right.

Yet.

--- **4** ---

Mike Russo clicked off the military phone aboard the helicopter, breaking the connection with Bob Ward, the news director for Channel 9 TV out of Fort Smith. Ward had been ecstatic to hear that he was finally going to learn the truth about Harbinger, and that in learning it he'd have a scoop that would shock the world.

Mike had liked Ward since he'd first met him, nearly ten years ago. The newsman had always been the type to put friends and common decency ahead of thoughts of his own career. And in all those years, Bob Ward had lived up to his agreement not to ask about the Harbinger Project. Mike was happy that he could finally tell his friend the truth.

Mike turned to the chopper's pilot to relay the information he'd gotten from Ward.

"We're cleared to land directly on the station's roof. The pad'll only hold one helicopter though. Might as well send the other back to base. You know where this place is, right?"

The man nodded. "Twenty minutes maybe. This news guy'll be there to meet us? You're going live with the Whoun?"

Mike shook his head. "He'll be there but we'll tape it. Broadcast it later. As people are waking up to their morning news."

The pilot didn't say anything else, only got on the radio to the chopper that was trailing them. The third helicopter had already been dispatched to a hospital with the wounded.

Now, Mike watched their last escort peel away. He felt a spurt of fear to see them leaving but told himself it was silly. Everything was over but the easy part now. Besides, he still had Warkind and soldiers in *this* chopper with him. He got out of the copilot's chair and went back to the cargo area to see his wife and kids, and the infant Whoun who was about to become the most famous being on earth.

--- 5 ---

Leonard was searching the second floor of the parking garage for an unlocked door when he saw the van arrive below him at the main building's rear entrance. Three men got out and went into the building with armloads of equipment. Leonard knew why they were here--for Mike Russo and the Whoun--and he felt a sweet tremor course his lean frame.

He took two quick steps, leaped over the shiny red guardrail and dropped twenty-five feet to land behind a row of shrubs and the square shapes of trash bins. He crouched there, until the men came back to get more equipment. Then he followed them inside, following quietly as any hunting tiger, until they led him to a recording studio. Their excited chatter told him he was in the right place, and he slipped around a corner in the hall to wait and watch.

Leonard smiled, the skin splitting in a seam along the line of his jaws. He'd found a way in. And he hadn't even had to kill anyone. His teeth were disappointed.

--- 6 ---

As soon as Mike stepped off the helicopter onto the roof of the WLOS TV building he saw Robert Ward waiting for them. He rushed across to the man, waving at the others to stay inside the chopper for the moment. Ward met him with a firm handshake and a smile.

"About time you came clean, Mike."

Russo grinned. "Wait till you see what I've brought, Bob. Hope your sense of wonder is intact after all these years of hanging around in the gutter."

"Then wow me," Ward said.

Mike grinned again, waved his hand toward the helicopter. Kyle Dupree and Melissa Bowers got off first, Kyle limping slightly on his injured leg. Joshua and Caleb were next. Behind came Helen Russo with the infant Whoun in her arms. But Ward couldn't see the baby clearly because of the blankets that wrapped it.

Ward glanced at Mike curiously. "I don't under--" he started to say. That was when Graye and three other Warkind sprang from the chopper onto the landing pad.

The newsman got very silent, his mouth shocked wide, his eyes bright with a combination of excitement and curiosity and fear.

"The baby is one of them too," Mike said.

Ward spoke without turning his head, his eyes still glued to the Warkind.

"My God, Mike. We've got to get them on tape right now. *Right now!*"

Mike nodded. "That's what I wanted to hear."

--- 7 ---

Warkind, Leonard's senses shouted.

He smelled them in the corridor, like rusty nails, coming toward the TV studio. And he smelled something else. A new signature. The Mother had borne her child. Its scent quivered deliciously on the air. The fact of the birth would make Leonard's job easier; the presence of the Warkind would make it harder. But he could deal with that.

Leonard moved quickly out of the hall, finding a room, twisting off the lock, shutting the door behind him without a click. He knew his scent was different than a Warkind's and not nearly so strong, but if those beasts got a good whiff of him they'd be coming on the hunt.

He should have expected Mike Russo to bring his pets along. It was only that he himself was so used to secrecy. But Russo *planned* to blow the Harbinger story wide open, and for that he needed something huge and dramatic. The Warkind were both.

Leonard had to sketch out an alternate course of attack now, though. He couldn't go charging straight at the Mother. Not with the Warkind between him and his goal. They'd be strong and quick enough to stop him before he got to the infant, before he could access its blood and reverse the process accelerating inside his body.

Leonard's gaze crawled around the room, which was lit only by reflected light through the windows. The studio where he wanted to be was only a dozen yards away. But there were walls and Whoun destroyers between.

He didn't want to die. Not beneath Warkind claws. Nor from the killer that lived within him now.

Sudden cramps locked his muscles, dragged him to his knees. He fought not to scream, as the skin split on his forehead, and down the sides of his face, and over his shoulders. He felt the warmth of blood and pus trickle into his mouth. White knuckles ruptured through the backs of his hands.

No! Not yet! There's time. There has to be time.

He wrapped his arms around himself, leaned to rest his raw forehead on the carpeted roughness of the floor. Yellowed knots blossomed across his back and down his sides, each one a crucifix of pain that pulsed in rhythm with his hammering heart.

"Time, time, time," he whispered like a mantra.

Cold in the Light

And instead of a scream, his throat purled a growl. He lifted his head, lips writhing. The whites of his eyes had filled up with blood from torn veins, turning his pupils into black voids against a background of bruised crimson.

But he saw through those eyes to the plastic panels in the ceiling behind which the dead lights hid. And he rose, found a desk to climb on. He slipped a few panels aside, tore out the fluorescent tubes and their metal frames, found the struts above that would support his weight. He climbed in, began to slide through the crawlspace, toward the TV studio.

All across his body, small explosions of blood and tissue continued, muscles contracting and expanding. Sharp things poking through, unfolding. Something being born from beneath the flesh.

--- 8 ---

Mike Russo was dead calm as he got ready to speak, the cameras rolling on him, all of it going to tape for early broadcast on the morning news. Bob Ward was there, with two cameramen. Only one light shone, throwing Mike into relief against a surrounding darkness.

The Warkind were in the shadows behind Mike, with Helen, his sons, the Whoun infant, Kyle Dupree, Mel Bowers, and three soldiers standing farther away to one side. None of them had heard the story he was about to tell, and he wondered briefly what their reaction would be. Then he put the wondering out of his mind as he began to recall events of great promise.

"In December of 1972," he said, "Apollo 17 landed in the Taurus-Littrow region of the moon. The history texts report that the crew brought back 225 pounds of lunar samples, assumed by everyone to be dust and rock. Most of it wasn't.

"Buried in the side of an impact crater the crew found an artifact, which they at first took to be a leftover from an alien civilization. They were wrong.

"The artifact was a rectangular box of an unusual metal. About the size of an office refrigerator. When opened, on Earth, it was found to contain an incredibly intricate mechanism. And inside the mechanism, packed in individual cryogenic cells, were 10,000 embryos of a species never before encountered.

"But they were not alien.

"A number of symbols were discovered inside and outside the box, believed to be a written language of some kind. Though they remain untranslatable, a few of those symbols *resembled* English letters. We found what looked like a 'W,' an 'H,' an 'N.' The race was soon being called the 'Whoun.'

"In 1978, after intense research and debate among a select few scientists, it was decided to incubate some of the embryos. We already knew the Whoun had originated on earth, and that they were genetically related to the mustelids, the biological family that contains minks, weasels, and otters. We had discovered much about their DNA. With that knowledge, we chose one hundred embryos for our study. Those embryos are now adults."

Mike stopped talking and stepped to one side a little. In a glass enclosed overlook booth was another man, a light-and-sound technician. He fiddled with some knobs. Behind Mike a light bloomed, bringing the Warkind into view. Mike had told the man to keep the light dim, and he did. But still the Warkind blinked in the semi-brightness, and opened their mouths to snarl. The cameras caught it all and Mike knew how effective this scene was going to be.

"Our theory," Mike continued, "is that the Whoun evolved during the Miocene epoch, about ten to twelve million years ago. And that they reached a high level of intelligence but failed to develop a tool culture or any sophisticated technological civilization.

"And then. We suspect. They left."

"Possibly, that exodus occurred around the time of the so called Great Ice Age, which triggered changes in human evolution too. That would have been between one and four million years ago. We have no idea how the Whoun managed to develop the technology to escape earth. *If* indeed they did. We do believe that the embryos were placed on the moon deliberately, but it is possible that it was *not* the Whoun who placed them there."

Mike motioned Helen forward and his wife walked up to him carrying the swaddled infant Whoun. He let her hold the small bundle, but moved his hands to unwrap it slowly in front of the cameras, wanting the machine eyes to have a good long look.

"This is the first infant born on earth among the modern Whoun. It--"

Cold in the Light

A shriek belled out from overhead. The lights flashed into brilliance. Mike heard the infant cry out as if it had been struck. He heard the Warkind roar. He looked up.

Glass shattered in the overlook booth. The light-and-sound technician came windmilling through amid a rain of small, crystalline shards. Mike saw the man hit the floor and bounce, saw the twisted angle of the neck and the uncoiling of purple intestines from a horrid wound to the stomach.

Then he saw the shape that followed the tech down from above, a hurtling, liquid movement that dropped like some spider/scorpion mix. It landed softly, launched itself on all fours toward where Helen stood with the Whoun infant. Mike tried to yell. As he saw the thing coming. As he saw that it still wore the remnants of clothing. And he realized it had once been a man.

Before it erupted like a scream in his face.

--- 9 ---

Kyle saw the light flash on in full intensity, saw Graye and the other Warkind collapse as if they'd been axed, their hands clasped over their heads and eyes. He heard the scream of the dying technician and saw the shape of the man's killer spill from the overhead room and throw itself toward the Russos. He was already drawing his Sig 9mm, was pushing Mel behind him. The soldiers stood cold. The cameras were rolling.

The attacking thing looked like a hybrid of Warkind and human. Smaller than a Warkind. But faster. And not bothered by the brightness. Its skin was mottled white and yellow and black.

Kyle glimpsed a jutting jaw with the cheek tissues torn back at the sides to reveal scarlet-painted teeth. War-spikes grew on the misshapen hands and dark quills had burst through the scalp and back. The creature wore the shreds of a suit coat and tie.

Kyle leaped forward. Knew he was too slow. The thing struck Mike Russo, knocking the man flat, then spun toward Russo's wife--Helen. She cringed, tried to duck away. The hybrid grabbed her, tore at her hands and arms, at the bundled form she held there.

The Whoun infant!

The woman screamed. Kyle was coming, slowed by his injured leg, his gun seeking a target and not finding it. Helen was between him and creature. Adrenaline shouted to Kyle's muscles, exploded down his spine. He saw Kargen again. Kargen looming over Mel. Kargen charging him in the Darkhome.

Helen Russo was battered hard, but for that moment held onto the Whoun baby. Kyle heard the hybrid's savage growl, saw its war-spike draw back for a blow that would decapitate the woman who held what it wanted.

"No!" Kyle shouted, pausing in his rush to steady his aim, shoving the 9mm out in front of him to risk a dangerous shot.

Mike Russo intervened, coming off the floor with blood on his forehead, shouting a rage of his own, hurling himself onto the back of the hybrid. Kyle saw the man's hands rising, falling, tearing at the monster's face.

Helen fell back with the infant in her grip, shrieking her husband's name. Kyle reached her, leaped past as the hybrid turned on Mike Russo and slapped him to his knees. Its mouth dipped for the man's throat. Russo clubbed it savagely in the face, too angry to be afraid. And for just a second the awful shape froze.

That left time for Kyle to arrive, time for him to lash out with a boot, smashing the hybrid in the shoulder, flipping it away from Russo and onto its back on the floor. His foot came down. He straddled the thing's legs, his eyes hot in their sockets. The creature started to rise, limbs thrashing. Kyle kept seeing Kargen.

"See you in hell," he whispered, as he punched the Sig forward and emptied the clip like a hard rain into the hybrid's body.

The creature jerked and jarred as the bullets poured into it, pulses of red spraying. Then it fell back, skull thumping on the floor, the strange body lurching into a tonic spasm.

Kyle stood there still as Michael Russo dropped onto his hands and knees and crawled over to the hybrid, mouthing words over and over that finally registered.

"Leonard. My God, Leonard. What did you do?"

The vicious look on the hybrid's face faltered, returned, faltered. Died. The body relaxed...slipped into something much more human. And Kyle heard the being's response to Russo, the voice like an exhaled breath. He listened in horror.

"Mike. Almost...Mike. I wanted--"

Silence.

Russo grabbed the being's shoulders. "Wanted what, Leonard? What?"

The creature sighed, its eyes turning brown. Half human now. Half monster. The arrogance fading. "Test...the embryo. Its blood. Wondrous. Serum--"

The last word spilled ever so quietly into the room.

"Leonard!" Mike shouted. "Hold on." He rounded on Kyle. "Call an ambulance dammit! Right now! Call one!"

Kyle didn't move, only stared at Russo. "No use, he said.

And when Mike looked back at his old mentor it must have been clear that Kyle was right. Leonard Suskind was dead, the eyes glazing over like a skim forming on cream, the arms dropping to the floor with the click of war-spikes on linoleum.

Kyle turned away, hearing Russo weeping, as if someone had just poured the scientist's last drop of innocence on the floor.

--- **10** ---

Only two of Kargen's war-band were left. Both were hurt; both were torn and leaking. But when the soldiers and their Warkind allies had gone, the two came down into the place where Kargen had died, and they carried away the bodies of their Pod leader, and of the Mother of the first Whoun infant. They took them to a Darkhome, to the one that had been excavated on the Harbinger grounds by Kargen himself.

In that place, in the last hours of night, they cleaned the bodies of flesh. With war-spikes and claws. With mouths and stained teeth. And when the bones were all purified, they built a cairn from them on a flat stone that Kargen had hauled in for his seat.

Within the Darkhome were many other bones, embedded in the walls and descending from the roof--the skeletons of minks and weasels toward the center, with the bones of bear, mountain lions, and wolves radiating out like broken rays from a cold sun. The whole made a mandala, created by Kargen. And now in the heart of that mandala, at the point of integration, the skulls of Kargen and the Mother sat facing each other with black sockets. The two living Warkind squatted and watched.

When day came the two survivors slept, the sweet odors of meat and blood all over them. In the warming shadows of evening they rose again, and it seemed to them that all their wounds were healed and free of pain.

In the revelation of that moment, the two went out together into the forest and dragged down a buck deer with its antlers wide spread. They brought the body back fresh and opened its throat over the skulls, letting the still-heated blood flow down in red streamers over the white heads, letting it flow down into the gaping, hollow mouths and across the teeth of those who had healed.

Afterward, they went to find others of their own kind.

To teach them.

To make them believe.

Cold in the Light

EPILOGUE (Late May)
----

*In the watching ruin, the eyes settled
to rest, sated for a brief red moment,
the lips coated with fear and despair.
And a glorious evil. Once again the
hunters waited, patience their weapon.*
--In the Memory of Ruins

--- 1 ---

Tru Maclang sat on a lawn chair in his back yard, his feet propped up on the leftover stump from a lightning blasted oak he'd had to cut down two years ago. Beside him, his wife Carlene had put a TV tray on which rested a chilled glass of sweet tea.

It was warm for May, the sun kind on his face. He didn't seem to be able to get enough warmth after the events of the past few weeks. He shifted a little in his chair, reaching to get his glass, wincing as his ribs twinged. They had knit well. As had his punctured lung. But both still troubled him and he imagined they would for a long time to come.

There were other things that troubled him more, though. Images of Warkind and of blood. And thoughts and fears he'd never before had. His world had been an orderly one before the Whoun. There were crimes and punishments, work that gave pleasure. There was the love of a good woman.

Then the skin had fallen off the world and he'd seen the underneath. How many more projects like Harbinger were being hidden? How many scientists like Leonard Suskind were out there?

And closer to home. What had happened to Kargen's body? And Raina's? Why had they never been found? Why had there never been a complete count of how many Warkind were missing?

The night was a scarier place with those questions in it.

Tru leaned his head back a little, looked up through the lacy leaves of his weeping willow tree. Patches of blue broke through the green. He'd found himself looking at the sky a lot recently, because he had one more question that only the sky could answer.

According to Michael Russo, no one knew whether the Whoun race still existed. But if they did they were most likely in space. Somewhere. Somehow. Outside the solar system.

Tru figured the Whoun for survivors. He figured they *were* out there. And he wondered.

How long before they came back?

--- 2 ---

Mike Russo looked up from the lab desk when Helen walked into the room. She crossed to him with a tray of milk and sandwiches, and set them down on his work bench. He caught her arm as she started to turn, and pulled her face down to his, drawing her into a kiss. He held her there, her hair tickling his cheek. Until she pulled back and smiled at him.

"I hope you're not planning to work in here all day and ignore me," she said.

He grinned. "Not likely. The data on the Whoun infant is already in the computers. I should have an answer to the riddle that Leonard left us in a few minutes."

She shook her head and gave him a look of mock pity. "I don't care about any riddle. I want to know what you plan to do *after* you solve it and save the world. Again."

Mike grinned a second time. "Well...then I'm coming downstairs to ravish my wife."

"Good answer," Helen said.

She kissed him on the forehead and turned away, walking to the door without a backward glance, though they were both aware of how he watched her hips sway beneath her jeans.

Helen had been gone only a moment when the computer on the desk beeped and the screen began to fill with graphs and tables and plots from the analysis on the Whoun infant. Mike's attention shifted back to wondering what Leonard Suskind could have meant in speaking of the "wondrous" blood in the infant's body. The answer should be here, in the graphs he now studied, the tables he scrolled through.

At first he didn't see it. Then he did. And he saw how brilliant Leonard had been as a scientist, and how the man had let himself be seduced by the lust for youth and power. Like so many before him.

The infant Whoun was Kargen's child as well as Raina's. Perhaps he should have guessed it, Mike thought. It explained much. Kargen had been several standard deviations above the Warkind average in IQ. Leonard had sought the perfect blend of Warkind strengths and the creativity and intelligence of the Typicals. And in doing so he had found something even greater. The infant had the blood of a god. Perfect health. Perfect immunity against disease. And it was transferable.

Coupled with the genetic manipulations that Leonard had worked on his own body, Mike suspected that if the scientist had been able to mix the infant's blood with his own he would have become almost superhuman. No sicknesses, rapid healing, speed and strength and sensory capabilities beyond anything humans had ever possessed. And a life span increase marked in hundreds of years.

Michael Russo stared at the secret on the screen, a secret that only he knew. His heart jackhammered in his chest; his mouth filled with a dune's dryness. *The power here*, he thought. The chance to change the world. What every true researcher desired.

And the money! To make up for having no job anymore and little prospect of getting another that he wanted.

What matter that the infant Whoun would be prostituted in the name of human glory? What matter that wars would be fought and blood shed for a share in wealth that belonged to another race of intelligent beings?

Mike stared and stared, fingernails biting into his palms. Until, in the house below, Mike heard a sound, the sound of his wife singing. He hadn't heard her so happy in years, and he reached to the computer and typed in a command that would reformat the hard drive and erase every bit of data it contained.

Then he smiled, and got up, and went downstairs to make love with his wife.

--- 3 ---

In the late evening, Kyle and Mel drove up to Deerhaven Lake and parked near the picnic area. Though the day was fine--with only a light breeze and warmer than usual for May--there were no other people there. Kyle got out of the car and went around to help Mel with the picnic basket and the blankets. His limp was barely noticeable.

The wind ruffled the surface of the lake and the water was that deep, deep blue it gets before it turns night black. Kyle didn't ask why they had come here so late for a picnic. He just followed as Mel led the way down toward the water and along a narrow levee to a quiet and grassy spot beyond. There were ashes of old campfires there. A few beer bottles. But that didn't detract from the serenity.

Mel knelt to spread the blanket and Kyle squatted beside her to help, wincing slightly as his injured left leg twinged. He wondered for a moment if the wound that Kargen had given him would ever heal completely. Then he forgot about it as Mel touched his shoulder.

"Let me," she said.

Kyle sat back, watched Mel smooth the blanket down. He reached and pulled out a small rock that made a bump in the fabric, then waited while Mel opened the picnic basket and set out crackers and sandwiches and a bottle of Arkansas muscadine wine.

They ate and drank as the sun went down over them and the world darkened, and the frogs came out to sing. Kyle noticed how Mel looked up from her food when the first frogs sounded. He didn't ask her why.

The breeze came up a little cooler and Kyle took the extra blanket they'd brought and draped it over Mel's shoulders. She shivered anyway and Kyle scooted closer to her and put his arms around her--feeling silly and good, young and old, all at the same time.

"You're beautiful, Melissa," he said.

She grinned at him, a quick grin that disappeared as fast as it came. She kissed him on the cheek.

"I have to tell you a story," she said.

"You don--" Kyle started to say. Then stopped himself. Those words were so typical and so foolish. So wrong. Because, of course, she did have to tell it. And he had to let her.

Kyle's fingers slid up and down her arm, until she grasped his hand and held it.

"OK," he said after a moment. "Tell me a story. A true story."

Mel slipped her hand out of his, but quickly leaned forward to kiss his cheek again, to let him know that it wasn't wrong to touch her, just wrong right now to hold her. Instead, she put her hands in her lap to twist together, and she looked at the lake, darkening now toward a metallic sheen.

Kyle lit the two citronella candles they'd brought along to keep off the mosquitoes and to provide some light. He waited for Mel to begin.

"When I was little," she said at last, "our school used to come here on picnics. We'd have fishing rodeos sometimes. You know. Where the kids win prizes for the biggest catch. Or the most. Perch maybe. Minnows usually.

"I liked coming here. And when I was older I came a lot. On Saturdays and Sundays. Riding my bike. When I was fifteen I met a boy here one summer."

She looked at Kyle, watched his eyes. "He was black," she said.

Kyle tried to keep his face blank, to not let her see any reaction that might shut off the flow of words, because he sensed that if he dammed them up now they'd never come again. And that would be his loss because Melissa would go out of his life after that. He didn't want her to ever go out of his life.

Mel looked down at her hands, began worrying at her nails with her thumb.

"His name was Deacon." She laughed a little. "Such a big name. Like a football player name. But he was just a little guy. Kind of clumsy. A year older than me. He was staying across the lake that summer, in one of the summer houses. Like the one where we stayed when..."

"I remember," Kyle said.

Mel shrugged. "Anyway, we met right here. This is kind of a narrow section of the lake. And he had rowed across. Was walking when I saw him. When we saw each other.

"We talked. He was interested in different things than most of the people I'd met. Most boys I knew. He liked poetry. He could play the piano. Though I never heard him play. He had the hands and I would watch his fingers move sometimes on their own when he was talking. And you could see that he would be good when he played.

"After a while I started coming here to meet him on the weekends."

She stopped for a moment. Then went on.

"Nothing ever happened between us. He kissed me once. Very quick and furtive, with his eyes open like he thought he'd have to run afterward. I wanted to kiss him back, but I didn't really know how. Mostly we just talked. Sometimes until evening.

"One night when we were here. Sitting on this levee. A truck pulled in. I knew who it was. Three boys from my school. Seniors. They'd been drinking."

She stopped talking again, the silence stretching until Kyle had to break it.

"They saw you with Deacon," he said.

"Yes. Deacon tried to stand up to them. But they were bigger than he was. They didn't even hit him or anything. Just sort of pushed him around. Called him...names."

She looked again at Kyle. He knew what names they'd used. But it was Mel it had hurt.

"They pushed him in the water. One of them busted out the bottom of his rowboat. They called me names too. In front of him. I could see how scared he was, but I was scared too. I couldn't say anything.

"One of the boys wasn't from here originally. His family brought him. I heard it was because they wanted to get him away from the city where he'd gotten in trouble. They thought being in the country would help. But that wasn't what happened.

"That boy told Deacon they were going to fuck me. And that Deacon could watch. I tried to hit him but he was a lot bigger and faster than I was. He just pushed me away and told the other two to hold me. Then he told Deacon that the two of them would have to fight for me.

"Deacon was crying. I remember that so clearly. And then the boy, the leader, told Deacon to just walk away. And that as long as he didn't say anything there'd be no reason to bring up how he was cozying up to a white girl.

"I didn't think Deacon would do it. I didn't want him to. But he walked away. Then he ran. And they raped me. All three of them.

On the levee with the water lapping the banks. And the frogs croaking.

"They left me here afterwards and I rode my bike home. I didn't tell anyone what had happened. Told Mom and Dad that I'd fallen off my bike to explain the bruises. But within a week there was a story about me all over town. Not the real one. But a story where I was letting Deacon make love to me and was sleeping around. My dad believed it. I don't know about Mom but she acted like she sided with Dad.

"A couple of weeks later I found out I was pregnant. My dad assumed it was Deacon's. I remember how he ranted around the house about not having a mixed breed grandson. And about how I was going to have an abortion and learn what it meant to be true and straight.

"So I ran away from home. I don't know now if I would have let the baby be aborted if things had been different. But I wasn't going to let my father make me abort a child and think it was something it wasn't."

Again Mel stopped, her breathing loud in the near quietness by the lake. Kyle waited, wanting to reach out to her but knowing that she wasn't ready yet to invite him in.

"I had the baby in a motel in Texarkana," she continued. "And I gave it to a nun there who ran an orphanage. A few years later I checked on the baby. It was a boy. A beautiful boy. He'd been adopted by a good family and I never wanted that to change. I didn't try to see him."

"And then you put yourself through vet school?" Kyle asked.

"Yes. But I had help from people. I got a job working with a vet. He and his wife helped runaways a lot. In Memphis. And the time passed."

"Why did you come back?"

"Mom and Dad died a year ago in a car wreck. I came back then. Though they'd already had the funeral. I came back to see their graves. And, of course, they'd left the house and everything to me. I sold it."

"Did they know you were OK? Before..."

"Yes. I was always a dutiful daughter. I called them several times. Called Mom at least. To let her know I was OK. She always wanted me to come home. Or begged me to let her send me money. But I really was doing all right. I know I was lucky.

"Dad would never talk the first couple of times. But one time he did. And he was crying. I almost came home then. But I was still young enough to want to hurt them."

Mel started to cry herself then. And Kyle moved closer to her, not willing to let her fend him off this time. He put his arms around her and he said nothing, just let the weight of his body tell her that he was with her.

She cried for ten minutes. Twenty minutes. Kyle felt the time pass and didn't care. He held her. Till she lifted her fevered face up to his and he kissed her as she wanted to be kissed. Then, for longer than she had cried, he made love to her. On the banks of the lake, with the stars slowly uncovering themselves in the sky and the frog chorus orchestrating their songs all around:

He made love to her.

And held her against the darkness.

--- 4 ---

The infant Whoun opened his eyes when the smell hit him, rank and sheered and violent. His body responded, though his newly minted mind had no names for such odors. It was dark and warm where he slept in the Harbinger compound, and he rolled over and pulled himself to his feet, using the railing that surrounded his rest-place.

In the shadows, his yellow eyes made out the shapes of the beings that gathered around him. He didn't know how they had gotten here but they were huge, filled with odd low growls and the clicking of claws and spikes and teeth.

He watched them. Not afraid. But not understanding why they suddenly dropped onto all fours and bared their throats before him.

And he heard what words they said to him. What they called him.

"Kargen! Blood-lord!"

Though he didn't understand that either.

Yet.

About the Author

Charles A. Gramlich grew up on a farm in Arkansas near the Ozark Mountains where Cold in the Light is set. On a long walk one afternoon he stumbled upon a tiny valley in the mountains where the trees seemed to gather around like dark and menacing angels, and where the sunlight chilled his skin. He never went back to that place, but he was never quite the same either.

Charles lives in the New Orleans area now. He's in his 40s, married, and has a teenage son named Joshua. He teaches psychology at a local university. Charles has had two previous novels serialized in science fiction and fantasy magazines, and has sold a lot of stories and essays over the years in fantasy, horror, and other, much stranger, fields. When not writing he can often be found cruising the back roads of Louisiana on his motorcycle, looking for a place where angels brood and the light is...cold.

Printed in the United States
815900001B